The Promise

Lucy Diamond was born in Nottingham and has lived in Leeds, London, Oxford and Brighton. She now lives in Bath with her family. *The Promise* is her sixteenth novel.

LUCY DIAMOND

The Promise

MACMILLAN

First published 2021 by Macmillan
an imprint of Pan Macmillan
The Smithson, 6 Briset Street, London EC1M 5NR
EU representative: Macmillan Publishers Ireland Limited,
Mallard Lodge, Lansdowne Village, Dublin 4
Associated companies throughout the world
www.panmacmillan.com

ISBN 978-1-5290-2702-0

3 5 7 9 8 6 4 2

A CIP catalogue record for this book is available from the British Library.

Typeset in Dante by Jouve (UK), Milton Keynes
Printed and bound by CPI Group (UK) Ltd, Croydon, CR0 4YY

Visit **www.panmacmillan.com** to read more about all our books
and to buy them. You will also find features, author interviews and
news of any author events, and you can sign up for e-newsletters
so that you're always first to hear about our new releases.

For Martin,
the one I love the most.

Prologue

It was almost midnight and the Thames was rolling along, black as tar, wrinkling and smoothing itself beneath the starlit sky. The houseboats were shadowy shapes at their moorings as frost scattered icy glitter across rooftops and railings, silvering each trembling blade of grass. High above, a crescent moon gleamed, as lustrous as wedding satin.

A man walked unsteadily down the river path, hands shoved in his pockets, head bowed. His world seemed to have tilted on its axis and he wasn't sure how to right himself again. First there had been the breathless phone call that afternoon – *I've got something to tell you* – leaving him with the prickling sense that luck was slipping between his fingers, that maybe the charm he'd always relied upon might not be enough to rescue him this time. Then, feeling cornered, he had lashed out needlessly, hurting people he loved with his words. Now he was left with a rising tide of dread that he couldn't shake off.

What was he going to do? Had he blown everything?

A scouring wind skimmed off the river against his face and somewhere in the distance a fox shrieked, as high-pitched and unnerving as a child's scream. The man hunched deeper into the collar of his coat, wishing he was already at home, the front door bolted, warm and safe in bed, the heating pipes cooling with their soft clicks and creaks. But did he even deserve to be there any more, after what he had done?

Suddenly there were footsteps scuffling behind him. A shout. 'Oi! Mate.'

He turned. And then—

Chapter One

It wasn't as if Dan had been deliberately avoiding Zoe since the funeral. All the same, when he glimpsed her and Bea at the far end of the supermarket aisle, his first thought was to swerve away and hide. Sweat prickled between his shoulder blades. Adrenalin spiked in jags through his blood. Every instinct he possessed told him to get out of there, fast, *run* – but then he pictured himself fleeing like a criminal, hunched low in the driver's seat of his car, and knew he would feel even more of a scumbag than usual. Which was saying something.

Lurking behind an end-of-aisle stationery display, he felt a wrench inside as his gaze fell on Bea. She was wearing a grubby unicorn onesie, with the rainbow-striped horn at a dejected angle on the hood, trailing after Zoe, who was pushing the trolley. Were those tears streaking his niece's round face? Yes, he thought, they were. Bea was usually a happy-go-lucky resident of her own magical daydream world; Dan remembered her on her sixth birthday blowing out the candles on her cake and saying that she wished she could be a *real* unicorn when she grew up. Beatrice Rose Sheppard had always been everybody's poppet, the apple of her daddy's eye, all dimples and bouncing. Although not today, clearly.

Come on, Dan. Stop being a coward. Say hello at the very least, he ordered himself.

He hurried to catch up with them. 'Zoe – hi.'

Shame stabbed him below the ribcage as he noticed how thin and pale she appeared, how faraway her gaze. There had always been a wholesome sheen about Zoe, with her golden hair and rosy cheeks, but today she bore the dull skin and deadened expression of someone who'd just clawed her way through the worst weeks of her life. 'Hello, Bea,' Dan added weakly when Zoe didn't answer immediately.

'Hello,' muttered Bea, eyes damp. Then her lower lip slid out, pink and quivering, and she stamped a foot, back in argument mode. 'But why *not*, Mummy?' she pouted.

Ignoring her, Zoe gave Dan an unfriendly look. 'I thought you were meant to be in South America' was all she said.

Dan hung his head. 'Didn't go,' he replied. Obviously. His suitcase was still half-packed on the bedroom floor, where he hadn't been able to face putting away the neat piles of new shorts, T-shirts and hiking socks, although he had at least managed to claim back most of the money from the untaken flights. It seemed like a dream now, that whole itinerary he and Tiggy had discussed and planned: the mountains he'd intended to climb, the temples and jungle and beaches he thought they'd be visiting, the fiestas and full-moon parties she had been so excited about. Dan's great adventure to show the world there was more to his life than spreadsheets and calculations. Typical, he hadn't even made it as far as the airport, though. Having arranged three months off work, he had barely been anywhere, other than the coroner's court, the crematorium and his own miserable flat. He swallowed, aware of the awkward pause that was building between him and his sister-in-law. 'So how are you both doing?'

Stupid, stupid question. Stupid, stupid man. How were they *doing*? It was three weeks since Patrick had died; they were probably doing about as abysmally as Dan. Worse, if anything. He'd last seen them at the funeral, after which he had borne both Zoe's gaze-avoiding reproach (*This happened on your watch*) and the louder, shriller version from his mum ('I don't understand. Why did you let Patrick go off like that? Over a stupid argument. Honestly, Daniel!'). He had ended up repeating *Sorry* and *He went before I could stop him* on a miserable kind of loop, before resorting to desperate self-defence: *Look, you know what Patrick was like – he was totally out of order, all right? I was angry!* Except that this had been greeted by the pursed lips and judgemental head-shaking that were somehow worse than any yelled accusations. *Yes, and now he's dead,* his mum's silence said. *Dead – and you're the one to blame.*

'Oh, you know,' Zoe replied, voice flat. 'Limping along. Bea, stop that now, come on,' she added, when the little girl showed no signs of ending her grizzling.

'But I want it,' whined Bea, leaning against a rack of magazines. There was one with free plastic fairy wings attached that she kept plucking. 'I want it, Mummy, very badly. Pleeeeease?'

'No,' snapped Zoe. 'I've said no, and that's that. Get your hands off it before you crease the pages; you're not having it. Enough!'

Bea slumped against the trolley as if she'd been shot. 'It's not fair,' she howled, fresh tears springing from her eyes. 'You're so mean to me. I hate you.'

You could practically hear Zoe's teeth grinding as she tried to hang on to her patience. 'I said *enough.*' Her knuckles were white against the trolley handle, her face tightening as an elderly woman walked past and made a disapproving tut. 'And I mean it. Any more and I'll get cross.'

Dan opened his mouth. He wanted to say, *I'm sorry.* He wanted to say, *I know this is all my fault.* He wanted to say, *Let me finish that shopping for you, let me do something to help. I'll buy that magazine for Bea – I'll buy all of them – I don't mind.* 'How are the boys?' he asked instead. Bea was now kicking the trolley mutinously, a pink light flashing on her scruffy white trainer with every kick; a cross, defiant unicorn with a flushed face and blazing eyes.

'They're fine,' Zoe said, but in a beaten-down voice that meant they were not fine. Well, of course they weren't fine. 'Anyway,' she went on, shrugging, 'I'd better go. I need to pick Gabe up from his football club in' – she glanced at her watch – 'Christ, in twenty-five minutes actually. I should crack on. Sorry,' she added as a harassed-looking man tried to squeeze past them with a full trolley. 'Get out of the way, Bea.'

'Right,' Dan replied, clearing his throat, wanting to say more; to say anything that might build a bridge between them. Or at least begin papering over the crevasse. 'Er. Maybe . . .'

But she was already walking away, calling 'Bye' in a stiff, sod-off sort of voice over one narrow shoulder, the wheels of the trolley squeaking in protest as she swung it into the next aisle.

Dan stood there, clutching the wire supermarket basket, remembering the first time he had ever met Zoe; how he and Patrick had been in The Ram, not realizing that some God-awful karaoke evening was about to begin. 'Jesus, let's get out of here,' Patrick had groaned when the opening chords to 'Atomic' started up and they saw the three women clustered expectantly around a microphone. But then his face changed as he looked again. 'Check out that blonde one,' he said, eyes glued to her, and they'd both fallen silent as she gave it her best Debbie Harry. She was taller than her friends and slender, in tight jeans and boots, with long yellow hair that swung around her shoulders as she moved, and an animated face that you couldn't help but warm to. 'I'm in love,' Patrick said as the song ended and there was a ragged round of applause. Then he added, 'I'm going to marry that woman' and got up, making it to the bar just before she did. 'Allow me to buy you a drink, Ms Harry,' Dan heard him say. 'Or can I call you Debbie?'

The rest, as they said, was history.

She'd always been fun, Zoe, that was the thing. Originally from south Wales, she was giggly, kind and gorgeous. Dan had secretly fancied her himself until he grudgingly had to admit that she and his brother made the perfect couple. 'Patrick Sheppard has been tamed at last,' their mates teased, all raised eyebrows and disbelief. 'Who'd have thought?'

More than tamed, though; Patrick had met his match. 'She makes me want to be a better man,' he confessed to Dan after a few pints, early on in the relationship. 'To try harder. To be good. Do you know what I mean?' Dan knew exactly what he meant. Because Zoe herself was good through and through, smiling and golden; a person who shone her attention on you like a lamp and made you feel warm in the glow. She listened properly, remembering tiny threads of conversation and then restringing them the next time you met. *Did you get that commission you were hoping for? How's Rebecca's dad? What was the film like – is it worth seeing?*

Once, just after Dan had split up with Rebecca, Zoe had paid a surprise visit, only to find him blind drunk and unshaven with the curtains pulled at four o'clock in the afternoon. He'd been embarrassed to see her looking so pretty and clean in his grungy living room, and half-expected her to start flinging wide the curtains and forcing coffee down his throat. Instead she'd cracked open a beer with him, slouched companionably into the sofa and said, 'Go on then, tell me all about it.' He'd ended up feeling a fraction better about everything as they talked, as if one person in the world might understand, after all.

But today . . . Today she looked terrible. Her radiant face seemed to have caved in, all the sparkle bleached away, her shoulders drooping with an unbearable weariness.

He had done that to her, he thought. He had done that.

The guilt was so monstrous that he had to lean against the nearby rack of greetings cards because he suddenly felt unsteady, as if the ground was shifting beneath him. He dropped the wire basket to the floor with a metallic clatter and left the supermarket, smarting with shame.

Driving home, Dan felt detached from the world, which probably wasn't recommended in the Highway Code. This was how life had become since the accident, though: observing time passing like an outsider, the days and weeks dragging by in a sludgy sort of numbness where nothing touched him. Having haltingly explained to Tiggy that he could no longer join her on the South America jaunt, he'd spent most of the time in bed like an invalid, unable to manage anything much besides sleep or staring at the walls. Well-meaning people kept assuring him that time was a great healer, but as February turned into March, and early blossom began appearing on the trees, Dan couldn't say that he had noticed any meaningful personal change. The shock of his brother's death still throbbed like an aching wound, hot with infection, the horror as fresh and new as ever. He missed Patrick so much. And yet the missing-him was tangled up and tainted with the last evening they'd spent together; with how it had all ended.

If he shut his eyes at any moment, day or night, Dan would find himself back there, walking home alone, with the lamp posts casting their cones of orange light through the darkness, the sound of bassy reggae from a passing car rising and falling, the smell of frying onions and spicy meat from the kebab shop on the corner. The night air was cold against his face, in contrast to the alcohol and rage boiling his blood, and his fists were still clenched. How he'd hated his brother in those last few minutes, truly hated him – and yet how he wished now that someone could have told him, warned him: *You're making a huge mistake, one you will always regret. Turn round, go back, patch things up. Otherwise you'll never see him again.*

There had been no such warning, no such premonition, though. Instead, he had continued home, alone and seething, while Fate had been left to play its cruel trick. And now they all had to live with the consequences.

He hadn't cried properly yet, not even at the funeral. Sure, his throat felt tight for a while, especially at the sight of Zoe and his mum breaking down in tears, hands over their faces, but that was it. A rock of sadness had appeared inside him instead – the burden of having been the last person in the family to see Patrick alive, plus the solid ache of his loss. 'Thick as thieves, you two,' his mum had often said fondly during their childhood, ruffling their hair – or sometimes rolling her eyes with frustration if they were trying her patience. He was an only child now, though.

Arriving home, Dan sank to the floor in his hallway, breathing in the stale air that told tales of too many takeaway dinners. He remembered with a pang the fixed set of Zoe's jaw, the numb exhaustion scored into her face, and felt ashamed. Patrick's death had dropped a huge and terrible crater into her life and yet there she was – limping along, as she put it, filling a supermarket trolley with food for the kids, while Gabe was at football and Ethan was presumably taken care of elsewhere. Meanwhile here was Dan, with no kids and very few responsibilities (did the spider plant count? probably not), wallowing in self-pity as if he was the only one affected by his brother's death. Some days he hadn't even got dressed or left his bed. Had Zoe been afforded that luxury? Of course she hadn't.

How would Patrick have reacted in a similar situation, he wondered, if, for instance, a mate of his had died suddenly, leaving a wife and kids behind, shell-shocked and struggling? If Patrick had come across them in the supermarket, the child weeping, the mother defeated-looking, he'd have scooped them up in the next instant – Dan knew it. He would have hoisted the tearful child onto his shoulders, come to the rescue, taken charge. *Okay, I'm here now, I'll help you,* he'd have said in that direct way of his, before leaping into action and heroically saving the day.

Whereas Dan . . . Well, he'd done nothing. He'd scurried from the building, having provided no support or solace whatsoever. What a loser, he chastised himself. What a selfish coward.

He found himself thinking about the occasions when he'd been round at his brother's place, having arrived before Patrick got back from work; how the whole house became charged up with new energy and noise the moment Patrick let himself in with a bellow of 'I'm home!' The younger kids would swarm all over him like monkeys, shrieking with laughter, Zoe's face lighting up as he came to kiss her. How quiet the house must be now, without him. How empty it must feel.

And yet Dan hadn't been round there once since the

accident. He had bottled picking up the phone or sending a text because he didn't know what to say. What kind of a brother-in-law did that make him? What kind of uncle? It was shoddy of him. Really shoddy.

Suddenly he was sick of feeling sorry for himself. Sick of doing nothing. He got to his feet again, grabbing his bike helmet and keys. Patrick's death had broken Zoe and the kids. What sort of man was he if he didn't at least attempt to put things right?

'Oh,' said Zoe, with a distinct lack of enthusiasm, when she opened the door and saw him there. 'Hello. Twice in one day.' She was wiping her hands on a grey-and-white striped tea-towel and it was only then that Dan realized, too late, that it must be getting on for five-thirty and she was probably busy making dinner. Of all the things he had pondered on, cycling along the river path to Kew, this one had not occurred to him. *Good start, Dan*, he thought with a sigh.

'Hi,' he said. She was still unsmiling, he noticed in dismay. 'Okay if I come in? Just thought I'd . . .' He trailed off, embarrassed. *Just thought I'd pop round and see how you all are*, he'd been about to say but the words sounded trite, when it had taken him this long to bother. 'Thought I'd say hi,' he said weakly instead. 'Again.'

She lifted a shoulder, her mouth a flat line, as if she

didn't especially care what he did, but held the door wider for him nevertheless.

'Thanks,' he said, lugging his bike up the steps.

Taking care not to leave an oily mark as he leaned it against the cream-coloured wall, he found his eye falling on a framed photograph hanging nearby: of Patrick and Zoe signing the register on their wedding day. There was Patrick in his best charcoal-grey suit, a white carnation in the button-hole, his thick dark hair neatly cropped. His face was tilted as he gazed at Zoe with such love, such adoration, it burned Dan's eyes to see it. To have and to hold, till death do us part. *Oh, Patrick*, he thought, suddenly desolate again. How was it possible that his brother was no longer present, wandering through to slap Dan on the back and offer him a beer? *All right, mate?*

Yeah, not bad. You?

'Sorry,' he said, realizing he was standing there in silent mourning. He'd been right about the quietness of the house, he thought. The atmosphere was like a held breath. A suppressed sob. 'Um, yeah. So I thought . . . Can we talk?'

'Sure,' she said, unmoving. She *did* hate him. She didn't even want him to go any further into the house.

'Could we . . . ?' The words stuck in his throat.

Patrick and Zoe had always been the most generous hosts, pressing food and drink on you, urging you to stay – There's no rush, sit down, help yourself! – but today resentment radiated from her in waves. *Go away, go away,* her body language said. *You should have stopped him. He'd still be here, alive, if it wasn't for you.*

Dan forced himself to finish his sentence. '. . . maybe go in the kitchen?'

'Okay.' She turned and walked down the hall into the large, light-filled kitchen. He remembered them having this extension built, back when Gabe had just been born; how the flapping sheets of blue plastic over the end of the wall had frightened Ethan, who must have been four at the time. This room was the heart of the home, the long oak table set more often than not with a couple of extra places for friends. The layers and texture of family life that had silted up were visible everywhere: framed holiday photos and Art Deco posters alongside the crayoned drawings on the walls; a collection of spotted mugs clustered colourfully along the dresser, mingling with various wonky school-made pots; the fridge boasting certificates for good spelling, football skills, an art commendation.

Today the room had a different feel. Perhaps it was the meanness of the late-afternoon light that left it drabber than usual, but there was definitely a new air of neglect about the place as well. Some of the plants on the windowsill appeared shrivelled and stalky, their leaves miserably brown in places. There was a box of recycling by the bin – cardboard and empty yogurt pots and tin cans – waiting to be sorted. And random stuff lay everywhere: library books and unopened post, a pair of shin-pads, a roll of gaffer tape, a broken necklace, a spelling chart . . . A Lego knight lay face-down on top of the butter dish and Dan stood it up again, wondering where the children were. It felt as if he'd entered an alternative universe; one out of sync with real life.

'Sorry about the mess,' Zoe said. She sounded defiant, as if she expected criticism. 'I'm in the middle of dinner.'

'Yes. Sorry,' he replied like an echo, unsure what else to say. There were sausages spitting in formation under the grill, he saw, a pan of potatoes foaming on the hob, and a chopping board on the side with a mound of peeled carrots. 'Can I . . . do anything?' He hadn't even brought a token gift, he realized, cursing himself. No flowers or wine, no peace offering at all.

'It's fine,' she said. 'Do you want a drink? I'm going to carry on with this, if you don't mind.'

'Not at all,' he replied. He couldn't bring himself to say yes to a drink, despite the dryness of his mouth. He couldn't take anything else from her. 'Um. So,' he began, 'I just—' He broke off, trying to remember the speech he'd composed on his way here. It had seemed plausible back then, noble even, but now the right words seemed to have slid out of reach. 'I came round to say that I'm sorry I've not been over for ages, but I do want to help,' he managed to get out. *I'm sad too,* he wanted to say. *I've been a complete mess. Today is the first time I've shaved in a fortnight.* 'I want to support you and the kids,' he went on. 'You know, be there for you all. So if there's ever anything I can do, then—'

'MUMMY! He *hit* me,' yelled Bea just then, bursting into the room like a small raging tornado. 'Gabe hit me with the remote, right here.' Bristling with self-righteousness, she pointed to her temple, where a red mark bloomed. 'See?'

Zoe's shoulders stiffened. 'Gabe,' she shouted tonelessly. 'What have I told you? If you can't share, the screen goes off. Do you hear me?'

'You said he'd be *banned* from the Xbox if he did it again,' Bea was keen to remind her. 'You need to ban him now, Mummy. Tell him!'

'I'm busy at the moment,' Zoe said, not turning round as she chopped through another carrot.

'Hi, Bea,' said Dan. This was his chance to do something useful, he realized. 'Shall we set the table together to help Mummy?'

'That's Ethan's job,' she said, flouncing out again. 'Gabe! Mummy says you're in *big* trouble,' they heard her yell. 'Really, really BIG. If you touch me again, you're *dead.*'

Zoe flinched at her daughter's words but before Dan could say anything, Ethan walked into the room. 'What's for dinner?' he asked. 'Oh, hi, Uncle Dan.'

Ethan was tall and reedy, pale-faced with large square glasses and tufty ginger-brown hair. He was a quiet boy, thoughtful and artistic, who gave the impression of creating whole worlds up in his un-walled mind. He'd been such an earnest toddler, head always cocked as he asked one brain-bending question after another. Now he was fourteen and still a quirky sort. Patrick had worried about him starting secondary school – *He's not like the other kids, they'll kick the shit out of him,* he'd agonized once to Dan – but so far Ethan seemed to be surviving unscathed.

'Bangers and mash,' Zoe said shortly.

'Hi, mate,' said Dan. 'How's school?' Then he promptly cringed at his own remarks because: one, Ethan was not a 'mate' kind of person; and two, no kid ever liked being asked *How's school?*, the most boring question in the world. 'Are you working on a new sculpture at the moment?' he added quickly, as if needing to prove that he had actually met his nephew before.

'Nope. I've stopped going to the club.' Ethan grabbed some cutlery from a drawer and began dumping it around the table.

'Oh. That's a shame,' said Dan, straightening a fork. He vaguely remembered that Ethan had been overjoyed to be offered a place there – some edgy creative space in Wandsworth where they made all sorts of weird and wonderful artworks from wire and scrap metal and clay. 'How come?'

'I don't think we need to go over this again,' Zoe said, sweeping the chopped carrots into a pan of boiling water.

A muscle clenched in Ethan's jaw and he banged down the last knife with such force that it spun in a circle. Then he stormed out of the room.

'Good one,' Zoe muttered, rolling her eyes.

'Sorry,' Dan said for what felt like the hundredth time since he'd arrived. 'I didn't realize.'

Zoe swung round, eyes glittering. 'No, Dan, you didn't, did you? You didn't realize because you've no idea what's been going on.' She slammed a lid on the pan of carrots and the blue flame beneath it jerked and trembled in response. 'Coming round here and bleating *Sorry* over and over again, like that's going to change anything. Well, it's not good enough. You're too late!'

'Sorry,' he said before he could stop himself, then grimaced. 'But, look, I do want to help. I—'

'No, *you* look,' she said, folding her arms across her chest, but then Bea was barrelling into the room once more, wailing this time.

'He twisted my arm right behind my *back*. It hurts! I think it's *broken!*'

Zoe became rigid, as if she was on the verge of shattering into pieces. 'You want to help?' she asked Dan, so fiercely it felt like an attack. 'You really want to help?'

'Yes, of course,' he said. She was going to ask him to have a word with Gabe, he guessed. Or pour glasses of water to go with dinner. Or come back tomorrow and run the lawnmower around the garden, which was looking pretty unkempt.

'Great,' she said, her voice clipped. She held her hands up in the air, signalling surrender. 'Then it's all yours,' she said. 'Dinner, the kids – everything. I'm going out.'

'What . . . where?' Dan asked in surprise, but Zoe was already striding towards the door.

'MUMMY!' screamed Bea, racing after her. 'Don't go! Come back!'

'What the hell . . . ?' asked Ethan, as first his mother and then his sister charged past him.

In the hall, Bea had body-slammed Zoe and was now clinging around her legs. 'Mummy, no,' she cried. 'Don't leave me.'

'Stop being so dramatic,' Zoe said, stuffing some keys in her jeans pocket. 'I'm not going forever. I just need a break.' She unwound the little girl's arms from her knees. 'Be good for your uncle,' she added on her way out.

'MUMMY!' Bea howled as the front door closed. Through the red and green teardrop shapes of its stained-glass window you could see Zoe walking quickly down the path, then turning onto the pavement. Dan blinked and she was gone completely. Meanwhile Bea was rolling around on the carpet, wailing and snotty. She had lost one parent already, Dan remembered. He had to be kind with her, rather than impatient.

'It's all right,' he said, kneeling down. He put a wary

hand on her shoulder as if she were a wild animal, but she shook him off with a sob. 'Mummy'll be back soon. She's just gone for a walk. Do you want to help me dish up tea?'

'No! I just want *her*!'

'She's not allowed to dish up,' Ethan put in unhelpfully. 'Too babyish. She'd only spill something or burn herself.'

'Would NOT!' Lying face-down, Bea kicked out, almost scoring a direct hit to Dan's groin.

'Hey,' he yelped, backing away. 'Don't worry,' he said from a safe distance. 'Come on, hop up now and . . .' He struggled to think of something she could do. 'You can help me mash the potatoes. I bet you're a great masher.'

Bea said nothing, but kicked wildly again and thumped the floor for good measure, the rainbow tail of her unicorn onesie bouncing with each movement. 'I want Mummy,' she sobbed. '*Mummy!*'

'Leave her,' said Ethan, turning back towards the kitchen. 'She's just trying to get attention. This is what she does, like, every day. It's so boring.'

Dan hesitated, feeling powerless. Bea sounded genuinely distraught; he couldn't simply abandon her there. What else could he offer his niece other than potato-mashing? 'Um . . .' he began, his mind unhelpfully blank.

But before he could think of anything, there came a shout from the kitchen. 'Uncle Dan? Did you know that the sausages are on *fire*?'

Chapter Two

Dinner wasn't exactly the most tempting meal of Dan's life. The sausages were blackened. The mash was lumpy, the carrots woody and underdone. 'This is dis-*gusting*,' pouted Bea, her eyelashes still spangled with tears.

'It's pretty gross,' agreed Gabe, who had curly brown hair and wore a mud-smeared football kit. He added a massive splodge of ketchup to his mash and stirred it together. 'Pink mash. Yuck,' he said, with undisguised glee. 'Now it looks like a road accident. Brains everywhere.'

'*Gabe*,' said Ethan. 'Shut up.'

'Make me,' jeered Gabe, holding up a fork full of pink mash and letting it drop in soft, wet dollops onto the plate. 'Braaaaains,' he crowed, sneaking a look at his brother.

Ethan scowled and Dan found himself wondering where Zoe was and how long she intended to stay away. Also whether his woefully late appearance at the door had been the final straw after the worst three weeks of her life.

Bea pushed her plate back in mutiny and Dan felt

compelled to act fast, before the meal plunged to even more dismal depths. 'This *is* a fairly rubbish dinner,' he said, before quickly adding, 'My fault – not your mum's', in case anyone saw fit to dob him in for it later. 'So where's the nearest chip shop round here?'

His words were like a magic spell, as all three of their heads whipped round towards him. Yes, okay, he was desperate, and guilt had made him a pushover.

'It's on Sandycombe Road,' said Ethan. 'Like, five minutes' walk? Four, if we're quick.'

'Are we really going to have chips?' asked Bea, with an air of faint suspicion. 'Actually really and truly?'

'CHIPS!' cheered Gabe, who seemed to have no such doubts. He stabbed his knife and fork vertically into the revolting pink mash, then leapt off his chair and struck a superhero pose. 'CHIPS TO THE RESCUE!'

His enthusiasm was infectious. 'Chips are my actual favourite!' Bea squealed. Even Ethan jumped up from the table with a newly eager air.

'What are we waiting for?' asked Dan, and they abandoned the rubbish dinner and set off. First lesson in childcare: buy them off with fried food, he thought, with a wince as they headed along the road, hoping very much that they wouldn't bump into Zoe on her way back. *Sorry, Zoe. Sorry, Patrick. Just filling your kids up with grease and salt because I couldn't even manage to keep the sausages from catching fire. Looking on the bright side, though, I didn't burn the house down, right? Not yet, anyway!*

Still, at least everyone had cheered up. Bea was skipping and twirling around each lamp post singing about chicken nuggets, while Gabe gave Dan a lengthy account of that afternoon's school football club. He seemed to have scored about eighteen goals, according to his version of events, including several headers, an overhead kick and one from the halfway line. 'Unbelievable,' Dan said each time, which about summed it up.

Ethan was the only one who was silent and Dan shot him a look. 'Everything all right, E?' he asked.

Gabe, interrupted from a story about an amazing volley that had resulted in him getting his first hat-trick, glanced across at his brother. 'Oh,' he said, scrunching up his nose. There was something appealingly Just William-ish about Gabe, with his unruly springy hair and freckles, plus his almost permanent air of dishevelment. 'It's cos I'm talking about football. It makes him really angry. Because he's got anger-management problems. And—'

'Shut up, dumb-arse,' said Ethan, elbowing him, whereupon Gabe promptly jostled him back.

'See?' he cried, dodging away as Ethan glowered and made a proper swing for him. 'See that, Uncle Dan? Anger. Issues. That's what his teacher told Mum. And I – *ow!* See? And now he's *hitting* me.'

'Come on, less of that,' Dan said, to no effect whatsoever. 'Boys!' He was relieved to see the lights of the chip shop ahead, like a welcome beacon, as the two of them began scuffling in earnest. Gabe had always had a knack of winding his older brother up, but Ethan looked positively murderous this time as he hit out at Gabe.

'Enough, you two, we're here now, pack it in,' Dan said, grabbing them both and pulling them apart. 'Right then, guys – what do you all want?'

'I'm not a guy actually,' Bea reminded him. 'But I would like chicken nuggets and chips, please, Uncle Dan.'

Ethan was still white in the face, whereas Gabe looked sweatily bullish. Clearly the magic offered by a bag of chips couldn't solve everything, although the two boys did stop trying to punch each other long enough to mumble their requests at least. Small mercies.

Back at the house, as everyone tucked in with rather more appetite, Dan kept glancing over at the clock as it ticked through the minutes, with no sign of Zoe's return. He had one ear tuned to the sound of the front door while the kids chatted, wondering if she still accidentally listened out for Patrick coming home at this time of day. You would, wouldn't you? Some habits were so ingrained they were muscle-memory, wired into your cells. After Rebecca left, Dan hadn't been able to sleep in the empty bed because he kept waiting for her to get in beside him. He still thought about her on what had been their wedding anniversary and her birthday, the memories less painful every year but bitter-sweet nonetheless. But anyway. He was trying his best to keep her out of his head, especially after . . .

Don't go there, he told himself quickly. He had wasted enough time agonizing over her lately.

It was half-past six once they'd finished eating. Now what? Dan wondered. Would Zoe be back before the kids' bedtime or was he meant to do that too? 'Does anyone have any homework?' he asked, at which their faces fell. 'Or we could play a game of something?' he added hastily.

Ethan sloped off upstairs, whereas Gabe claimed he needed to 'finish the level' of the Thor game he'd been glued to on the Xbox earlier, which left Bea, who told Dan that she *did* want to play something: unicorns. This involved Dan crawling around the playroom while Bea rode imperiously on his back, occasionally casting spells that allowed them to fly to various magical lands together. She seemed so much more cheerful that he didn't dare complain about the friction burns he could foresee appearing on his hands, although he did feel tremendous relief when Gabe called through to say that it was seven o'clock and bedtime for 'baby Bea'. After the inevitable argument with her brother about how she wasn't a baby, and he was a *pig, actually,* she eventually acquiesced and trudged upstairs. Childcare was exhausting, thought Dan, as he supervised his niece's teeth-brushing in the bathroom a short while later. How had Zoe managed to deal with this alone, day after day? Managing the turbulence of her children's grief on top of her own, soldiering miserably through each long evening without her husband there – it seemed unthinkable. Barely possible.

'Oh, am I meant to be giving you a bath?' he asked, belatedly noticing a line of animal flannels along the edge of the tub.

'Hmm,' said Bea, through a mouthful of foaming toothpaste. 'Usually I have a bath, *then* brush my teeth. You got it wrong actually, Uncle Dan.'

'Oh dear,' he said. 'Never mind. You can go to sleep stinky this once, I'm sure.'

'Girls don't *stink*,' Bea told him, outraged. 'Anyway,' she went on as if something had just occurred to her. 'How can I *sleep* without a story from Mummy?' She rinsed her toothbrush and made a big show of spitting flamboyantly into the sink. 'And the Daddy song?'

'What's the Daddy song?' Dan asked, following her into the very pink, bunting-adorned princess kingdom that was her bedroom. The walls, the curtains, the carpet all glowed a warm rosy hue, with a sparkly fairy-tale palace painted above the bed. Dan found himself imagining Patrick up a ladder painting the walls and hanging the pastel bunting, and felt the hairs on the back of his neck tingle. How he had doted on his little girl.

Unzipping her unicorn onesie and tossing it to the floor, Bea began singing, her voice high and sweet, although becoming somewhat muffled as she peeled off her school uniform and her jumper got stuck around her head. 'Daddy, I miss you, every every day. You were my favourite, in every every way. Please come back to meeee. Love Bea.'

If Dan had been feeling sad before, his grief now threatened to choke him. How could a six-year-old come to terms with losing a parent, when previously the world had been nothing but magic and fairy tales? He could hardly bear to imagine. 'That's a lovely song,' he croaked as she hoisted up a pair of pyjama bottoms, then attempted a wobbly headstand on the bed. 'Really special. Did you make it up yourself?'

Her legs crashed down and she giggled, then put on her pyjama top. 'Mummy helped a *bit*,' she conceded, negotiating the armholes. 'Like – one word. And some of the tune. But I did the rest.'

He gave her a hug because he couldn't find the words for a moment. 'I miss him too,' he said, her small body crushed against his.

'He was your brother,' she said, pulling back after a few seconds and looking at him. They were so close that he could see every blonde eyelash. Her blue eyes were steady and appraising, just like Zoe's, but her slightly pointy ears and expressive eyebrows were most definitely from her dad.

'Yes.'

Bea shrugged, wrinkling her nose. 'I don't mind if *my* brothers die,' she said, heartlessly. 'But I miss my daddy. A *lot*. This much,' she elaborated, stretching her arms wide.

'He was funny, wasn't he?' Dan said.

'Yes, he was *really* funny. And he would throw me around sometimes. Really high in the air, so it was like flying.' She wriggled out of his arms and leapt on the bed. 'And he gave me piggybacks and let me tickle his hair. And when he laughed, he did this: HUH-HUH-HUH.' She threw back her head in an uncanny impression of Patrick, and Dan shut his eyes briefly because he knew exactly what she meant.

'He was a good daddy,' he agreed. His emotions were swelling and heaving like a rising tide; he needed to change the subject before he was dragged under. 'Right then,' he said. 'You'd better hop under those covers, quick, and go to sleep.'

She snuggled beneath the duvet and stretched up her arms for a last cuddle, winding them around his neck as he leaned in. 'Goodnight, Daddy,' she said in his ear and he stiffened. Had it been a slip of the tongue, he wondered, or was she pretending, for comfort? Either way, his heart was cracking.

'Now you say, "Goodnight, little Bea",' she instructed, her breath warm and minty against his neck.

The rock in his throat was becoming more boulder-like

by the second and he had to really force it back down before he could speak. 'Goodnight, little Bea,' he echoed.

She let go and rolled onto her side. 'Buzz-buzz,' she murmured, then shut her eyes.

Dan said nothing for a moment, in case further orders were issued, but she remained silent and, almost immediately, her breathing began to deepen and lengthen. He gazed at her with a pain in his chest. *Goodnight, Daddy,* he heard her say again and the poignancy of the words took his breath away. However she might be working through her grief and pain, coming up so close to it felt pretty shattering.

Oh, poor you, scoffed Zoe in his head. *It's all about you, isn't it, Dan?*

By the time he had left Bea's bedroom and returned downstairs, it was seven-thirty and dark outside, but there was still no sign of his sister-in-law. He wondered what she was doing now; if she was with friends in a noisy bar, or within the soothing sanctuary of someone's house; if she was steaming drunk or crying, or both.

'Gabe?' he called, going into the living room, then stopped at the sight of his younger nephew fast asleep on the sofa, still fully dressed and clutching the game controller. Gabe's face – usually so animated – was softened with sleep, his mouth slack, his thick, full eyelashes quivering mid-dream. Dan found himself thinking back to when Gabe was born, how he and Rebecca had looked after Ethan while

Zoe was in labour, before Patrick's jubilant phone call had finally come: *Little boy – well, not so little really, he's nine pounds three ounces, an absolute whopper!* Trust Gabe to start life with a bang.

Dan remembered that day particularly for how much he'd loved hanging out with Ethan. It was the first time he and Rebecca had had sole responsibility for a child, and he'd really enjoyed it. They'd gone to the park and played in the sandpit together, then, back at the flat, Dan had found a leftover roll of wallpaper, spreading it across the floor so that they could draw a complicated road network for Ethan's toy car to drive along. Having been a bit apprehensive about entertaining his small, solemn nephew for possibly a day or more, Dan felt a glow inside as it became clear that the boy was relaxed and happy, chatting away as they drew. *I'm doing all right here,* he told himself, praising Ethan for his scribbly contributions. *I can do this.*

Later they took Ethan to the hospital to meet his new brother, witnessing at first hand the warmth and wonder of the maternity ward: Patrick and Zoe so delighted, Zoe's mum and stepdad arriving from south Wales, his own parents there too, everyone celebrating. All the joy gave Dan an unexpected pang of envy for what Patrick had: the children, the family life, that whole future they were building for themselves. It must have shown on his face that evening, because when he'd turned to Rebecca with the question half-formed on his lips, she'd shaken her head before he'd even managed to ask it. 'Oh no,' she said. They were in bed together, her long auburn hair loose about her shoulders, and she wagged a finger forbiddingly. 'Stop right there. I know what you're going to say, and the answer is *No way*. Stretchmarks and stitches? Not for me.'

If he'd been listening for it, Dan might have heard a ghostly bell tolling a faint warning just then, but in the next second she'd whipped the covers back to reveal her flat belly and small perfect breasts, which distracted him.

'I'm not ruining these, either. After all the Pilates I've done? And that sodding fasting? It would be a tragedy.' Needless to say, he'd agreed with her at the time. He would have agreed with anything she'd said at that precise moment, let's face it.

Nine years on, anyway, newborn baby Gabriel had grown into this scrappy, charming and opinionated child, who was now spark out on the sofa. Dan scooped him up with the same tentative care as when he'd held him in the maternity ward for the first time, but there was not a murmur. Not a flicker. All that football, plus a plate of fat vinegary chips, had done for him.

The landline started ringing as Dan was halfway up the stairs and he froze, dreading the noise disturbing Gabe, but the boy slumbered on, oblivious. After a few rings the answerphone kicked in and a cross-sounding woman launched into a message. 'This is Mrs Henderson from Townley Street. I've left so many messages on your mobile, I've given up and got this number from Directory Enquiries. And you're still not answering! If you have a shred of decency, then please call me back. The boiler's playing up again and we've been without hot water for two weeks. It's not on!'

Presumably the woman was one of Patrick's tenants, who had no way of knowing that he had died, Dan realized. Having worked in the building trade since leaving school, Patrick had made a lot of money, fast, by buying up derelict properties, renovating them and then selling them on at vast profits. More recently he had accumulated six or seven West London flats and kept them on as rentals. The plan had been to earn some easy money on the side of his main building work, but he'd often grumbled about his tenants' inability to change a light bulb without phoning him to complain about it. Still, a broken boiler was a different matter. Dan figured that Patrick's work mobile was no doubt as dead as he was, and almost certainly full of other similar messages.

On went poor unlistened-to Mrs Henderson, ranting into the answerphone while Dan continued up to the landing, his sleeping nephew surprisingly heavy in his arms. Gabe's small bedroom was next to Bea's, and was plastered with posters of Fulham Football Club and various superheroes in action poses. As Dan lowered the boy gently onto the bed, he noticed that someone – Zoe? Gabe himself? – had Blu-tacked a photo on the wall nearby at pillow height, of Patrick and Gabe at a Fulham match. There they were together, holding an end each of a black-and-white scarf above their heads, both of them open-mouthed with a cheer, by the look of it. They had the same lips, Dan noticed, wide and full, prone to forming shouts and smiles in equal measure. His heart ached as he saw a smudgy fingerprint on the photo and imagined Gabe lying there, reaching to touch his dad's face before he went to sleep every night. He was too old for a Daddy song of his own, but he still needed something, clearly. Didn't they all?

Gently rolling the *Star Wars* duvet out from underneath Gabe, Dan peeled off his nephew's football socks before deciding to leave the rest of his kit on for the night. It was Friday, so there was no school in the morning at least. He pulled the duvet up to Gabe's chin, shut the curtains and left the room.

Two down, one to go, he thought, padding downstairs, where the irate tenant was still voicing her displeasure into the answerphone. 'I said to the Citizens Advice Bureau, this is the worst landlord I've ever had – he's an absolute disgrace, completely unreliable and—'

Complaints about a dodgy boiler were one thing, but having the house filled with slurs against his brother was too close to the bone. Hurrying down the last few stairs, Dan snatched up the receiver. 'He's dead,' he said coldly.

'He's *dead*. And I'm sorry you've got a problem with your boiler or whatever, but your landlord – my brother – died last month, and that's why he's not been answering your calls. Got that?' And then he slammed the phone down again, before sinking to the bottom step, his hands rising instinctively to cradle his own head.

He took several deep breaths, taken aback by his own burst of temper. He'd always been the calmer of the two brothers, the one to pause and think carefully rather than allow his impulses free rein. Tonight, though, he felt raw, uncontained, his emotions highly charged after the hours spent with his niece and nephews.

He rubbed his face, his temper dropping away as quickly as it had flared up – how was this woman to know what had happened? Then, with a groan of regret, he reached forward, took the phone again and pressed last-number redial. 'I'm sorry,' he said when she replied. 'I'm Patrick's brother Dan, I shouldn't have spoken to you like that. We're all still a bit at sea without him.' The phrase seemed wholly inadequate. *We are broken without him*, he should have said. *We are drowning in his loss*. Then he cringed at how inappropriate these words were. 'It was very sudden and unexpected,' he finished, hoping she wouldn't ask any questions.

The woman – Mrs Henderson, had she said? – took a moment to respond. 'I understand,' she said. 'And I'm sorry too, for saying those things and upsetting you. Not to mention sorry that . . . that you've lost him.' She hesitated. 'I just . . .' But then her voice trailed away almost immediately, as if forbidding herself to start complaining again. *Not now. A man has died, remember.*

'I get it,' he said, filling the space. 'You're fed up and nobody's returned your calls or helped you. Fair enough.' And then, because he didn't feel he could really ignore the problem now, he added, 'I could have a look at the boiler for you. Not tonight, obviously, but maybe tomorrow?'

'Oh, *would* you?' Her relief was almost palpable. 'I'd really appreciate that. I've got young children, you see, and we're having to go next door or to friends' houses to shower and – well, it's been going on for a fortnight now and my friends have been wonderful, but we can't carry on like this. It's really getting me down.'

'Of course it must be. And I'm sorry,' he said again. 'Let me take down your details. What time tomorrow would be best for you?'

He reached around for something to write on and saw another pile of unopened post sitting there on the hall table. He flipped the letters over, to see that most of them were addressed to Patrick. 'Go on,' he said to Mrs Henderson, jotting down her details on one of the envelopes and reflecting on how hard it was to lose someone when the rest of the world hadn't yet caught up with the news. All those people you had to keep telling again and again, before they stopped ringing and writing and asking for things. All the mailing lists and databases a person ended up on – how every entry had to be deleted, one after another. It was bad enough trying to handle the shock yourself, but for Zoe, having to repeat the news endlessly to person after person and then feeling obliged to respond to *their* shock and condolences and questions . . . It must scrape off the top layer of skin each time, the wound unable to start healing.

But he could take some of that away for her, he realized. He could deal with this stack of post, if she wanted him to. Go through the phone calls jamming up Patrick's work mobile and the landline answerphone and make sure the grim word got out: to tenants, to the bank, to suppliers. He could take on that responsibility.

Wow, my hero, Zoe said sarcastically in his head. *It's really the least you can do, you know that, don't you?*

It was a start, though. It would be something at least.

By now it was past eight o'clock, and after making arrangements with Mrs Henderson – 'Call me Ruth' – all Dan felt like doing was cracking open a beer and sinking into the sofa, but with Zoe still absent, he had to keep a clear head. Do his bit. So he went up to Ethan's room and knocked gently on the open door. 'Hi,' he said, poking his head round.

Ethan was plugged into some computer game or other, headphones on, bony shoulders tensed, peering intently at his laptop. Killing things, judging by all the flying sparks and explosions on the screen. Dan moved a little nearer, into his nephew's field of vision, until Ethan eventually noticed him and jerked round.

'Oh. Hi,' he said, glancing from Dan back to the game just as a masked gangster shot his character in the head.

'Oof,' said Dan as gore splattered the screen. 'Sorry. Er . . . Just wanted to see if you're all right.' He sat on the edge of the bed, hands between his legs. 'If you needed any help with homework or anything.' Not that it looked as if much home-work was in the offing. His gaze travelled around the room, taking in the metre-high papier-mâché hand that was giving him the middle finger from the far corner, the large Escher prints and a metallic collage of the London skyline on the wall, plus the life-size bust of a Greek god wearing a purple party hat by his bed. 'You've got some cool stuff in here,' he commented.

'Thanks,' said Ethan. 'I don't have any homework.' Then he grimaced. 'Well – some revision for exams, but . . .' He shrugged as if to say, *Who gives a shit about exams?*

'I can help with that, if you want.' Dan guessed that exams and schoolwork didn't feel so important any more, when you'd lost your dad. 'We could go through it together?' He was desperate to help, he realized. Desperate to make up for the evening of Patrick's death, when he'd been oblivi-ous, striding away, all self-righteous and cold. How many

hours of exam help, how many Daddy songs, how many
carries up to bed would it take, though? If he could fill in a
few of the gaps that Patrick had left, it would be *something*,
he figured. Right?

Ethan didn't seem particularly bowled over by the offers
of assistance, though. 'Nah,' he said, closing down the game
on his screen. 'It's okay, thanks.'

'Well – another time, then,' Dan said. 'Hey, what was
that all about earlier anyway, you and Gabe scrapping on the
way to the chippy? Did I miss something there?'

Ethan's face became mask-like. 'He's a dick,' he said
shortly.

Dan tried again. 'Was it something to do with the sculpture club you were going to? The one your mum didn't want
to talk about?' he guessed. Anger issues, Gabe had taunted,
but Ethan had never been an angry child before now.

His sigh in response was world-weary. 'Yeah. It's Wednesday afternoons, the same time as one of Gabe's football
sessions, so Mum can't pick me up. She doesn't want me
coming back from Wandsworth on my own because I
couldn't possibly manage a bus *and* a Tube without being
mugged or stabbed or getting lost.' He rolled his eyes, a
proper glower setting in. 'Like, I *am* fourteen! Everyone in
my year goes all over London on their own. But Mum's got
really weird about us doing anything that's not completely,

boringly safe. And obviously Gabe can't give up his precious *football.'*

It was the longest speech he'd made since Dan had got there, and it took Dan a moment to work through all the resentment simmering within. He nodded, not wanting to take sides or go against Zoe's decision. As for Gabe and the football, he remembered Patrick once joking that Gabe was like a dog – he needed running several times a day, every day, otherwise he became hyper and unmanageable. Zoe had laid down the law here and he understood why, but all the same it didn't seem fair on Ethan.

'It wouldn't take that long to cycle back,' he said, think-ing aloud. 'Half an hour to get here from Wandsworth?' But he could tell from Ethan's expression that Zoe wouldn't permit cycling, either. Too dangerous. Too much of a risk. He got it. When you'd lost your husband so shockingly, so suddenly, of course you were going to be paranoid about bad things happening to your kids too. 'How did you get home before?' he asked. 'Did your dad pick you up?'

Ethan nodded, eyes faraway. Remembering fun times in the front of Patrick's van, no doubt, just the two of them, having a laugh, music blasting. Patrick commenting on attractive women walking past, then winking at his son. *Don't tell your mum I said that!*

'I could take you instead,' Dan offered. 'Wednesday after-noons, did you say?'

Ethan's face lit up. 'Really? Do you mean it?'

'Sure. Absolutely.' As a financial tech consultant, Dan's days were usually spent finding new solutions to clients' tech problems, with little time for much else. But seeing as there were two full months left of his sabbatical, he was free to help out, for now at least. Frankly, he would be quite glad of an excuse to leave the flat and be useful to somebody, he realized.

'Oh my God.' For the first time since Dan had seen his nephew that day, there was a flash of genuine happiness on his face. 'I'm so . . .' His chin wobbled. Ethan had always been such a quiet, self-contained kid. Had he been over-looked in the fallout from the family's tragedy? 'That would be amazing. Thank you. Are you sure?'

'I'm completely sure.' Dan wondered if it would be too much to ruffle his nephew's tufty hair, but at the last moment held back. Ethan didn't strike him as a touchy-feely person and this was strange new ground they found themselves on. 'Do you know, earlier on I was thinking back to when Gabe was born,' he said suddenly. 'You might not remember, but I was looking after you that day and we ended up drawing together for hours on this great long roll of wallpaper. It started off as a series of roads for your car, but then we added all sorts of weird and wonderful buildings and creatures. Jungles, mountains, cities . . .' His eyes felt hot, thinking back to the sweet, solemn little boy Ethan had been then, how he'd leaned over that paper so intently as they worked on it with their felt-tips. They had created their own world, albeit imaginary. How ironic that Dan had inadvertently destroyed Ethan's actual world all these years later.

Ethan's face was screwed up in concentration. 'I think I do remember,' he replied. 'We rolled the paper right out and it stretched across the room.'

'It did! Spot on.' They smiled at each other, a tentative, fragile sort of smile but it counted nonetheless. 'Well, I'll leave you to it,' Dan said. 'And when your mum gets in, I'll tell her about our Wednesday-afternoon plan, yeah?'

'Yeah. Thanks.'

'No problem. Oh – and don't forget to brush your teeth before you go to bed, will you?' he added, realizing that Gabe had gone to sleep with his teeth unbrushed. Oops.

Ethan raised an eyebrow. 'I'm not a baby,' he said.

'No. Of course you're not. Okay, I'll leave you to it.'

Dan went back downstairs, feeling very much as if he deserved a beer by now and hoping that Zoe might have a few in the fridge. Then he saw his bike in the hall and remembered that he still had to cycle home. Presumably, anyway. Assuming that Zoe did eventually reappear. He stood gazing at the front door, wishing he could hear her key in the lock, that she would come back again now. She had made her point: she'd escaped from the house and kids for a few hours, she'd caused Dan to sweat.

She *was* going to come back, wasn't she? Like . . . tonight? She wasn't going to stay away for the whole weekend or anything?

It was dark outside, headlights gleaming through the black as cars cruised along the street, trying to find parking spaces. The weather forecast he'd heard earlier had predicted a heavy frost tonight, and already the pavements were glistening with the first icy traces. He pulled the living-room curtains shut, a swarm of anxious new thoughts invading his head. Standing there in the kitchen earlier, her face sharp with stress and blame, Zoe had seemed at breaking point. What if she'd really had enough and had done something stupid? You heard about people who simply couldn't go on without their partners, who were so destroyed by grief and anger and loss they could no longer think straight.

He went through to the kitchen, feeling uneasy as he pulled down the striped blind, checked the back door was locked. Zoe had thrown up her hands in defeat and marched out of there, deaf to Bea's wails, no hesitation whatsoever. Had she even taken any money with her? he wondered now. Where *was* she?

Clearing up the detritus from their fish-and-chip takeaway, he washed up the pans from the first aborted dinner and set the dishwasher running. He found himself thinking back to when he and Rebecca split up and he'd rented a temporary flat on Shepherd's Bush Road; how for a while he had been the archetypal bachelor slob again, wallowing in misery and grime, letting the mess accumulate around him and not caring. Ironically it had been Patrick coming round and saying, 'Jesus Christ, Dan' and 'This is a shithole' and 'God, pull yourself together, will you? Are you having a nervo or something?' that had snapped him out of it.

He wiped the surfaces now, wondering if he should do anything about all the clutter piled up around the room and whether it was any of his business to sort it out, or if Zoe would react angrily and take his interference as criticism. He chucked out the shrivelled brown daffodils that had died of thirst in a dry vase, relocated from the fruit bowl to the compost bin a couple of mouldering satsumas that had developed interesting verdigris-like patterns, and cleaned the worst of the dust from the window-ledges with some kitchen roll. Should he carry on? Maybe if he'd been a better brother-in-law, in and out over the last few weeks to help with shopping and childcare amidst the family's storm of grief, he would know the best course of action. He'd have earned the right to take charge and rearrange her kitchen. Not today, though. Not yet.

He went into the living room and sat down. The house was as quiet as a morgue. He switched on the TV, volume low so as not to disturb anyone, and flicked through the channels, but nothing good was on. He fiddled with his phone, wondering whether or not to call Zoe, but was too wary of her shouting at him again. He sent a text instead: *Hope you are okay. The kids are all fine. I'll stay here till you get back. D*

No reply. He leaned against the soft cushions, suddenly weary. He'd managed a lot today; the most, in fact, since Patrick had died, and there was plenty to process. He shut his eyes. All he could do now was wait for Zoe to come home.

Two streets away, Zoe was on her best friend Clare's sofa and making decent inroads into her third glass of wine. 'I'm never going home,' she announced, as the doorbell rang, heralding the arrival of their Indian takeaway. 'Is that okay, Clare? If I just stay here and you look after me? You don't mind, do you?'

Clare got up to answer the door. 'It's going to be okay, Zo,' she said as she left the room.

Zoe slumped like a bag of damp sand, her teeth furry from the wine, her limbs loose and alcohol-sodden. 'It's going to be okay,' she repeated to herself in a tiny whisper, but even as she was saying the words, she knew they couldn't possibly be true. How could anything ever be okay again, without Patrick?

Chapter Three

'Let's have a look, then,' Dan said, peering at the controls on Ruth Henderson's boiler the following morning and hoping he looked vaguely knowledgeable. It was a vain hope, no doubt, after the precious little sleep he'd had the night before: he'd ended up dozing off on Zoe's sofa sometime around midnight, waking up several hours later when she crashed back into the house, incoherent and smelling strongly of wine. He'd lain awake afterwards for what felt like ages, the sofa fabric prickly against his face, as his mind looped ceaselessly, too wired to stop. In the wake of Patrick's death, he had gone about things all wrong, he kept thinking. He had to figure out how he could start making amends.

Step number one on the atonement trail had begun right here: the small, cold kitchen of the Henderson family, in a scruffy terraced street behind Charing Cross Hospital. Dan stared uncomprehendingly at the dead boiler, trying to remember the YouTube videos he'd watched twenty minutes earlier, detailing how to restart the pilot light. Wondering if he might blow the place up, if he fumbled a crucial part of the job. Getting out his phone to check would not exactly fill Mrs Henderson with confidence, he imagined, but it was preferable to the house collapsing in rubble.

Zoe had been quiet that morning when she emerged, bags under her eyes, her face pale and creased as she knotted a raspberry-pink towelling dressing gown around her middle. 'Sorry about last night,' she mumbled, before going through to the kitchen to make coffee. Dan, who had been awake since half-six when the unexpectedly bright March sunshine jabbed through the thin curtains, couldn't tell if she wanted to talk or for him to leave without further discussion. But he'd been so absent over the last few weeks, he felt he should at least stick around for coffee. He'd done enough flaking out recently.

'That's okay,' he'd said, going over to the window and pulling up the blind. The garden appeared dishevelled after its wintry battering, the lawn mossy from all the rain they'd had. 'Did you have a good time?'

She glanced at him suspiciously as if wondering whether he was taking the mick. 'Yeah,' she said after a moment. 'Went to my friend Clare's. Put the world to rights over approximately seventeen bottles of wine. Not feeling quite so triumphant this morning, but it seemed a good idea at the time.' She put a mug of coffee on the table in front of him, steam twining up like tendrils. 'Thank you for holding the

fort,' she added. 'And sorry if I . . . said anything I shouldn't
have when I got in.'

'You were fine,' he replied, deciding it was probably the
gallant thing to gloss over her return. 'Zo . . . I won't leave
you in the lurch again,' he went on. 'I mean it. We're still
family, aren't we, you and me?'

The words rang in his head now as he carefully took the
front off Ruth Henderson's boiler. Families stuck together
and stood shoulder-to-shoulder when times were bad. Zoe's
face had sagged with relief when he offered to take over the
care of Patrick's landlord affairs while still on sabbatical,
starting today. Her lower lip had wobbled when he said he
could drive Ethan to the sculpture club every Wednesday, no
problem at all. And she had nodded several times, quite
hard, when he offered to come back later tomorrow so that
she could give him a list of everything else that might be
helpful. 'Thank you,' she said quietly and for a moment he
felt . . . not forgiven exactly, but as if he had done something
good for once. Worthwhile. He would do anything she
asked of him, he'd vowed there and then. Whatever it took
to prove he was sorry.

In the meantime, he really needed to get this boiler
working again. Okay. Gas valve – that must be it. The words
On, Off, Pilot were printed on the knob.

'Oh,' said Mrs Henderson from behind him. 'If you're
trying to start the pilot light, we've already done that a

thousand times. My neighbour found a YouTube video and we followed the instructions. But nothing happened.'

'Ah,' said Dan, feeling like an idiot. 'In that case . . .'

'The problem's clearly not with the gas supply, as the cooker's still working fine. And it's not the timer that's faulty, either. We've checked all those things.' Her smile was rather fixed as he withdrew his head from the cupboard, her eyes flicking upwards as they heard the raggedy cry of a baby starting up from above their heads. 'I did try what I could, while I was waiting for your brother to get back to me.' She grimaced. 'Sorry. I don't mean to—'

'It's all right. I know.' He looked down at his feet for a moment, then decided he should come clean. 'Look, I'm sorry, I can't fix this for you. I work in finance, not as a boiler engineer, so your guess is as good as mine here. I should have realized you'd have tried everything yourself. So what I'll do,' he said quickly as her face fell, 'is call an emergency heating engineer right now and book someone to come out today. I'll wait in for them, if you've got stuff to do.'

Upstairs the baby's crying was becoming louder, rising to a crescendo, and then a small girl with wild red curls and a knitted blue rabbit in hand rushed into the kitchen, breathless with self-importance. 'Mum! Phoebe's woked up.'

'I know, love, I'll be there in a minute,' said Mrs Henderson. 'Could you be a really good helper for me and just go in there and pat her tummy very, very gently? Say hello in a kind voice?'

For a stupid split-second, Dan thought she was asking *him* to do these things, but then the little girl whirled around, the blue rabbit's legs flying out behind her, and they heard her pounding upstairs on her mission. 'Thank you,' Mrs Henderson said to Dan. 'That would be great. Getting someone out today, I mean. And if you could wait in for them too, that would be even better. My husband's coming back from a conference later, and there's not a crumb of food in the house, so we really need to—' She broke off as the crying upstairs reached a new, more urgent pitch. 'I'd better see what's happening,' she said, hurrying from the room.

It turned out that getting an emergency heating engineer to call on a Saturday was going to be very, very expensive. It also transpired that, following the recent cold snap, there were many boilers that had suffered similar deaths and Dan could be waiting hours for someone to fix this one. 'Fine,' he sighed, knowing he had no choice. In fact the more costly and inconvenient the experience was going to be, the better in some ways, he thought, accepting a mug of stewed tea from Mrs Henderson – Ruth – and assuring her that no, he didn't mind hanging around for the engineer while she went to the supermarket, it was no problem. Any cost – money or time – that he could pay was some tiny coin of penitence to deduct from the gigantic debt of guilt he was surely destined to carry around forever.

This was the balance sheet of his conscience from now on, he thought, as Ruth departed with the kids and the house fell quiet. Working in finance, he knew his way around a set of company accounts, and had always found satisfaction in tallying up income and outgoings; all those crumpled receipts and invoices being converted to clean, clear, final figures. In his case, because of what had happened with Patrick, he was probably in the red for the rest of his life, but he could at least attempt to rack up a hefty number of good deeds in counterbalance, to show the universe he was truly sorry.

Just at that moment there was a knock at the door and he opened it to see a man holding a toolbox with an expectant air. 'I'm here about your boiler?'

Showing the engineer through to the chilly kitchen, Dan experienced the first flicker of optimism he'd felt in a long time. Whatever it took, however much it cost, he was going to step into his brother's shoes and pick up the reins of his life. He would fix this. All of it.

Chapter Four

'Patrick Christopher Sheppard was the best of all men,' Zoe murmured to herself as she walked along. 'A loving father, husband and son, who was liked and respected by every-one . . .' Her throat tightened as she thought of his handsome face; the laugh she'd never hear again, the lips she could no longer kiss. It was one of her ongoing regrets that she hadn't felt able to give a personal eulogy at Patrick's funeral.

Others had stepped up: her father-in-law, Derek, had made a stilted speech about his son that didn't capture any of Patrick's warmth and love of life – although that was Derek for you, she supposed; a man who wouldn't recognize human warmth unless his house was on fire. Dan had also spoken during the service, stammering about what a great brother Patrick had been, along with a couple of anecdotes, but he had been whey-faced and uneasy, talking without any real conviction. Zoe had sat there in her new black suit with her head down, anger rising at what a bad job they were both doing. Did she want to hear the opinion of Derek who, according to Patrick, had been such a cold-blooded father he was practically reptilian? No, she did not. Did she want to hear funny stories from Dan, whom she still blamed for Patrick's death? No, she did not.

And so the service had come to an end without anyone standing up and giving the whole-hearted, loving, sincere tribute that Patrick deserved. Nobody had been able to convey his humour, his charisma, his energy. At the time Zoe could hardly croak out a sentence without breaking down and so she had failed him too, with her silence. Still, between now and the summer, she planned to perfect the most beautiful tribute to her husband and declaim it as she scattered his ashes. It was the least she could do.

'I knew, as soon as I saw him, he was special,' she practised aloud. She'd been twenty-five when they met in a grotty pub where Patrick teased her about her karaoke skills, bought her a drink and then proceeded to charm her and make her laugh, pretty much for the next seventeen years straight. At the time she'd been wary of men – she'd had her heart broken a couple of times by previous crappy boyfriends, and was of course scarred by her own philandering dad walking out on the family – but Patrick was different. He was just *good*. She had trusted him instinctively and her instincts had not let her down.

Today was Monday, the start of a new week, which always seemed particularly tough: seven more dreary and joyless days without her husband, and absolutely nothing to look forward to. *Keep going, Zoe. One foot in front of the other*, her friend Clare had encouraged on Friday night. *Hang in there, my love,* her mum had urged on the phone the night before, but it was so bloody hard getting up some mornings. So hard to chivvy the kids into their school uniform and out of the front door, when she felt like staying in bed all day with the covers pulled up over her head.

Zoe was a primary-school teacher although, after Bea was born, she'd switched to working on a supply basis only, finding that juggling her own three children with the thirty in her class, day in, day out, was too much to handle all of a sudden. Since Patrick's death she had stayed away from the classroom altogether. His life insurance had recently come through – a generous package – which had taken the pressure off financially, thank goodness, but it had also taken away any incentive she might have had to work again. 'How are you feeling about getting back into teaching?' Clare had asked the other evening, once the wine had loosened them up. 'Or is it too soon to ask? Only it might be a distraction, that's all. It might . . . help?'

Zoe knew the question was meant kindly and that Clare was just trying to haul her back towards normality. The problem was, she couldn't imagine ever feeling like standing in front of a class of children and talking about phonics or times tables or the Victorians again. The Zoe who put on a nice blouse and skirt every morning, who kissed her husband and children goodbye before heading to work, the Zoe who was able to inspire and educate a class of nine-year-olds . . . that cheerful, carefree woman had vanished. Instead here was this angry, weeping mess of a person who shouted at her kids and forgot things, who couldn't sleep at night for worrying about what was to become of them all. When she eventually fell asleep, she would dream of Patrick – often that she was diving into the river, trying to rescue him. Sometimes she would spot his body in the water and be heaving with all her might to haul him up to the surface from the murky depths – uselessly, helplessly, because at some point in the nightmare she would realize that he was already dead and she was too late. Other times she would glimpse him drifting away from her, slipping through the reeds and shadows. 'Wait!' she'd yell, silver bubbles rising from her mouth as she tried to reach him. 'Stop!' But he never did and she could never catch up, however hard she swam in those dreams, however desperately she shouted his name.

She would wake up, panting and gasping for air, as if she too had been submerged under the muddy Thames. And a few seconds later she'd realize that here was another awful day, and the horror of real life would swing into place once more. *What happened to you that night?* she wanted to cry to him. *What actually happened?*

'Maybe,' she replied to Clare's question. 'But not yet. It's too soon.'

Too soon, as if this was merely a temporary loss. As if she wouldn't always feel this way. That didn't seem remotely likely right now, when she felt like half a person, a crumbling wreck of a survivor. At home she was clinging on to her sanity, but all around her chaos threatened to break in. The house was becoming grubbier by the day because she didn't care enough to hoover and mop. It was so chaotic that Liz, Patrick's mum, had taken to silently sorting and ironing laundry whenever she popped round. Squirting bleach around the loo now and then. Sliding a casserole or a crumble into the fridge for Zoe to reheat. These acts of kindness only made Zoe feel ashamed, though, as if her mother-in-law was judging her on her slovenliness; the lingering smell of bleach a reprimand that she was failing her family.

If you'd asked her a month ago, Zoe would have said that she was the one who did everything around the house, but it was becoming apparent there were plenty of chores that Patrick had taken care of after all: cutting the front hedge, for instance. Cleaning the compost bin. Managing bills and washing the cars and taking stuff to the tip. One of the brackets on Gabe's curtain rail had come loose and Zoe hadn't got round to fixing it yet. It was the sort of job that would have taken her husband five minutes, but she felt nervous about using the drill (which size bit did she need?

which colour Rawlplug?). Her car insurance was due for re-
newal and usually Patrick shopped around to find a good
deal for her, but she would have to do that herself this time.
As for his car, she supposed she'd have to sell it, but she
didn't even know how to go about such a thing. Sure, she
could ask her stepdad or brother, but even that felt like another task to add to her list. The sum of it all was over-
whelming. Impossible. Far easier, somehow, to do none of
it, to let herself sink further into the mess, until it eventually
consumed her.

Recently she had taken to walking for hours at a time
while the kids were in school, haunting parks and streets
like a mournful ghost, in an attempt to compensate for her
intake of crisps (which was getting dangerously out of
hand), as well as to escape the messy house. She dragged
herself around the Botanic Gardens some days, dimly noticing the narcissi nodding their pearly heads and trying not
to think about how many times Patrick had given her daffodils over the years. She'd kept the last bunch he'd bought
her for weeks after his death, unable to throw them out.
Dan must have binned them, she'd realized the other day,
and it was all she could do to stop herself scavenging
through the bin, trying to salvage a few brown petals.

Today she had walked as far as Chiswick and abandoned
her eulogy attempts as she drifted like a wraith past the
shops on the High Road, trying to remember how to act like

an ordinary person. Other women knew what to do, she thought dully, pulling her scarf tighter around her throat as she saw clusters of them sitting inside cafés or holding up clothes to show one another in boutiques. Other women jogged together through parks and green spaces, their gleaming trainers pounding along in sync; they pushed grizzling tots in buggies alongside one another and invited each other round for coffee, chat-chat-chat. Zoe could no longer move in these circles with such thoughtless ease, though; she had become an outsider, unwelcome. Turned out that when you lost your husband and all-time love of your life, other people found you awkward company – they were afraid of being too happy or glib in your presence; they felt they had to adopt hushed tones and touch your arm as they tilted their heads to one side. *How ARE you?* Always the *How ARE you?*s, eyes wide with concern. It was driving her nuts, frankly.

The worst thing – one of the many worst things – was that she would always be marked out in this way now. Always branded as poor Zoe, poor widowed Zoe. *So sad, wasn't it, have you heard, oh my God, I couldn't believe it. Do you think it was suicide? I heard a rumour that they had money troubles, you're kidding, who would have thought it?* Oh, she'd heard all the whispers, seen the nudges and glances, however sympathetically people might act to her face.

Ignore them, she reminded herself. *Don't get paranoid on top of everything else.* She was outside and in the fresh air – well, as fresh as it got on Turnham Green Road anyway – and she had managed to survive all the way to eleven o'clock this morning without crying. Also – silver lining! – yesterday Dan had reappeared and even though she still hadn't forgiven him (and probably never would), he was at least offering support, which she had grudgingly accepted. He'd collected a mountain of paperwork and post that had built up, untouched in Patrick's absence, and had taken the lot away, promising to deal with everything. This was progress, she supposed. A tiny step forward through the misery.

Just as she was daring to feel positive, however, a man walked past her with the same aftershave that Patrick had always worn, and she found herself instantly floored by the familiar scent. The blood drained from her face at the spicy, woody fragrance; the heavenly smell that brought to mind all those nights when he'd worn it: restaurant dinners and parties, nights in the pub, his arms around her. She'd been spraying the cologne onto his pillow every night so that she could hug it, and the bottle was nearly empty. Would it be ridiculous of her to buy more? She just missed him so much. She was lost without him. So lost!

A sob escaped her, then another. Here it came: the desolation, roaring up inside as if it had been lurking beneath the surface the whole time, waiting for her to crack. She put her hands over her eyes and leaned against the nearest shop window, legs shaking. What was she even doing here? So much for hiding in plain sight amongst the yummy mummies of Chiswick – now she had outed herself as a grieving wreck, a woman who fell apart at a single floating waft of Givenchy, tears coursing down her face in public. She didn't know what to do with herself. There was nowhere to hide and yet she couldn't pull herself together, she couldn't stop crying, she—

'Are you okay? No, you're not, I can see you're not. Come inside the shop – come and get your breath back for a moment.'

A woman was talking to her, her face quite close, although Zoe's eyes were too full of tears to really see anything. An arm slipped around her back, then she was gently led through the shop door. 'Just a minute, let me . . .' said the woman, and Zoe was dimly aware of her closing the door behind them and flipping a sign to *Closed*. They were in a small homewares boutique, full of beautiful cushions and throws as well as shelves of vases and ceramics, the sort of place she would never dare bring her children for fear of expensive accidents.

The woman who had rescued her guided her towards a rather lovely pink velvet armchair with elegant wooden legs. 'Sit down,' she encouraged.

Zoe sat. 'I'm sorry,' she gulped, mortified that this was happening. She put her head in her hands, still trembling with emotions, and tried desperately to pull herself together. 'God, I'm so embarrassed and sorry,' she managed to say.

'You're fine, don't worry – just have a moment,' the woman said, grabbing a box of tissues from behind the counter. 'Here, take these. Can I make you a coffee? Peppermint tea?'

'No, thank you,' sniffled Zoe, hiccupping as she tried to force her breathing under control. She'd always teased Patrick for being a hypochondriac – *Call an ambulance! My husband has a cold!* – but if she'd had any clue that he was actually going to *die* on her, she'd have tended to him far more lovingly. Why hadn't she cared for him more, when she had the chance? Why had she ever been mean to him, argued with him?

'A biscuit, then? You look very pale, if you don't mind me saying. Mind you, don't we all, after this horrible winter. Here, take one, you'll be doing me a favour. I'll only eat them all otherwise,' said the woman, waving a packet of chocolate digestives under Zoe's nose. She was wearing a short, loud patchwork skirt, Zoe noticed, with a silky black top and a chunky copper necklace that clinked like tiny cymbals whenever she moved.

The smell of the digestives was surprisingly uplifting. Zoe was ravenous after the walk, she realized; and, come to think of it, had forgotten to eat breakfast in all the palaver of the Monday-morning school rush earlier. 'Thank you,' she said, taking a biscuit and nibbling the edge. Sugary crumbs exploded in her mouth and she took another bite, resisting the urge to cram the whole thing in at once. It was delicious and made her feel the tiniest bit more able to function. 'Sorry,' she said again, aware of how peculiar her behaviour must appear. 'I lost my husband recently. Or, rather, he died – I haven't just mislaid him somewhere.' She grimaced, risking a look up at the other woman, braced for a wary what-have-I-got-myself-into? expression on her face.

But her rescuer gazed back with compassion instead, her chocolate-brown eyes sincere. She was younger than Zoe, mid-thirties at a guess, and pretty, with long chestnut hair and freckles. 'Oh God,' she said. 'How awful. I'm so sorry. You must be going through hell.'

Zoe had to press her lips together because there was so much sympathy in the other woman's voice that she could hardly bear it. Also because 'hell' just about summed up her life these days. 'I am,' she admitted shakily. 'It's been the worst thing ever. And I smelled my husband's aftershave on another man just now and . . .' She could feel her face rushing with hot colour. 'I know it sounds silly, but it caught me off-guard. Little things keep doing that.'

'I bet they do,' said the woman. 'It must take ages to process a loss like that.' She waggled the biscuit packet temptingly again. 'Have another,' she urged. Then, as Zoe dipped her hand obediently into the crinkling wrapper, she said, 'Do you want to talk or would you rather sit and get your breath back? You're welcome to stay here as long as you like, obviously, but I could call someone to pick you up if that would help?'

Calling someone and drawing any more attention to her tearful breakdown was the last thing Zoe wanted. The idea alone was enough to propel her to her feet, knees still wobbly, but determined to hold fast. Forget the biscuits, it was time to go. A customer was at the shop door now, peering through the glass as if wondering what was going on inside and Zoe's cheeks burned. 'It's fine,' she said, which wasn't true but never mind. 'Anyway, I'd better . . .' She gestured towards the street outside, real life waiting for her re-entry. 'I'll leave you to it. But thank you.' She forced her mouth to smile and walked quickly towards the door. *Nothing to see here – I am absolutely fine. One hundred per cent okay; do not ask another question.*

'No problem,' said the woman from behind her, but Zoe didn't turn back. *Keep walking, keep walking,* she ordered herself and her body obeyed, taking her out through the door again and into the street, quickly past the shop window, where the woman was probably still staring worriedly at her, and away. Anywhere. Just away, and fast.

'I've lost the plot,' she said to herself, not sure whether to laugh or cry. 'Were you watching that, Patrick? I've totally lost the plot without you.'

Chapter Five

Two days later, Dan parked along the street from a large, noisy comprehensive school and peered through the windscreen, feeling slightly overwhelmed as hundreds of kids poured out, all loud voices and massive bags, jostling and barging. No, not all of them, he corrected himself, because in the wake of the gobby ones, shoving and yelling, he noticed some quieter kids with their heads down, plugged into music, detaching themselves from the boiling teenage mass as it thundered along. He suspected his nephew Ethan might be part of the latter grouping. He remembered it well from his own secondary-school years.

Parked up near the postbox, he texted Ethan now, as per their arrangement. *Silver Ford Focus.*

Ruth Henderson's boiler aside, this was pretty much the first useful thing he had done since his sabbatical had begun, Dan realized, leaning his right arm against the window. In fact, if he was honest with himself, it was possibly the most useful thing he'd done all year. In recent months he had felt something of a zombie, wearing the same three suits on rotation, taking the same Tube journey each morning and evening, buying the same sandwich from the same deli when it came to lunchtime. Sometimes he would be sitting there at his desk and he'd blink and find himself unable to remember what day of the week it was. What season, even. Sometimes, also, he felt as if he were the only unmoving constant in the office. Around him colleagues were getting married and having children, leaving for other jobs, taking interesting-sounding courses, planning holidays, seeking sponsorship for the marathons and charity bike-rides they'd signed up to. He, meanwhile, just . . . existed. It had been that way ever since his divorce, in hindsight. When everything went to pot in your private life, it was surprisingly easy to throw yourself into work, say yes to every job, however dull it might be, and turn that into your world instead.

The sabbatical had been due to change that, of course. All staff were encouraged to take one after ten years' service to the company and it had been the managing director herself who had told Dan, quite forcibly, that they were expecting him to take a break. It was good for staff well-being, she said. They would pay him for the time he was off; this was an incredibly generous offer that most other members of the company had been delighted to accept. There must be something he wanted to do other than work, surely?

He wasn't sure at first. In fact he floundered around in the empty desert of his imagination for quite some time. Dan wasn't the most adventurous of souls, after all; his Hammersmith flat was a mere three streets away from the house where he'd grown up. But then, just before Christmas, he got chatting to Tiggy, one of the secretaries, who'd recently given in her notice, planning to head off to South America in February for the trip of a lifetime. 'Sounds amazing,' Dan said, hearing her describe her itinerary with breathless gusto. 'I'd love to go there.'

'Seriously?' She'd peered up at him through her cat-eye glasses, then smiled with a sudden new radiance. 'Why don't you come too, then? My travel buddy's just dropped out, the selfish cow, and it won't be as much fun on my own. And aren't you meant to be taking three months off?'

Tiggy was ten years younger than Dan, she was outspoken and sarcastic and had a pink streak in her hair; in short, she was not the sort of travelling companion he would have picked for himself. And yet . . . Was it idiotic that he had felt unable to refuse? His polite attempts at deferral were deflected by her increasingly persuasive line of reasoning: *Yeah, but you said yourself it sounded amazing and you'd love to go there – this is your chance! Look, it's all sorted – you just need to book your flights. Remember how shit it is in this country in February? Like, the worst, right? Well, forget that, because you could be on a beach instead. Drinking cocktails.*

Learning to surf and scuba-dive – apparently there's a wicked place you can dive at Easter Island . . .

Nobody was more astonished than Dan when, by the end of a fifteen-minute coffee break, he'd actually said okay, he'd think about it. It was partly the fact that Tiggy was so relentless and enthusiastic, but also partly because he kept eyeing this version of himself that went off and did exciting things, like climb mountains and scuba-dive, and rather liked it. Besides, she was right about February; he'd always found it the most miserable month of the year too.

'Blimey, you must really fancy her,' Patrick teased the following weekend, when Dan mentioned that he was considering taking this mad, impulsive trip with a colleague he barely knew. Dan had protested – Tiggy was so *not* his type, the idea was laughable – but the more he thought about getting on a plane and exploring cities and jungles and ancient temples and beaches, the more he was seduced by the idea of an adventure. Why not? He had never done anything like this before. Never been the reckless type. Never even been particularly brave. Since his divorce, his life had shrunk to a narrow tunnel, all safety and routine. Earning plenty, but never spending it. The thought of breaking out of his comfort zone and striding towards a new horizon . . . well, it appealed greatly, actually. Did he dare?

Yes, he dared. Encouraged by Tiggy (badgered by Tiggy, some would say), he dared. He'd be forty in the autumn and this could be his chance to finally do something extraordinary. And think how impressed – and maybe even jealous – Rebecca would be, if she got to hear about him gallivanting to a whole new hemisphere with another woman. A younger, cooler woman. She'd always nagged him about being too closed-off, too cautious – but you could hardly get *less* closed-off and cautious than travelling to the other side of the world. Right? 'Okay,' he told Tiggy the following Monday at work. He even sounded quite breezy about it, he reflected, thrilled by his own boldness. 'I'll join you.'

And so the plan had come together. A three-month tour, all carefully researched and mapped out. Obviously there were spreadsheets. He had downloaded guidebooks and travellers' tips, he had worked as hard on his itinerary as he had done on his MBA. They established a few ground rules, too – or, rather, Tiggy had laid down the law. 'Just to make this clear. One: no sex,' she said, tapping a pen against her teeth.

'Of course,' blustered Dan, caught between wanting to agree vehemently, which might insult her, and not agreeing hard enough and possibly creeping her out. His whole face remained hot as she went through her other stipulations: two, they could go their own separate ways at any time; three, they . . . Actually he had stopped listening by then because he was still so mortified by the no-sex rule. He didn't even fancy her, and yet now he was left feeling like some dirty old pervert.

To cut a long story short: he hadn't gone to South America. He'd been a week away from getting on the plane, from becoming that man, when Patrick's body was found, at which point the world had telescoped right back down to its narrow boundaries once more. 'You should still go,' his parents had urged him, but of course, in the shock and tumult of the aftermath, Dan hadn't felt able to. And yet . . . well. This might sound risible, but in some ways it had been a relief to cancel the trip, now that he had an excuse not to go. A relief, because although he hadn't said this aloud to anyone, he'd been kind of nervous about spending so much time out of the safe bubble of his usual routine. He'd been increasingly nervous about spending so much time with Tiggy as well. The more he had got to know her, the more he'd realized how different they were, personality-wise. She would probably want to go to wild parties and snort drugs off beefy Brazilian men's chests all the time, whereas he . . . wouldn't. He would only have been a disappointment to her, ultimately. A weight, dragging her down.

'You what? Oh, *man*,' Tiggy sighed when he rang to tell her that he was no longer going, choking on the words in his shock and grief as he explained why. 'Shit, Dan. So sorry to hear that. And gutted for you about the trip, too. But look – leave it a month and come out when you feel like it, yeah? It would probably do you good to get right away from everything. Yeah?'

Yeah, he had replied dully, but he knew even then that he wouldn't. His trip had already vanished like a mirage, a vivid dream that he couldn't clutch onto. He'd had a post-card from her that morning in fact, from Valparaíso – *Wish you were here!* she'd written and it hardly seemed real that in another universe he would have been there too.

Anyway. Whatever. Here he was now instead, doing something practical at least: punctual and ready to commit himself to the first uncle–nephew bonding session of the new post-Patrick world. Zoe had texted him the address earlier and Dan had felt a jolt of – what? nostalgia? heart-ache? – as he realized where the SculptShed was located: two streets from the road where he and Rebecca had rented their first flat together, back in the good old days of opti-mism and love. Mind you, in hindsight, their differences had been apparent even then – she liked to stay in bed for hours at the weekend; he didn't. She liked friends dropping round any time of day or night; he didn't. She didn't care how the dishwasher was stacked, while he knew for a fact that his way was more efficient. They had teased each other for these things, though, and none of them had really mattered until, years later and married, they all suddenly mattered. Mattered too much for her to want to be with him any more, apparently.

Enough about Rebecca, he told himself. He needed to stop looking back over his shoulder and face forward again.

Today was all about being positive, taking another step to redress the balance and put things right. Forget his travel plans; Dan intended to devote the remaining two months of his sabbatical to filling in for his brother. He couldn't bring him back but he could walk in his shoes when possible, blot up some of the pain caused by Patrick's absence by being the very best replacement he could. True to form, he had already drawn up a spreadsheet over the weekend to track his progress. *The Patrick plan,* Dan had titled the document, and as soon as he'd printed it out he felt more in control, as if he had a purpose again.

If he could complete at least one task that Patrick would have done for his family and business every single day, he would help ease the burden all round, he'd figured. It was now almost the end of March, and he wasn't due back at work again until early June. Just think what he could achieve in that time! And maybe by then they might all have navigated their way collectively into the second phase of the bereavement at least, the shock and devastation having begun to lift.

The spreadsheet was now pinned up on Dan's fridge – he was trying not to think about how it resembled all the sticker-based reward charts that Patrick and Zoe had used with the kids to encourage good behaviour. He tried also to block out Patrick's voice in his head, teasing him for his methodology. *Life isn't a spreadsheet, Dan! You can't fit people into boxes and charts.* To which Dan found himself replying, *Each to his own.* He had never before come across a spreadsheet that had let him down.

At the top of the page he'd listed all the best things about his brother that he wanted to emulate – a great dad, a loving husband, a successful businessman, and so on. Then, in neat, typed columns below, he had thought up a number of ways in which he could try to fill in the gaps Patrick had left. So far these included:

Time with Ethan – lifts to and from his SculptShed group every week. They could chat each way, man-and-boy stuff that Ethan couldn't tell Zoe about. Maybe stop for a sneaky burger on the way back sometimes, to cement the bonding. Ethan could confide in him, lean on him as a substitute father figure. Or so Dan hoped.

Time with Gabe – Dan was less clear on what this might entail, although he sensed his younger nephew would prefer it to be something exciting and possibly dangerous. Or football-related. They could watch the occasional Fulham match together, like Gabe had with Patrick. Go mountainbiking, maybe, or find some other adrenalin-charged activity?

Time with Bea – he had even fewer ideas how he might fulfil this category, but he'd assured Zoe that he was up for it, whatever his small niece might want to do. If she needed chaperoning to dance lessons or an afternoon doing arts and crafts together or . . . He bit his lip, already out of suggestions. See: this was why he needed to put in the effort, he told himself. Get to know his own relatives again, like a proper uncle.

Also on the list: being there for Zoe. This was similarly hard to quantify, but he would endeavour to help out whenever needed, although he would have to take care in his approach. He cringed, remembering how she had given him the side-eye on Sunday when he offered to mow the lawn. 'I *can* use a lawnmower, Dan, I'm not completely clueless,' she'd scoffed in reply. 'Besides, the grass hasn't really got going yet this spring, it's been so cold. And aren't you meant to let lawns grow a bit longer anyway, these days, for wildlife reasons?'

He'd had to back off, message received that his suggestion had been clumsy, but then she'd added, 'You can do the hoovering, though, if you're desperate to save me from the rising tide of chores', thus pointedly notifying him of his gendered ideas of help. Had he been patronizing? he wondered glumly to himself, heaving the battered red Henry around the living-room floor moments later. He prided himself on being modern and switched on, in terms of equality, but he'd immediately leapt straight to old-fashioned ideas about men's jobs and women's jobs, and Zoe had rightfully called him out for it. He would keep working on that though. Maybe he could—

He jumped as the car door opened in the next moment

and there was Ethan, hunching awkwardly to peer inside. 'Hi,' he said.

'Hello, mate, had a good day? Hop in,' Dan said, starting the engine as Ethan detached a weighty-looking backpack from his shoulders and clambered into the passenger seat.

They set off into the school-run traffic, which was fulsome and slow-moving. A weak, irritating drizzle freckled the windscreen as they headed towards the A3. 'So how was your day?' Dan asked. *I care*, he wanted his nephew to hear. *I'm interested. I care so much I have typed up an entire list of ways I'm going to atone for your dad's death and I've pinned it up on my fridge, okay?* No, he probably shouldn't say that out loud, but all the same, he was determined to show that he was in it for the long haul. 'What lessons did you have today then?'

'Crap ones,' Ethan replied, looking completely uninterested.

'Hmm,' said Dan, wondering if he should comment on his nephew's language, but unwilling to start wielding joyless authority so early on. He wanted to be the cool, friendly uncle rather than priggish twerp, after all. He braked at a pedestrian crossing and they watched as an elderly man swung himself across on a pair of crutches, seemingly risking his balance by putting up a hand in thanks. 'So what are the non-crap lessons then? *Are* there any non-crap lessons?' Dan asked, raising his own hand at the old man in return – no rush – then glancing back at Ethan, who shrugged. To be fair, he'd probably have given the same response at that age. *Daniel shows promise but never quite manages to apply himself* – that had been the recurrent theme of his school reports. Come to think of it, that had pretty much been the recurrent theme of his entire life. 'How's your week going, then?' he asked, rather lamely, to which Ethan lifted a shoulder and mumbled, 'All right,' without divulging any other details.

Right. This wasn't going to be as easy as he'd hoped. After a full day at school and in the unfamiliar surroundings of his uncle's car, perhaps it wasn't surprising that Ethan didn't seem ready for any instant bonding or confiding.

'I'll put some music on,' Dan said as the silence stretched thickly between them. He switched on the radio, feeling like a failure as Five Live obligingly filled the void with sports commentary. 'Are you interested in athletics? Find a music channel, if you want,' he added, changing gear as he approached a roundabout.

For a moment he thought Ethan was going to ignore him, but then the boy took his phone out of his blazer pocket. 'Or I could link my phone to your Bluetooth – play something from that?' he suggested.

'What? Yeah, sure, whatever. You can educate me.' He felt a burst of intrigue as Ethan fiddled around, linking the devices together. What would he choose to play? Some bratty teen-pop? He couldn't imagine it somehow. Death metal? Unlikely.

In the next moment, however, thunderous piano chords burst from the speakers, fast and furious. 'Beethoven,' Ethan said, turning up the volume a little.

Okay, so he hadn't been expecting that. Dan was an ignoramus when it came to classical music; he preferred something with a chorus that you could sing along to, a beat you could hammer out on a steering wheel when stuck in traffic. All the same, he was able to feel the urgency of the music, the tempo so frenetic you could hardly imagine how anyone's fingers could gallop across the keys so quickly. The air swelled with a crescendo. 'Wow,' he said. 'You're into this then, I take it? Do you play yourself?'

'No,' said Ethan. 'I just like it.'

They drove along, listening to the rippling movement of the piece, Ethan with his eyes shut, Dan thinking back to the box of paperwork he'd picked up from Zoe, promising to sort it out. She'd given him Patrick's work phone too, which was full of unanswered messages and unlistened-to phone calls. 'Would you mind? It's just been one thing after another,' she had said apologetically, but Dan had been only too willing to take it off her hands, not least because it was another task that he could add to his secret plan, up on the fridge.

Clearly he was not going to be undertaking any building work or dishing out quotes to people who had requested it, but he was pretty sure he could deal with Patrick's tenants for the time being. How hard could it be, after all? Chances were, he wouldn't hear much from them anyway, he'd figured. So far, he had at least been able to delete the increasingly desperate calls from Mrs Henderson regarding her boiler, but there were others that needed attention: the family in Shepherd's Bush whose back door had been kicked in by a would-be burglar and now wouldn't lock properly; a man giving notice on his flat in Acton; and an elderly-sounding woman ('It's Rosemary, darling') who'd said she'd heard a mouse several times now and could he pop round? Dan had phoned them all back, feeling a stab of alarm when he realized that darling Rosemary's number was stored on his brother's phone as 'Pain In Arse'. Having booked an emergency locksmith to go out to the Shepherd's Bush flat as soon as possible, he was also faced with the slightly more onerous task of dropping round to the so-called Pain In Arse tomorrow morning.

'Hey, did your dad ever mention one of his tenants called Rosemary?' he asked Ethan now, curious. He had to raise his voice to be heard over the music, which seemed to be whirling up into an all-guns-blazing ending.

'Rosemary? Yeah, all the time. Moaniest old cow he'd ever met,' Ethan replied. 'Um. Uncle Dan? We've missed the turning. We should have gone left then.'

'Whoops – sorry. Not concentrating,' he said, swinging round at the next junction and doubling back. He'd been heading for his old address on automatic pilot, he realized; the memories of all those journeys mapped into his brain on a deep cellular level, clicking straight back in again, as if he'd never been away. You could take the bloke out of Wandsworth . . . as they said.

SculptShed – when they eventually arrived – looked pretty unimposing from the outside, resembling a characterless industrial unit with big metal shutters, set in a no-through road not far from the High Street. Nonetheless, Dan could hear hiphop music breezing out from an open window, the screech of what sounded like an angle-grinder, as well as shouts of laughter, and couldn't help feeling intrigued. 'Do I need to come in and make sure you're—' he started asking, but Ethan edged away, shaking his head and saying, 'No, it's cool. I'm fine from here, thanks.'

In other words: on your bike now, old person; don't go showing me up in front of my arty mates. Understood. 'I'll meet you back at the car afterwards,' Dan replied, walking away.

He had ninety minutes to kill now, and nothing to do. This was the problem with taking a three-month sabbatical to go travelling and then never actually going because your brother had died; the days tended to mock you with their emptiness. He'd worked out last night that, had things been different, he and Tiggy would have been on their way to Argentina by this point, which had prompted a sorrowful few minutes forlornly imagining another version of himself hiking to see the Perito Moreno Glacier or eating an amazing steak in Buenos Aires. Never mind.

'Dan's midlife crisis,' Patrick had teased him in the pub that last night, when Dan had shown him pictures of the salt flats in Bolivia that he was looking forward to seeing, and described his plan for hiking the Inca Trail to Machu Picchu.

'Jealous, much?' Dan had retaliated, only to see a glimmer of what looked like resentment on his brother's face. Yeah, Patrick *was* jealous. For once, Dan was doing something that Patrick had never done. For once, having the family and business and nice house looked kind of pedestrian and safe in comparison to Dan's big old adventure right there on the horizon. Not that Patrick would ever have admitted as much, of course.

'What, jealous of you? No chance,' he'd scoffed instead.

Whatever. It was academic now anyway, because Dan had never even made it to Heathrow, and Patrick had sidestepped the whole jealousy issue by dying like that. He always had to go one better, didn't he? Always had to have the last word. Dan stared down at the pavement as he walked blindly along, because he would have given anything to have Patrick back for some brotherly mick-taking in the pub again, even if the conversation had descended into something altogether darker by the end of the night. But there was no chance of that ever happening again. What a waste.

Without being aware of it, Dan had walked to the street where he and Rebecca had once lived together all those years ago, and he gave a start as he realized where his feet had taken him. Ground-floor flat, 21 Windermere Road. Good times.

He remembered what a dump it had been initially – a cheap dump, with a horrible avocado-green loo and sink in the bathroom and the smell of mildew in the tiny kitchen. The cushions on the brown corduroy sofa had been torn and were prone to leaking sad little clouds of stuffing, while the bedroom carpet sported what looked like a massive bloodstain in the middle. But over time it had become a cosy nest – their nest, which they repainted and decorated and made homely. Rebecca's red mirror-work Indian throw had transformed the sofa, and a rug from Camden Market had hidden the dodgy stains of the bedroom carpet. The kitchen was brightened up with framed pop-art prints and cacti on the windowsill; they bought retro lampshades and cushions, and stuck a big map of the world above the mantelpiece, with colourful drawing pins pushed into all the places they wanted to explore.

Standing in front of the house now, he half-expected to see a spectral version of himself shimmering there, striding up the path and letting himself in. The happy old Dan who smiled at strangers, who was in love with his beautiful girl-friend, who had big plans for the future and no idea that in years to come she'd get an eye-popping promotion at work and move into a new circle of confident, charismatic friends. By then they'd taken the plunge and bought a fancier place in Clapham, and he quickly began to feel left behind. As if he disappointed her. 'Can't you try a bit harder?' she'd asked him once, exasperated, when he'd accompanied her to a glamorous work do at Gibson Hall and found his small-talk to be lacking. He'd felt shy, out of his depth, while she cruised through the crowds with ease, pulling away from him in more ways than one.

The irritating drizzle had now turned into a more determined pattering shower. As the raindrops began soaking his hair and sliding beneath his collar, Dan swerved away from the building, heading back along the wet pavement and ducking into the nearest pub. Their former local – except that it had been transformed since its old-man-and-his-dog days of tobacco-coloured walls and sticky carpets. Nowadays it was a smart gastropub with tasteful claret paintwork and flagstone flooring. Everything changed while you looked the other way, he thought, walking up to the bar and ordering a coffee.

The pub was quiet and Dan was able to sit by the window, gazing out at the buses trundling down the High Street, the school-uniform-clad teenagers on their bikes apparently unbothered by the rain, shoppers with umbrellas, people walking along staring at their phones. He pulled out his own phone for something to do and opened Facebook for the first time in weeks. There were several photos posted by Tiggy – most of which seemed to be variations on a theme: her sandwiched between two bronzed, buff and oiled men on a beach – and he snorted faintly with a mixture of affection and regret. There were still loads of unopened condolence messages about Patrick that he hadn't been able to face reading properly or replying to, including . . . oh God. He actually flinched as he saw her name there. Including one from Rebecca herself. Speak of the devil and she will appear. Before he could think better of it, he clicked on the message: *Devastated to hear the news about Patrick,* she had typed a fortnight ago. *He was always so full of life. Thinking about you and the family.*

His jaw tightened and he had to put the phone down quickly, because a flood of emotions threatened to overwhelm him. So many feelings. Too many feelings. *Don't think about it,* he ordered himself. *Don't think about her.* He'd become so adept at blocking out painful thoughts in the last month, like a blanket thrown over a birdcage; he hadn't so much as peeked beneath it. But today . . .

Maybe it was having just been back to Windermere Road, feeling the past put its hand on his shoulder, but it wasn't so easy today. Suddenly he found himself clicking through to Rebecca's page, needing to know what she was doing with her life. They had split up three years ago, and although Dan had steadfastly avoided finding out too much about her since

then, he'd been unable to miss the headline fact of her remar-
riage last summer to some broad-shouldered alpha male
called Rory. At the time Dan had only been able to bear a few
glances at the photos, but Rory looked the sort of man who
flew helicopters for fun and saved children's lives in between
sealing massive global deals during office hours. He definitely
would have one of those massive expensive watches, if he
could find one big enough to go around his thick strong
wrist, of course. 'It's okay, I don't care – I'm over her too,'
Dan had declared to anyone who would listen during an
eight-pint bender on her wedding day, shortly before everything got really messy and blurry.

He glanced at the screen again now and saw that her most
recent update was a cryptic one. *Big day tomorrow! Cross your
fingers for me.* Ugh, he thought, closing the app immediately.
She was probably having an interview for CEO of the world
this time, for even more money and status. Amazing celebratory holidays with Rory and all their high-flying friends. His
face burned as he felt rejected all over again. He certainly
wouldn't be crossing anything for her, he thought.

Outside, the shower had already eased off and the pavement glinted damply as the sun sent tentative rays slicing
through the pigeon-grey clouds. A bus had to brake hard at
a distracted cyclist, issuing a disapproving honk, while a
cluster of women with prams walked along together, all

wearing Lycra and enormous colourful trainers, their pony-tails swinging behind them in unison.

Then Dan realized that Patrick's work phone was ringing from his jacket pocket and scrabbled to pull it out. *Pain In Arse*, read the screen, and he let out a muffled groan. Sometimes he couldn't help thinking the universe had it in for him.

'So how did you get on? What were you making today?'

Coffee finished, a demanding tenant temporarily placated and all thoughts of Rebecca firmly stashed back in a mental folder marked *Do Not Disturb*, Dan and Ethan were heading back towards Kew. As before, though, the conversation, like the traffic, was not exactly flowing freely, although another furious concerto currently thundered from the speakers.

'It's a group project,' Ethan said, all shrugs and mumbles.

'Of . . . ?' Come on, kid, give me something to work with here, Dan thought, trying not to sigh as he turned up the fan heater. Ethan had seemed so pleased on Friday when Dan had offered him a lift. What had changed since then?

'It's a person. Made of metal,' Ethan replied, as if long sentences were beyond him. Even his body language seemed closed-off, unwilling, Dan thought, glancing across: the boy's knees were turned towards the door, away from Dan, as if he didn't want to look at his uncle. Had something happened at the club? Was someone picking on him, maybe, or giving him a hard time?

'Everything all right?' he asked as they joined the South Circular, along with half the vehicles in the capital, by the look of things. It was a stupid question, he realized, as soon as the words were out of his mouth. Of course Ethan wasn't all right. When would Dan remember to stop relying on such inappropriate and banal conversational prompts? 'Listen, I know no one will ever take the place of your dad,' he said, 'but you can talk to me, okay? Think of me as . . . I dunno, as a substitute for him, yeah?'

Dan had to overtake a van in the next moment, so couldn't be entirely sure, but he thought Ethan might have muttered, 'Puts the "tit" in "substitute"' or something along those lines.

Startled, Dan looked over at him again. 'What's wrong?' he asked. 'Just say it, whatever it is.'

There was a loaded pause. 'It's about when Dad died,' the boy eventually mumbled, looking down at his own hands.

Ah. Shit. They were going there, were they? 'What about it?' Dan asked, feeling as if he had stepped onto a tightrope. *Don't look down. Keep breathing. Baby steps.*

'I heard Mum saying . . . Well, nobody's really explained what happened,' Ethan said, the words tumbling out in a rush. His usually pale face flushed and a hard edge appeared in his voice. 'And I heard Mum say that she blamed you, basically. For Dad dying. She said it was your fault. And I just wondered . . . I mean, was it? Is there something I don't

85

know?' His hands curled into fists. 'Because I need to know,' he finished gruffly.

Dan's mouth was dry suddenly. If Patrick could see his boy here now, fierce and brave, asking this really tough question of his uncle, he would be so proud of him, Dan thought with a pang. But in the meantime, what was he supposed to say in reply? Moreover, why did they have to launch into such a difficult conversation on the heaving South Circular, where he was stop-starting along in first gear? 'It was an accident,' he began. 'Your dad . . .' Then he hesitated, wary of saying too much. 'What did your mum tell you about that night?'

'That he fell into the river and drowned.'

'Yes.' Up floated Patrick's body from Dan's nightmares: pale and bloated, eyes half-eaten by the fish, weed streaking his dark hair. He hadn't actually seen Patrick on the mortuary slab himself, it had been poor Zoe who had gone to identify the body, but his imagination had filled in the gaps with vivid enough detail. 'That's what happened. Unfortunately.'

'So . . . why does she think it was your fault?' Ethan's knee was jiggling with the stress of the conversation, his voice low but tense. Fists still clenched on the knees of his school trousers, as if poised to start raining vengeful blows at any moment. 'I mean, you didn't push him in, did you?'

'No! Christ, is that what you've been thinking? No! Absolutely not. I didn't push him in. I wasn't even there.'

Ethan's shoulders went limp as he exhaled audibly. 'Right,' he said. 'Sorry. But why does Mum think—'

'Because . . .' Now they were getting to the nitty-gritty. 'Because he was supposed to be staying at my place that evening, not walking home on his own.'

Ethan took a moment to digest this. Uncle not a murderer. No need for filial vengeance. Stand down. Wait, though – another question. 'So why didn't he? Stay at your place, I mean.'

And here it was: the very point Dan's conscience had been grappling with again and again, endlessly, every bloody day, since Patrick had disappeared. 'Because . . .' Bile rose in his throat and he forced himself to remember the scene – the two of them stumbling out of the pub, worse for wear, Dan angrily striding ahead, telling Patrick he should go home because he wasn't welcome; he didn't want to see him. How his brother had shrugged and walked away, leaving Dan bristling all over with impotent rage. Typical! Patrick couldn't even argue properly, just when Dan really needed to have it out with him.

His fingers tightened on the steering wheel as he tried to find adequate words in reply to Ethan's question. 'We had an argument,' he mumbled eventually, the same weak line he'd bleated to Zoe, to his parents, to everyone else who'd asked. 'You know the way that brothers do? Things got said in the heat of the moment.' He risked a look at Ethan, whose expression was tight and pinched, hard to read. He didn't look won over by his uncle's defence, that was for sure, although the 'brothers' bit would surely have struck a chord. 'Look, I wish to God I could change things, rewind that evening and do it all differently, but I can't,' he said, the words bursting out with unexpected earnestness. 'But it was nobody's fault. Just one of those terrible, unlucky things that happens.'

The music had reached a crescendo, fittingly enough. Ethan said nothing. Dan was pretty sure he didn't care about luck, or whose fault it was; he only cared that he no longer had a dad, that his world had been shattered one dreadful February night. *I will make this better,* Dan vowed to his nephew in his head. *I promise you. I will never stop trying to make this better for you, for the rest of my life and yours.*

Chapter Six

The following morning Zoe scrolled idly through a news website on her phone as she sat in the doctor's waiting room. Yet another sleepless night and she was starting to feel as if she was losing the grip on her sanity. Her eyes were sore, her brain jangled; her entire body felt heavy and cumbersome. She was fantasizing about sleeping pills that would knock her out, send her into oblivion. *I need help*, she imagined saying to the doctor when it was finally her turn to be seen. *I can't go on like this. A few days ago I burst into tears on the pavement and had to be rescued by a kind shopkeeper. What can I do? When will I start feeling normal again?* She hoped she wouldn't embarrass herself by crying, but she couldn't rule it out. Her tear ducts seemed permanently on standby these days, always ready for an impromptu weep.

'Do you want me to come over at the weekend?' her mum had asked on the phone last night, sounding anxious, as Zoe poured her heart out. God, it was tempting to say yes. There was a part of her that longed to retreat into the sanctuary of her mother's arms very much – to hide her face against her, like she'd done as a little girl, prone to shyness – but she'd said a regretful no in the end. She had to manage, for the sake of the children, take charge of the situation rather than ducking responsibility. Besides, if she leaned too hard on her mum, she might never be able to get up again.

'Mari O'Connor,' she heard a woman saying at the reception desk just then and turned her head to see a mum she knew from school standing there. Oh, great. Now no doubt there would be a sympathetic How-*are*-you? conversation and Zoe would not be able to reach the end of the first sentence without losing her dignity. She bent over her phone, hoping Mari wouldn't notice her in the corner, praying that she would be called in for her appointment now, to avoid any awkwardness.

She heard Mari's footsteps and smelled her strong jasmine perfume, but no such How-*are*-you? was forthcoming. Glancing across the small room, she was just in time to see the other woman notice her then quickly turn her head away. Zoe felt her hackles rise. This happened a lot – people pretending they hadn't seen her because they felt uncomfortable around a grieving widow – and in many ways it was even worse than the irritating How-*are*-you?s. And guess what, *she* felt pretty bloody uncomfortable every minute of the day. 'It's only because they don't know what to say,' Clare had soothed when Zoe moaned to her about it. 'And there *is* nothing good to say, really, other than *I'm so sorry this has happened to you – how can I help?*'

'So why don't they say that then? Rather than crossing the road to avoid me, as if I'm some kind of plague victim? Like I won't notice them slinking away, the cowards!'

She was sick of people shunning her out of their own weakness. Okay, so ten seconds ago she might not have wanted any kind of conversation, but now, contrarily, she felt compelled to force one. 'Hi, Mari,' she said pointedly across the busy waiting room. *I see you.*

Mari looked up at once, guilt all over her face. She had strawberry-blonde hair and the porcelain sort of skin that showed up even a faint blush in full fiery Technicolor. 'Sorry, I was miles away,' she said, which was such a transparent lie that Zoe had to struggle to hold back her sardonic snort. 'How *are* you? We all miss Patrick so much.'

'Zoe Sheppard?' called the doctor just then, appearing in the doorway, thank God.

'Bye, Mari,' said Zoe, getting up from her seat and walking away, her nerve-ends bristling. *We all miss Patrick so much* indeed, she thought crossly. It was Mari's husband, John, who'd been friends with Patrick; not Mari, who barely even knew him. Some people simply loved to cash in on another person's unhappiness, though, and appropriate it as their own. She had a sudden flash of memory from the funeral:

Mari sobbing there at the back of the church, thin and beautiful in her black mourning dress. How dare she? Zoe thought now, following the doctor into her room and sitting down. Shedding those fake tears, which were not even rightfully hers to shed!

Dr Gupta looked at Zoe's notes on the computer, then back at Zoe. Here came that professional compassion, thought Zoe, noting the doctor's tilted head and concerned gaze. Any second now.

'So, Zoe, how *are* you?' said Dr Gupta. Bingo. 'How can I help you today?'

'There. Can you hear it? Just there.'

Over in Shepherd's Bush, Dan had, with some trepidation, gone to see Rosemary, the eighty-something-year-old woman who had been the bane of his brother's life, by all accounts. Having expected to be confronted with a sour-faced old gorgon in her lair, he had been surprised at the small, rather sweet-looking lady who answered the door, dressed in a crisply ironed ivory blouse with a tweedy skirt, tendrils of long white hair spilling from a chignon. Her lipstick was immaculate and he could detect a faint floral perfume from her as she walked across the living room.

'Do you hear it?' she asked as he followed her. 'The mouse?'

'Mrs—' He had forgotten her last name. He definitely

mustn't call her Mrs Pain In Arse. 'Rosemary – if I may,' he went on. 'I think it's a squeaky floorboard rather than a mouse.' He moved his foot up and down on the salmon-pink rug, demonstrating. 'See?'

She crossed her arms across her narrow frame and for a moment he thought she was going to put up an argument – she had been absolutely insistent on the phone that there was a rodent problem – but then her shoulders sagged and she looked down at the carpet. 'Oh.'

'I can see why you thought it was a mouse,' he said quickly, not wanting her to feel embarrassed. 'It's a very mousy sort of squeak.' He pressed his toe down again, nodding at the sound.

'I suppose it'll mean the carpet coming up,' Rosemary said, pursing her lips. Was it Dan's imagination or did she seem pleased at the prospect? 'You'll want to fix it, won't you? I mean, in case it gets worse.'

'Um . . .' replied Dan, who didn't really see the point of going to so much trouble for a squeaky floorboard. 'Well, I'm not sure it's an *emergency,* but—'

'I'll put the kettle on,' she told him, whisking away before he could complete his sentence. 'While you're here, you can look at the kitchen sink. There was a funny smell coming from it the other day.'

So much for this being a quick visit, Dan thought, an hour or so later, having drunk two coffees and repeatedly refused a third slice of fruitcake. As soon as he fixed – or discounted – one 'problem', another would mysteriously arise. 'Oh, you *are* clever,' she praised him, when he changed the light bulb of her bedside lamp. 'Thank you, dear,' she cried in apparent delight, when he replaced the washer on the bathroom tap. And then, just as he was standing up to go – no, really, he absolutely had to leave now – she caught him off-guard by saying, 'So where's Patrick anyway? Not that I'm complaining. You're much nicer. But is he on holiday or something?'

Poleaxed, Dan sank back into his chair. He'd assumed she already knew. 'Oh,' he said, swallowing hard. It felt as if there was a sticky paste of fruitcake behind his teeth, gumming up his entire mouth. 'He died,' he managed to say. 'I'm his brother. Sorry, I thought I'd said.' He ran his hand through his hair. 'I've lost track of who knows and . . .'

She froze, aghast at her own faux pas, and they both sat there for a moment looking at one another. 'Goodness gracious,' she said eventually, her eyes widening in sympathy. 'I'm very sorry. How did he . . . ? I mean, you don't have to tell me, of course, but . . . was it sudden? It must have been. I only saw him – well, last month. I did wonder why he wasn't answering my calls, but thought he might be on holiday or perhaps he'd lost his phone or . . . Good heavens. What *happened*?'

That question again. Twice in two days. Dan thought of

Ethan's guarded face, the tension shown by his knotted fingers, his clenched body language. Still, Dan wasn't obliged to disclose anything to Patrick's tenant in the way that he had to Patrick's son. 'It was a tragic accident,' he told Rosemary, not meeting her eye. He pushed his chair back and got to his feet. 'Very sad. Now if you'll excuse me, I really do need to—'

'And him a family man, too,' she exclaimed, her hand flying up to her mouth. 'I'm very sorry to hear this news, Daniel. Very sorry indeed. Patrick's been extremely good to me over the years. Very fair. Had a bit of a temper on him now and then, obviously, but . . .' She checked herself. *Don't speak ill of the dead now.* 'You must all be devastated. His poor children. And his parents! How terrible to lose a child. They must be heartbroken.'

Dan swallowed, thinking about his mum sobbing at the funeral while his dad remained dry-eyed; the twisting of a checked handkerchief between his fingers the only sign of his agitation. 'Yes,' he mumbled.

'And you said it was an accident, did you? What sort of accident?'

Dan tried to wrestle back a grip on the conversation. 'If you don't mind,' he said, 'I'd rather not talk about it.' And – thank goodness – that seemed to do the trick. Before she could ask him anything else, he walked to the door, although she got up immediately to follow him. A vision flashed into his head of him trying to leave the premises with Rosemary clinging to his legs to stop him, the questions ongoing. 'Thanks for the coffee,' he said, making it all the way down the hall without being rugby-tackled. 'Nice to meet you.'

'See you soon,' she called as he made his escape.

Not if I can help it, he thought. He put up his hand and kept walking. Quickly, before a lasso could be used to haul him back again.

The rest of Dan's week turned out to be unexpectedly busy. His long, empty days spent lying in bed were a thing of the past, now that he was working through all the outstanding problems Patrick's tenants had raised recently. New locks were put in place for the family on Adelaide Grove. A leaving date was agreed with the Whitecliffe Road guy, who was moving out. A meeting arranged with the lettings agent Patrick had dealt with about advertising the soon-to-be-vacant property. Although Dan had vowed to step into his brother's shoes for the duration of the sabbatical, it felt as if he was literally following in Patrick's footsteps by taking on his work this way.

What was more, he felt as if his sabbatical had been invigorated, saved from the jaws of defeat and reconfigured with new purpose. With tenants to look after and his good-deeds plan in place, he was out every day, dealing with all sorts of people, having to find practical solutions to a wide variety of problems. It was surprisingly enjoyable. 'A change is as good as a holiday,' his mum had always said, and he was starting to see the wisdom in this.

Admittedly the paperwork was proving less fun to tackle, namely because Patrick didn't seem to have any sort of system as far as Dan could tell. He'd set up direct debits for the basics at least – gas, water, electricity and council tax – but there were also plumbers and electricians and locksmiths to pay, some of whom had taken to sending irate reminders. Having dealt with all the bills due that he could find, Dan noticed an emailed reminder from Patrick's accountant about the January–March quarterly VAT return documents needing to be sent in at the end of this month, and decided he should probably start gathering together the invoices and receipts required.

It was while he was working through the bank statements, item by item, that he noticed one payment for which there was no corresponding paper trail: a monthly payment of several hundred pounds to an L. Fox, marked with the reference 'Maintenance'. A builder, kept on a retainer? he wondered. A painter and decorator? Cleaning service? It was odd because, aside from this particular payee, the other listed outgoings were fairly obvious. There were labelled receipts for a variety of goods and services: a carpenter, a plasterer, a carpet firm, two bottles of drain-cleaner, petrol. Also, the general maintenance – boilers and broken locks and squeaky floorboards – seemed always to have fallen to

Patrick himself, if the phone calls Dan had been receiving were anything to go by.

Perplexed, he turned to Patrick's laptop and tracked down a file labelled 'Accounts', where he scrolled through old spreadsheets to see if any further information was available. The payment went out on the first of every month and had been listed within a column marked 'General', which didn't help enormously. Still curious, he went further back through the files. Whoever was receiving these monthly payments had been doing so for years, he noticed, his pulse quickening. But where was the money going?

His imagination went into overdrive. Had Patrick been involved in a money-laundering scheme? Funnelling funds through his business account to a dodgy person or company? He wrinkled his nose, unable to quite believe this scenario. Patrick was the sort of bloke who would cut corners now and then, but Dan was pretty sure he was not an out-and-out crook. Maybe he was being blackmailed then? But by whom? Did Zoe know about this?

Something about it definitely smelled odd, he thought, continuing to scroll down. There didn't seem to be any paperwork to back up the maintenance service: no company invoices or correspondence whatsoever. How had Patrick even got this past the accountant? Then he eventually reached a spreadsheet dating back seven and a half years and noticed that the payment hadn't been made then. Okay. So the mysterious transfer had been leaving Patrick's business bank account for seven years and three months. The question was: should Dan pursue this little mystery or turn a blind eye? If Patrick had been in some kind of trouble – or collusion – and Zoe was oblivious, Dan certainly didn't want to get her involved in any extra drama. But all the same, seeing as he was sorting out the VAT return, he might be held legally responsible for anything underhand that later transpired.

He went back to the original email from the accountant and found a phone number. Sod it – he was going to find out what this was about, for his own peace of mind, if nothing else. 'Hi,' he said, when he got through to the right person. 'I'm preparing Patrick Sheppard's VAT return and wanted to query a payment, because I can't find any corresponding paperwork . . . Yes, it goes out as "Maintenance" every month. Could you let me know the payee, so that I can trace—'

Then he stopped midway through his own question, because it had just occurred to him that there was more than one kind of maintenance payment. One where it was for actual property maintenance, as he'd initially assumed. But there was also such a thing as a child-maintenance payment, wasn't there? Which meant that . . . Oh my God. No. Surely not?

'Her name's Lydia Fox,' the accountant said. 'The payee.'

'I see,' said Dan, his voice suddenly hoarse. He didn't want to know any more. Did he? 'Right. Thank you.' And then he hung up, a whole new and terrible picture forming in his head. Lydia Fox. *Fuck*. What had Patrick got himself into here? More to the point, what the hell should Dan do about it?

In the early hours of the morning Zoe felt warm breath on her neck and a small wriggling body in close proximity. She opened her eye a crack to see that Bea had crawled into bed beside her, at which point her brain caught up with the message from her nose: the faint smell of ammonia, which meant that Bea had wet her bed again. 'Did you have an accident?' she murmured, shuffling round to put an arm across her daughter and wondering what time it was.

'Yes,' came the reply. 'But don't worry, it didn't go on the toys. And I changed my pants.'

'Okay,' said Zoe, willing herself to plunge back into sleep. This had been happening a lot recently. Most nights since Patrick had died, in fact. *Everyone will get through the loss in their own ways,* stated the grief booklet her GP had pressed on her. So far Ethan's grief had manifested itself in silent withdrawal and occasional bursts of white-faced rage; Gabe's in loud dogged arguments; Bea's through crying jags, insistence on wearing her unicorn onesie whenever possible and wet beds. Zoe, for her part, still felt as if she were living through her own personal disaster movie, liable to be crushed by a rockfall at any given moment. Sometimes – and she wasn't proud of this – she even wished for said rockfall to hurry up and put her out of her misery.

'Try a nice lavender bath before bed,' Dr Gupta had advised, apparently loath to prescribe any sleeping pills despite Zoe's request. 'Make sure you're getting plenty of exercise – enough to make you physically tired by the end of the day. And how about talking to a therapist, just to unpack your thoughts to another person on a regular basis? There's a phone number at the back of the booklet I've given you, if you want to find out more – or, of course, I could suggest a couple of people who might be able to help.'

Zoe had thanked her politely, but she knew already she wouldn't bother. She didn't have the energy to start ringing round trying to organize therapy.

'Come back in two weeks and let's see how you're doing,' the doctor had said at the end, but so far Zoe hadn't got as far as booking another appointment. What was the point?

Bea's breathing became deeper and slower, and she made a few sucking sounds with her open mouth. It was too dark to see much more than her outline, but Zoe could imagine her daughter's face softening and becoming slack as sleep towed her under once more. Her poor babies: so confused, so traumatized, so bereft. Even now, weeks after the event, it seemed unthinkable that Patrick was no longer there to comfort them and her, to make them laugh, to pull them together. She didn't want to share a bed with her daughter every night; she wanted her husband beside her instead, the solid comforting mound of him under the covers, the faint sigh of his breathing as the nightly soundtrack of her life. She wished she could hold him once more – a thousand times more, a million – that they could be pressed so tightly together that his body would leave an imprint against hers, but he was gone. She would never be able to hold him again.

Other women she knew moaned about their husbands all the time – so lazy, so thoughtless, so selfish – and, sure, she had criticized Patrick for all of those things once in a while. Add to the list that he was reckless with money, a terrible flirt and that he always, without fail, left his dirty clothes on the bedroom floor rather than bothering to put them in the laundry basket, but she would gladly take all of that and never complain again, if she could just have him back. At least then she would get the chance to say sorry for the last fight they'd had.

Don't think about that now, she told herself hurriedly. On nights like this when she lay awake in the dark, her thoughts almost always circled back round to the awful things she had said that final evening, as if it was her own personal purgatory. Her very heavy cross to bear.

She forced herself to remember instead Patrick in one of his more heroic hours. When Ethan was a tiny baby, they'd lived in a grotty first-floor flat in Ealing, and a series of nasty notes began appearing through the front door. *Tell that brat to stop crying or I'll be over there myself to make him stop!* the notes threatened, or words to that effect. Ethan was three months old, and colicky, and yes, he did cry a lot, day and night, but Zoe was doing her best, she thought, reading the notes, ashen-faced. She went round and apologized meekly to the shrewish fifty-something woman who lived next door, but the neighbour gave her short shrift. 'Some of us have jobs to go to! I'll be complaining to the council if this carries on – get a social worker on to you.' Exhausted by the demands of early mothering and intimidated by the angry woman, Zoe had said nothing to Patrick, but then a few nights later after Ethan had had a particularly grizzly day, loud music came blaring through the wall around two in the morning, start-ling them all and making Ethan sob with wide-eyed fright.

'It's that woman again, I bet,' Zoe said, trying to reassure her terrified son.

'What woman?' Patrick had asked, getting out of bed.

Zoe hadn't wanted to drag him into the situation, but ended up showing Patrick the notes. It was like activating a superhero, or at the very least unleashing something primitive and fundamental inside him, the genetic code of which basically came down to: DEFEND WOMAN AND CHILD.

'Right,' he said, jaw set, before marching straight over

there to deliver a furious riposte to their neighbour. Off went the music almost immediately, although not before Zoe heard the woman shouting, 'Well, now you know what it feels like to be woken up in the night by a horrible noise. Annoying, isn't it?'

Patrick, once roused, was unstoppable. He was magnificent, in fact. 'How *dare* you,' Zoe heard him retaliate. 'How *dare* you write your pathetic little notes to us, threatening my son and harassing my wife? I've a good mind to call the police. Do you think you're helping at all? Making things better? Have you any idea how tired my wife is, how much we have been through recently? She lost two pints of blood when she gave birth, did you know that? No. Because you didn't bother to find out. People like you make me sick. And I don't want to hear another word from you on this subject, do you hear me? Not another word. Otherwise, God help me, I might end up doing something I regret.'

My hero, Zoe had thought back then as the door slammed behind him. The great protector. From the moment she'd discovered she was pregnant with Ethan, Patrick had been the most loving husband, the best dad ever. But now she had nobody. Now she was left to do everything herself, fight her own battles and mop up her own mess. Some random guy had rung the doorbell after dark a couple of evenings ago, asking for money, to which she'd politely said no and closed the door, but afterwards she found herself nervously listening out for his return and wishing that Patrick was there, just for the security. Sometimes when she was awake in the night, like now, she heard strange noises around the house and became convinced that someone was trying to break in. By now she had worked out a plan of action – wake up the kids and lock her and them safely in the bathroom while she dialled 999 – but even so, it was hardly a relaxing way to spend the wee small hours.

See? This is what I have to deal with now, because of you being stupid enough to die on me, she raged at him in her head. *Lying here wide awake, imagining the worst. Crying in the street the other day like a crazy person.* At least she had made amends on that front, she consoled herself. Earlier today she had slunk back to the boutique where the woman had been so kind to her and pressed a bunch of velvety mauve anemones into her hand, muttering hot-faced apologies. The woman had been lovely, thank goodness, telling her there was absolutely no need to say sorry and even scribbling down her number on a business card 'in case you ever want to chat'.

Still, not everything was resolved. Not by a long chalk. There was still the matter of what, exactly, had happened between Patrick and Dan that fateful night to get to the bottom of – something that Dan was resolutely not telling her.

'What were you even talking about in the pub?' she'd asked him after Patrick's death had been confirmed, when they were all groping their way through the ghastly new landscape of bereavement. She wanted to get to grips with every detail of those final known hours, examine every clue of behaviour that might explain why Patrick had gone off alone, and what might have happened to him. She also felt desperate to learn what Patrick had said about her, about their argument. Did Dan know about that, for instance? It sounded as if Patrick had left the world with two of his dearest loved ones angry with him, which broke her heart to imagine. But Dan was unforthcoming; shifty, even – staring at the floor, muttering that he couldn't remember all of it, they'd both drunk too much.

But you remember feeling angry enough to say that he couldn't stay at yours any more; you remember sending him off along the river path to his death? she'd asked sharply, only it had come out as more of a shout – a scream, possibly.

'Zoe, that's not helping,' her mum had said, putting a calm hand on hers, but Dan hadn't replied, merely flinching, then avoiding her gaze.

It had wormed away at her ever since, that downward stare of his, the way he had pulled up the drawbridge. *I can't remember.* Yeah, right. It was so obvious that he *could* but something was stopping him from telling her. What? Was he protecting her by not revealing whatever hateful, damning remarks Patrick had made about her? Was that why Dan had stayed away all this time? Did *he* now hate and blame *her* for his brother's drowning? God, you could go mad, spiralling down into paranoia over this, but she couldn't quite bring herself to ask the questions aloud. She did not want to be told that yes, her husband had gone to his death angry with her, resentful after their bust-up. It would finish her off. Destroy what little was left of her.

And now Dan had appeared at her door, wearing that penitent, hangdog look all the time, and she knew he was trying to do the right thing by her, but even so, the doubts and suspicion kept surfacing. What really happened that night? What was keeping Dan so tight-lipped? One way or another, she knew she'd have to get it out of him. Just as soon as she felt strong enough to cope with any unpleasant truths.

Chapter Seven

On Sunday it was Liz Sheppard's seventieth birthday, and the entire family was gathering for a celebratory lunch in The Plough – the first time they had all been together since Patrick's funeral. Dan could tell, the minute he saw her, that his mum had been crying because her mascara was smudged around the soft pouches of her eyes and she was blowing her nose. 'Happy birthday, Mum,' he said, hugging her.

'How can it be happy when my oldest son isn't with us any more?' she gulped and he tightened his grip about her, catching his dad's eye and exchanging a look of defeat. Was it unfair of Dan to say that he'd always felt like the second-favourite son? Throughout their childhood Patrick had consistently been the one to jump higher, kick harder, charm every person who crossed his path. Patrick was taller, better-looking, funnier, more successful, whereas Dan was . . . well, kind of a dork, he supposed. A loser.

Nobody had quite said aloud, 'The wrong son died' after Patrick's death, but Dan was pretty sure his mum had thought that at some point. Even now, weeks on, she could hardly look him in the eye.

'We'll make the best of it,' he said after a moment. 'We'll raise a glass to him. I'm sure he's looking down on you, from wherever he is.' Personally, he had no truck with any notions of an afterlife, but his mum, a Catholic, was a firm believer. 'And he'd want you to be happy today, wouldn't he? On your birthday.'

'A bereaved mother on Mothering Sunday, though. Did you ever hear of anything so awful?'

Shit. It was Mothering Sunday too? He glanced furtively around, noticing how full the pub was, with smiling women positioned at the head of every table. There was a shiny foil balloon on the next table saying *Best Mum Ever* – yes, and a list of 'Mother's Day specials' chalked up on the board beside the bar. Damn it. Mother's Day. How had he managed to miss that? 'A good excuse to celebrate what a great mum you were to him – and still are to me,' he said after a brief hesitation, wondering if he would be able to unpeel the envelope containing his seventieth-birthday card and add an extra Mother's Day message as well. Probably not. 'Let me get you a drink. What would you like?'

She blew her nose again and blinked. 'Dear me, I must look a fright,' she said, rummaging in her handbag for a compact mirror-and-powder thing. 'A large glass of Sauvignon Blanc, please, Daniel.' She peered at her reflection as she dusted her face. Liz Sheppard had always taken care over her appearance, with her chic silvery bob, statement jewellery and smart handbags. Today, however, she looked – well, pretty unkempt actually, although she would have killed Dan for saying as much. He wasn't usually good at noticing such things, but even he could see that her hair needed cutting and her navy dress was crumpled.

'A very large one, if you know what I mean.'

'One bucket of wine coming up,' he confirmed, before remembering the spreadsheet pinned on his fridge at home. Of course! He should have factored his parents into the plan too, in an attempt to fill up the gaps Patrick's death had left in their lives. He squeezed her shoulder gently. 'Listen, Mum, I was wondering. Is there anything that Patrick used to do for you that I could do instead?' he asked. 'Like . . . odd jobs or what-have-you?'

His mum sniffled, putting her compact away. 'We just miss him popping round, don't we, Derek?' she said plaintively. 'Every time someone comes to the door, I think it might be him, even now, but . . .'

'Yes,' agreed her husband when she trailed off, unable to finish the sentence. He was a taciturn man who used words with economy, as if speaking each one cost him money. Apart from when he lost his temper, of course, when he would spray them out full pelt. As a little boy, Dan had once been so frightened when his dad started shouting at his mum in the car about a wrong set of directions that he'd wet himself, the hot splash of liquid soaking through his trousers onto the vinyl back seat. He still remembered how his mum had sighed, 'Oh, *Daniel*' at him, when they eventually arrived and got out of the car, and how Patrick had instinctively put an arm around him.

'Popping round?' he asked now. 'What, at the weekend or . . . ?'

'No, during the week. He'd be driving by and he'd drop in for a cuppa. Sometimes he'd help out your dad, or he'd get me a bit of shopping if my legs were playing up or . . . You know. He was just there a lot.'

This was all news to Dan. Working in his glass box over in the City for long hours during the week, he had never once dropped round to see his mum and dad in this way. It hadn't occurred to him that Patrick might. 'Right,' he said, feeling as if he'd missed something obvious. 'I see. Well, maybe I should start doing the same.' He *would* do the same, he thought immediately. This very week he would manufacture an excuse to drive over to their small semi in Brentford and play a more active role in his parents' lives. 'In the meantime, let me get those drinks. Dad, what would you like?'

He escaped to the crush of sons and husbands at the bar, still mulling over the fact that he had perhaps neglected his parents in a way Patrick clearly hadn't. It was like discovering you'd missed out on a party that everyone else had been invited to – only in this case he should have thought to invite himself. Dan had always thought he knew his brother well, but here was something that he'd been unaware of. A *second* thing he'd been unaware of, rather, because he still hadn't been able to track down this mysterious Lydia Fox of the 'Maintenance' payments leaving Patrick's business bank account. He had searched for her through all the contacts on his brother's phone, trawled through email accounts and Facebook friends, but had found no trace. Whoever this woman was, it looked very much as if Patrick had wanted her to be kept secret. But who was she to him?

There had to be some rational explanation for the payments, he kept telling himself. There must be. His imagination had provided all sorts of lurid options that he didn't want to look at too closely: was she a mistress, tucked away in one of his flats? With Patrick paying her from his company account, as if she were some kind of business expense, some other service that was being supplied? 'Maintenance' made him think there must be a child there too, which added a whole other layer of complexity. But no. Patrick had behaved badly in the past – Dan was trying not to dwell too closely on that – but this was getting into the realms of bonkers fantasy, surely?

'Hello, lovey, your mum and dad sent us over,' came a voice just then and he turned to see his Aunty Mary and

Uncle Colin at the bar beside him. 'I'll have a small sherry, if you're buying, and Colin will have – pint of bitter, Colin?'

'Please,' said Colin, who was never one to disagree with his wife. If she'd told him he was having a Jägerbomb or a flaming Sambuca, he'd probably have nodded obediently.

'I thought we would be the last ones here today – Colin couldn't find his glasses as usual – but I gather Zoe hasn't arrived yet,' said Mary, with a sympathetic cluck. 'It must be very hard for her, the poor thing, especially when the children are all so . . . Ah. Here she is now.'

Dan looked over to see Zoe and the kids barrelling through the pub door. Zoe wore her usual frazzled expression as she gazed around, simultaneously ignoring Ethan and Gabe who were bickering furiously, as well as Bea, who was plucking at Zoe's sleeve with an urgent expression. Who was he not seeing? Dan wondered, unable to stop thinking about the maintenance payments. Another child, another partner? What on earth had Patrick got himself into – and how much, if anything, did Zoe know?

'Oh dear. She's got her hands full, hasn't she?' sniffed Mary, frowning as Gabe thumped Ethan's arm.

'Zoe! Over here,' called Dan, wondering in the next moment if the children had any idea it was Mother's Day. Damn it. If he'd known, he could have given Ethan a heads-up on Wednesday, chucked him some cash to sort out cards and flowers for his mum. But if even he, an adult, hadn't been on the ball, he was pretty sure the children wouldn't have organized anything themselves.

'Hi,' he said, waving as they approached. 'What do you all want to drink? Special Mother's Day glass of fizz, Zo?' *By the way, what does the name Lydia Fox mean to you, Zo?*

Zoe looked wan. 'Just a tea, please. Kids, what would you like?'

Ethan asked for a Coke, Bea a lemonade – no, orange juice; no, actually a fizzy apple juice; yes, definitely that – while Gabe asked for a pint of beer and then changed it to a hot chocolate when Zoe told him off for being silly.

'You do all know it's Mother's Day, right?' Dan said to the children, with a meaningful look over at Zoe.

'Uh-oh,' said Gabe, eyeing her. 'Nope. We didn't have a clue.'

'I thought it was Grandma's birthday,' said Bea, frowning.

'Well, it's that too,' said Dan, 'but—'

'It's fine, it's not a big deal,' Zoe interrupted. 'Don't start guilt-tripping them. Bea, let's find the loo, I thought you were bursting. Boys, help your uncle carry the drinks over, please.'

Dan opened his mouth to defend himself, then shut it again. He wasn't trying to guilt-trip anyone, he wanted to say; he was trying to be thoughtful. But she was already walking away with Bea.

'Who's next?' called the bar worker then, and Dan spun round to put in the order.

'Don't take any notice of Mum,' Ethan said gruffly. 'She's just in a bad mood today.'

'Yeah, we had to get the bus because the car wouldn't start, and *then* she said the f-word,' said Gabe, looking gleeful at the memory. 'Well, she didn't actually say "the f-word", she said "fuck", but—'

'*Gabe*,' said Dan warningly as his Aunty Mary started pulling her cardigan about herself, making *Goodness-me-how-disgraceful* faces. 'Language.' Then he motioned to the barman. 'Sorry, mate. Could you change that pint of lager to a Coke, please?' The pub was only a ten-minute walk from his flat; if Zoe's car was playing up, he could give them all a lift back home later on, he figured. 'Ta.' Then he took a twenty-pound note from his wallet, handing it to Ethan. Better late than never. 'Here – maybe you could pop out and get your mum something with this later on, when you're back in Kew. A bunch of flowers or a box of chocolates, that sort of thing. Say it's from all of you, yeah?'

Gabe's eyes went round. 'Wow! Twenty quid!'

'Yeah, for me to look after, not you,' Ethan told him, tucking it into his jeans pocket. 'Thanks, Uncle Dan.'

One more good deed to add to his balance sheet, he thought a few minutes later, carrying the drinks over to the table. Two good deeds, if Zoe said yes to the lift home. He wondered if he would ever be able to earn enough to achieve any kind of redemption. Right now, he doubted it.

Zoe had never really gone in for Mother's Day in a big way, so she'd been surprised, on waking up that Sunday, by how flat she felt without Patrick there, marshalling the children to bring her a tray of breakfast things plus a vase of whatever-was-alive in the garden. (One year she had been presented with a selection of twigs with a cake-ribbon tied around them; it had been a hard winter.) This year – nothing. She didn't have the heart to mention it to the kids; it didn't matter, she thought as she made the breakfast herself. But then the car wouldn't start and she didn't know what to do – and this made her miss Patrick more than ever. He was good with practical things, he would have figured something out. 'Can we go in Dad's van instead?' Gabe had piped up hopefully, but there wasn't room for them all in there – and besides Zoe had never liked driving it.

'Do we *have* to go?' moaned Ethan, kicking at the tyres of the useless car.

'Yes, it's Grandma's special birthday, and she's booked us all in for a nice lunch at the pub,' Zoe snapped, just as it started to drizzle. 'We'll get the bus.'

Once at the pub, she felt herself unwind a little. Liz gave her a hug and made a fuss of the children and even Derek tried his best, producing a 50p coin and doing tricks for Bea. She didn't have to cook, Zoe consoled herself. She'd washed her hair that morning and put on some lipstick and a nice top for the first time in weeks, and felt a shade more human again as a result. The children were on good form too, with Gabe in particular making everyone laugh with his impressions and general daftness. For a short while she was able to keep the sadness at bay and relax, enjoy the food and company. Even smile a few times. Who knew, she thought, hugging her in-laws goodbye when it was time to leave, that small pleasures could make such a big difference?

Best of all, Dan offered them a lift home, which was a relief to everyone after the bad-tempered bus journey over there. Then, back at the house, he poked around under the bonnet of her car for a while, before coming in to tell her that he was fairly certain it was a flat battery. Under his instruction, they managed to jump-start the engine, then he suggested that Zoe drive around for fifteen minutes or so to give it a decent charge. 'Call this your Mother's Day treat,' he said with a faint smile. 'Fifteen minutes' peace on a Sunday. Hell, go out for longer if you want. Put some music on. I'll hold the fort till you get back again.'

'Don't tempt me,' she said, before grudgingly admitting to herself that she was grateful to him. 'Thanks,' she added. 'I appreciate this.'

'No problem,' he replied, putting up a hand in farewell as she edged out of the drive.

It was quite a novelty to Zoe, driving aimlessly around with nowhere in particular to go. Usually sitting at the wheel meant a chore – either going to whichever school she was working in that week, a trip to the supermarket or ferrying the kids to an activity or birthday party, one eye on the clock, worrying about being late and – more often than not – trying to referee a bout of bickering and jostling that was kicking off on the back seat, without losing her focus on the road. None of that today. Complete silence and no distractions. Once she'd recovered from her initial nervousness that the car would give out on her, it was almost a relaxing experience. She turned on the radio and found some upbeat dance music, then whacked the volume up high. Hell, it was Mother's Day and nobody was around to criticize her singing. Forget Dr Gupta's advice about lavender baths and talking therapy – it turned out that belting out a great pop song felt better than anything, really cathartic. Right until a cheesy love-ballad came on and she found that tears were rolling down her face, anyway.

She arrived back eventually to find Gabe glued to the Xbox – she really needed to start enforcing stricter rules about that – and Dan taking part in one of Bea's tea parties, along with various teddies and stuffed toys that had been arranged in a circle. Ethan, hopefully, was upstairs doing homework, although the chances were he was plugged into a game too. Oh, well. She wasn't going to start picking fights today.

'All okay?' Dan asked, setting his miniature floral teacup down on its mismatched red plastic saucer with comedic daintiness.

'All good,' she replied. 'Thanks again. Can I make you a coffee or something?'

'I've just *made* him one actually, Mummy,' Bea protested.

Dan pretended to drain the empty teacup, smacking his lips for good measure afterwards. 'Delicious,' he assured Bea. 'Another coffee would be great,' he replied to Zoe, getting up. 'Thanks, Bea. That was exactly what I needed.'

They went into the kitchen and then something very weird happened. When Dan went to get the milk out of the fridge he stopped dead in front of it, peered closer at something, then said in a strangled voice, 'Wait – so you *know* her? This Lydia Fox?'

'What?' Zoe was confused for a moment until she saw he was pointing at a business card pinned up there with a San Francisco tram magnet, and she realized it was the one given to her by the nice woman in the gift shop earlier that week. 'Oh. No, not really. It's just some woman I met in a shop.'

'You met her in a *shop*?' For some reason Dan looked

completely taken aback. She'd go as far as to say stricken, even. Was there some law that had been passed about talking to strangers in shops, or what? Why was he acting so peculiarly? 'Recently or—'

'Yeah, a few days ago. Why?'

'What, she came up to you and . . . Is she *following* you or something?'

Zoe stared at him, unable to see where this was going – or, indeed, where it had come from. 'No. I just . . . *Why?*' she repeated. 'Do *you* know her then?'

Before he could reply, they both heard the front door slam and Ethan's voice. 'Gabe! Bea! Come here!'

Startled, Zoe swung round. 'Where's he been?' she asked, feeling as if she had lost track of her senses. She could have sworn she'd only been out for twenty minutes, yet she seemed to have returned to a parallel universe where nothing felt quite normal.

'Um, just out,' Dan replied vaguely.

In the next moment Ethan, Gabe and Bea marched into the kitchen together, Ethan holding a bunch of daffodils, Gabe clutching a box of Milk Tray and Bea brandishing her most beloved pink stuffed unicorn.

'HAPPY MOTHER'S DAY!' they chorused, all three of them beaming at their own cunning. 'You can *keep* my unicorn, if you really want,' Bea added lavishly, before appearing to regret such impulsive generosity. 'For today, I mean.'

Zoe actually felt quite tearful for a moment as she crouched down so that they could rush into her arms. The daffs were dripping on one shoulder, a corner of the chocolate box jabbed painfully into her boob, and Bea, scrambling to get on her lap, almost knocked her over, but it was a good moment. A really good moment. 'My favourite flowers, my favourite chocolates and most definitely my favourite children,' she said into their necks, as love spread through her like a balm.

It was only much later on that evening that she remembered Dan's strange behaviour with the shop-woman's business card, and wondered what that had all been about. Probably nothing, she decided, stuffing a chocolate fudge into her mouth. She wouldn't waste time dwelling on it, when the worst had already happened. From now on, the only way was up.

Chapter Eight

Lydia was dishing up platefuls of (disappointingly stodgy) macaroni cheese when her phone started ringing. It was Monday teatime and when she glanced over and saw a number she didn't recognize onscreen, she decided to ignore it. No doubt it would be some scammy call about a non-existent injury claim that she was supposed to have made, or the phone company trying to talk her into an expensive upgrade. No, thanks. Besides, the peas were about to boil over if she didn't attend to them this second.

'Tea's ready,' she yelled through to Jemima, who had been practising forward rolls up and down the living-room for the last twenty minutes. 'Bugger off,' she muttered as the phone began ringing a second time.

Jemima burst in, her bunches loose and wonky after her gymnastics, navy-blue school socks in wrinkles around her ankles. 'Oh, I forgot to say, Mum,' she began, hopping from one foot to the other. 'Guess what? Miss Sergeant's getting married in June. To a *lady*!'

'How nice,' Lydia said, pouring a glass of milk for her daughter and putting it on the table. Miss Sergeant was Jemima's kind, clever class teacher and the current object of hero-worship. The much-adored Miss Sergeant had been invited to Jemima's birthday party back in January. ('Please don't feel you have to come,' Lydia had whispered to her, taking her aside at pick-up time the day invitations came out. 'At all.') She had been the recipient of a very special Christmas card that had been laboured over for an entire weekend, and she also starred as the subject of countless anecdotes, observations and drawings. Lydia was pleased that her daughter had a great role model – it was a step up from Barbie, she supposed – but had been slightly taken aback by Jemima's breathless, unending enthusiasm for the woman. She hoped she hadn't raised some kind of stalker in the making, put it that way.

'I want to get married to a girl too, when I'm big. I just like them more than boys. Hey, Mum – idea! Why don't *you* get married to a lady?' Jemima said, dragging the stool over to the sink so that she could wash her hands. 'Then you won't be lonely!'

'I'm not lonely, darling,' Lydia said, spooning carrots and peas onto their plates and trying not to leap on the defensive.

'You are a *bit* lonely,' her daughter insisted. 'I heard you telling Bridget once. And you don't have anyone to talk to, when I go to bed. Maybe I should stay up late with you tonight?'

Ever the optimist, always ready to try her luck – that was her girl. 'That's kind, but I'm fine, thanks,' Lydia assured her, trying not to laugh. 'Besides, you need your sleep after all that gym. Remember you were saying you wanted to be as tall as Poppy at school? Well, you grow when you're asleep. So the earlier you go to bed . . .'

'I'll get taller and taller and taller!' Jemima hopped down and shook her hands, soapy water flecking her school skirt where she hadn't rinsed off the suds. 'But you *could* marry a lady. If you don't like men.'

Tenacity was her daughter's middle name. Well, it wasn't, obviously, but maybe it should have been. 'Who said I didn't like men?' Lydia replied mildly. 'Give those hands a proper dry, please.'

'*You* said you didn't. You said to Bridget, I hate BEEP men.' Jemima gave her the side-eye before sliding into her seat at the table. 'The beep was a rude word, by the way,' she added with uncharacteristic primness. 'And I *heard* it. I don't know *what* Miss *Sergeant* would say if she knew I had heard words like *that* from my *mum.*'

'Sorry.' Lydia put their plates on the table, then cupped her hands around her mouth and pretended to shout out of the window. 'Sorry, Miss Sergeant! It won't happen again, I promise.' She pulled a funny face at Jemima and decided it was time to move the conversation along now. 'So! Tell me more about what happened on the trampoline anyway. Did you say you were learning a new routine?'

'Yeah, but . . .' Jemima waved her fork, unwilling to be distracted from the more important matter at hand. 'You could marry Bridget,' she persisted. 'Why don't you?'

Lydia tried not to sigh as she dug into the macaroni. 'I'm happy with things as they are,' she said. 'Just the two of us. I thought you were too? In fact, I remember you saying—'

'If you married Bridget, we could live in her house, though. And I could share Rohan's bedroom. Can I?'

'Darling . . .' This was getting out of hand. 'To marry someone, you have to be in love with them, okay? You have to really, really like them—'

'But you *do* like—'

'And feel like kissing them all the time.'

'You and Bridget hug each other. I've seen you!'

'Yes, but . . . it's different. She's my friend. I'm not madly in love with her. I don't want to kiss her.'

Jemima pouted. 'That's not very kind. Poor Bridget!'

'She probably doesn't *want* me to kiss her,' Lydia pointed out. 'Anyway! I'm glad Miss Sergeant is getting married. Did she tell you anything about the wedding?'

'Not really.' Jemima looked thoughtful for a moment as she speared a carrot and swished it through some cheese sauce. 'Mum, can I tell you a secret? A really, really big secret that you're not allowed to tell anyone?'

'Of course. Anything. *You're* not getting married as well, are you?'

'No! Mum! Don't be so silly. The secret is . . .' Jemima looked around theatrically, as if double-checking they were alone for this revelation, then lowered her voice. Clearly it was a matter of extreme importance. 'The secret is . . . I'm going to ask Miss Sergeant if I can be her bridesmaid. And I think she will say YES!'

Later that evening, not long after Jemima had gone to bed, Lydia's phone started ringing again – the same number as before, she saw. 'This had better be good,' she grumbled, flicking a finger across the screen to answer the call. 'Hello?'

'Hi.' It was a man. A hesitant man, by the sound of the pause that followed. 'Is that Lydia Fox?'

A sales call, she guessed. 'Yes,' she said, still on her guard. 'Who's calling?'

'I think you knew my brother,' said the man. 'Patrick Sheppard?'

Lydia frowned. Patrick *Sheppard,* she repeated to herself, racking her brain but drawing a complete blank. 'Never heard of him,' she said.

'Really,' said the man. Was that sarcasm in his voice?

'Well, he's been paying you money every month for seven years.'

Paying money for . . . ? Lydia's hands felt clammy all of a sudden as the penny dropped. 'You mean Patrick Armstrong,' she said shakily. Shit! What was this about?

'No, I don't mean Patrick Armstrong. I mean Patrick Sheppard,' came the testy response. 'Look, I don't know what your game is, but leave my sister-in-law out of it, all right? If you're thinking of harassing her or—'

'*What?*' Lydia couldn't follow the conversation any longer. None of it was making sense. 'Whoa, hold on a minute. What are you talking about? I'm not harassing anyone. And the only Patrick I used to know was called Patrick Armstrong – or at least that's what he told me,' she said, with rather less conviction, as cogs began clicking and turning in her brain. After their split, Patrick seemed to vanish off the face of the earth. The maintenance money he'd paid her every month appeared on her bank statements as coming from PS Holdings Limited, but when she looked up the company to try and get an address, she'd found that it was registered to an accountant's office. An accountant who refused to give her any further information about the company. *PS Holdings*, she repeated to herself now. PS for Patrick Sheppard, maybe? Her head was whirling. 'I've no idea who your sister-in-law is,' she added.

'Well, she had your phone number on her fridge door, so that's obviously not true,' the man said.

He actually sounded aggressive now, as if he was angry with her. For doing what – existing? she thought crossly. Having fallen in love eight years ago? And what was all this rubbish about a fridge door anyway? Maybe he was some random weirdo. 'I think you've got the wrong number,' she said. 'Bye now.'

'Wait!' he said just as she was about to hang up. And despite the strangeness of this conversation so far, something gave her pause. This man knew about the maintenance money, after all. If he really was Patrick's brother – her Patrick – then what was his reason for getting in touch after so long?

'Sorry,' he said. 'Let me start from the beginning. I've been helping with Patrick's accounts and I'm ringing up about a monthly payment that goes out to you.'

Back to the payments again then. Something inside Lydia crumpled. Oh no. She hoped this wasn't heading where she thought it might be. Was Patrick trying to get out of paying her any more? 'Right,' she said warily, her heart stepping up a gear. She tucked her legs underneath her on the sofa, then changed her mind and swung them down. Stood up in the middle of the room and dug her toes into the soft rug, as if anchoring herself. *Here we go.*

'And – forgive me for asking – but I'm trying to work out . . . ah . . . your relationship to Patrick. Er . . .'

Lydia pulled a face even though there was nobody there to see her. Her *relationship* with Patrick? There hadn't been one since he had ditched her, then disappeared from her life. 'So why don't you ask *him* that?' she replied after a moment.

There was an awkward pause. 'He's not here right now,' the man said. 'He . . . Look, could we meet up, maybe? It might be easier to talk about this in person.'

Talk about what? 'This isn't some kind of trick, is it? Has he put you up to this?' She remembered the date all of a sudden and groaned. 'April Fool's Day – very funny. Hilarious. Who are you really? Did Bridget give you my number?'

'No!' he replied. 'It's not a trick or – or anything like that, I swear.' There was a pause, then he said, 'Look, I know this is all a bit out of the blue. But can we meet?'

'Is he going to be there? Is that what this is about?' Lydia asked. She was starting to feel nervous. If this was some long-winded preamble to Patrick telling her he wasn't going to pay her child maintenance any more, then he could think again, because she would find a solicitor and take him to court. Her career had come to an abrupt halt after Jemima had been born; the unsociable hours didn't work with a baby to factor in, plus the cost of childcare was only marginally less than her salary. She'd been a stay-at-home mum for five years, the two of them forced to live in her dad's spare room for the first year because she was so skint, only getting some part-time shop work from her godfather once Jemima was old enough to go to school. She needed the money from Patrick, that was the point. She relied, very heavily, on his monthly contribution to their daughter's upkeep.

'No, it'll just be me,' the man said. 'When are you free this week?'

She didn't like the sound of this. She didn't like the sound of it at all. She felt very much as if she might be walking into a trap, but all the same she was intrigued at the thought of Patrick coming back into her life. 'I finish work at one tomorrow,' she found herself saying. 'I could meet you in Gunnersbury Park café at about half-past?'

'Okay,' he said. 'Er . . . how will we recognize each other?'

'I've got a red mac,' she said, wrinkling her nose at how weird this was. At least if they met in the café there would be other people around, she thought, in case he turned out to be a complete nutter. And she'd have her bike with her, so if the worst came to the worst, she could just hop on it and pedal away, fast.

'I'll see you tomorrow,' he said, and that was that.

Hanging up, she slumped back into the sofa, pulling a plum-coloured velvety cushion across her middle and hugging it for comfort. She had no idea what to make of the man's strange accusations (harassment?) and his guardedness about Patrick. She hoped she wasn't getting involved in something unpleasant. Still frowning, she texted her best friend Bridget with the number that he'd called her on. *Bit random, but if by any chance I am not at school pick-up tomorrow, I have gone to meet the person who has this number. Please pass it on to the police if I am found dead in a bin bag a few weeks later.*

Bridget phoned approximately two seconds after the message had been sent. 'Whaaaat? Are you going on a date or something? What's his name? Tell me everything!'

Lydia felt herself collapse a bit inside, because this was probably going to be the exact opposite of a date. 'I don't know his name,' she confessed miserably, still clutching the soft cushion. He hadn't mentioned it and, in her fluster, she hadn't thought to ask. 'It's not what you think, though. I'll tell you more when I see you, but I don't have a good feeling about this.'

'Can I help? Do you need moral support? An angry kick-boxing friend beside you?' came Bridget's next questions and Lydia smiled weakly, before remembering the conversation she'd had with Jemima over dinner.

'No, but thank you. By the way, just so you know, my daughter would like us to get married and, to be honest, I'm finding it hard to think of a reason why not right now,' she said, and they both laughed. 'Thanks, Bridge. Sorry to go all dramatic on you; it's probably nothing, but . . . Well, I'll find out. Coffee on Thursday?'

'You bet, and they're on me, with brownies too,' Bridget

replied. She seemed reluctant to go. 'Call me if you need me, won't you?'

'Thanks. I will.'

Patrick Armstrong – or Sheppard, she supposed – had burst into Lydia's life like an unexpected firework, dazzling and beautiful, but over too soon. She had fallen for him so hard, so absolutely, it was as if her feet left the ground whenever they spoke. It had been a good time in her life, full stop really; she was living in a shared house with Bridget and two other friends, and worked as an events organizer at an arts space in Richmond. Life was one long whirl of fun – she loved her job and her friends, she was busy all the time and making the most of being young and single. And then one evening, introducing the first act at the arts centre's monthly open-mic comedy night, she caught Patrick's eye amidst the audience and the world started to spin even faster.

Oh, sure, she'd had boyfriends before, but with Patrick everything was different. *She* felt different for a start – free and uncontained – and he was a million miles away from previous loser boyfriends, who'd all been either emotionally stunted or hopelessly unfaithful. Patrick was a proper man: ten years older than her, confident, clever and handsome. He treated Lydia like a princess, taking her to gorgeous quiet restaurants and boutique hotels and art-house cinemas. Her housemates all developed crushes on him too when he stayed over the first time and made everyone poached eggs for breakfast the following morning. Who wouldn't fall in love with a man like that?

The only problem with a firework relationship was that once it had shot up unfeasibly high, bright and sparkling, it was fated to fall just as quickly back to earth again; scorched and extinguished, dead. And whatever future Lydia thought the two of them might have shared together, her dreams were immediately shattered when, five months in, she discovered she was accidentally pregnant. They were in The White Swan on a warm May evening when she broke the news, sitting out at a table by the river and, fool that she was, she'd been nursing a secret wild hope, ever since seeing the test result, that Patrick would take her hands and express his joy. *It's all a bit of a rush,* she imagined him saying, *but we can make it work, right? You're the one! This is meant to be.*

Instead, he could hardly wait to get away – and out it had all come: the harsh blurted truth about a wife and children, delivered in scant sentences like a series of gut-punches. *I've been meaning to tell you,* he said, his eyes sliding away from hers just to underline the lie. *Let me give you some money to get rid of . . . to take care of things.*

It all added up then, too late. Why he only ever came to her place; why he preferred those quiet, tucked-away restaurants and hotels on the outskirts of the city. How he'd never really said much about his family, and wasn't on social media. A fling, he'd called their relationship, when in her mind it had been true love, or at least heading in that direction. In hindsight, she'd been so dazzled by his brightness that she hadn't looked closely at all the small print. And okay, so they had only been seeing each other for a short while, but their split knocked the wind out of her sails so thoroughly that she'd never really recovered.

Angry to have been conned, heartbroken that she'd never see him again, she had entertained thoughts of revenge; of wrecking his life just as he'd ruined hers. But either he'd given her a false surname or he'd vanished from London, because he seemed impossible to track down, both online or through the electoral register. She had his phone number and that was it, she realized belatedly. He had kept her like a dog on a lead, and she'd been only too keen to trot along devotedly after him, willing to give him all the power.

Pride kept her from contacting him again, plus the few shreds she had left of her dignity. And maybe, if she hadn't been pregnant, she would have carried on with her life and bounced back from the disappointment there and then. Everything would have been simpler – she could have stayed in her job and her house, she would have met somebody else and written Patrick off as a warning to keep her wits about her, and not go diving in head-first thinking you were in love. Instead, she had been plunged into the quandary of what to do. If only her mum had been around to lean on, to ask! It had been the hardest, loneliest decision of her life. Then, once Frank, her dad, had finished threatening to track down Patrick and knock his block off, he'd said gruffly, 'You know, Lyddie, you were a surprise to me and your mum. You weren't planned. And you turned out to be the best thing ever for us. The most wonderful surprise.'

Perhaps, looking back, it had been silly of her to make such a massive decision swayed by sentiment, but it was the thought of her mum undergoing a similar dilemma and choosing to say yes to the baby – yes to Lydia's life – that clinched it in the end. Maybe it was the hormones as well, buoying her with optimism; whatever, she had said yes, too. Yes to single motherhood and all that it entailed.

As far as Patrick was concerned, she had at first ruled him out of the equation – she didn't need him! – until after Jemima's birth, when her dad encouraged her to get back in touch. *He's the child's father and he has a responsibility, like it or not*, Frank had said. *Whatever your feelings about him now, Jemima won't thank you for it later if you don't at least try. You have to contact the man, Lyddie, and that's that.*

He had a point, so Lydia had rather grudgingly sent Patrick a text message, along with a picture of Jemima. *Here is our daughter*, she told him. *We would both love you to be a part of our lives, whether that's in person or merely financially.*

Yes, if she was honest, she had felt a faint flicker of hope that he might change his mind when he saw their baby girl.

Because, come on, she was beautiful and it was such a cute picture of her round pink face, her rosebud lips pouting as she slept, those ridiculously long eyelashes. But Patrick rang up the same day and sounded terse, not clucky and admiring at all. 'Is that some kind of threat?' he began the call, before setting out his terms, cold and clinical. It was best if he didn't see the baby – he actually called her that, 'the baby', as if Lydia hadn't just told him her name, as if Jemima wasn't his own flesh and blood – but he would contribute towards her upkeep every month, providing Lydia stayed away. If she ever tried to mess up his family life, he would stop the payments immediately. Was that clear?

By now, of course, any hope had been completely snuffed out and whatever love she'd once felt had curdled to hurt and then to hatred. She loathed Patrick for responding with such unfeeling curtness, for laying out such horrible, mean-spirited parameters. If she'd been wealthier herself, she would have told him where to shove his payments. But she was not wealthy, so she was trapped in a corner, unable to do anything other than agree. Yes, it was clear. Yes, she understood. And so began their silent monthly transaction, of Patrick paying Lydia to keep them both out of his life. She had absorbed the sting of his double rejection and tried to remove him from her head – successfully, mostly, as motherhood kept her busy and distracted – as Jemima changed from a baby to a toddler to a little girl, and Lydia held it together, made things work. They had managed this far anyway, and she was proud of herself.

But now . . . Now her life was in danger of being stirred up all over again. Patrick – via this brother of his – was back in touch, and she couldn't help nervously remembering the terms of their agreement. How the payments would stop if she broke his stupid rules. Had she unwittingly let something slip? Jemima had asked questions now and then, but Lydia had never once blown Patrick's cover or intruded on his life. She didn't think she had, anyway. So why was he on her case now? What had changed?

Oh God. She was dreading this meeting. She knew already she wouldn't sleep well tonight. *Patrick Sheppard*, she thought to herself, glancing back at her phone and realizing that she could go foraging for more information about him, now that she knew his real name at last. It was like being handed the key to unlock a mystery – she could type his name into the search bar and go digging, gorge on pictures of his wife and children, see what else she could find.

Sometimes you could know too much, though. Sometimes this sort of knowledge hurt. Did she really want to torture herself by poring over the details of his life without her? Her hand hovered over the phone and then she snatched it away. No, she thought. She had come this far; she could live without knowing a little while longer, thank you very much.

She would deal with whatever new twist or turn was coming her way tomorrow.

She glanced across at Jemima's year-two school photograph on the bookcase nearby, taking in the dearly loved dimpled face that was half-Lydia, half-Patrick with a pinch of pure Jemima for good measure, and felt a twist of fear inside. Whatever this was about, she just hoped she could handle it.

Chapter Nine

'Patrick Christopher Sheppard was the best of us,' Zoe said to herself as she walked along the path. 'He made me laugh every day I knew him. He made me feel loved. So loved. And being loved by him was . . .' She hesitated, struggling for the words that adequately described her feelings. 'It was like standing in a pool of sunshine, feeling warmed right through. It was like winning the Lottery over and over again.'

The eulogy was still coming together, although she had reached the point where she just liked talking about her husband, even if she was the only one there to listen. She liked the idea of him looking down on her from wherever he was and hearing her praise. Anything to try and make up for their last horrible conversation, frankly.

She sighed, sinking into gloom. It wasn't as if the two of them had even really argued that much; they both had hot tempers, but weren't one of those couples forever scowling and muttering at each other, slagging each other off behind their backs. But their last minutes spent together had been in argument, and that was one of the worst things about Patrick dying. They had never been able to say sorry, never hugged each other and made up, and now they were stuck like this forever, with their cross words permanently frozen between them.

She had come to the Old Deer Park in Richmond for her morning walk today and the grass was thick and lush after all the rain they'd had, the trees splendid with their new, acid-green leaves, fresh and vivid. Blackbirds pecked busily at the ground, and the air was soft and damp, just the sort to leave her hair in a total frizzball by the time she got back home. Glancing up, she noticed that the sky had become a sulky grey, dismal and dreary, and she walked a little faster, wondering if she should have brought an umbrella. It had been the longest winter of her life and, in some ways, still didn't seem to be in a hurry to make way for spring.

'Where are the sodding butterflies anyway?' she had moaned to her friend Clare, two weeks after the funeral. Her mum and stepdad had gone back to Penarth and she didn't feel able to cope in the house alone with the kids, so Clare had camped out with her for a few nights, sharing the double bed. On this particular night they had drunk quite a lot of red wine, and Zoe had begun bemoaning the fact that everyone else, upon losing someone close, seemed to see a butterfly and take it to be a beautiful spiritual message from their loved one. 'When am *I* going to see a butterfly?' she had wailed.

'Er . . . in July, I should think?' Clare had replied, elbowing her. 'When they actually hatch? Because it's still March, remember.'

Zoe had blushed, feeling foolish, but the point remained the same. She'd read and heard so many stories of mysterious messages coming from 'the other side' following a bereavement; signs of comfort sent to those left behind. When was Patrick going to get his arse into gear and do the same? Should she take it to mean that he didn't care? 'Helen Baxter from school said she kept seeing feathers when her grandfather died,' she explained. 'Like, dropped feathers on the pavement everywhere. A huge white one was even on her doormat one morning. She was convinced it was him, sending them to her.'

'Sending her *feathers*?' Clare, always a bit of a sceptic about anything remotely woo-woo, didn't seem to find this particularly deep and meaningful. 'What, you mean those things that randomly float off birds all the time? So her ghostly grandad went plucking them out deliberately for Helen, did he, and scattered them around on her doormat? Sounds a bit of a weirdo to me. I only hope the poor woman doesn't have any kind of feather allergy.'

'Clare! It's not like that. Helen said she found it really comforting and nice, because she was so certain they were from him – it was as if her grandad was with her again each time.' Zoe had paused then, suddenly doubtful. It had seemed plausible enough when Helen told her about it, but in the face of Clare's cynicism, the words didn't quite add up any more. 'I wish Patrick would send me something like that. Just a sign, you know, that he was okay.'

Clare raised an eyebrow. *Do I really need to spell this out?* the eyebrow said. 'Darling, he's not okay, though, is he?' she reminded her gently. Zoe and Clare had met at teacher training college and Clare was a secondary-school science teacher through and through, with no capacity whatsoever for entertaining bullshit. 'He's d—'

'Don't say it,' Zoe pleaded. 'Indulge me. Please, Clare.'

They'd gone on to drink more wine, which resulted in a silly, verging-on-hysterical conversation about what, exactly, Patrick might leave for her by way of ghostly message – a pair of pliers, one of his many pairs of hated reading glasses, an odd sock – and then Zoe had started to cry, because she felt sad that she had washed all of his socks now and would never find another stray one. She'd even rolled them into neat pairs and put them back in his drawer, as if waiting for the next time he'd wear them. Every time she thought about those clean, unworn socks, her heart seemed to crack all over again.

Anyway, whatever Clare might say, Zoe was still looking out for her sign. How could she give up on the idea, when she was desperate to be reconciled with her husband after their last argument?

'I forgive you,' she called into the cold hushed air in the hope that he might reciprocate somehow. 'Did you hear me? I forgive you, it's fine.'

A woman with a fuchsia woolly hat walked by just then, accompanied by a Yorkshire terrier in a smart tartan coat, and gave Zoe an odd sort of look. The woman, that is, not the dog, although come to think of it, the dog had stared up at her rather quizzically too. Maybe the dog was a sign from—

No. Stop it. Don't go completely mad now, on top of everything else, she groaned to herself. Besides, if Patrick was going to come back and give her a message as a dog, he would not choose a Yorkshire terrier as his guise; he'd go for something infinitely more macho. A lurcher or a German shepherd. Maybe even a Staffie, if the afterlife had left him feeling particularly insecure.

Zoe found herself blushing at this crazy line of thought, glad that nobody could see inside her head and realize what a lunatic she had become. *Pull yourself together, Zoe. Best foot forward. Your dead husband will not manifest himself as a dog.*

Their argument hadn't even been an especially meaning-ful one. They were in the kitchen together while the children were in their various rooms; it was the golden hour when she was cooking dinner and everyone was home, all safely gath-ered in. She was listening to a funny podcast while she diced celery and carrots; there was a bottle of rather nice-looking white wine in the fridge, and it felt cosy to be indoors with the rain pattering against the windows, the blinds pulled down against the shadows. She remembered feeling content as Patrick came in, dumping a tool bag on the floor, his hair wet from the rain. He kissed her hello – their last kiss, as it turned out – and asked about her day. (Oh, if she had only known this was to be their last kiss, she would have made so much more of it! But she'd had garlic on her fingers and didn't want to get it on his shirt, so she had gone in for more of a peck, unattached, instead of a proper full-body smooch. This was another of her enduring regrets.)

Then she had told him, in full cheerful detail, about the school she'd worked in that day, and how, during a creative writing session, one of the six-year-olds had ventured a contribution to the class – a really imaginative, funny contribution at that. Afterwards, at break time, the teaching assistant Louise had told Zoe that the boy in question, Caleb, never usually spoke up in class. Never!

Patrick hadn't looked quite as impressed as he might have done at the end of Zoe's little spiel of glory. He'd shrugged a shoulder, put some bread in the toaster (even though she was right there, making his dinner, which would be ready in forty minutes) and pushed his lips out in a *So what?* face. 'What's the point of it all, though?' he said, offhand.

She should have left it then, rolled her eyes at him for bursting her bubble, but his question was so ridiculous and she actually felt kind of aggrieved, so she went on the counter-attack. 'What's the point of *education*?' she replied scornfully. 'Is that what you're saying?'

'I mean, writing a story. It's not exactly important, is it?'

God, what had put him in such a grump? He surely knew that this was a pretty big button to go pressing. 'Well, it *is* important actually. It's fun, for one thing. The children get to go wild with their imaginations. They create something together, as a class, so there's this lovely shared ownership and—'

'Right,' he said, cutting in. 'But that's not going to help them in the real world, is it?'

She gazed at him, stung. 'It will, if my lessons make them feel validated,' she answered. 'It will, if it helps them work as a team and feel confident that their ideas are encouraged, rather than dismissed. I did a whole module at uni about learning through play – if kids are—'

'Oh, at *uni*,' he mocked. 'I wondered when you were going to mention that. Going to university doesn't teach you everything, though, does it?'

The argument seemed to be getting bigger and nastier by the second, as if it were rolling down a hill and picking up speed. This latest angle was something they'd touched upon before; Zoe knew that Patrick had a chip on his shoulder about university, not least because she'd gone and he hadn't. He was smart but uninterested in school, passing his exams but leaving at sixteen in order to go straight into work. University of life, that's all you need, he'd claimed in the past. Whatever.

'No,' she said, feeling tired as she swept the chopped vegetables into the frying pan. 'Going to university doesn't teach you everything, Patrick.'

'Waste of money, if you ask me. I'm certainly not expecting our kids to bother with that sort of thing. Get out and get working, that's what they should do. Have a bit of pride in themselves, rather than loaf around being a student.'

She knew he was deliberately trying to get a rise out of her and another time she might have joked away the tension, steered the conversation to a safer zone. But he was starting to get on her nerves now. 'Well, I hope our children *do* go to university,' she said, adding a glug of olive oil to the pan and stirring everything together. 'I would love them to. They're all clever enough to do whatever they want. Why would you deny them that experience?'

She knew why, of course. He had confessed to her once that his worst fear was of the children growing up and moving ahead of him, intellectually. Being cleverer than him and looking down on him, their blue-collar dad with his van and toolbox. She had done her best to reassure him – of course they wouldn't! they admire you, they love you – but already Ethan was starting to favour her when it came to asking for homework help, as if he felt that his dad wouldn't be able to guide him through whatever he was stuck on. You didn't have to be a genius to recognize that this would injure Patrick's pride.

The argument had continued snippily on – and pointlessly on too, seeing as Ethan was still only fourteen and hadn't even thought about his further-education options. Zoe had always been able to get over a bust-up quickly – her temper would flare and then drop, and life would go on, but Patrick had a moodier temperament and could stew in a black cloud for a whole evening. She was glad when he reminded her that he was going over to meet Dan and stay at his place that night, to help him cut down a dead tree the next morning. Glad that she could have the evening to herself, when she could try to claw back the good, happy feeling she'd had before.

Of course the memory of this crucified her now. The fact that she'd wanted an evening in alone, when she no longer had any choice in the matter – when pretty much every single sodding evening was spent alone on her sofa these days, with a yawning gap at the opposite end where Patrick should be sitting, feet companionably against hers, putting the day to bed between them.

And then he hadn't come home the following day and she'd assumed it must be because he was still angry with her, simmering away, unable to put the row behind him and move on. When she'd phoned Dan that morning, only to hear that Patrick hadn't even stayed over, she had taken it personally again – fretting that he must be feeling so cross with her that he hadn't wanted to come home. It was only hours later on, when there was still no word from him, that a creeping realization had started to dawn on her that perhaps something even worse might have happened.

Her finger slid behind her right ear where there was a patch of dry, flaky skin that went up into her hairline. It had become a spot for Zoe to worry and pick at when she was feeling miserable, even though she knew she was probably making it worse. Almost home now, her cheeks flushed with the fresh air and exercise, she vowed to dig out some Vaseline or night cream to soothe the flare-up. Then she stopped dead on the pavement outside her house as she realized what was sitting on her doorstep: a large black cat she had never seen before, staring straight at her.

The breath caught in her lungs. '*Patrick?*' she croaked, incredulous.

At her approach, the cat's yellow eyes rounded with alarm and it dropped into a crouch before streaking away, over the low wall into the next front garden, where it vanished amidst the shrubbery.

She felt such an idiot as she searched for her keys and let herself in, leaning against the door, once inside. Thank God none of her neighbours had just seen her addressing a random cat by her dead husband's name. They would think she'd utterly lost the plot. She put her head in her hands and stood there for a moment. Crying on a stranger in a shop the other day, talking to a cat ... 'Get a grip,' she ordered herself through clenched teeth.

Chapter Ten

'Oh! Hello,' said Liz, as she answered the door and saw Dan standing there. 'Everything all right, love?'

'Hi, Mum,' said Dan. 'Just thought I'd pop round.'

She raised her thinly plucked eyebrows, apparently startled, and peered at him. 'Are you okay?' She wasn't quite stretching out a hand to check the temperature of his forehead, but Dan could tell that she was considering it. 'Is something wrong?'

'No!' He felt slightly nettled that she had to ask. 'I just thought I'd . . . you know. Drop in. Say hello, see how you and Dad are.' Clearly she *did* feel she had to ask, seeing as he hadn't actually done this for ages, he realized, stabbed by guilt as she finally allowed him in over the threshold.

'Well, what a nice surprise. Lovely!' she said, recovering herself. She patted her hair fretfully – it was straggly and out of shape, Dan noticed in dismay. Had she even brushed it that morning? 'Derek!' she yelled up the stairs. 'Our Daniel's here. Dropped in to say hello.'

'Is he all right?' came her husband's muffled response from somewhere above them and Dan felt the smile on his face begin to stiffen like setting concrete.

'Come and see for yourself,' Liz ordered, ushering Dan through to the living room.

Although, on retiring, Liz and Derek had moved out of the small Hammersmith house where Dan and his brother had grown up, the living room had been transplanted pretty much straight from there to here. The two sage-green sofas, one big, one small, formed an L-shape around the television, flanked by the same nest of walnut tables that a young Dan had made dens with, and a bookcase where well-thumbed Wilbur Smiths cosied up alongside rank after rank of Danielle Steels. Even the fake-coal gas fire was similar to the one that Dan had sat in front of after bathtimes, bundled up in his *Star Wars* dressing gown with a mug of bedtime cocoa. The same pictures were displayed along the mantelpiece and shelves: old school photos of the boys with gappy teeth and bowl haircuts, Patrick and Zoe's wedding day, Dan's graduation, the grandchildren on Christmas Day and a black-and-white picture of Liz and Derek's own wedding, a blizzard of confetti frozen in the air around them as they smiled shyly from the frame.

Also there was . . . yep, Dan's least favourite photo, the one of Patrick getting him in a headlock on Brighton beach when they were boys. The two of them had always got on pretty well as kids, but sometimes Patrick liked to remind Dan who was boss, by force if necessary. In the photo both of them were grinning, although if you looked closely (as Dan had done) you could see the flash of humiliation on Dan's face, the grin actually fragile and fake. He could still hear even now his brother's mockery – 'Baby! Baby!' – when Dan had become tearful.

Glancing behind him to find the room still empty – his mum was making drinks in the kitchen – he moved the picture out of view, behind a larger one of the family celebrating Liz and Derek's fortieth wedding anniversary. That was better.

'So,' said his mum, walking in with a tray of tea things, 'what brings you over here then? Do sit down, Daniel, no need to stand on ceremony.'

'I . . .' He couldn't say again that he was just dropping in, he was starting to feel like his own echo chamber. He pulled out one of the tables from its nest and moved it near the sofa, so she had somewhere to put the tray. 'It struck me, on Mother's Day, that I haven't seen you very much lately. Too busy with work stuff. So while I'm not in the office, I thought I could come over a bit more often – you know, like Patrick used to.'

Liz's fingers trembled a little on the teacups. Her face was pale and make-up-free and she looked small and shrunken in an oversized grey cardigan and navy trousers. 'He was a good boy,' she said automatically. It seemed to be her default response: you mentioned Patrick's name, she told you how good he was. Perhaps Dan was feeling paranoid and defensive, because he found himself wondering if it might also be a slight dig at him in comparison. Was *he* a good boy too?

'Yes,' he agreed helplessly. 'But now that he's not around, maybe I can stand in for him, if you like. Do the things Patrick used to do for you.'

'You don't have to *stand in* for him, love, you're your own person,' she reminded him, pouring the tea. Her fingernails, usually glossily painted, were nude today and looked old and yellowy. When did her hands get so gnarled? Dan thought with a churn of sadness.

'I know, but . . .' He squirmed. 'I just want to be helpful.'

'I see.' She passed over a mug, then sipped from hers. 'DEREK,' she called. 'TEA!' Then she glanced towards the window. 'Weather's on the turn,' she commented.

'Yes,' he agreed. There was a small gap of silence and then he asked, 'So is there anything then? That I can do, I mean. To be helpful. Any little chores or . . . I could nip over to the shops for you, or fix anything that's broken . . .'

His dad appeared in the doorway then, with his usual air of detached disinterest, and Dan found himself trailing off mid-sentence. *I love my kids so much,* Patrick had once said down at the pub, staring into his pint glass. It must have been a few months after Bea was born and he'd been jubilant all evening, if clearly exhausted, yet had suddenly become introspective. Maudlin, even. *I would do anything for them, you know. But it makes me sad, in a weird way, because I know our dad didn't feel the same way about us. Do you know what I mean?*

Dan had felt startled at the time – nobody wanted to be confronted with the idea that a parent hadn't loved them – but he had to admit that Derek Sheppard had never been a cuddly sort of a man. Had he ever even slung an arm around his boys? Kissed his wife in public? He had worked for years as an archivist in what had then been Middlesex Poly, and always looked as if he'd rather be leafing through old papers than actually interacting with another human being.

'Hello, son! Fancy seeing you here. To what do we owe this great honour then?'

Even a simple question had the ring of sarcasm when it came from his dad. Dan opened his mouth, but his mum beat him to it. 'He's popped round to be helpful. To do our chores,' she explained.

'Has he?' His dad frowned as if this was a bad thing, some-how impertinent, and Dan felt himself wanting to retreat, just as he had throughout various childhood battles. Then he looked out of the back window where – thank heavens! – the lawn seemed kind of shaggy. Zoe might have rejected his mowing offer, but his dad had always grumbled about keep-ing the lawn in check. Surely this was his opportunity?

'I could mow the lawn for you?' he suggested.

His parents looked at one another, unspoken questions flitting between them. Then his dad shrugged. 'If you want to,' he replied.

'That would be very kind, Daniel,' his mother said.

Dan smiled at them both and drank his tea, but he couldn't shake off the feeling that they were . . . well, humouring him. Not taking him very seriously. Had he got this wrong somehow?

Heaving the mower out of the shed a short while later, he turned his head to see them both still in the living room watching him. His mum put up a hand in a wave and he returned the gesture. This was a good, helpful thing to do, he reminded himself, as his dad opened the back door to show him the extension cable. Definitely worthy of an entry on his good-deeds spreadsheet. For that alone, any awkwardness could be borne, he decided.

Over in Chiswick, Lydia was struggling to concentrate. Just off the High Street, the shop she worked in, Soft, sold a mixture of cushions and throws, as well as ceramics, woodblock prints and jewellery by local artists, and she usually found it a soothing place to be. Encouraged by Jonathan, her boss, who was always telling her that her talents were wasted working for him, she made many of the cushion covers herself, from soft tweeds or muted Liberty prints, and there was always something to be done, even with a dearth of customers like today. But her thoughts were still whirling from the phone call last night and now, as she looked around, she found despair leaking in. Would working here be enough to support them if Patrick decided to change the status quo? Was she about to receive a rude and scary financial wake-up call?

Lydia had always loved making things, ever since she'd been a tiny girl. Back as a sixth former, she'd been offered a place to study Costume Design at university, and had pored over details of the course's modules – corsetry! tailoring! millinery and many other delights – so long and hard that even now she could picture the creased and grubby page in the prospectus. But when her mum, Eleanor, became ill that year, school work no longer seemed a priority, and while her friends were revising, Lydia spent her days doggedly nursing her mother, willing her to get better. 'Of course I'll get better,' Eleanor had said, squeezing Lydia's hand. Her squeeze had been as faint as a fairy's, though, barely there. 'Just as soon as I've beaten this, we'll go to Australia to celebrate, do you hear? I've always wanted to show you my favourite beaches, take you around my city. What do you think?'

It was the most precious offer of Lydia's life, but it had never come to fruition. Eleanor's condition worsened and she went into hospital and then, only weeks later, she came home again because there was nothing more that could be done for her. She had lost her hair and Lydia camped out by her side, cooling her hot bald head with a damp sponge and holding cups of water up to her cracked lips for her to sip. Studying didn't get much of a look-in. Lydia didn't even wait for her exam results to know that she'd missed out on a place at university, but she was so numb with grief, she no longer cared all that much. Nothing seemed to matter, compared to losing the person she loved most in the world.

She'd done bits and bobs of work, and she'd always got by, working in retail and as a PA for a while, before landing the arts-centre job, which she'd loved. But of course when Lydia became a mum herself, all that had ground to a halt, until Jemima started school and Jonathan had offered her some part-time work. She'd kidded herself at first – hey, it was still a creative environment, she was working with artists, perhaps she could progress to helping select new pieces for the shelves – but the reality turned out to be far less scintillating; she spent most of the time on the till or directing out-of-towners towards the Tube. Jonathan had been her mum's best friend when Eleanor first came over from Sydney and did his best to be the supportive godfather, encouraging Lydia to take evening classes and get back into education, but at the end of the day she had to be pragmatic. Yes, but how would she afford it? And who was going to look after Jemima? It wasn't as easy as he seemed to think.

Crossing the room to add new stock to the shelves, Lydia

caught sight of her reflection in the mirror and did a double-take, before sheepishly recognizing herself. Usually she wore colourful vintage-style outfits that she had made herself, but today she had deliberately chosen more sober clothing for the occasion. Her one and only black knee-length skirt, with a smart blouse in olive green, prim gold studs at her ears, black court shoes. She wanted to look like the sort of person who'd say, 'I will have to consult my lawyer about this', who would be taken seriously, should any disagreements arise.

A woman in a stylish grey trouser-suit with clicking high heels came into the shop just then and went on to make several purchases: one of Martha Mackie's gorgeous fox-shaped copper brooches, a framed print by Ivo Cooke of swallows in flight, and a 1950s-style lampshade that Lydia herself had rather coveted, made from sailcloth, with a repeating boat design. 'Lovely choices,' Lydia said, wrapping everything up carefully and ringing them into the till. Most people paid by card these days, especially when the total amount due was well over two hundred pounds, like now, but this customer pulled out a burgundy mock-croc purse and began counting out a fat stack of notes in payment. 'Ten, twenty . . .' she said, pushing them over to Lydia.

Once the shop was empty again, Lydia's thoughts kept turning to all the cash that was now sitting there in the till. All the things you could buy with it. If she ended up hitting rock-bottom financially, would she be tempted to start pocketing money from future cash sales like this, and not running the payments through the system? Would Jonathan even notice if she helped herself? His sixtieth birthday was coming up and he was distracted, planning an elaborate party and obsessing about cocktails and outfits. It wouldn't be hard to sneak the odd hundred here or there, if need be . . .

The doorbell jangled again as a new customer came in and Lydia snapped to attention, horrified that her thoughts had taken such a deceitful turn. She had always prided herself on her honesty; she had never stolen anything in her life. What the hell was wrong with her? Was it the prospect of meeting Patrick's brother later on that was prompting such weird behaviour? If so, the sooner it was over with, the better.

Back home after vising his parents, Dan found himself staring out at his own garden, most notably at the dead sycamore that still loomed there. Whenever he walked into the kitchen, like now, his gaze was drawn to it through the window, the diseased branches rattling like bones in the wind, lifeless and leafless. A taunt. It should have been cut down and removed back in February, with Patrick as planned, but . . . Well, events, and all that. Events.

He'd been standing pretty much right here when Zoe had rung the morning after his and Patrick's last night at the pub. He almost hadn't answered when he saw her name flash up on the phone, rolling his eyes at the thought of his brother wimpishly getting his wife to ring up and apologize. *Patrick feels really bad for what happened* . . . Yeah, well that wasn't going to cut it. This time Patrick had gone too far. But she turned out to be calling about something else altogether.

'Sorry to bother you, Dan, but could you get my husband to give me a ring, please?' she asked. 'Not now, if he's wielding a power tool or up the tree, obviously, but just when there's a good moment. He's not answering his phone.'

Dan had snorted, guessing that Patrick must be on his way round after all then, probably stuck in traffic. Ha. He'd get short shrift if he tried knocking on the door like nothing had happened. In fact he'd be lucky to escape without any chainsaw wounds, the mood Dan was still in. 'He's not here,' he replied curtly.

'Oh,' said Zoe. 'What time did he leave then? I thought it would take you two longer, I have to say. Right. Maybe that's why he's not answering. Is your garden looking better for the surgery?'

They were talking at cross-purposes, Dan realized, frowning. 'No – I mean, he's not been here at all. He didn't stay last night.'

There was a moment of baffled silence, then they both spoke at once. 'So he didn't—' Dan began.

'He's not been here, either,' Zoe said at the same time. There was a small hesitation before she gave a nervous sort of laugh and asked, 'So where did he spend the night? Or shouldn't I be asking that?'

'He – well, I assumed he was going back to yours,' Dan said. This, admittedly, put a new spin on things. Where had Patrick gone?

'He didn't come back. I'm not at work today, I was hoping to—' Zoe broke off. 'So what happened then? Why was there a change of plan?'

Dan gritted his teeth. If this was Patrick disappearing in a massive huff in an attempt to manipulate Dan into guilt, then he simply wasn't going to rise to it. He refused to feel guilty about anything, when Patrick was the one squarely to blame. 'We had a bit of an argument,' he said. 'He was walking back along the Thames, last I saw, so I assumed he was heading home.'

'From Hammersmith? Why didn't he get a cab?'

She had a point. But Patrick probably just wanted to skulk off alone, Dan figured, rather than accompany his brother back to the main road. He might even have slunk into The Dove nearby for a consoling whisky before going any further. 'I dunno – it all got kind of heated,' he admitted. He was *not* going to feel bad about this, he reminded himself. He was *not*.

'Well, what about? What was so terrible that he didn't go back to yours?'

Dan hesitated for a moment, his eye caught by the starling

that was back in the garden, hopping about thuggishly, head cocked.

'Dan?' Zoe prompted and he had to think quickly. No way could he tell her the truth. Absolutely no way.

'It was nothing,' he said eventually. 'Too much to drink. Have you tried his business phone? Maybe the battery's flat on his other one.'

'Yeah, it's in the house somewhere – I can hear it ringing. Bloody hell. Where *is* he then? Let me know if he turns up, won't you, and I'll do the same.'

Dan hadn't been too worried at first, assuming his brother must have spent the night at a mate's house, where he was now sleeping off the booze. No doubt he'd appear at Zoe's shortly with a bunch of daffs and a series of excuses, and charm a smile out of her. He was good at that. *Dan said you'd had a bit of a row,* Zoe would venture after a while, but he would brush it off. *Not important,* he'd reply. But it was important to Dan, all right.

The day lengthened and turned into evening, and still no word came from Patrick. Liz rang, having been contacted by Zoe, wanting to know what the argument had been about. 'I hope you haven't gone and upset him,' she'd chided. 'You know how sensitive he can be.' This was Patrick all over, Dan thought, rolling his eyes. The only person who could wallow about in shit and come up smelling sweet. Sensitive, indeed. Last night Patrick had been about as sensitive as a brick through a window, in terms of how he'd spoken to Dan. All the same, Dan was beginning to feel a creeping dread that something was badly wrong. Because Patrick wasn't one to flake out and vanish for hours on end like this. Yeah, he might be unreliable at times, but he was wedded to that phone of his, for starters; it was completely out of character for him to ignore calls and messages, to stay away.

By the time Dan spoke to Zoe again and outlined his worries, she was already one step ahead, having contacted local hospitals, friends, family and, minutes earlier, the police. 'I don't understand what was so bad that he didn't stay at yours,' she fretted. 'Are you keeping something from me? Or covering for him? Because I need to know now, all right? Forget brotherly loyalty or whatever code you've got going on – I need to know he's okay, Dan.'

The questions had left him squirming. He'd cobbled together some lines in response – so flimsy you could have blown them over with a single puff – but even as he said them, he could tell Zoe didn't quite believe him. They had more important things to dwell on, though: namely, that the hours were passing and there was still no word from Patrick. Looking back, Dan could hardly remember how they dragged themselves through that time, how they filled the strange expectant days that followed, as the dread ratcheted up with every tick of the clock. It had felt as if they were collectively going out of their minds. People didn't simply *disappear* like that, he kept thinking – not grown men, with a family and a business, and all the trappings of a great life.

Four days later, the police were in touch again. A man's body had been found washed up in Vauxhall and, when Zoe was asked to go and identify it, she was able to confirm that yes, it was her husband. Her late husband, Patrick Christopher Sheppard, who was dead and not coming back. The police wanted to speak to Dan, as the last person known to have seen him alive that night. Was Dan to blame? It felt that way. Guilt assaulted him like a knee in the balls, closely followed by the twin blows of shock and grief. Patrick had gone from their lives just like that, and they would never be able to see one another again, let alone make up and put things right.

He still dreamed about that final glimpse of his brother. Dreamed that they were on the river path together, and that he – Dan – had had a change of heart, calling Patrick back. 'Don't be daft, you can stay,' he said in these dreams, gruff with reluctance. 'Not that this means I forgive you. Because I don't, you piece of shit. But you can stay, all right?'

That was what brothers did, wasn't it? They stuck together through good and bad, *thick as thieves*. But it hadn't happened that way. In real life, Patrick had kept on walking, while Dan had been unable to find the words – or grace – to stop him.

It was a living nightmare. None of them could take the news in at first. Dan found himself obsessively wondering

how his brother had ended up in the river, what awful chain
of events had led to this terrible, horrible outcome. Patrick
had always been a strong swimmer, confident in the pool or
sea. He was fit and healthy – his death a mystery. Not knowing how he had died, what had happened in those last
moments of his life, was torturous. Had he been frightened
when the end came? Had he even been conscious? Dan kept
picturing his brother's face sinking below the surface, the
river swallowing him up. He had once seen a dead dog wash
up by the side of the Thames, over in Greenwich, and he'd
never been able to forget its bloated, distorted corpse, its
misshapen head with empty sockets where the fish had
eaten its eyeballs. He kept imagining Patrick's lifeless body,
dirty and sodden, dumped on the muddy riverbank by the
tide, and it was the worst image in the world.

The post-mortem revealed a head injury, but it was
explained to them that this could have been from Patrick
falling and hitting his head before entering the river or,
equally, an attack, a mugging, that had left him reeling and
unbalanced. And where exactly had he gone into the river
anyway? Dan walked and cycled the Thames path fairly
regularly and found himself retracing his brother's likely
steps there over and over again. Large stretches of the path
had railings or shrubbery that separated pedestrians from
the water, but there were other areas with nothing to prevent a man from falling and drowning. Or, for that matter,

throwing himself in deliberately. But he wouldn't have done that, would he? Not Patrick. He loved life, or so Dan had always thought. He certainly had plenty to live for.

The usual weary sadness had descended, and Dan dragged his eyes away from the garden now. Really, he knew he should hire a tree surgeon to deal with the sycamore for him, just get rid of the thing once and for all. One of the neighbours had asked the other day, rather pointedly, when it would be removed, but the dead tree had become so tied up with Patrick's last night and Dan's guilt that he felt a mental block there, paralysing him from taking action.

He went to find his car keys, trying to shake off his unhappiness. In half an hour he was due to meet Lydia Fox and he'd have to explain a potted version of his brother's death to her, as well as finding out what had been happening with her and Patrick all these years. He felt on his guard, deeply suspicious. Deeply loyal to Zoe, too. But when he'd spoken to this Lydia the day before, the conversation had been very odd. Patrick must have given her a false name (Armstrong, indeed, he scoffed to himself – typical; he was surprised Patrick hadn't told her his surname was Testosterone, frankly) and she sounded wary about their prospective meeting, as if she didn't trust Dan's motives.

To be fair, she *should* be wary, though, because he fully intended to warn her well away from Zoe and the children. Seeing that business card with her name on it on Zoe's fridge had nearly given Dan a coronary and he'd immediately leapt to worst-case conclusions – that Lydia planned to blackmail Zoe or con her somehow, that she was up to no good and needed to be stopped. He had been cursing himself for having blurted out his shock like that, in Zoe's kitchen – *Wait, so you know her? This Lydia Fox?* – because after that he hadn't been able to pocket the business card and take it away, for fear of drawing attention to it even more. He'd had to sneakily photograph the details when Zoe went to answer the front door, his mind racing. But clearly Zoe didn't know Lydia was anything other than a woman she'd met in a shop, and Dan wanted it to stay that way.

Today he would make it very clear to Lydia: do not speak to Zoe. Keep your distance. Oh, and that money Patrick's been paying you? It has to come to an end now, because I can't let Zoe find out that you exist. Got it? By the way, if you were wondering why he hadn't been in touch with you, it's because he died.

God, he wasn't looking forward to any of this. Dan wasn't the sort of unreconstructed bloke who flinched and vanished to the bar when anyone started talking about their feelings, but all the same, such talk made him feel uncomfortable. Itchy around the collar. This was going to be one of the most excruciating conversations of his life, he could already tell. He hoped this Lydia person wouldn't start crying and freaking out. *Why don't you ask* him *that?* she'd said, when he'd mentioned her relationship with Patrick. Present tense, as if it was possible to ask Patrick anything now. It sounded as if she still thought he was alive – unless she'd spent last night frantically googling him, now that she knew his real name, of course.

They had arranged to meet at the café in Gunnersbury Park, a modern, low-built space, all chunky wood and glass amidst the trees, and as Dan loped across the grass towards it, he could feel his blood pressure rising, shots of stress percolating through his veins. What was he walking into here? Who was Lydia, and what kind of hold had she wielded over Patrick? He kept picturing a hard-faced woman with a cold glare, while labels like 'home-wrecker' and 'bunny boiler' looped in his head. Maybe she had been *blackmailing* Patrick? Maybe she'd pinned something dastardly on him and had him pay for it ever since?

He sighed, unable to fully believe any of these ideas. There had to be a rational explanation to all this, surely; something he hadn't thought of. Who knew, in ten minutes the two of them might be laughing at his stupidity and misunderstanding.

Anyway – enough second-guessing. Right now he needed to focus on the matter in hand: how he was going to make all of this go away, for Zoe's sake. Whoever this Lydia was, and whatever her game, he would waste no time in clearing everything up, once and for all.

Chapter Eleven

The path was wet following a heavy shower earlier and the trees still dripped percussively as Dan approached the café entrance, the air fresh with the scent of pine. The sodden picnic tables outside were deserted, but the lights were bright inside the building, drawing him on. *I've got a red mac,* Lydia had said, as if they were meeting on a blind date, and Dan, getting out of his car ten minutes ago, imagined how boring his own description would have been in comparison. *Jeans and a navy hoodie.* That really marked him out from every other middle-aged bloke – not.

As soon as he walked in, he saw her: long chestnut hair falling about a heart-shaped face, small neat features, both hands cradling a steaming mug. The red mac was drying on the back of the chair next to hers, with a cycle helmet dangling from one side. She looked up, her gaze meeting his, and something quickened inside his body, an unexpected chemical reaction. Because she was pretty, he guessed, rather than the mean, unpleasant version that his imagination had conjured up. He hadn't anticipated her looking quite so . . . well, quite so sweet.

'Lydia?' he asked, walking over with trepidation. It must be her. The only other people in the place were an elderly couple sharing a huge slab of Victoria sponge, plus a young man with damp dark hair, who was hunched over a sketchbook, pencil in hand.

She offered a small, polite smile in response, although he could see how apprehensive she was. 'Hi,' she said. 'You look like him,' she blurted out, then her cheeks turned pink, as if she'd gone in too personal too soon.

He ignored the remark, unsure how to answer it. Until he knew more about Lydia Fox, he didn't want to get too cosy. Coolly detached: that was his game today. 'Can I get you anything? Another drink?' he asked. *Because it's the only thing I'll be offering you today,* he thought. *Other than a one-way ticket out of my family's life, that is.*

She shook her head, so he went to the counter and ordered a latte. 'With an extra shot, please,' he asked, feeling in urgent need of caffeine. Anything that might help him get through this.

He sat down opposite her and opened his mouth to begin, but she beat him to it. 'I don't know your name,' she said.

'Oh. It's Daniel,' he replied. 'Dan.'

'Dan,' she repeated. 'Hi, Dan. Actually, I think I remember him talking about you now.' She offered him a wary smile, but Dan's face didn't know what to do in response. A grimace was about the best he could manage. *Don't start trying to make friends with me,* he thought, remembering Zoe's drooping shoulders in the supermarket. Remembering how much he owed her.

'Hi,' he said. 'So—'

'So what's all this about?' she said over him.

His mouth was dry and he gulped some too-hot coffee, with a tiny prickle of irritation that she kept taking the reins of the conversation when he was the one who should rightfully have been steering. Now he felt wrong-footed before he'd even begun. 'It's about Patrick,' he replied stiffly.

'Yes,' she said. 'I gathered that much.' Her eyes were dark brown and anxious, she was gripping her mug. This would all have been far easier if she looked less like a worried fawn, Dan thought, bracing himself for what was to come.

'I don't think you know what's happened – I'm pretty sure you don't – so I'm just going to tell you,' he began. The coffee and adrenalin were both doing a good job of making his pulse accelerate. 'And I'm really sorry because this is horrible news, but . . . well. The thing is, he's died. Patrick's died.'

There. He risked a direct look at Lydia and she stared back, her face sagging in shock.

'He . . . what? He's *died?*' Shit, so clearly this was the first she'd heard about it. Where did she think Patrick had been all this time then?

'Yes. He . . .' Six weeks on from the event, it still wasn't any easier to say the words aloud. 'He drowned.'

'He *drowned*?' She clapped a hand to her mouth and blinked several times. When he looked at her again, he could see that her eyes were glistening with tears. 'Oh my God. I'm so sorry. I can't believe it. That was the last thing I expected you to say.' A tear broke free from her lashes and rolled down her face, dragging a streak of sooty mascara with it.

'I know.' He stared at the table. 'He was walking home one night, he'd had a few drinks, we think he just got unlucky and fell in the river, but . . .' He shrugged unhappily, forcing himself to say the next words. 'We don't know what happened. He was on his own, see, so . . .' Emotion caught up with him. *He was on his own.* Patrick had died on his own, water pouring into his lungs, his body sinking below the black surface of the river, when he should have been in Dan's spare room snoring and muttering in his sleep. It was a terrible, terrible way to go.

'That's awful. That's so tragic. I'm so sorry,' Lydia said again, anguished. Her face had already been pale, but it was chalk-white suddenly. Dan hoped she wasn't going to faint or throw up or have some other extreme physical reaction. 'Oh God, and now Jemima will never get to know—' she added, but bit back the rest of the sentence before she could finish it.

Jemima. He felt sick. So much for he and Lydia laughing

about his misunderstanding, as he'd hoped. It seemed as if his first guess had been right all along. 'That's your kid?' he asked, feeling something crumbling inside him. Oh, Patrick. He couldn't quite believe it.

'Yeah. And Patrick's. Your niece, I guess.'

Dan blinked. *His niece.* Christ, he supposed she was. He hadn't thought of it like that. He had been so caught up in his need to protect Zoe that he hadn't considered much else. 'Um. Yeah,' he said, taken aback.

Now Lydia was rummaging in her bag – for a tissue, he assumed, until he realized she was looking for her phone, to show him a photo. No, he wanted to say, one hand up like a police officer stopping traffic. Don't show me. He needed this woman and her kid to be forgettable, anonymous. A part of Patrick's life that he could effectively close down and sever. But it was too late.

'Here,' she said, holding up the phone. A girl with brown hair in bunches smiled out at him, a gap between her two front teeth, freckles sprayed across her nose. 'This is her. She's seven.'

The girl's face was animated and expressive; it looked as if she was in the middle of laughing or sharing a joke, and again Dan felt a zap of connection because she looked remarkably like Bea. They could practically be sisters, he thought, before remembering that, *duh,* in a half-sense, they were. Her hair was a different colour – more like Lydia's chestnut than Bea's sandy-blonde – but the nose was the same and her smile was just like Patrick's. He found that he had a lump in his throat. Before now, this girl – Jemima – had been nothing more than a shadowy possibility that Dan had struggled to believe in, but now she was real. A human being: Patrick's other daughter. Dan was unnerved by how much this had thrown him off-course.

'She's lovely,' he said brokenly. 'She actually really looks—' He was about to blurt out 'like my other niece' but he couldn't. He couldn't link them aloud like that, for Zoe's sake. Did Lydia even know that Patrick had other children? He had to tread carefully here, not let his mouth run away with him.

Time to change the subject. 'So you and Patrick – when did you . . . ? How long were you . . . ?' He couldn't even finish his own questions. Part of him didn't want to know any details, because on some level he still kept expecting it to be a trick, not true. At the same time, another part of him needed to establish the basics, to peg this story into some kind of frame. He needed, also, to understand why it had happened. How Patrick could have done this to Zoe and the kids.

'How long were we together? Five months or so,' she replied. 'He dumped me when I found out I was pregnant. It wasn't planned, admittedly, but Patrick really didn't want to know. Washed his hands of me the same day and said never to contact him again. Which was nice.' Her expression hardened – he had hurt her, Dan could see – but when she caught him looking at her, she dropped her gaze. 'Sorry. It feels wrong now, to say anything bad.'

Dan was unable to keep up. 'Wait – how old did you say Jemima was?'

'She's seven. And amazing.' Her face was a mixture of pride and defiance, as if daring him to dispute this. 'I had no idea Patrick was married, that's how naive I was – but all the same, when I got pregnant . . .' She flushed. 'It was an accident, like I said, but I didn't want to just get rid of her. He told me to – he said he'd pay for . . . you know. An abortion.' She stumbled over the word. 'But I decided to keep her.'

This was all happening too quickly for Dan to stay on top of. 'You didn't know Patrick was married,' he repeated, trying to piece the story together in a way that he could comprehend, find a narrative where his brother didn't appear like such a bad guy.

'No! Because he didn't mention it, and I assumed – well, you *do* assume, don't you, if someone's flirting and flattering you, that they're not already hooked up. It didn't cross my mind that he was married, not for a second.' Her voice rose. 'What – do you think I'd have gone out with him if I knew he had a wife?' She gave a mocking laugh, her eyes so stony, Dan was starting to feel unnerved. 'I'm not like that,' she said, jabbing the air. Then her lips trembled and she put a hand to her face. 'I can't believe he's dead. Sorry. It keeps hitting me. I know it was a long time ago – I haven't even seen him since then, but I always kind of hoped that Jemima would meet him one day, all the same. That he'd love her as much as I do.'

Dan still felt miles behind, bogged down by his earlier assumptions. Lydia wasn't, in fact, a home-wrecker. Probably not an evil blackmailer, either. 'So you weren't together any more after she was born,' he said. Surely he had got this wrong somewhere. 'He and Jemima . . .'

She shook her head. 'Never met. He wasn't interested.'

You could see how much this had wounded her, but she was proud too, because as soon as she'd made herself vulnerable by saying the words she shot him a look that said, clear as anything, *Don't you dare pity me for this.*

But it was too late, because he did. He felt terrible for her. Really hurt on her behalf. 'Sorry,' he mumbled, appalled by his brother's atrocious behaviour. 'That's . . . pretty crap.' Not seeing your own child, *ever.* Not even once. It was more than crap, it was abhorrent. What had Patrick been thinking?

'His loss,' Lydia said, and her face was so tight, so fierce, that it looked as if she might punch your head in, if you dared suggest *she* might have lost out on anything.

'Yes,' Dan agreed. He couldn't help thinking of how much Patrick had loved his three children, how enormously proud he had been of each of them – and how secure and happy they had been with him as their father. Yes, it was Patrick's loss not to know this fourth, secret child of his, but Christ, it was the little girl's loss too, that she'd never been part of her dad's life. Not that Dan would dare to venture anything so tactless, mind, while Lydia still looked so combative. 'God, I'm really sorry,' he said again. 'I had no idea.'

She shrugged, clearly not wanting his sympathy. 'We manage.'

There was a momentary silence and then he remembered how he had got her number in the first place: the final mystery to clear up. 'One other thing,' he said. 'The card you gave Zoe – that was how I got your phone number. It was up on her fridge.'

'This is your sister-in-law?' she said tartly. 'The one I'm supposedly harassing?'

He lowered his eyes. Ah yes. He'd forgotten he'd bandied that particular accusation around. 'Sorry,' he said again. 'I was confused. How do you two know each other, though? I wasn't sure what to say – Zoe mentioned that she'd met you in a shop or something?'

Lydia shook her head blankly. 'I don't think I know anyone called Zoe,' she replied, adding with a sarcastic side-eye, 'I'm pretty sure I'd have remembered meeting Patrick's *wife*.'

'The business card was from a shop in Chiswick.' Dan

got out his phone and showed her the photo he'd taken of it, with Lydia's name and phone number handwritten there. 'Unless Zoe has somehow tracked you down herself and—'

But Lydia's face had cleared. 'Oh God,' she said. 'That was Zoe?' She put a hand to her mouth, eyes wide as the pieces fitted together. 'Okay, it makes sense. She was crying in the street – I had no idea who she was and I looked after her, basically, until she felt better. She did say that she'd lost her husband recently.' She blinked, aghast. 'Then a few days later she came back – she'd brought me some flowers. Unless she's an amazing actor, I think it must have been a total coincidence.'

They stared at one another. How did that even happen in a city like London?

'She seemed so upset, I gave her my number, in case she wanted someone to talk to,' Lydia went on. 'Honestly, that's all it was. I felt sorry for her.' She bit her lip, gazing down at the table. 'She's very pretty,' she said, almost to herself. Then she frowned. 'So what do I do if she rings me up for a chat? I can't pretend this hasn't happened, can I?'

'Can't you?' Dan replied weakly. The situation was getting more complicated by the minute. So much for cutting Lydia neatly out of the picture before Zoe got a sniff of her. Too late for that.

Lydia seemed shocked. 'No!' she told him. 'What, lie to a grieving widow, when our kids are half-sisters and brothers? Wait – what are they, by the way? Boys or girls? These are Jemima's half-siblings and I don't even know their names.'

Dan hesitated. It was as if Pandora's Box had cracked open and he was powerless to close it again. Would it be disloyal of him to tell Lydia their names? But how could he refuse when, as she said herself, they were the half-brothers and -sister of her own daughter? 'Ethan, Gabe and Bea,' he mumbled.

She nodded, digesting the information. 'Nice,' she said after a moment. 'Wow! Jemima did always want to have brothers and sisters. So how old are they?'

This was all going too fast. Becoming too messy. He owed it to them, and to Zoe, not to say any more. Right? 'Well, the thing is . . .' he began helplessly, floundering for how to dig his way out.

Her eyes narrowed as she scrutinized him for a long uncomfortable moment. Then she leaned back in her chair. 'Oh, I get it. Silly me. Let me guess: you didn't come here today wanting to play Happy Families; you actually came to tell me there'll be no more money, hard shit – the wife wants me to fuck off back under my rock.' There was an awkward beat of silence, then she barked a mirthless laugh when he didn't correct her. 'Right. As I thought.'

Dan swallowed because all of that was exactly why he had come here, of course. But meeting Lydia had made him feel differently. She was no longer merely a name on a bank statement; she was a person with feelings, someone he'd witnessed go through suspicion, disbelief, sadness, anger and pride, all in a matter of minutes. What was more, she was the mother of Patrick's other daughter. 'No, it's not that,' he heard himself say. Like it or not, this child – Jemima – was family. If he dismissed her and Lydia now, he would be acting in the same callous way as his brother. It turned out he couldn't do that.

But what would this mean, in practical terms? he wondered in the next breath. How could he possibly square the situation with Zoe? Oh, by the way, your kids have got a half-sister – surprise! Patrick's been paying her off for years, and I know he's dead now, but she should still get something, right? Maybe from the life insurance?

Lydia's face looked pinched and defiant. 'I don't want his money anyway,' she said, chin up, before he could speak. 'I did tell him not to bother in the first place, that we were fine without him, but . . .'

'I'll find a way,' Dan blurted out, a hot wave of shame washing over him in the next second as he imagined Zoe's face if she ever got to hear of this conversation. *You told her what?* 'I mean . . . I could ignore the direct debit that's already set up, pretend I hadn't seen it, so that the monthly payment keeps on going out to you—'

'No, thanks.'

'Or – look, I'll give you money for your daughter myself. I'm her uncle, like you said. Surely I—'

'No. We don't need anyone's charity.' She was pretty magnificent in her anger, it had to be said. She stood up, snatching her damp mac and cycle helmet from the chair, no longer looking him in the eye. 'Forget it. Thanks for letting me know and everything. You've done your bit. We'll be fine. Sorry to hear about your brother,' she added as an afterthought.

And then, before he could react, she was walking stiffly away, without a single glance back. Dan found himself marvelling at how angry a person could look just from the rigidity of their shoulders, while simultaneously shrivelling inside at how badly the encounter had ended. Cut them loose, get rid, he had told himself half an hour ago. Yet it wasn't quite as simple as that. In fact, he was pretty sure this wasn't going to be simple at all.

Chapter Twelve

'Ah! You made it. Not chopped up in a bin bag or held hostage in some perv's flat. Relief!' cried Bridget as Lydia arrived at the school gate later on.

Lydia's smile felt kind of wobbly in reply. 'Relief' wasn't exactly the word she would use about how she felt right now, but yes, at least she wasn't dead or kidnapped, she supposed. A fairly low bar for a silver lining, but she needed to take the positives where she could find them today. Her emotions were still in turmoil. *Patrick is dead, Patrick is dead*, she kept repeating numbly to herself. When she wasn't agonizing over her stupid, blurted-out refusal of his money, that was. What had she been *thinking*? 'I made it' was all she said.

'Aaaannnnd?' Bridget prompted. She was a big woman, and loud with it, the sort of person who naturally attracted attention. Even now there were people looking over at them.

Lydia put a finger to her lips and edged away from the crowd. 'I've just met Patrick's brother,' she said in a low voice.

'Patrick,' Bridget repeated, frowning, then her eyes bulged as the penny dropped. 'Whoa, whoa, whoa! What? *The* Patrick? You're seeing his *brother* now?'

'No! Not like that. Really not like that.' Lydia glanced round to make sure nobody could hear them. 'He asked to meet me because . . . well. To tell me that—'

The school caretaker had come to unlock the gates and the waiting parents began streaming through them towards the various classrooms. Lydia and Bridget hung back.

'He died,' she finished bluntly. 'Patrick. He drowned.' Foolishly, tears had come to her eyes because it was so strange to say these words, and for them to be true.

He had always been so rudely *alive*, that was the thing. Full of vitality, so quick and strong and sexy. He lit up a room merely by walking into it; she couldn't take her eyes off him. For a long time after their break-up she kept expecting to bump into him, would scan groups of people, wondering if Patrick's face would be among theirs. But she hadn't seen him again, and now she never would. He had gone.

'Oh my God. Babe, I'm so sorry. How are you feeling?' Bridget gathered her up in an embrace, and for a few brief moments Lydia allowed her emotions to assail her, the memories sweeping in through her mind. All those shared moments of happiness.

The first time he'd come over to her place, for instance: a Tuesday afternoon when they'd both bunked off work. *I've got a migraine coming,* she had told her boss, heavy-lidded, before practically skipping down the road to catch the Tube. She and Patrick had fallen into bed together an hour later, with the sun streaming through the window onto their bodies. How glorious it had felt, how perfect. Afterwards, lying there in each other's arms, the sultry sound of someone practising a clarinet had wafted in on the breeze. 'This is our theme tune,' he'd said, moments before the musician had played a wrong note, at which they both burst out laughing.

The evening he had surprised her by waiting outside her office one sunny day, with a picnic and cold bottle of cava. They sat in Richmond Park and fed each other fat scarlet strawberries, and she thought she might very well die from sheer contentment. She still found herself thinking about him whenever she ate strawberries.

The weekend they'd spent in the South Downs together, staying in a 900-year-old castle with mullion windows and a view of the moat. They had imagined themselves king and queen, and she had told Patrick she loved him for the first time. 'Oh God, me too. You have no idea how much,' he replied with such earnest sincerity she almost couldn't bear the intensity. *This is it,* she had told herself, heart melting as she woke before him on the Sunday morning and drank in the gorgeous sight of her sleeping man. *This is the one. Always and forever. I love him!*

(It had killed her, once she knew the truth about him, to

wonder what he'd told his wife on all these occasions. Working late? Stag do? Poker night with the lads? She would probably never know now. But how could anyone live with themselves, lying so blatantly to the person they supposedly loved?)

On it had gone, anyway, happy time after happy time, until her pill let her down – in hindsight, it must have been a bout of food poisoning that was to blame – and then came the positive pregnancy test. Shortly after which, of course, he had done his vanishing trick, neatly removing himself from her life as if snipping himself out of a picture.

'I feel . . . a bit strange,' Lydia confessed now, disentangling herself from Bridget and delving into her pocket for a tissue. 'Like . . . it wasn't as if he was ever going to leave his wife for me or anything, and I knew it was over – he didn't make any bones about that. All the same, though, I feel for Jemima. Because now she'll never meet him.' She blew her nose. 'Speaking of which – we should go and get the kids.' If they talked any longer, she'd end up admitting that she had told Patrick's brother to stick his maintenance payments, and Bridget would give her seven shades of hell for it. Plus there was the whole business about accidentally having met Patrick's wife that she needed to digest in private too.

'I suppose so,' said Bridget. She gave Lydia's hand a squeeze. 'You know where I am, though, if you need me, yeah? Or if you and Jem want to come back with us now for a cup of tea?'

'Thanks,' said Lydia, 'but we'll be okay. I just need to get my head around it, I think.'

'Sure thing,' said Bridget, as they joined the steady procession of parents through the gate. 'What was he like then, the brother?' she asked, elbowing Lydia. 'Another good-looking sod like Patrick?'

Lydia smiled faintly. 'He was . . .' She had to stop and consider the question for a moment; she had been so taken up by what Dan was saying that she hadn't really formed much of an opinion on those terms. What was it Patrick had said about him, all those years ago? *He got the brains, I got the looks* – or something along those lines. 'They do look alike,' she said. 'You can tell they're brothers. Same eyebrows.' She pulled a face at how irrelevant this was, under the circumstances. 'He was all right, I suppose. We got off on the wrong foot at first, but then he was okay. Mind you, I stormed off at the end, because—' She clammed up, cursing her own runaway mouth. Hadn't she just vowed not to get into this particular part of the conversation?

'Because . . . ?' prompted her friend.

Lydia shot her a rueful look. They were almost outside the classroom now and there were too many other parents around for her to take the story any further. 'I'll have to tell you later,' she said. 'If you promise you won't be cross with me.'

Bridget groaned, giving her a stern look. 'Lydia Fox, what have you gone and done now?'

Chapter Thirteen

'Mummy,' said Bea through a mouthful of sandwich.

'Yes, darling?' It was Wednesday afternoon and they had retreated to the car for the last twenty minutes of Gabe's football practice. The temperature had dropped outside and Zoe was worried about Bea's cough getting worse if they stood around for much longer in the slicing wind. Now sitting in the passenger seat as a treat, still wearing her pink fleecy hat, Bea had remembered she had some of her packed lunch left over from earlier and was tucking in.

'I was just wondering. Do you think there are any sandwiches in heaven?' she asked, as strands of grated cheese fell onto her school skirt.

'Try not to drop bits, love – look, it's going everywhere,' Zoe said, suppressing her irritation as Bea promptly brushed them all off her knee and into the footwell.

'Do you, though?'

'Do I think they have sandwiches in heaven? Um . . .' This had been happening a lot recently: Bea asking very specific questions about heaven, as if she was trying to pin down the precise details in her head. 'I guess so.' Zoe studied her daughter's expression. 'Are you thinking about Daddy?'

'Yes, because he does like bacon sandwiches so much. I hope he has lots of them. And ketchup! Is there ketchup in heaven?' She licked some butter off her finger, her face turned expectantly to Zoe. There was a small frown between her eyebrows, as if the ketchup issue was worrying her.

'Oh, I should think there'll be plenty,' Zoe replied, in as hearty a voice as she could manage. She was always left feeling uneasy about these conversations. Having set out to be vague and reassuring in her talk of heaven, being pinned down on the specifics – like the ketchup stock issues – felt a lot like lying. But what was the alternative? *If it's comforting to Bea, then I think that's okay*, her mum had reassured her on the phone, and Zoe was inclined to agree.

'What if there's just brown sauce, though? He doesn't even like that. Or if they say: sorry, no bacon, it's only tuna today. He hates tuna!' Bea had always been the most tender-hearted of her children, and her blue eyes were filling at the thought of her dad being deprived so cruelly. 'He'll be sad, won't he? And hungry!'

Zoe put her hand on Bea's. 'I'm pretty sure that heaven is a really nice place where nothing bad happens,' she said firmly. 'So it's always sunny, with plenty of bacon sand- wiches, and Daddy will feel very well looked after, and not sad or hungry at all.' She was making the afterlife sound like a great holiday, with an endless breakfast buffet and fantastic room service, she realized. Still, there were worse analogies.

'But he'll miss us, though, won't he? Because we miss him.'

'Yes, but some people think that when you're in heaven, you can look down at the world and see everyone you loved there, and still be a part of their lives. Sort of.' Okay, so now she was getting into murkier waters. Having read up on what to say to bereaved children, she knew that this notion could be soothing, but also potentially alarming to the more literal-minded.

'So he can see me on the *toilet*? Or getting told off at *school*?'

'Well . . .' Trust Bea to go for the most prosaic examples. Maybe the idea wasn't as soothing as Zoe had hoped. 'I don't think so,' she hedged. 'But I like to believe that, if I'm talking to him, he can hear me. Which makes me feel a bit better.'

Bea considered this for a moment. 'What sort of things do you say to him?'

This definitely wasn't the time to confess to all the angry remarks Zoe had made to Patrick during her darkest hours. 'Well, I tell him that I miss him, and I wish he was here. Sometimes, when I go to the cemetery, I tell him things that have happened at home – what you and the boys have been up to.'

Bea chewed the last corner of her sandwich, pondering this. 'Can we talk to him now?'

'Yes! Absolutely.' Zoe squeezed her hand. 'What would you like to say?'

Bea rubbed a wet circle in the condensation on the window, so that she could see out, and peered up towards the sky. 'Daddy!' she said in her bossiest voice. 'Can you hear me?' There was a pause while they both listened.

Stupidly, Zoe found herself waiting for a sign once more: a patter of raindrops on the car roof, a feather dropping from the sky onto the windscreen. Nothing, of course. 'I'm sure he can, darling, carry on,' she said.

'Daddy, it's me, Bea. I've got something *very* important to say to you,' she continued, still gazing through her peephole. 'This is it: don't look at me when I'm on the toilet, okay? Don't! Because that would be rude. Okay, Daddy?'

Despite the situation, Zoe found herself wanting to giggle all of a sudden. Bea looked so severe and disapproving, she was even wagging a finger. 'Anything else?' she managed to say in a strangled voice.

'Um ... I miss you, Daddy! Really a *lot*! L-O-T,' she spelled out for good measure. 'I did well on my spellings this week, by the way, and . . .' She paused, frowning as she searched for inspiration. 'And Gabe got in trouble with the head teacher for—'

'Okay, let's not tell tales to Daddy,' Zoe interrupted.

They could be here all day if this turned into a supergrass session. 'Let's just say nice things, all right?'

Bea cupped her hands to her mouth. 'I LOVE YOU, DADDY! You're the best! But remember what I said about the toilet, okay?' She cocked her head as if listening, then nodded in satisfaction. 'He said okay.'

'Good.'

'And that he loves me better than the boys.'

'Hmm.'

'He *did*! He *said* that to me.'

'Well, maybe keep that bit as a secret, okay? Look, here comes Gabe now. Hop into the back again and put your seatbelt on, darling, that's it.' She smiled at Bea. 'Well done. Let's do that another time. I bet Daddy really loved hearing your message. Hi, Gabe! In you get. Let's go home.'

That evening, Dan sat in front of his laptop and set about updating his Patrick-plan spreadsheet. *Filed accounts with accountant,* he typed in the 'Business' column. *Sorted paperwork. Paid bills,* he added, dating each entry. It was remarkably satisfying to see the new entries accumulating, each one small but valuable. Was it really only a week since he'd decided to embark on this plan? In that time he'd so far chalked up ten good deeds, which averaged out as 1.428 per day. Call it 1.43. Whichever, it felt like excellent progress, as if he was genuinely making a difference. In fact, if he carried on at this rate, over the next two months he'd have completed at least eighty Patrick-related tasks and, with each one, he hoped to lessen the pain and stress felt by Zoe and the kids.

Wait – there was more. *Lift to/from sculpture club,* he typed in the 'Ethan' column, which made eleven Patrick deeds. Or should he count it as two separate jobs? he wondered, before deciding that was probably pushing it. His nephew had been more communicative this week, chatting about the work they were doing at the club and recounting a couple of anecdotes from his day at school over the crashing chords of another concerto. 'Did you and your dad listen to this sort of music together?' Dan had asked during a break in the conversation, feeling curious. He couldn't picture it somehow.

Turned out, his instinct was correct. Ethan had snorted. 'You're joking, aren't you? Dad always said it was gay.'

'Seriously?' Dan asked, flummoxed. 'Meaning that classical music is gay, or that people who listen to it must be?'

'Both. You know what he was like.' Ethan lifted a shoulder as if he didn't care.

Dan hadn't been entirely sure how to reply. 'Seems a bit small-minded,' he commented eventually. He didn't want to bad-mouth his brother in front of his own kid, but calling a whole genre of music 'gay' seemed like something from the Dark Ages. Also kind of pathetic.

'Yep. Well, that was Dad,' said Ethan. 'He thought Art was pretty gay too. Me wanting to go to SculptShed . . . *What's wrong with you, lad? When I was your age I was playing for the rugby team, not bending bits of wire together.'*

His impression of Patrick was uncanny and Dan cringed. 'God,' he said, staring through the windscreen. 'Well, I don't think like that. And most people don't think like that. At all,' he felt compelled to say. There was silence for a moment. 'You know, maybe he was just trying to push your buttons, wind you up a bit,' he went on, wanting to give his brother the benefit of the doubt. Patrick wasn't a bigot, after all. He really wasn't.

'Yeah, maybe,' Ethan said, sounding unconvinced, and before Dan could think of anything else to say, they had arrived in Wandsworth and Ethan was getting out of the car. On the way home, things were more convivial at least, with the two of them laughing companionably together about this and that. Patrick wasn't mentioned again.

Arriving back in Kew, Dan pulled on the handbrake. 'Same time, same place next week, I take it?' he asked.

'Oh – no, it's the Easter holidays next week. The club's closed for a fortnight.'

Damn it, thought Dan, picturing his schedule up on the fridge. He would fall behind with his numbers now. Unless . . . 'Maybe we could do something else together,' he suggested. 'Go to Tate Modern – or if you want some sculpture inspiration, we could find some of the Henry Moores around London?'

It was gratifying to see his nephew's eyes light up in response. 'Yes please,' Ethan said at once. 'That would be cool.'

'Great. I'll talk to your mum. Get something arranged,' Dan told him, before waving goodbye and driving off again. He felt warm inside all the way back to Hammersmith. Who knew that a child reacting to you with such obvious pleasure could feel so good? *See, Patrick? I'm there for him,* he thought. *And guess what – I'm going to do loads of so-called gay Art stuff with him, because he loves it, and so do I. So chew on that one for a bit, pal.*

Moving on, anyway: tomorrow he planned to spend the day clearing out the recently vacated flat on Whitecliffe Road before painting it throughout. Friday, he would add a second coat of paint, finishing the job over the weekend if need be. Then he'd get back to the letting agent about renting it out to new tenants and – boom. More money arriving in the business account for Zoe, thanks to him, as well as more good deeds totting up.

The big question, though, and one he was struggling to get to grips with, was whether or not to include Lydia on the spreadsheet. He couldn't decide. Did meeting her count as something to be ticked off on Patrick's behalf? Theoretically, yes, but did it benefit Zoe in any way? No, absolutely not – in fact quite the reverse, seeing as Dan had flip-flopped so abruptly on his initial plans. The sticking point was that he liked Lydia, he'd realized. His instinct was that she was a decent person, not someone grabby and out for what they could get. Listening to her account of things, it seemed she was more victim than villain in the situation; a woman who had been shoddily treated and deserved better. But hers was only one side of the story, he reminded himself, still unable to quite believe it. Maybe the truth hadn't actually been as black and white as she'd made out. Maybe, in fact – here came his imagination again, cranking into action – maybe she'd tried to entrap Patrick, tricking him, lying to him. Deliberately getting pregnant to try and force him apart from Zoe, or something. Or maybe – yes, this could be it! – maybe it had been a one-night stand, a foolish mistake that Patrick had been feeling terrible about ever since, and Lydia had embellished the whole thing, fantasized that they'd had some kind of relationship.

But then he remembered how anxious her eyes had been, how sincere her shock and grief. Dan had only spent thirty minutes with her, yet he was pretty sure she wasn't a bunny boiler with a game plan. She looked as if she'd genuinely fallen in love with Patrick, and had her heart broken. Which meant that . . . Oh bloody hell. He did believe her, that was the problem. His instinct was that she had been telling the truth.

'What were you thinking, Patrick?' he groaned aloud.

You weren't supposed to speak ill of the dead, but some-times that was impossible when you discovered their darkest secrets. Perhaps this happened about everyone when they died and the skeletons came tumbling forth from previously locked closets: you were left feeling shaken, as if maybe you hadn't known them as well as you thought. It was even more disconcerting when you'd spent your life looking up to that person, seeing them as someone to emulate. But for Patrick to behave as he had towards Lydia – it was really bad. Sleazy and just wrong. No wonder he had decided to keep the whole saga to himself. And no wonder, also, that Lydia had been so wary when Dan phoned her up and men-tioned Patrick's name. Jesus.

His fingers still hovered over the empty spreadsheet boxes while he tussled with the dilemma. *Meeting Lydia*, he typed, but then changed his mind almost immediately and backspaced through the letters again. He'd gone to meet her with the intention of resolving matters but the situation didn't feel quite finished. To him, anyway, but she had been pretty fierce as she left, telling him in no uncertain terms that she didn't need any charity from him, then marching off. Would that really be the end of it? Although of course if it was, it would make life a damn sight easier for him, he figured. Problem solved. Direct debit stopped. Zoe never had to know.

But then he remembered the business card on Zoe's

fridge. He'd have to pocket it, the next chance he got, to prevent any contact between them. Whatever happened, he must not let Zoe call Lydia. Imagine the fallout if Lydia blurted out the truth to her, told her everything. She'd seemed so wound up when she left the café, Dan had felt rattled ever since. Who knew what she was capable of? 'You see?' he complained aloud to his brother. 'You see what a mess you've made of everything? You twat.'

His phone beeped just then, a text from his friend Steve: *Blue Anchor tonight or we're staging an intervention. Come over — it's been too long. Will be there from 8.*

Dan checked his watch to see that it was seven forty-five already. Sod it, he was thirsty and Steve was right, he hadn't seen any of his mates for weeks. Plus, if he went on agonizing about Lydia and Zoe all evening, he would lose the will to live. *Meeting Lydia,* he typed, then set the spreadsheet printing before he could change his mind again. Done. If she wanted to draw a line under things, then that suited him just fine.

On my way he texted back.

The Blue Anchor was an eighteenth-century pub on the riverside with good beers and even better chips, and as soon as Dan walked through the door twenty minutes or so later, he felt a wave of relief sweep over him. Pub. Mates. Beer. Conversation about sport, work, funny stories. Nothing bad could happen here. No difficult dilemmas to resolve, other than what to drink. And Christ, did that first pint taste good.

'Someone's got a thirst on,' commented Neil as Dan drained his glass.

'Making up for lost time, aren't I?' Dan replied, getting up from the table. 'Who wants what?'

He was going to get wasted, he decided as he ordered a round of whisky chasers for everyone as well as their pints. He was going to drink and drink and drink, until he stopped thinking about Patrick and Zoe and Lydia. Alcohol would blur them all away tonight: bring it on.

This plan worked for a time too; really well, in fact. The four men had known each other since their schooldays and were able to veer into long, enjoyable reminiscences about events from twenty years ago, such as the night when, having taken a load of magic mushrooms, they re-enacted the Abbey Road photoshoot, stark naked at two in the morning. Or even further back, when they were in a chemistry lesson together and one of them – Neil thought it was Steve; Steve blamed Mark – had set fire to Victoria Postlethwaite's blazer with a Bunsen burner. And then they were into a round of 'What Happened To . . . ?', starting with Victoria Postlethwaite herself (last seen working in a Harvester, still as hot as – well, as hot as a Bunsen burner, Mark reckoned), before the conversation took a detour to football, then on to a heated discussion about chocolate bars of the Eighties.

It was exactly the kind of easy-going bollocks he needed, Dan thought, as he bought another round. His fifth – or was it sixth? – pint, and the rest of the world was starting to soften around the edges, as if viewed through an old movie camera, slicked with Vaseline. 'Cheers, boys,' he said, feeling a sudden rush of love for them – huge boundless love for these men who had released all the stress and strain inside him with their banter and teasing: Neil with his daft buzz cut, which wasn't doing much to disguise his slowly vanishing hairline. Marky Mark with the same Pixies T-shirt he'd had for at least two decades and the loudest laugh in the room. Steve, once a proper goth with a dyed black Mohican and lip piercings, now a rotund dad of twin girls who'd recently taken them to some teenybopper concert and realized, to his horror, that he knew all the words of the songs. Thank God for friends who came and scooped you up, who reminded you that the world could be all right, just when you'd forgotten how to laugh.

'Cheers,' they chorused. But then Steve, no doubt thinking he was being sensitive, felt the need to lift his pint again. 'And to Patrick,' he said solemnly.

'To Patrick,' the others chorused, drinks in the air.

Dan felt his mood collapsing like a flicked house of cards. He didn't want Patrick at the table, not tonight. 'Nah,' he said. 'Let's not.'

Steve looked uncomfortable. 'Sorry, mate,' he said. 'We

don't have to talk about it. Just . . . well, he was a great bloke, wasn't he?'

But Dan no longer knew what to think about his brother, let alone how to respond. Lydia's hurt face rose in his mind, followed by poor Zoe's loving ignorance, and then he was flashing back to the argument he'd had with Patrick the night of his disappearance, feeling the gut-punch all over again. The pure pain of betrayal. 'Not always,' he replied thickly, the alcohol skidding through him. 'Turned out he wasn't always that great, you know.'

The others looked confused by this response and afterwards the evening kind of fell away from Dan, without him ever being able to pick it back up. He was drinking faster and faster, as if his thirst would never be quenched. He was stumbling on his feet, crashing into the wall on the way to the Gents, so hard that he'd have bruises on his arm for almost a week afterwards. He started arguing with Mark about – he couldn't even remember what, only that the other three all exchanged glances and then Neil said, 'Taxi for Mr Sheppard' and . . . He didn't swing a punch, did he? God, he might have done.

Anyway, the next thing he knew, the pub was closing and Mark was frogmarching him home. Dan vaguely remembered trying to shove him away, but Mark had a tight grip because he had started going to the gym loads when his wife left him two years ago, and Dan was too drunk to fight back properly. And then . . . Oh no. He had the horrible feeling he started to cry right there in the street, telling Mark he was sorry, and that everything had gone wrong. Then there was a gap, a blank in his memory, and they were back at Mark's flat, not his, and Mark was putting him in the spare room.

The next morning when he woke up, head jangling, mouth like the Sahara, he realized he must have thrown up in his sleep, because there was vomit all over the floor and down the side of the bed. He lay there, stinking and sweaty, as moments from the night before smashed into his memory like blows to the head. Rock-bottom all over again, he thought miserably. Every time he felt as if he was inching out of despair, down he tumbled once more, all the way to the depths.

His stomach churned. Bile rose. He only just managed to get out of bed and sprint to the bathroom before he was sick again. Shivering and clammy, he remembered that he was supposed to be painting the flat on Whitecliffe Road today, and didn't know whether to laugh or cry. Or vomit once more.

'I suppose you think this is funny,' he growled to Patrick between retches.

Chapter Fourteen

Thursday morning was cool and grey, the sky almost pearly in the east as the sun tried to break through the cloud cover. Ethan had left the house in a bad mood, having discovered that Zoe had forgotten to wash his rugby kit ('What do you even *do* all day?' he'd snapped at her, stuffing his still-muddy shirt into his bag with a kind of fury). Half an hour later, setting out with Gabe and Bea towards the primary school, Zoe still felt tightly wound, with Ethan's criticism continuing to echo through her head. *What do you even DO all day?*, as if he felt nothing but contempt for her inadequacy. He was grieving, she reminded herself, and this was yet another sign that things had changed, that she was not the organized, capable mum she had been two months ago. She was a mess and they both knew it. This didn't really make her feel any better, on second thoughts.

'Mummy,' said Bea, swinging her book bag as they walked along, 'do you think there are unicorns in heaven?'

'Er, *no*,' Gabe answered scathingly before Zoe could find

an appropriate answer. 'Cos unicorns aren't *real*, dumbo. And neither is heaven. It's just a story for little kids and religious people.'

'Gabe!' scolded Zoe. 'Don't call her names. And don't say that about heaven.'

'Why not?' he challenged. 'Do *you* believe in heaven? Cos I haven't seen any proof that it even exists, like photos or maps or anything. So how does anyone actually *know*?'

They were walking past a bus stop at that moment and a stout middle-aged woman waiting there caught Zoe's eye, but not in a good way. She was wearing a badge that said 'Jesus is Love' and Zoe hustled the children past her fast, in case the woman was tempted to join the conversation.

'I don't have *proof*, Gabe, because I haven't been there myself, but lots of people believe that it—'

'I think Daddy would *like* to meet a unicorn,' Bea put in serenely, chewing the end of her plait as Zoe floundered mid-sentence. 'They could be friends. I'm going to call his unicorn Snowdrop because she's all white and pretty.'

'Lovely,' said Zoe weakly, giving up on the heaven answer.

'Not real, not real, not real,' Gabe taunted his sister.

Bea glared at him. 'They *are* real, and me and Mummy are going to see a *film* about them on Saturday, in the *cinema*, so there! REAL!' she retorted, stabbing her brother with her finger for good measure.

Gabe gave the scathing laugh of a nine-year-old who knew

absolutely everything. 'Yeah, a *cartoon*,' he scoffed. 'It's not like a *documentary* about unicorns. DERRR!'

'That's enough,' Zoe said, wishing that her children – particularly this gobby middle one – wouldn't take such enormous glee from winding each other up.

Gabe was still in goading mode, though, cackling at his own superiority. 'Did you actually think it was going to be a wildlife film with, like, David Attenborough standing there with a bunch of . . .' He could hardly get the words out for laughing so much. 'With a bunch of *unicorns?*'

Bea's face darkened, never a good sign. Then she stopped dead in the street with her hands on her hips. 'Right, I'm telling Daddy about this now,' she announced, before gazing up at the sky, her little chin sticking out. 'Daddy, did you see that? He's being mean. Tell him!'

In the very next second a car horn beeped, loud and indignant, as if answering her command, and Bea's eyes grew round at the sound. 'See!' she exclaimed, vindicated. 'That was him, telling you to stop.' She went right up in her brother's face. 'BEEEEP,' she yelled, then skipped off along the pavement. 'Thanks, Daddy,' Zoe heard her say.

Gabe glanced across at Zoe, looking chastened. 'That *wasn't* Dad,' he said, but you could hear the uncertainty in his voice.

Zoe shrugged. 'Who knows?' she said lightly. Maybe Patrick was more willing to offer a sign to Bea than he was to her; to dish out a warning beep here and there to keep Gabe in check. He'd always stuck up for his daughter in the past when the boys' teasing tipped over into unkindness, after all, and it wouldn't hurt Gabe to think twice about his behaviour. She put a consoling hand on his shoulder. 'Anyway, look on the bright side,' she reminded him. 'You're going to play with Jack on Saturday, aren't you, so you don't have to see the unicorn film with us. Could be worse, right?'

Once Zoe had seen the children safely into the school playground, she walked back down the road. 'I take it you're still not replying to *me*,' she muttered aloud, staring up at the sky like Bea had done. There was no corresponding beep from any vehicles, though, no sudden burst of sunshine, no sparrow nodding meaningfully at her from the nearest tree. No acknowledgement whatsoever. 'In your own time,' she added.

She was being fanciful, she told herself as she walked further along. As fanciful as her six-year-old daughter, who at least had an excuse for it. This was not really Dealing With It, this was a blatant coping mechanism, a means of kidding herself that he was still around somewhere, amidst the chilly April morning air, able to hear her. Moreover, it was a coping mechanism that didn't even work properly, seeing as she never got anything back from him. Still, talking to Patrick was clearly helping Bea, at least. Zoe had heard her chatting away after her bedtime the night before and, when Zoe put her head round the bedroom door to remind Bea that she was supposed to be going to sleep, her daughter had replied, 'I'm just telling Daddy a bedtime story. In case he's missing me.' The room was dark, save for the toadstool lamp beside the bed, which glowed softly pink, but Zoe could make out the little girl's smile through the shadows, pleased with her own kindness. It was enough to crack a person's heart in two. How could she deny Bea this one-sided conversation? Besides, it kept Patrick real for her; it kept him a part of her life, which could only be a good thing.

She didn't feel like going straight home this morning; she had found that the act of walking through her own front door often sapped her energy and left her unable to do very much other than wander mournfully around the empty rooms, occasionally sinking onto one of the children's beds and putting her head in her hands. *What do you even do all day?* Ethan had sneered, and the honest answer these days was: not much. His words still smarting in her head, she found herself veering towards the cemetery, which was a fitting place for a widow, she supposed.

'Hello,' she whispered as she walked through the gates. She and Patrick had never explicitly discussed their preferences in death, blithely assuming they would have decades left together before they needed to consider such things, but when it came to making decisions about his funeral and other arrangements, she had known, instinctively, that he would not have wanted to be buried. He was tall and out-doorsy, and had never liked being confined in small spaces. Lifts, budget-hotel bathrooms, small cars: they all gave him the heebie-jeebies. It was silly of her – he was dead, after all, and technically unable to care much either way – but she couldn't bear the thought of him in a coffin, buried under the ground. She'd opted for cremation instead, and currently had what was left of him in a small urn on top of the ward-robe. 'I can't leave him on the mantelpiece or anywhere downstairs,' she'd had to tell Liz, after her mother-in-law had hinted several times about keeping Patrick's ashes some-where more visible. 'The kids will only knock him over and spill him everywhere.'

Her own mum wasn't entirely happy that Zoe was still holding on to the urn, either. 'You really should scatter those ashes,' she had said, more than once. 'It might help, love, let-ting him go.'

'I will, I'm going to,' Zoe had said. 'Don't rush me.' That pot of ashes was all she had left of her husband; she wanted his final send-off to be perfect. She was planning to bring him on holiday to Pembrokeshire with them that summer anyway. Take a walk along the headland with the kids, and let him fly with the wind as she gave her eulogy and they talked about their fondest memories of him. Patrick loved holiday-ing there; they both did. They'd gone a couple of years ago, staying in a house right on the beach at Freshwater East, and it had been one of the happiest weeks of her life. She liked the thought of him resting there.

That was all ahead of her, though. In the meantime, she had paid for a memorial plaque with his name on in the Garden of Remembrance, here in the grounds of the cemetery, and it was a peaceful place to visit. The flowerbeds were beautifully tended, with the cherry trees just coming into bloom. There were benches to sit on too, if you felt like lingering a while, and the calm kind of hush that made the rest of the world seem far distant.

'Patrick Christopher Sheppard was a loving father, husband and son,' she murmured to herself as she walked along. 'A kind, honest man who we all adored. Such a wonderful father. The best of all men. The best man in the world . . .' It was no good. Every time she tried to sum him up for her eulogy, the words felt inadequate. How could a few bland phrases do justice to the years they had shared together, the way that all of his tiny kindnesses and acts of love had built up in tissue-thin layers to create something solid and indestructible? She still missed him so much all the time. She missed his easy company, his whistling around the house, his habit of pulling her to him in an embrace, the knack he had of making her feel better, whatever kind of a day he'd had. Even after Bea's birth, when Zoe had been stunned by an unexpected cloud of post-natal depression that had brought her to her knees, Patrick had been able to reach her, the only person who still managed to connect with her in that fearful shadowy place. He'd taken her hand and not let go until he'd helped pull her through the darkness.

She held her hands up in front of her now, wishing he was still here to clasp one within his warm, friendly fingers. To hook an arm around her shoulders and let her lean against him. To make her laugh with a story about one of his tenants, or something one of the lads at work had said or . . .

'Zoe? Are you all right?'

Oh, shit, there was Mari, one of the mums from school, on the path, presumably having just heard Zoe muttering her eulogy under her breath, like a weirdo. While holding up her hands and staring at them! Imagine if this got round the school playground – it would spread faster than melted butter.

She's obviously not handling it well. Talking to herself in the cemetery like a fruitcake. It's not a good look, is it? Poor woman. I hope the children are okay. Do you think someone should have a word?

'Zoe?' Mari prompted. She was wearing a gorgeous pale-blue coat that made her look like some kind of ice-queen, Zoe registered distractedly, before snapping to attention.

'Yes! Sorry. Miles away,' she said. 'Yes, I'm fine, thanks. Are you?'

'Not bad,' said Mari, although the wind was making her eyes run and she dabbed at them suddenly. 'Listen – maybe we should have a chat sometime. Get together. It would be good to talk.'

'Oh,' said Zoe, feeling uncomfortable. 'I'm not sure.' She already felt so talked *about,* that was the problem. She'd removed herself from a couple of parents' WhatsApp groups recently because she couldn't cope with other people's comments and clumsy approaches, however well-meaning. What did they know about grief? How many of them had had to deal with the death of a husband? They had no idea – and clearly neither did Mari, if she thought Zoe wanted to chat about her feelings. 'I'm not much company right now. But thanks anyway.'

She made her goodbyes and hurried away, trying to keep a lid on her emotions. One day she'd feel normal again, she comforted herself. One day she'd be able to make conversation like the other mums, drop round for coffee with them, eat cake and swap funny stories about their children. But not yet. Not today. Right now, all she could manage was putting one foot in front of another, in order to trudge along through each minute and hour.

'You're doing great,' she told herself fiercely. 'Mari's not important. Just keep going.'

Chapter Fifteen

On Friday evening Dan was gazing at his good-deeds spread-sheet, in particular the blank spaces in the 'Gabe' and 'Bea' columns, when Zoe rang. 'I know it's short notice but I don't suppose you could have Gabe for a few hours tomor-row, could you?' she asked. 'He was meant to be spending the day with his friend Jack, but Jack's brother fell off the climbing frame at the park and has fractured his wrist – they're operating first thing in the morning. I'm a bit stuck now because Ethan's out, doing a workshop at the Tate, and I promised Bea ages ago we'd go to see some terrible uni-corn movie that Gabe would rather die than watch, so—'

'It's fine, I can have him,' Dan said when she paused for breath. It was as if Fate had made an intervention, right there. He was not about to refuse Zoe anything, not least because of the extra guilt he'd been carrying around since meeting Lydia. The still-to-be-resolved, what-the-hell-am-I-going-to-do? guilt, which was becoming more onerous with every day that passed. He was feeling so queasy about the whole thing that he'd probably have agreed to commit a series of crimes on Zoe's behalf, if she went on to request such a list. 'Whenever you like,' he added for good measure.

Zoe exhaled with noisy relief, and the sound of it made Dan feel better. Needed. This was the first time she had specifically asked him for help since Patrick's death – perhaps ever, now that he thought about it. She had come to him, and he had been able to say yes. Plus, hadn't he just been thinking that he needed to find something he and Gabe could do together?

'Oh, thank you,' Zoe sighed. 'Thanks so much. I really appreciate this.'

'No problem. What time do you want me to get him?' He was positively jaunty by now. *The middle of the night? Five in the morning? I'll do it. You want me to walk to your place barefoot along a path of burning coals and broken glass? Absolutely.*

'About ten, is that okay? Sorry – I hope you're not having to rearrange anything around us or change your plans.'

'No, not at all,' he assured her. This wasn't entirely true. He'd planned on finishing painting the Whitecliffe Road flat on Saturday, it having taken far longer than he'd anticipated – admittedly, largely because he'd been so hungover on Thursday that he'd hardly been able to open the emulsion bucket without retching. Today had been more productive at least, but there was still all the woodwork left to gloss and . . . Well, never mind, there would be time on Sunday. 'Ten is fine,' he said. 'I'll think of something fun we can do together.'

'Oh, gosh, don't feel you have to. You can stay in the house and play computer games all morning with him, if you'd rather. Whatever's easiest, Dan.'

How was it possible to feel simultaneously pleased by another person's gratitude, yet also sick to the stomach with shame at your double-crossing? Whatever, Dan was absolutely not about to cop out and play computer games with his nephew, when he could seize the opportunity to be Super Uncle and Kind Brother-in-Law. 'Leave it with me,' he said. 'See you tomorrow morning.'

That grandiose sort of posturing was what had led to Dan now shepherding an extremely excited Gabe towards his first skateboarding lesson at a skate park just off the Westway. Gabe liked dangerous activities; he was a bold, reckless and well-coordinated boy. The moment Dan had seen 'skateboarding' come up in his 'fun things to do with your nephew' Internet search, he had thought: *Bingo.* Okay, so Zoe didn't look completely thrilled by the prospect when Dan arrived earlier and made his big announcement – she had turned a little pale, if anything, and started talking anxiously about broken bones – but unfortunately for her, Dan had made the rookie error of airing his suggestion in front of Gabe as well, resulting in a whoop of 'YES!' from the boy, followed by a frenzy of karate kicks and 'KAPOW!' noises around the kitchen. It would have taken an utter kill-joy to forbid the trip now, and so Zoe had dubiously agreed, albeit with pleas to return her son in one piece rather than in an injured mash.

'Fancy having a go yourself?' the instructor joked to Dan when they arrived and set about registering Gabe and hiring the necessary kit. Dan was about to laugh and say, 'No, thanks, I value my limbs' when Gabe looked up at him, eyes shining, and said, '*Do* you, Uncle Dan? Oh, go on!'

When was the last time anyone had looked at him like that? As if he were a king or a rock star, someone important. Here was his nephew specifically asking for his company, flattering him with hopefulness – was it any wonder Dan heard himself replying, 'Um . . . sure, okay' without properly thinking about what he might be letting himself in for?

In hindsight, this was rookie error number two. No turning back now. Five minutes later, they were both rigged up in brightly coloured helmets, elbow and knee pads and choosing their skateboards, before being greeted by a terrifyingly young instructor called Aki. Oh, shit. Dan was already regretting his decision to take part. Was it too late to backtrack? All around them, kids in hoodies and skate pants were whizzing up and down ramps of varying sizes and gradients, leaping and twisting in mid-air from the half-pipe and – most alarming of all – rattling along steep rails with apparent ease. It was a massive place, with indoor and outdoor sections, a skate shop and a café, which looked particularly tempting right now. Damn it.

Having been guided to the beginners' area – an almost entirely flat section of the skate park that was shunned by anyone over the age of eight, they waited for Aki, who had stopped to back-slap a couple of moon-faced teens in over-sized tartan shirts. Gabe fidgeted with barely contained excitement, stepping from foot to foot, eyes wide with the thrill of so many cool kids in the vicinity. 'This is *awesome*,' he breathed happily.

'Too right,' Dan agreed, trying to mask his sudden rush of dread with a stern talking-to. *Here we are, uncle and nephew, and we're going to have a great time,* he reminded himself. *We are cementing a new bond together; we're starting something really good that will last forever; I am stepping into the role of Number One Male Adult in his life, and I will not fuck this up.* What was it he'd heard Ethan mutter that first time in the car? Something like 'Puts the "tit" in "substitute"'. Well, he wouldn't be doing that, either.

He glanced up at the sky. It wasn't as if he believed in an afterlife, but he liked the thought of Patrick looking down and seeing them here together, appreciating the expression of utter joy on Gabe's face and maybe chalking up a tick for Dan. Dan found himself thinking of the photos by his nephew's bed, of Gabe and Patrick together at various football matches. Patrick had always been sure-footedly sporty, able to catch and throw and kick with skill; it was obvious that Gabe had inherited the same physical competence. If Dan was ever going to attempt to compensate for the loss of Patrick, then this was the least he could do. He must not let the kid down.

'Okay, guys!' Aki said, clapping his hands together. He was short but stocky, with insane muscles rippling through his shoulders whenever he moved; dressed in a thin hooded top and baggy shorts, his feet in massive dark-blue Nikes, the exact name of which Dan felt he was twenty years too old and not nearly cool enough to know. Gabe immediately fell silent, staring up at Aki with something bordering on love, or at least Massive Great Crush. Dan was not one to cast aspersions on under-tens, but he felt quietly confident that his nephew never gave the teachers at school such devout attention.

'Let's get started,' Aki said. 'First up: how to stand on your board.' He elbowed Gabe with a wink. 'We'll see who's better, shall we – you or the old guy?'

Dan prickled all over at being called 'the old guy', but Gabe sniggered disloyally. 'That's my Uncle Dan,' he said, blushing with the honour of speaking to his new hero.

'Uncle Dan, hey?' Aki grinned and raised an eyebrow at Dan, who couldn't quite bring himself to grin back. Wanker. He tried to pull a face that said, *Yeah, whatever, I'm not intimi-*

dated by you, but felt his teeth baring in more of a snarl. 'Okaaay,' said Aki, clapping his hands together. 'So: standing on the board. One foot in front of the other, yeah? Most people like to have their left foot at the front, so that the right can do all the pushing. But it's up to you – there's no right or wrong way about it. See how I'm keeping my back foot at an angle? That helps my balance. You try it for me now, little dude.'

Gabe stepped confidently onto the skateboard, following Aki's instructions. There was a slight wobble and a brief arm-flail, but then the boy found his balance with a triumphant grin. *Easy*, his face said.

'Boom!' cried Aki, reaching over for a high-five. He was already getting on Dan's wick. 'Now your turn, Uncle Dan. Let's see what you've got.'

Patronizing twat. Dan stepped onto the board, praying it wasn't about to roll away beneath him or tip up, or anything embarrassing. One foot in front of the other. There. What was all the fuss about? He was only raised two inches off the ground. Big deal!

'No sweat,' said Aki. 'Cool as a cucumber. Okay, now let's get moving. I'm going to push off with my back foot, slow and strong, and we'll walk the boards around for a little while. Like so. See? Hey – you paying attention there, Uncle D?'

'Sure,' said Dan, momentarily distracted by the sight of a small girl with plaits poking out from a pink baseball cap. Seeing her had made him think about Lydia's daughter – this unexpected niece he'd just discovered he had – and then his thoughts had turned to Lydia herself, and her pale, anxious face frowning at him over her coffee. What should he do? he fretted for the hundredth time, as Aki demonstrated how to scoot along on the skateboard, and he and Gabe followed behind. Their fraught conversation had nagged away at him since then. How he wished he could have handled the situation better. How he wished, moreover, that he had remained ignorant of Lydia's existence altogether. But the genie was out of the bottle now and there was no way of persuading it back in there.

Anyway. He needed to concentrate. Satisfied that his pupils could competently walk a skateboard along, Aki now wanted the two of them to shift into the riding position with both feet on the board. 'Back straight, knees a little bent, find your balance,' he ordered, sailing around them in a wide loop on his own board to demonstrate. But then his attention was dragged elsewhere and he whistled under his breath. 'Back in a minute, guys,' he said, before skating across the park towards a young woman with a swingy black ponytail and a heart-shaped bottom encased by tight white jeans.

'Look, Uncle Dan, I'm doing it!' Gabe crowed with breathless glee, having pushed off. He rocked perilously backwards and forwards for a moment, arms windmilling, before righting himself. 'I'm skateboarding!'

'Nice one,' Dan cheered, glad to see his nephew so

happy and excited. When he thought back to how peevish the boy had been the other week, winding up his brother, surly to Zoe and glued to the computer game he was playing, it was like looking at a different child altogether. *Check this out, Patrick. Are you watching? I'm doing good here, I swear.*

Flushed with self-congratulation, he hopped on his own board, wanting to share the moment, only to lose his balance almost immediately. It was harder than it looked and he'd pushed off too strongly to control what was happening beneath his feet. 'Whoa,' he cried, desperately trying to maintain equilibrium. But then somehow or other he was tipping over and falling, and as he put his right foot down, his ankle rolled under with a sickening crunch. 'Fuck!'

'Uncle *Dan!*' said Gabe in shocked delight, coming to an abrupt stop. 'Uncle Dan, I *heard* that.'

Pain was shooting around Dan's body like pinballs in a machine and he was unable to speak for a moment. Breath hissed out from between his clenched teeth as he lowered himself to a sitting position on the floor, clutching his wrenched ankle. Shit, had he broken it? He was in agony. Fuck! He could practically hear Patrick laughing at him from wherever he was watching. Wait – no, that wasn't Patrick, it was actually Aki, racing back to them.

'What the . . . ?' roared the man-child. 'Are you kidding me? I turn my back for two minutes and you go and injure yourself, D?' He squatted next to Dan and prodded the ankle knowingly. 'We're gonna need some ice here. A whole bag of ice.' He looked up at Gabe. 'You okay, kid? Hey, don't worry. Happens all the time, especially to the old guys. You're not gonna hurt yourself though, right?'

Gabe's expression of glee had turned to one that looked very much like embarrassment. 'Mm-hmm,' he said, eyes hooded, his gaze flicking to Dan and back.

Oh God, thought Dan, picturing the scene from above: all the cool, edgy kids whizzing around fearlessly while the middle-aged has-been lay crippled and contorted on the cold concrete floor. This was not the fun experience he had planned for either of them.

'Ice,' said Aki again, rising to his feet. 'And a chair. You'll live, don't worry,' he added, as he hurried off.

When Zoe got home later she found Dan sitting there with one foot up, ice-pack resting on his ankle, while Gabe eagerly told her about his lesson in a single unceasing sentence without taking a breath. She didn't know whether to laugh or cry. Or whether she should just roll her eyes up to the ceiling and yell, 'I could have told you this was a stupid idea from the start!'

Okay, so she felt a grudging amount of sympathy for Dan, who was white-faced with pain and looking very sorry for himself as Gabe regaled them with full details of his glories on the skateboard, but her overriding reaction was one of exasperation. Because nobody had *forced* Dan to go along to the skate park in the first place, had they? Certainly nobody had insisted that he have a go himself. And now Gabe was hyped up with this exciting new pursuit, and guess who was going to have to be the mug who took him along from now on? Zoe, that was who. Zoe, who already had a million other things to be dealing with, and who was only surprised that reckless Gabe hadn't been the one to break a bone or rip a ligament. When she had already lost one member of the family and was trying her hardest to keep the rest of them safe from harm. Marvellous. Just marvellous!

'Sounds fun,' she said, taking off her shoes, feeling light-headed as she bent down. She'd had another poor night's sleep and, following her morning spent watching the God-awful unicorn movie with Bea, she wanted nothing more than to sit for five minutes on her own and drink a cup of tea in peace, eyes shut, zoning out. It appeared she might have to wait a while before such a thing was possible. 'Mmm. Great,' she murmured when Gabe finally paused for breath. Then she got a grip on herself. 'Coffee, Dan?' she asked, feeling bad for her churlish thoughts when the guy was only doing her a favour, after all. *Make an effort, Zoe.* 'Do you need me to take you to the walk-in clinic – have some-one look at that?' she asked, mentally crossing her fingers that the rest of the day wouldn't be spent in a noisy A&E waiting room. 'Were you able to drive back okay?'

'He did swear a few times in the car,' said Gabe the snitch. 'You *did*, though, Uncle Dan,' he added, when Dan shot him a reproachful look.

'Sorry,' mumbled Dan, hobbling through to the kitchen after her. 'Braking was kind of painful,' he admitted. 'But it's just a twist, nothing serious. Might even teach me to remember my age. Coffee would be great, please.'

Zoe felt herself soften a little. 'Thanks for taking him. You know, I bet Patrick would have done exactly the same thing. Exactly. In fact he'd probably have come home having bought them each a skateboard and all the gear.' She shook her head affectionately, finding it all too easy to imagine the scene. Patrick had always launched into new hobbies with the greatest enthusiasm, as the rowing machine, ice-cream maker and box kites still gathering dust in the cellar could testify.

Dan's face cleared at her comment. She would go so far as to say that he actually looked delighted. 'Really? So I was just . . . doing what Patrick would have done?'

'God, yeah.' She laughed. 'Sometimes I wasn't sure who was the biggest kid in the family. Do sit down,' she added, glancing back from the mug cupboard to see him hovering awkwardly by the fridge. 'Keep the weight off that foot.'

They made chit-chat while the kettle boiled, and Zoe felt her tension start to ebb away. She had always liked Dan after all; he was a good guy, even if, like his brother, he sometimes rushed into a so-called great new idea without actually thinking it through. He told her about painting one of Patrick's flats, and how he was getting to know the tenants from wading through the backlog of all their recent complaints. She hadn't realized quite how hard he had been working on their behalf and her heart swelled with gratitude.

'Thank you,' she said humbly, adding milk to his coffee. 'That's really good of you. Obviously let me know how much I owe you for the paint and everything. I've been meaning to log into the business account and start getting to grips with it, so having to transfer some money over to you will force me to pull my finger out.'

His eyes darted away for some reason, though. 'Don't worry, it's fine, you've got enough on your plate,' he said.

'As if! I'm not having you paying out of your own pocket,' she told him, passing his mug over. 'In fact – wait there,' she added, digging in her purse and getting out the company credit card Patrick had given her. 'Use this for anything you buy online from now on, okay? And save any other receipts for me, so that I can settle up. By the way, I've been meaning to ask: was all the paperwork there with the accounts? I know you said you were going to sort out the VAT return; I hope everything was in order.' She smiled at him. 'No dodgy payments, I take it? Patrick not up to anything naughty behind my back?'

She'd intended the questions to be light-hearted – she *was* joking! – but Dan spluttered on his coffee at her words. Was she going mad or did a weird expression flash across his face even? 'Um . . .' he said, raking a hand through his hair.

'Dan, I'm *kidding*,' she laughed, although she couldn't help peering at him, wondering why he was hesitating like that. Her laugh died away as confusion set in. 'Everything all right?'

He shook his head, recovering himself. 'Yes! Sorry. Yes, all fine. The accounts – of course. My mind went blank for a moment. I was thinking about my own accounts; forgot I'd even taken a look at Patrick's. Yes. No problems. Very straightforward. I've sent everything off to the accountant, just waiting to hear what's owed on the VAT.'

He was talking quickly, seemingly keen to convince her, but Zoe wasn't fooled. Not for an instant. The hair on her arms stood up on end, her mouth becoming dry as he continued in this poor, rambling attempt at covering up. But *what* was he covering up? *Was* there something untoward about Patrick's paperwork?

Before she could investigate further, he had already changed the subject to an idea he'd had about taking Ethan to see some sculptures over the school holidays, and began reeling off a list of ones that were scattered around the capital – from a Barbara Hepworth piece on Oxford Street, to a Rodin at Westminster Palace – and she found herself caught up in his enthusiasm. Yes, Ethan would be thrilled to have his uncle taking this level of interest in him. Then Dan was offering to take Bea out on her bike, because Gabe had mentioned that this was something she and Patrick had always done together, and Zoe's eyes became quite moist with a rush of gratitude, followed immediately by guilt. She wasn't managing to do enough for them; she was still dragging herself through life like a zombie, performing the basic functions but little more, she reprimanded herself. *What do you even DO all day?* she heard Ethan jeer again. Meanwhile, here was Dan, taking care of Patrick's landlording on top of his own life, and still managing to add a bit of flavour and excitement to her family.

'Thank you,' she said, humbly. 'They'd love those ideas.' *Must try harder. Must find the energy*, she told herself as he finished his coffee and hobbled out of the front door. She'd plan a trip to her mum's, she decided on the spur of the moment. Maybe for Easter weekend, cheer everyone up a bit at the seaside, not least her own self.

It was only later on that her thoughts returned to the strangeness of her and Dan's earlier exchange about the accounts; how he'd faltered and stiffened, every inch a guilty reaction. What, exactly, had Dan been hiding? Or was she better off not knowing?

'Don't think I've forgotten,' she muttered to herself with a frown.

Chapter Sixteen

'You did WHAT? Are you CRAZY?' Bridget had all but shrieked to Lydia, when she came over for the full story of the Dan encounter a few evenings ago. 'You told him – wait, let me get this straight. You told him you didn't need any more money from Jemima's dad? You *said* that?'

Lydia put her head in her hands, unable to bear her friend's appalled reaction. 'Don't,' she begged. 'I know it was stupid. I just . . . lost my cool.'

'You lost your cool? Yeah, and now you've lost your income, you pillock. How will you manage now?'

The question had barely left Lydia's head all weekend. Money management was something she'd really had to work at – which was why she was so furious with herself for refusing Dan's offer, in a misplaced fit of pride. Dread sank through her whenever she tried to work out what she and Jemima would do without Patrick's monthly contribution, what they would need to sacrifice. She kept finding herself glancing over her possessions, as if pricing them up to sell:

TV, laptop, bike . . . It wasn't like she lived a lavish lifestyle, by any means. What might she get – a few hundred quid for the lot? That would vanish with the next gas bill. So how else could she scale down their costs? Jemima's gym classes were one of their biggest expenses, but Lydia would rather find herself a second job or take out a loan than tell her daughter she had to give them up. No way.

Maybe the two of them could start sharing her bedroom and let Jemima's room out to a lodger. (But who? And how would Jemima feel about this? She'd hate it. So would Lydia.) Otherwise they could look for somewhere smaller and cheaper to live, she supposed, maybe move further out of London – but that would be such an upheaval, so much stress to bear alone, especially if Jemima then had to change school and all the rest of it. Take on another job? She might have to. Perhaps something she could do at home in the evenings: admin tasks or envelope-stuffing or . . . There had to be some way round the problem, surely. Otherwise she'd end up back at her dad's again, like a washed-up failure. She couldn't bring herself to go there a second time.

Clearing up once Jemima was in bed on Sunday evening, her gaze drifted miserably to the small framed piece of paper that lived on the kitchen wall where she could see it every day. One of the most precious things Lydia owned, she had found it after her mother died: a crumpled list she must have compiled back when there were still dreams and plans to be made for the future. *Favourite places to take Lyddie,* the title read in Eleanor's gorgeous swoopy hand-writing, followed by a series of entries detailing her most beloved Sydney beach, the café where she'd been a Saturday waitress, the sewing shop where she'd bought her vintage fabric and honed her dressmaking skills, the house she'd grown up in and other vital stops along the way. 'An adven-ture, just us two,' her mum had promised her, and Lydia had kept the list as a talisman, vowing that one day she'd make it there with Jemima and they would see all of the sights in her mother's memory.

Except they wouldn't be going there any time soon, now that her finances were about to be decimated, obviously.

God, she wished her mum hadn't died. Not only so that they could hang out on Bronte Beach together or revisit Eleanor's other old haunts, but so that Lydia could ask her what to do, turn to her for some much-needed advice. 'Now let's think this through together,' Eleanor had always said, whether they were discussing Lydia's first crush as a plump twelve-year-old or choosing which subjects to study in the sixth form. There was something about being taken ser-iously that Lydia always found thrilling, as if she mattered, was important. Not that it happened very often these days, mind you. She did her best, but sometimes she felt as if she was destined to be a nobody, or at least nobody special.

She dried her hands and poured a glass of wine, trying to

be positive. Maybe this was actually the shot in her arm she'd been waiting for, she told herself; her chance to be a bit braver and push herself forward for a better-paid and more interesting job. Working in the shop was easy, and had been a useful first step back into employment, but it wasn't exactly what she wanted to do for the rest of her life. There must be other, more lucrative options open to her. Perhaps in time she'd look back at this as a turning point in her life, where she took the wheel and steered herself boldly in a whole new direction. Why not?

Sipping her wine, she began scrolling through the list of part-time jobs available on a recruitment-agency website. Okay, so on a first glance there appeared to be a lot of driving vacancies. Also a ton of telesales 'opportunities'. Some shift work at a processing plant (processing *what?*). Cleaning jobs. Nothing exciting was really leaping out at her, it had to be said.

Yet, she told herself bracingly. Nothing exciting *yet*. Maybe if she adjusted the filters, it would help narrow things down. She went through and unticked every category of job except one marked 'Creative', then clicked Search and scanned the results.

Telesales in an ad agency.

An administrator for a theatre.

A PA role at a business-magazine company.

An internship within a gallery – *Travel expenses paid!* read the ad, as if that would make up for the apparent lack of salary on offer.

Waiting staff for a hotel near Heathrow.

And that was it. Nothing that would fit in with her single-mum set-up and – perhaps more to the point – nothing that called out to her. Spirits sinking, she chastised herself for ever thinking this might be easy; as if her dream job would even be available to her. *Wanted – Costume Designer for West End theatre. We pay really well and will help you sort out any childcare issues, and don't mind if you don't actually have any proper experience. Can you work a sewing machine and sketch cool outfits? Do you love clothes of all kinds? Then you're our woman! Or man, obviously, because we are fair like that. Call us!*

Yeah, right. Meanwhile, back in the real world, she was looking at minimum-wage jobs, unsatisfying roles and long hours across town. That was if she was qualified for them in the first place, she realized, noticing that even the internship required applicants to have a university degree. They probably didn't want someone who had failed their A-levels and was dyslexic and actually pretty rubbish at maths. Would Jonathan even give her a decent reference? He was always teasing her about how disorganized she was, how flaky. Just the other day she had been about to sell a beautiful vase to a customer for six pounds rather than sixty because she'd typed the number in wrong. If it hadn't been for the customer pointing out the mistake, she wouldn't even have noticed.

Panic was starting to set in and she forced herself to get a grip. *Okay. Think, Lydia.* She could take on some evening work to tackle at home while Jemima slept. Data entry. Call-centre stuff, customer service . . .

As she removed the search filters again and scrolled down and down, her optimism crumbled even more. There had to be something else she could do, which would fit in with Jemima and her home life – but if that job existed, she sure as hell wasn't seeing it on this website. Despair enveloped her like a toxic cloud. Why couldn't she manage to be a proper grown-up like everyone else? Sometimes she felt as if she was still that seventeen-year-old girl sobbing at her mother's funeral; as if a part of her had broken that day and she'd never quite managed to move on, blossom into an adult. She must be emotionally stunted or something, because she'd never even managed to have a proper loving relationship, apart from Patrick, and look at how that had turned out. What was wrong with her? Why was she so bad at adulthood?

She closed the laptop, feeling shaky. More to the point, without the money from Patrick, she and Jemima could be in all sorts of trouble. What was to become of them?

Chapter Seventeen

Dan's ankle was thankfully much better by Monday and, as he sat eating breakfast that morning, he felt relatively cheerful as he considered the last few days. His good-deeds spreadsheet had a whole new crop of entries, acting as tiny individual validations. The flat on Whitecliffe Road was newly painted throughout and ready to be let again. It had been raining overnight but the sun was shining once more, casting golden streaks of light on the last wet drops that speckled the windows. He'd topped up the bird feeder recently, and it now provided a buffet to a whole host of feathered visitors. He watched them as he ate, appreciating the free show. Back when he'd been an office drone, he'd never had time to sit and contemplate anything other than the news on his phone, or the list of meetings he had lined up that day, before heading out the door.

A different sort of agenda lay ahead of him this week. There had been three new calls waiting for him when he checked the messages on Patrick's business phone earlier, all from Rosemary, his most demanding tenant. Apparently her burglar alarm had started flashing at six o'clock that morning and still hadn't stopped. It almost certainly meant that the battery was on its way out and needed replacing, but she had sounded increasingly worried with each message, and he had a feeling that the calls would keep coming until he went to deal with it. That was first on the list. Later, he needed to chase up Patrick's accountant about the VAT bill. He cringed anew as he remembered Zoe asking, all innocence, about dodgy payments from Patrick's account. He was pretty sure he'd managed to bluster through a response without arousing her suspicions, but nevertheless, it had felt a perilous moment before he'd eventually twigged that she was joking.

He hadn't yet decided what to do about the direct debit due to go out to Lydia next week, but he'd managed to swipe the business card with Lydia's details from Zoe's fridge at least, pocketing it surreptitiously while she was making him a coffee, so he had prevented one horrendous phone call at least. The card was on the kitchen table in front of him now, like a ticking bomb, and he picked it up and turned it between his fingers, corner by corner, still unsure what – if anything – he should do. *Soft,* read the logo on the card, followed by a W4 address: the Turnham Green end of Chiswick, according to the map on his phone. Lydia had written her name and phone number on the card, plus a little heart.

Curious, he glanced at the website, discovering that it was

a small arty boutique, apparently owned by a Jonathan Browning. Lydia's husband or partner, maybe? Did she own the business or just work there? If the latter, then he doubted that she was being paid a huge amount of money. Maybe she was an heiress or had a massive trust fund or had married someone stinking rich, and therefore didn't need mainten-ance money from Patrick, but having met her, Lydia didn't strike him as someone who led an opulent lifestyle. The phone on which she'd shown him photos of Jemima, for instance, was not a top-of-the-range new model, he seemed to remember. He was pretty sure she hadn't been wearing a wedding ring, either, and she definitely hadn't mentioned any kind of partner, wealthy and shop-owning or not. Women tended to do that when they wanted to make very clear that they were not into you, in Dan's experience.

He put his phone back down, thinking. Patrick might have betrayed Zoe emotionally, but in practical terms he had been very thorough about providing for her and the children. The life insurance he'd arranged had paid out a substantial amount on his passing; the rest of the mortgage cleared in an instant, and lump sums were granted to Zoe, Ethan, Gabe and Bea. Nothing for Jemima, his other daughter, though. Zilch. In death, as in life, she had been airbrushed from the picture. It didn't sit comfortably with Dan. But what was he supposed to do?

To distract himself from this conscience-wrestling, he

phoned Rosemary and assured her that he would go over and look at her burglar alarm. He was about to head off when there was a sudden thud at the window. Swinging round, he was just in time to see the shape of a medium-sized bird – a blackbird perhaps, or the starling he'd seen the other day – batter itself against the glass and drop from view. Oh God. It happened sometimes, birds mistaking windows for air, but there was still something horrible about the soft, meaty thump of flesh meeting glass. He hurried over to peer through the window, but couldn't see the bird anywhere on the ground below. Presumably it had managed to swerve dazedly around and back up into the blue, stunned but somehow aloft.

Hopefully he could do the same, he thought, leaving the room.

'Oh, thank *goodness*. You're so clever. I didn't even *think* about the battery, I was convinced the alarm was flashing because someone was in my flat. A burglar, I mean.' Rosemary gave a small self-deprecating laugh, but her demeanour was subdued. 'I was scared.'

Over on Everlake Road, it had taken Dan a matter of minutes to remove the dying battery from Rosemary's burglar alarm, nip out to the nearest corner shop and buy a replacement, then reattach the device to her wall. Switching it on, to be rewarded by a steady green light rather than a flashing red one, Dan felt something of a fraud to have Rosemary's praise heaped on him when the job had been so straightforward.

'No trouble at all,' he told her, returning the screwdriver to Patrick's toolbox and fastening its clasp. Then, perhaps with more rashness than was wise, he added, 'Any more problems, let me know.'

'Oh, I will. You are good to me, Daniel. A very kind-hearted young man.' She beamed at him. Dressed in a Victorian-style blouse with high collars and tiny pearl buttons, plus a tweedy skirt, she resembled some sort of excellent lady detective from the 1920s. Dan found himself wondering what she'd done for a living when younger. A teacher? A no-nonsense matron?

'It's no trouble,' he repeated weakly with the polite sort of smile he'd always used for aunties and friends of his mum, although he wished she hadn't called him kind-hearted. What with keeping secrets from Zoe and his apparent inability to make a decision about Lydia, he didn't feel at all kind right now.

'And it's no trouble for *me* to put the kettle on,' she replied. 'Tea or coffee?'

He relented because it seemed almost impossible not to. But also because he was starting to feel fond of her. Patrick might have found her annoying but it was obvious that

Rosemary was pretty lonely, at the end of the day. Lonely and rather endearing. 'Coffee, please,' he said.

As he followed her through to the small, gleaming kitchen, Rosemary came to a sudden stop. A magnificently fluffy ginger tomcat was lounging on the table licking a paw with a leisurely air. 'He's not mine,' Rosemary said, hurrying towards the table. 'Come on, Desmond, what are you doing here? Off you go now. Off!' The cat – Desmond – ignored her until she clapped her hands at him. Only then, with a contemptuous glare over one beefy shoulder, did he leap from his perch onto the windowsill, squeeze his considerable girth through the open window and saunter out onto the fire escape. 'Naughty boy,' Rosemary said unconvincingly.

Dan chose to pretend he hadn't noticed the saucer of half-eaten cat food on the floor by the wall. He glossed over the fact that Rosemary had given the cat a name, and that a cushion on one of the kitchen chairs was coated in quite a lot of ginger fur. He was pretty sure Patrick's rental agreements all stipulated that pets were not allowed, but he couldn't summon up the energy to get into a discussion about it. Besides, he had no problem with cats. 'These things happen,' he assured her, thinking about Harvey, the over-friendly tabby that had repeatedly treated as an invitation any open door or window of the Wandsworth flat that he and Rebecca had shared. Harvey would stroll in as if he was a resident there too, friendly and purring, butting his soft head against your legs.

Rosemary busied herself making drinks and arranging a Jenga of sugar-sprinkled shortbread on a plate. Dan's gaze was drawn to the photos on the fridge, mostly fashion pictures, rather unexpectedly, although there was also a photo of a middle-aged couple pinned up with a flamingo-shaped magnet. 'Are these your children?' he asked, peering closer.

'No,' she said, without turning round. 'I don't have children. That's Alan, my nephew, and his wife, Maureen.'

From where Dan was sitting, he could see that Alan and Maureen were probably in their early fifties, and smartly dressed. Alan wore a large expensive-looking watch on his wrist and a smug expression. Maureen sported a bright pink-and-orange flowered dress and a tight perm, and was smirking as she sipped a cocktail through a straw. Dan knew you shouldn't judge on appearance, but all the same, he didn't find himself warming to the pair. 'Nice,' he said, as she set two coffee cups on the table and gestured at him to sit down. 'Are they local?'

'They're in Richmond,' she said, offering him the shortbread.

'Ah, that's handy.' Handy for Dan too, if Rosemary could start ringing up smug Alan rather than him every time she was worried about her burglar alarm or squeaky floorboards. But maybe her nephew was the type who'd sooner jerk a fat thumb in another person's direction and pass the buck. *Land-lord's job, ain't it?* he imagined the man in the photo saying.

'Well, yes, I suppose so, although they're very busy. Always very busy. I've said to them: The door's always open! I do love a visitor – but they have so many friends and Alan's got all these business trips and . . .' Her voice faltered for the first time and Dan felt sorry for her. Also kind of vindicated for reading the photos correctly.

'That's a shame,' he said, so that she didn't have to finish the sentence. Clearly smug Alan and smirking Maureen couldn't be bothered to make time for Alan's lonely old aunt. His own relative! And yet . . . Dan grimaced. And yet wouldn't he be doing the exact same thing if he took Lydia at her word and blanked her and Jemima? They were his relatives too, like it or not. Jemima was his *niece*.

His expression must have changed because Rosemary squinted at him across the table. 'Everything all right, dear?'

He hesitated. 'Not really,' he admitted.

'You can tell me,' she said and for a moment he was almost tempted to blurt out the whole tale: that bad-tempered last night in Hammersmith, Patrick's shocking death, his own determination to make everything right, the discovery of Lydia . . .

'Well . . .' He shook his head. 'It's a long story. Family stuff, you know.'

'I see,' she said, her eyes softening. They were very blue,

he noticed; the blue of Wedgwood plates. Despite every-thing, he felt himself unbending. Maybe she would be a good person to talk to: someone objective. Wise, even. And who else could he tell his secrets to?

'Well,' he said again, still undecided. Then the window rattled and there was Desmond barging his bulky way back inside again, as if refusing to put up with his banishment for a second longer. Manoeuvring onto the windowsill, he dropped to the kitchen floor and walked straight over to the food bowl with an unmistakable swagger of ownership.

'Oh! Desmond.' Rosemary's face became suffused with guilt as the cat began daintily licking the jelly from the chunks of meat. 'Now you mustn't think he's mine,' she gabbled, not quite able to meet Dan's eye. 'I did put a bit of food out for him this morning, because he was wailing so plaintively I thought my heart would break, but—'

'It's fine,' said Dan. Cats were total bullshitters in his opinion. Wailing plaintively, indeed, he thought. This one had spotted a sucker, all right. 'Honestly, I don't mind. As long as he's not ripping up the furniture or anything.'

'Goodness, no. Absolutely not. I would forbid any behav-iour like that in an instant,' Rosemary assured him. Her lower lip wobbled momentarily, then she reached across the table and patted Dan's hand. 'Thank you, darling. It's just nice to have someone to love, isn't it? Something, I should say.' She gazed fondly at the cat. 'I've been leaving my window open so that he can come and go, and I'm always pleased to see him,' she added in a rush of confession.

Dan found himself thinking hard as she went over to make a fuss of the creature. Life was short – too short to be a wanker to people. Whatever Lydia might have said, he wanted to do the right thing. He didn't want to be like Alan, the ignorant nephew who was content to forget about his lonely aunt. He didn't want to be like Patrick, either, and whitewash inconvenient relatives out of his life with excuses or money.

'You were about to tell me something, I think,' Rosemary said, straightening up once more. That blue gaze of hers was so direct, it was hard to look away. 'Let me guess – is it girl trouble? Somebody breaking your heart?'

But Dan, having made his decision, was keen to get going. Cramming a last piece of shortbread into his mouth, he rose to his feet. 'It's not girl trouble,' he confirmed. Well, it kind of was, he supposed, but the story was far too complicated to wade into now. 'I think I've just worked it out for myself anyway. Thanks all the same.'

And then he said goodbye and left, blinking a little as he stepped outside into the light.

Chapter Eighteen

'So what are we pricing these at, Jon?' asked Lydia, kneeling on the floor of the shop, carefully unpacking some bubble-wrapped ceramic hares to put on the shelves. They were beautiful objects, smooth and weighty, about the size of a butternut squash and each one perfectly unique, with their comically long ears and expressive large eyes.

Jonathan was standing at the card carousel, slotting in a bunch of greetings cards. *Bon Voyage! Good luck with your exams! New baby boy!* they exclaimed. 'Two hundred quid?' he said, glancing over his shoulder at her.

'Two hundred? Seriously?' Lydia rocked back onto her haunches, goggling from her boss back to the hare in her hands, then gripping it a little tighter, now that she knew how much it was worth. Two hundred quid – honestly, some people had more money than sense. She would rather run down the street without a bra on than shell out two hundred quid for a posh ornament.

'What, you don't think you can sell any at that price?'

He raised an eyebrow at her, competitive as ever. Tall and broad, with close-cropped salt-and-pepper hair, Jonathan had become Eleanor's best friend practically the day they met, working in a West End theatre together, making costumes and props. 'Tenner says I shift more of them than you do.'

Lydia snorted. 'You're on,' she replied. 'In fact, I'm going to put one in the window now, and if anyone comes in and asks about it, we'll be counting that as my sale. Okay?'

He laughed. 'That's my girl,' he said.

It was the first Monday of the school holidays and Lydia had organized a complicated childcare swap system with Bridget over the fortnight, calling in a couple of days' help from her dad too, in order to make up the hours here and there. Thank goodness for the safety net of friends and family, but all the same, sometimes the net beneath her felt threadbare and liable to fray. It would only take one snag, one tiny break, and the whole thing would unravel, leaving them falling to the ground. Lydia had booked four days off next week, but would be looking after Bridget's son during that time, which sometimes felt harder work than being in the shop. So be it. This was how life went and women managed, propping one another up as best they could.

Clambering into the window, she fiddled around with the display to find the optimum place for the hare. She had rearranged the stock there the week before for an Easter theme, building a 'set' with old wooden crates filled with paper straw and putting together a clutch of felted chickens, a set of gorgeous watercolours of spring flowers, and some smooth, cold marble eggs in shades of rust, pewter and jet. Mina, one of their nicest artists, had made a batch of delicate ceramic flowers too, which Lydia had arranged in a large spotty jug. With a few pastel-toned cushions, and a fringed throw in a soft heathery shade, it all looked very appealing, even if she said so herself.

She moved a couple of striped earthenware pots from a central crate and positioned the hare there instead. Perfect. The April sun shone warm and bright through the window as she rearranged the felted chickens into a line, to better show them off. There. But then, crouched in the window, just as she was about to stand up and clamber out again, she saw someone approaching the shop and her heart gave an uncomfortable thump. Oh, gosh. That wasn't ... that wasn't Patrick's brother again, was it?

'Shit,' she muttered under her breath. It was. It was actually him, walking down the street, peering at the shop fronts as if hunting for one in particular. A particular person, even. It must be a huge coincidence, surely, because he couldn't be looking for her, could he? By now he was almost at the shop and she was still crouching there, frozen awkwardly, as his gaze fell upon her. Then his face cleared and he gave her a tentative smile. He *was* looking for her. But why? What now?

'Everything all right?' asked Jonathan.

'Um . . .' *No.* 'Yeah,' she said. 'Well, I'm not sure actually.' Her instinct was to hide behind one of the crates, but it was too late for that, far too late. The shop bell was jingling with his arrival and so she had to deal with the embarrassment of climbing out of the window and jumping back onto the shop floor in front of him, brushing fake straw off her indigo shirt-dress. Oh Lord, it was all over her tights as well, she realized, plucking frantically at herself. This definitely wasn't the 'Talk to my lawyer' look she'd been able to present to him the other day.

'Hello there,' Jonathan said to Dan, professional as ever.

'Hello,' Lydia added, trying to sound calm. She forced herself to look at him. Just an inch shorter than Patrick, she reckoned, narrower shoulders. A paler, dilute version of Patrick's smouldering dark handsomeness. *I got the looks, he got the brains,* Patrick joked again in her head and she swallowed hard. The problem with brainy people was that they sometimes tripped you up, outsmarted you when you least expected it. 'And what brings you into our shop?' she asked, unable to help drawing herself a little taller in the hope of taking up more space. 'Tell me this is not some spooky random coincidence.'

'Um, hi,' Dan said, with a polite nod in Jonathan's direction. 'It's not a spooky random coincidence,' he confirmed, turning back towards Lydia. 'I nicked your business card from Zoe's fridge. Thought I would pay a visit rather than try and do this on the phone.'

This? What was 'this'? 'Sounds ominous,' she said, feeling alarmed.

'Not at all,' he replied, holding up his hands as if to show her he wasn't carrying any weapons. Which was marginally reassuring, but only just. 'Are you due a lunch break around now by any chance?' he went on. 'Maybe we could go to a café, have a chat.'

She hesitated, then glanced over at Jonathan, who shrugged. 'Up to you,' he said, his gaze flicking from Lydia back to Dan. She could tell her boss was wildly curious to find out what this was about.

Lydia felt as if she had no choice. 'Okay,' she said warily. 'What's the plan?'

'Pub?' Dan suggested, gesturing down the road.

Oh God. Whatever he wanted to say to her was serious enough that he needed alcohol to get through it. She gave a nervous smile. 'Sounds good to me,' she lied.

'So,' Dan began, once they were sitting down together in the nearest pub with a lunch menu each. A melancholy Rod Stewart ballad drifted from the speakers and he found himself wishing he'd given slightly more thought to their meeting venue than simply having steered her this way on impulse. There was a neglected air about the place – the carpet was threadbare in patches, the table between them looked greasy, with a discarded sugar wrapper in the centre, and the padded blue bench they were sitting on had a small tear in its fabric that revealed foam beneath, the colour of an overripe banana. With a potentially tricky conversation bearing down on him, Dan felt unable to concentrate on the list of sandwiches and light bites, and abandoned the laminated menu. 'Listen, I'm sorry to turn up out of the blue like this,' he went on. 'But I've been thinking.'

There was an understatement. Ever since he had stumbled upon the existence of Lydia and her daughter, the knowledge of them had been a lit match in his hand; a lit match that had the capacity to burn a lot of stuff down.

Her face was polite, but anxious too, probably wishing he hadn't come barging back into her life, let alone her shop. She was wearing a belted purple-blue dress and knee-high rust-coloured boots that creaked when she crossed her legs. Her hair was thick and brown, as shiny as a conker as it fell around her face. *Concentrate, Dan*, he reminded himself.

'Basically, the long and the short of it is, I don't think it's fair,' he went on, picking up a creased beermat and spinning it around, just to give his fingers something to do. 'Even though you said you don't want Patrick's money and all the rest of it, that doesn't sit right with me. I kind of think you should still have it.'

'Right,' she said, gazing steadily at him. You could tell she was waiting for the 'But . . .' to follow.

'Yeah.' His next words came out in a rush. 'Because his other kids have been looked after, financially. Like, massively looked after. Big lump sums waiting for them when they're eighteen. Which is quite right, you know; they've lost their father and all. But . . .' He hesitated, then went on. 'But your daughter should be looked after like that too. She was his child as well. And I know you said you didn't need the money now – and I totally respect that, if you really feel that way – but you could always put the monthly payments into a trust fund for her, or something. Start a savings account for when she's older, in case she wants to go off to uni or whatever. What do you think?'

His pulse raced as he waited for her to respond. He tried not to think about Zoe and how her face would collapse if she ever got to hear about this conversation. Was it even legal, what he was proposing? Patrick's business account was still active, as Zoe was one of the company directors and co-signatories, and Dan had reasoned to himself that he wasn't *doing* anything, as much as *not* doing it. Not cancelling the standing order, which – now he came to think about it – he probably wouldn't have permission to cancel anyway. So maybe the status quo was best for everyone. Christ, he hoped so.

'God,' said Lydia, looking dazed. 'I . . .' Her eyes glistened with emotion. 'Are you serious?'

'I'm serious,' he replied. 'I feel bad about this. Patrick's my brother – *was* my brother – but it sounds as if he was a bit of a shit to you. And, look, at the end of the day your daughter is my niece, like you said. We're family. Sort of.'

Lydia nodded. Her lips were pressed so tightly together, the colour blanched from them momentarily. She drummed her fingers on the table and Dan's eye was caught by a silver ring she was wearing, which looked like a tiny Viking helmet. 'What about—' She stumbled over the words. 'His wife? I can't imagine she's very happy about this.'

Ah. Yes. 'She doesn't know,' admitted Dan. 'She's had such a rough time lately, I don't think it would be a great idea to tell her just yet.' He was saying these words as if they came from a place of thoughtfulness, but he knew that it was largely down to sheer cowardice. 'I don't want to deceive her, but on balance, it might be best if I keep shtum and let the payments continue as before.' He pulled a face, feeling conflicted. Had he just nominated himself for worst brother-in-law ever? The other day, when Zoe had talked about reimbursing Dan from the business account, he'd managed to dissuade her, but this wasn't sustainable, he knew. There would come a time when Zoe wanted to take over from Dan and became the one sorting through statements for the accountant. How could he protect her from finding out about Lydia then? He'd have to invent some maintenance company maybe, then switch the direct debit to come from his own account. God, it was all so complicated. There were so many variables.

Lydia exhaled as if she had been holding her breath. 'Thank you,' she said. 'I'm not quite sure what to say, other than thank you. That's really decent of you.'

He looked down at the table, not feeling very decent at all. Wanting to be fair to Lydia was one thing but the business account was now Zoe's money, he reminded himself. Wasn't it actually pretty schmucky of him to turn a blind eye to the maintenance payments? Pretty weak? Yet what else could he do without alerting Zoe to the existence of these new family members?

Lydia was still talking, the colour returning to her face. 'To be honest, I'd been regretting acting so high-and-mighty last time we met, telling you to shove the money and all that. It's not as if I'm rolling in the stuff. All the same, what you're proposing . . . I don't want to come between you and your sister-in-law, or cause any trouble.'

This was welcome news at least. 'I don't want to cause trouble, either,' he said, 'but hopefully she won't find out – not immediately anyway. I can sign off the accounts and pretend I never poked my nose into them. I know it's not the ideal solution, but . . .'

They exchanged a shaky smile across the table. 'Well, thank you again,' she said.

'No problem.' Dan hoped these words would turn out to be accurate. 'And obviously if there's ever anything I can do for you or Jemima, please say.' He was still fiddling with the beermat he realized, putting it down abruptly. 'Since Patrick died, I've been looking after his kids more than before and . . .' He shrugged, feeling bashful. 'Well, I don't have children myself, and I've actually really enjoyed getting to know them a bit better.'

'That's nice,' she said, her eyes crinkling at the edges. 'You and Patrick – were you close?'

'Sort of. In that big-brother, little-brother way, I guess,' he replied. 'I always looked up to him – he did everything first, whereas I was forever trying to catch up. But yeah, we did get on, most of the time.' His face froze, remembering their last terrible argument, and he went on quickly, 'We were pretty different, but it was always just the two of us, growing up. Now I'm the only child and it feels really odd.'

'I bet,' she said. 'I always wanted a brother. I wouldn't have minded a sister, for that matter. Being an only child is a bit rubbish sometimes.'

Another tentative smile was exchanged. 'Are you from round here?' he asked, suddenly interested in finding out about her. 'You sound very West London. Not that that's a bad thing – I grew up in Hammersmith myself.'

'South Acton,' she replied. She had delicate freckles, he noticed, carefully dotted across the bridge of her nose. 'Let me guess, you were one of the William Morris boys.'

He laughed in surprise. 'Got it in one. Did you go there?'

'No, worse luck, I went to a dump in Ealing, but my friend Bridget was madly in love with a boy from William Morris, so we ended up going to a lot of parties with sixth formers from there.' She rolled her eyes. 'Those were the days, eh? Wild and irresponsible.'

'We thought we knew it all,' he agreed. 'I was going to be a pop star – for about five minutes anyway. I had the hair gel and everything.'

She burst out laughing. 'Seriously? I was going to be a fashion designer. I could have made you some cool outfits.'

'That must have been where I went wrong,' he said. 'My outfits were definitely not cool enough.' He glanced down at his faded blue grandad shirt and jeans. 'Still aren't, for that matter. Damn it.'

They seemed to have arrived at a friendlier footing, as if by swapping teenage stories, the armour had dropped a fraction from their bodies. 'Do you still have family locally?' Lydia asked after a moment.

'My parents are over in Brentford,' he said. 'I've been trying to pop in when I can,' he added. This was a bit of an exaggeration, but he was planning to go back again this week, so it wasn't a complete lie. He wanted to impress her, he realized in the next moment with a jolt of self-awareness, or at least beef up the evidence that he was a good guy.

'I bet they appreciate that,' she said, eyes soft. 'I can't imagine how tough it must be for all of you, dealing with the loss, I mean.'

He nodded. 'It keeps taking me by surprise,' he admitted. 'And not a good surprise, either. Like, going over to Mum's house, I think of him all the time. Whenever I walk past the pub where we spent the last evening of his life, I'm back there remembering it. Even seeing the dead tree in my garden brings him to mind.'

'A dead tree? Why, did he kill it or something?'

'No, he was supposed to be helping me cut it down and get rid of it, the day after . . .' The rest of the sentence failed Dan unexpectedly, and he stared down at the maroon carpet trying to find the words. 'The morning that he . . .' He shook his head, tongue-tied. 'We were supposed to be cutting it down together,' he said eventually.

She seemed to understand. 'And you don't feel you can now?'

'I've got some kind of block about it,' he mumbled, hoping she wouldn't find this – *him* – too weird. He had already surprised himself by being far more open with her, emotionally, than he would have been if the two of them had met a few months earlier. Grief seemed to have left him raw, scraping off a topmost layer that usually protected him from exposing his feelings with this much honesty. 'Anyway.' He grabbed a menu as a distraction. 'I'm supposed to be getting you lunch here. What would you like? And should we be concerned about ordering food from a place that can't spell "potato"?'

She peered at the other menu. 'I've always loved a jacket spud with an actual toe,' she remarked. 'But I'm game to risk my life, if you are?'

He laughed again. Despite everything, there was something so likeable about her, so warm. 'Bring it on,' he said.

Chapter Nineteen

On Wednesday, Dan had arranged a day out with Ethan, suggesting an art walk, from the Greenwich peninsula over the Thames and up into Queen Elizabeth Park, that featured all sorts of interesting-looking outdoor artworks. It was a blustery day, with gusts of wind strong enough to blow a seagull off-course, but the sky was bright and clear, and the Thames was Air Force blue when they arrived in Greenwich. As soon as they caught sight of the first piece on the trail – a huge steel construction that resembled an inverted electricity pylon, nose-diving to the ground – Ethan's face lit up and Dan knew he'd backed a winner.

'Whoa,' the boy marvelled, staring at the vast sculpture in awe. 'How do they even keep this thing up?'

It was a serious piece of engineering, no doubt about it. With the gleaming towers of the Isle of Dogs in the distance and the rumble of building works around the O2 arena ever-present, the sculpture felt outlandish and witty, a piece of crash-landed nonsense amidst so much industry. 'It's called

"A Bullet from a Shooting Star",' Dan read from his phone, 'and it weighs fifteen tonnes. And get this, it took one hundred and twenty tonnes of concrete, and foundations going twenty-five metres deep, to anchor it in place. Bloody hell.'

They gazed at it together, wowed.

'I love it,' said Ethan, taking photos from different angles. 'Even if the stuff we're making at SculptShed seems, like, totally lame now.'

'It's great,' Dan agreed. 'Ridiculously great. And all this fencing around it makes it feel like something from outer space, that's dangerous to get close to. Watch out for aliens. You never know when one might be creeping up behind you . . .'

'Uncle Dan!' Ethan yelped, laughing, as Dan made a sudden grab for him.

'*Take me to your leader*,' Dan droned in his best alien's voice.

Further around the peninsula they passed an artwork that was, effectively, a slice of a rusting sand-dredger, resting in the shallow waters of the Thames, with the water and wind passing freely through the open lower deck. The blank-faced skyscrapers that glinted on the other side of the river made the dredger seem like a relic from the past, industrial and derelict compared to the moneyed towers beyond.

'Cool,' breathed Ethan, peering over the railings. 'It's like one of those cross-section diagrams. Dad would have loved this,' he added wistfully. 'He loved poking around old docks and shipyards, didn't he?'

'He did,' agreed Dan. They stared down at the river together, the wind tugging at their jackets and hair, and Dan tried not to think about his brother's lifeless body in the water, tossed about by the current. 'Let's keep going,' he said, repressing a shiver.

They walked on around the O2 arena, with the sticky-looking mudflats to their left and the cable cars crossing the river ahead of them. Next on the art trail was a faintly disturbing bronze sculpture of twisted mannequin limbs on a massive scale ('Whoa!' was Ethan's response), and then they came to Antony Gormley's enormous Quantum Cloud piece set on a platform a small distance out in the water. The sculpture initially reminded Dan of a murmuration, a huge gathering of birds in the sky, although as they drew closer he changed his mind, deciding it was more reminiscent of a metal dandelion clock with a man's figure visible within.

'It reminds me of static on a screen,' Ethan decided, 'with someone trapped inside.'

'There's something eerie about it,' Dan agreed.

'Apparently it questions the reality of the self to the world and evokes the quantum age, suggesting an unstable relationship between energy and mass,' Ethan read from a description he had found online.

'Exactly what I was about to say,' Dan replied. They stood

staring at it for a while, the wind rustling through the rushes at the edge of the river. 'Although right now, I've got to say, my stomach is suggesting an unstable relationship between hunger and lunch. Shall we find somewhere to eat?'

Over packets of sandwiches, sitting on a bench nearby, Ethan caught Dan up with the news from his world. So far during the holidays he'd been to the cinema with a couple of mates, Zoe had taken him and his siblings bowling and to a climbing wall, and they'd been over to see Dan's parents for Sunday lunch. Dan, who had become finely tuned to the atmosphere in his brother's family, like a human seismometer alert for emotional tremors, felt cautiously satisfied. That all sounded pretty good, he reckoned. Zoe was getting everyone out and about, they were having fun together rather than moping around. Like a normal family, in fact.

News delivered, Ethan became distracted, as a series of beeps sounded from his phone and he peered down at it, reading messages and laughing softly.

'Who are you chatting to?' Dan asked after a minute, when it appeared he had been forsaken in favour of some digital bants.

'Oh! Sorry, Uncle Dan. Just a friend,' Ethan said, his thumbs a blur of movement as he fired off a reply. There was something joyful and open about his face as he read another message and laughed again. 'I sent him some of the photos I took earlier and he . . . We're chatting about them.'

Dan gazed out at the Gormley sculpture again as his nephew caught up on his social life. From this angle, you couldn't see the man within the cloud of shapes any more; there was the strange conundrum of it being simultaneously invisible, yet there. Just like Lydia had been until now, he reflected, then pulled a face at the way his mind had leapt so quickly back to her. In truth, though, he had thought about her a lot since their pub lunch. Things had taken a turn for the confusing, as he and Lydia had chatted more and he'd realized that . . . well, if he was honest with himself, he'd realized that he liked her. Okay, fancied her a bit too. Not that anything could, or would, ever happen between them, when she and Patrick had already had a relationship and there was this whole minefield of a back-story looming large. It was unthinkable. Anyway, wasn't there something a bit pathetic about the idea of latching on to Patrick's ex, as if he was trying to prove a point or something?

(*Was* he trying to prove a point? Was this his lame attempt at retribution, after what Patrick had told him during their last evening together?)

Don't think about that, Dan. He was not thinking about that. Oh God, but suddenly it was impossible to think about anything coherently, to order his thoughts in any kind of sensible format. All he knew was that he had enjoyed talking to Lydia. That she was pretty and funny. That she had tiny, beautiful freckles, and noisy boots and long graceful fingers. Even her ears were sweet, he had noticed at one point, when she tucked her hair behind them. Like small, perfect shells. But he shouldn't be noticing these things at all, he reminded himself in anguish. He must not think of her in any way other than—

'Uncle Dan! I said: can I open the crisps now?'

'Yes, sure.' God, he had totally zoned out just then. 'Sorry, I was miles away.'

'I could tell. I should have nicked your Maltesers,' Ethan said. He shoved a handful of crisps in his mouth and crunched. 'Dad always used to say, whenever I looked like that, "What's her name then?"'

Dan nearly choked on his sandwich. Had he been that obvious? 'Well—' he blustered, but Ethan was still talking.

'I didn't have the heart to tell him I preferred boys,' he said with a brittle laugh. 'Good old Dad. Always there with the assumptions.'

Dan struggled to swallow the half-chewed bread in his mouth. Whoa. Had he heard that correctly? Had Ethan just coolly dropped a gigantic coming-out bomb into the conversation? Bloody hell. He thought frantically, knowing that whatever he said next had to be exactly right: support-ive and accepting and loving. He felt a flush of pride too. Ethan trusted him, he realized. He trusted him with this big, important piece of news. 'Do you think your dad knew how you felt?' he asked, trying to sound casual. 'About . . .

preferring boys, I mean.' He risked a glance at his nephew's face to see that Ethan was staring out at the river, looking remarkably untroubled.

'Nah,' he replied, the wind lifting a lock of his gingery hair, then dropping it again. 'Mum knows, but I asked her not to tell him. He would have been disappointed in me, I reckon.'

There was just the slightest tension around his jaw to give away the fact that Ethan was not quite as nonchalant as he aimed to appear. Dan ached to hug him. He actually felt a pain in his own chest. Should he hug him?

'He might have been surprised,' he said gently instead. He didn't want the hug to stopper the conversation before it had run its course. 'And it might have taken him a bit of time to get his head round the idea, but I know he wouldn't have been disappointed in you. Definitely not. He was proud of you, E.'

Ethan made a scoffing noise in his throat, before attacking the crisp packet once more. 'Not sure about that,' he muttered.

'He was your dad – he loved you,' Dan said. Whatever unthinking macho crap Patrick might have come out with about classical music being 'gay', he was not a complete dinosaur when it came to love and all its variations. 'Okay? He loved you so, so much, and would have carried on loving you whatever you told him about yourself. Hundred per cent.'

Licking the salt off his fingers, Ethan folded the empty

crisp packet into a neat triangle. He still didn't look wholly convinced. 'Maybe,' he said with a shrug.

There was silence for a moment, bar the rushing of the wind and the tinny clatter of an empty Red Bull can that went bouncing along in front of them. 'Remember the first time I picked you up from SculptShed and you asked me about what happened, the last night I saw your dad?' Dan said. 'And you were quite fierce with me because you'd over-heard your mum saying stuff, and you asked me outright: was it my fault that he'd died?'

Ethan looked down at the ground. 'Yeah, sorry about that,' he said gruffly. 'I just—'

'No – no need to apologize,' Dan put in. 'I'm not saying it to make you feel bad. It was more that when you rounded on me like that – and it was pretty brave of you to do so, by the way – I sat there thinking how proud your dad would be of you, for taking it up with me. For daring to ask that question.'

'Well . . .'

'Genuinely. I swear. I thought how proud he would be if he could see you fighting his corner, tackling a difficult con-versation on his behalf.' He glanced across at his nephew again, deciding that this was the right moment to throw an arm round his shoulders. There. 'And if you'd told him what you've just told me, he'd have recognized that took guts too. No doubt about it.'

They sat there for a few seconds together, gazing out at the sludgy Thames and the big sky and glittering sky-scrapers, and Dan thought to himself: Yes, he was pretty sure that had gone okay, he was pretty sure he had said the right thing. Until Ethan wriggled out from under him, saying, 'Okay, this has gone weird. Shall I open the Maltesers now?'

Dan laughed. 'Yeah, I reckon. Then we should get going. Next stop – the cable car. I've never been on it before, have you?' He grinned, feeling a burst of boyish excitement at the prospect. Maybe he wasn't doing *all* of this from the good-ness of his heart.

Walking along together, chatting about cable cars and ferries and boats, it was almost as if their earlier conversa-tion hadn't happened. But it had, and it felt special, like Ethan had trusted him with something really precious. Dan hugged it to himself for the rest of the day.

Chapter Twenty

Hey, Dan, read the back of the postcard. The front showed a manky-looking alpaca – or llama? – amidst tufty grass with mountains in the background. *Bolivia is awesome! Went to Salar de Uyuni – tons of flamingos and mad cacti. Soaked in hot springs under moonlit sky necking singani (white grape brandy – lethal). Off to a national park somewhere tomorrow – apparently you can go sandboarding! And see jaguars! Love Tiggy x*

It was hard to read the postcard without a stab of envy, but Dan contented himself with the fact that, as the Easter holidays progressed, entries on the Patrick spreadsheet were accumulating thick and fast. He dealt with a dodgy radiator and a broken light fitting for a couple of the tenants, and was delighted to hear there had already been several viewings on the Whitecliffe Road flat that he'd spent so long painting. 'No takers yet, but there's lots of interest,' the estate agent oozed. After the success of the art trail with Ethan, he'd taken Bea for a bike ride the very next day, and promised Gabe that he would sort out another skateboarding session soon – solo this time. He also offered to babysit for Zoe on Friday night, for which she eagerly thanked him.

The goals he had set himself, the list of Patrick's best qualities he had drawn up – great dad, loving husband, successful businessman – Dan was able to look at them now and think yes, he was filling the gap. He was stepping into the absence and being there when it counted. Not such a loser after all, he told himself with a nod of satisfaction.

In short, he was feeling – dare he say it? – pretty pleased with his own efforts as he parked outside his parents' house on Thursday afternoon, ready for another shot at the casual drop-in. Caring son? Tick. This time he had come prepared with a bunch of flowers for his mum, a book he was lending his dad, and a load of photos on his phone to show them, of Bea on her bike from earlier on. She and he had spent quite some time beforehand decorating said bike to look like a unicorn and she had pedalled along, shouting, 'Fly, Mirabelle, fly!', which had been outrageously cute. He couldn't help noticing people smiling and pointing out the unicorn-bike, plus its adorable rider, to one another. But then he found himself thinking about Jemima, Lydia's daughter. Was she a unicorn-lover too, with a similarly rich imaginary interior life? Did she and Lydia go out for bike rides together? Was she exuberant like Bea or a more introverted type like Ethan?

The questions persisted all morning with no easy answers. Should he phone Lydia again? he wondered. Ask if he could meet Jemima? Maybe he could dig out some photos of Patrick for her, put a potted biography together, just so that when in the future Jemima asked – as she was sure to do – some serious questions about her dad, Lydia had something to show her. Besides, it would be an excuse to contact her once more, he thought eagerly, before remembering Zoe and immediately feeling disloyal. He sighed, knowing it would be a huge betrayal: of her and his own brother as well. What was he getting himself into here? Whose side was he on anyway? And yet doing nothing didn't seem an option, either – it felt like the coward's way out.

Arriving at his parents' house, he was distracted from the dilemma when he noticed that the picture he hated of him and Patrick had been moved back to centre stage in the display once more. He slid it behind a large photo of the grandchildren while Liz went to put the flowers he'd brought in water, then sat there in the overheated living room being the dutiful son while she told him her news. He'd forgotten how long it could take her to tell a fairly boring story about some fairly boring people that he had never met, nor had any inclination to meet, but he did a passable job of looking interested and engaged all the same. Or so he thought anyway, but he must have drifted off for a moment or two because suddenly she flung her hands up, exclaiming, 'You're not listening to a word I'm saying, are you?'

'I am,' he protested.

'I know you're not, because I just told you that Arthur next door got engaged to a golden retriever and you said, "That's nice".' She folded her arms across her chest, eyeing him suspiciously. Liz Sheppard had always had a laser-like gaze, able to spot from a mile away the telling signs that a son was bunking off school, not eating his vegetables or keeping something from her. 'He's not engaged to anyone, by the way, least of all a dog,' she clarified. 'But now I'm wondering what's going on with you, up there.' She tapped the side of her head and gave him her most penetrating look. She wasn't quite shining a bright torch into his eyes, but she might as well have been. 'Go on, let's hear it. What's on your mind?'

'Mum! It's nothing.' He really needed to work on his poker face.

'Is it a girl? *Is* it? Only I was saying to your dad the other night, it would be nice if you could find someone new. Move on from Rebecca, once and for all.' Then her lips clamped together with a guilty expression as if she had spoken out of turn.

'What?' asked Dan. 'Why are you looking like that?'

'Ah . . .' Liz and Derek Sheppard had been together since they were sixteen and were of the generation that stubbornly insisted marriage was for life, however disappointing the relationship might turn out to be. She had never said as much, but Dan knew that she'd been deeply troubled by his divorce, seeing it as a failure of catastrophic proportions. 'Well, now.'

'Mum, just say it. What's happened?'

Liz shifted slightly in her seat, folding her hands in her lap. 'I bumped into her dad on the High Street last week, who told me she . . . well, she's having a baby.'

There was a moment of silence as Dan remembered Rebecca's last cryptic post on Facebook. *Big day tomorrow!* Presumably she'd been going for a scan or something. Not a job interview. He swallowed. 'A baby.' His stomach churned. How could she? he thought. How *could* she?

'I don't want children,' she had told him, the last time he had broached the subject, some years after Gabe's birth. In fact it must have been when Patrick announced that he and Zoe were expecting baby number three, when Dan's feelings about fatherhood had become a permanent ache. It turned out that Rebecca hadn't changed her mind on motherhood, though; far from it. 'I just don't want to be a mum,' she'd said. 'Sorry, Dan. But I think it looks really boring, to be honest. And bloody hard work.'

Dan had accepted her decision – you couldn't force someone you loved to have a child they didn't want, after all – but in private had felt devastated. Because seeing Patrick and Zoe with their children didn't look boring at all to him. It looked really lovely. Joyful. Meaningful.

'Must be strange for you,' his mum said, her forensic stare now one of concern.

Strange – that was one word for it. Cheated – there was

another. So maybe Rebecca had wanted kids all along, only not with *him*. Having a baby with hunky Rory was a far more appealing prospect, obviously. 'Yes,' he managed to croak, trying not to show how much it hurt. 'Oh, well. Nothing to do with me any more.'

She wasn't a touchy-feely sort of mum, Liz – she'd always been more inclined to whack her boys with a tea-towel, growing up, rather than shower them with displays of affection, but she reached over now and squeezed his hand, which was about as sentimental as she ever got. 'There's someone much better out there for you,' she said. 'I know it, Daniel. You're a good lad, I've always said so. Our family has gone through a terrible time lately, but there are better days ahead, you wait. We'll get there, eh?'

'We will,' he said, comforted by her uncharacteristic tenderness. Then he changed the subject. 'Let me show you some photos of Bea, before I forget,' he said, pulling out his phone. Seeing her face soften with fondness and love as she scrolled through the pictures, it dawned on him belatedly that she and his dad also stood to be greatly affected by the discovery of Lydia and Jemima. This was another grandchild for them to dote on, another piece of Patrick for them to love. Surely they'd want to know her, to fold her into the family? Wouldn't it be wrong of him to deny them this?

He stared down at his knees, his thoughts in a tangle. Living with his secrets felt like being trapped inside a lie, betraying people he loved. But what was he supposed to do?

'So whatever he says to the contrary, Gabe has to be in bed, lights out, the works, by nine o'clock at the absolute latest, okay? Otherwise he will be vile tomorrow and we'll all know about it.'

'I am deeply insulted,' said the vile one, who was trying to balance a tennis ball on his head across the room.

'Don't worry, I have my cattle prod,' said Dan. 'I'll make sure he gets enough beauty sleep.'

'Hey,' grumbled Gabe as the tennis ball fell off his head and rolled along the carpet. 'I don't need *beauty* sleep, actually. Yuck. Who wants to be *beautiful*?'

'Ugly sleep then,' said Zoe, pulling a face at Dan. She was having a rare girls' night out with her friends and staying over at Clare's, which she'd been looking forward to ever since Dan had offered his babysitting services. Putting on a proper face of make-up and spritzing herself with perfume had been surprisingly uplifting, but now that she was all dressed up and about to leave, she was having nervous flutters about the whole idea. There was a part of her that was desperate to drink cocktails and strut her stuff on a sticky dance floor, just let go and leave her grief at the door for one night – but there was a different part of her that was scared

about doing so. Scared to be out in the bright lights, surround-
ed by people drunkenly having fun, when she was this bruised
and damaged version of her old self, vulnerable to everything.

Besides, what sort of a look was it for a grieving widow to
be dancing the night away? What did it say to the rest of the
world: that she didn't care? She was dreading bumping into
one of the school mums, for instance, and having it whispered around the playground that she was a heartless bitch.
Earlier that day she'd been back to the GP and confessed her
worries aloud on this score, but Dr Gupta had been very
clear. 'You are still allowed to be happy even while you're
sad,' she'd said firmly, looking Zoe straight in the eye. 'In
fact I really encourage you to find happiness whenever you
can. It doesn't demean or define your grief in any way. Quite
the opposite. Moments of happiness will be what get you
through this time and out the other side, okay? Now then.'
She'd steepled her fingers together, her gaze steady. 'How
about the therapy we discussed last time? Have you taken any
steps to talk to a professional?'

'Not yet,' Zoe confessed, remembering how the booklet
was still at the bottom of her handbag, where it had been
stuffed two weeks ago.

'I think it would help, if you can take that step. What
have you got to lose?'

'Anything else?' Dan asked now, and Zoe jerked back to
the present.

'Um. No. I'll be back by ten tomorrow morning. Any problems, check with Ethan first, then ring me. Bea will hopefully stay asleep now, but if she has a bad dream, try reading her a story in a slow voice. She might wet the bed – sorry – but if it's the middle of the night, just grab a sleeping bag from the cupboard; let me show you—'

'Don't worry, I can manage,' Dan interrupted, putting a hand on her arm as she made a move towards the stairs. 'Honestly. It's only a night. I'll look after them. Go and have a good time.'

'What if there's a burglar?' called Gabe, who was now trying to roll the tennis ball along his arm. He had been prac- tising this all week, with the result that there had been a constant backdrop of small thudding sounds and disap- pointed groans coming from whichever room he happened to be in.

'There won't be any burglars, but if any are mad enough to try, we'll water-pistol them out of your window,' Dan replied, which earned a delighted 'Cool!' in response.

Zoe wished she wasn't going at all now. Burglars, wet beds, over-excited children . . . There were too many things that could go wrong. Plus she was already having second thoughts about her dress; it was a clingy black number that clung a bit too tightly after all the crisps she'd been eating, and she'd just remembered that it had a habit of riding up her thighs. Also her roots were coming through where she hadn't been to the hairdresser's lately and . . . Oh, what was the point? She should stay home, she wasn't ready for this.

'They'll be fine,' Dan said, reading her expression. 'Go on, shoo. Go wild, have fun and don't come back tomorrow without a storming hangover at the very least.'

She smiled faintly. Sod it, she was only going out with her old uni friends; they wouldn't care about her dress or her hair, she reminded herself. Also, if she ended up a mess, they would have her back, just as she'd have theirs. 'Okay. Thank you,' she said. 'I'll do my best. See you in the morning. Bye, boys. Be good!'

And then she was walking through the door with her overnight bag and breathing in the cool evening air. The street lights were gleaming smudgily through the darkness, she could smell the topnotes of amber from her perfume, and a frisson went through her suddenly at the sheer novelty of being out on her own at this time of night. It had been ages. Months. She could do this, she told herself, as she clutched her bag a little tighter and set off.

Several hours later Zoe was in a club called Market, slightly unsteady on her feet after necking too many Happy Hour bargain drinks. To her relief, the evening had been really fun so far. First, they'd had dinner in a Mexican restaurant, where everyone had swapped funny stories (even her!) and caught up on the gossip, and then, since arriving at the club, they'd been dancing like they were eighteen again, making up daft routines and pratting about. Dare she say it, she actually felt wonderfully normal again, as if she'd been allowed out of her misery prison for a brief carefree holiday. It was so good to lose herself in the music and dance! Now she was at the bar, still absent-mindedly swaying to the beat while she waited to be served.

'You've got very sexy legs, darling,' she heard, and turned to see that a man wearing a horrible fake-leather jacket had appeared beside her.

'Pardon?' she said. He had a sweaty face and his eyes kept flicking from side to side as if he was on something. Mid-forties, scrawny, weaselly-looking, she thought.

'SEXY LEGS. YOU.' He jabbed a finger at her. 'YOU'VE GOT SEXY LEGS.'

Zoe stepped back because spit was flying in her face. 'Oh, right. Thank you,' she said automatically. Then she turned towards the bar, willing the barman to look at her and take her order, fast. Also wishing that she hadn't just said thank you to the weasel, like it made any difference what he thought, like she was grateful.

'Very sexy. Wouldn't mind having those legs wrapped around me,' he leered.

She ignored him. He wasn't easy to put off, though, looming closer.

'Oi. I'm talking to you. I said, I wouldn't mind having those sexy—'

'I heard what you said.' She put her elbow down on the sticky bar, trying to establish a barrier between his space and hers, wishing he'd go away. Her fleeting joyfulness was in danger of evaporating. 'But I'm not interested.'

He leaned against her shoulder; she could smell his gross sweet aftershave mingled with the stink of beer. 'You're not interested?' he repeated. She wasn't looking directly at him, but felt his mood change in the next instant. An angry exhalation, followed by: 'Well, fuck you, then. No need to get up yourself, darling, I only said you had nice legs. Jesus Christ. Tight bitch.'

Once upon a time she might have been cowed by his nastiness, but life had been so dire recently that she no longer felt anything could touch her. *You think that will upset me? Think again, mate.* 'I don't give a shit what you think about my legs. It's not your place to comment on them,' she retaliated, but he wasn't listening.

'I gave you a *compliment*, and that's all you can say: *not interested*?' He was shouting now, full blast, spit raining everywhere. 'When you're dressed like that? Prick-tease, that's what you are. All I'm trying to do is give you a compliment. Why do you have to be such a bitch?'

God, she hated it when men thought you owed them the goddamn world just because they had made some pervy comment about your body that you hadn't even asked for in the first place. 'I don't want your compliments. Don't you get it?' she yelled back, suddenly furious. Out came all the anger she'd been squashing down since Patrick's death, a torrent of hot rage. How dare he? 'I'm not a bitch, I'm not a prick-tease, I'm having a night out with my friends. What part of that do you not understand? Four mojitos and a gin and tonic, please,' she added frantically, seeing the barman glance her way.

'Fucken' bitch,' said the man, but at least he staggered away from the bar and left her in peace, no doubt intending to latch straight onto some other woman, in the hope of a better reception. Ugh. Good riddance.

She felt her strength falter with the relief of his disappearance. Her hands trembled as her anger subsided and she had to grip the bar, tears prickling her eyes. *It's okay. You're okay*, she told herself. *Don't get upset about a waste of space like him.* All the same, his whiplash flip to aggression had been horrible. She wanted to go home all of a sudden. Her skin was too thin for confrontation, and she felt bruised from the encounter. Plus her feet were killing her and the music was too loud. She wished she could transport herself to the safety of her sofa this minute, with the comfort of having her babies sleeping soundly mere metres away.

'Four mojitos and a – what was it, a vodka tonic?' the barman bellowed just then.

'Gin and tonic, please,' she replied, dabbing a tissue to

wasn't prepared for the boy to be quite so monosyllabic this time, all shrugs and gaze-avoiding, despite his best attempts. Hoping to engage, Dan suggested that the two of them go to a classical music concert sometime – 'You could educate me!' – and when that received a subdued response, he mentioned that there was a good zombie film on tonight and maybe they could watch it together?

'Nah,' Ethan said, offhand. He was staring at the screen of his laptop, playing a shoot-'em-up game, and glanced around in an *Are you still here?* sort of way a moment later. Dan took his cue and left. Well, he'd tried, he told himself, trudging downstairs again in defeat.

Feeling useless, he opened up Facebook on his phone and was unable to stop himself from seeking out Rebecca. Since his mum had told him the news about her, bitterness had taken root inside him. How dare she happily get on with her life, after what she'd done? It was like someone walking away from a car crash without a backward look. *I don't care about you.*

Oh Christ, there it was: a photo of a black-and-white ultrasound scan, along with Rebecca's caption: 'Thrilled to announce that Rory and I are going to be parents. Due Halloween, can you believe! No rude comments!!'

Bile rose sourly in his throat. Talk about smug. '*Thrilled to announce*', as if she were a member of the Royal Family or something. How was it that Rebecca could have behaved so deceitfully, betrayed him so terribly, and yet good things still happened to her? You could argue – as he had done in his own head many times – that if it hadn't been for Rebecca's treachery, Patrick would still be alive today. Life would have carried on as normal and Dan would currently be discovering the Bolivian salt flats with Tiggy, sporting the best tan of his life, instead of attempting to be the human sponge for his brother's family and soak up all their grief.

'Screw you,' he said under his breath. He felt mad with hatred suddenly, consumed by it. He couldn't remain silent. He was too resentful, too worked up.

He skipped back to the message of condolence she'd sent him – *Devastated to hear the news about Patrick* – and, before he could stop himself, typed a reply, fingers shaking. *You've got a fucking nerve, Bex. He told me, you know, about the two of you. Your shitty little secret. So don't you dare give me your fake sympathy and crocodile tears. I couldn't care less what you think.* And then, just for the hell of it and because he was too full of rage to pause long enough to think twice, pressed Send.

Fuck it, he'd had enough of turning the other cheek. He'd had enough of being blamed for what had happened to Patrick when there were other people in the equation. It wasn't all *my* fault, he thought, slamming his phone back down again.

★

The next morning, after a terrible night's sleep, Dan couldn't help feeling as if the children had conspired to give him one set of challenges after another. Or maybe this was, in fact, merely a true reflection of what it meant to be a parent. First of all, Bea woke up at the crack of dawn and, as Dan peered blearily in the cupboards for cereal boxes, sighed, 'Daddy always used to make *pancakes* when it was the weekend.' Perhaps guilt over his message to Rebecca had left him vulnerable to such emotional manipulation (so far no reply) or perhaps it was the chance to do something Patrick-related for his niece and chalk up another good deed. Whatever it was, seconds later there was Dan googling pancake recipes on his phone and whipping up a lumpy batter.

Then, when the boys eventually shambled downstairs, Ethan looking particular peaky as if he had been up all night shooting gangsters on his laptop, Dan felt obliged to nourish them with rounds of scrambled egg on toast. *See, I can look after them – I can do a good job,* he told himself doggedly, only for Gabe to throw a forkful of scrambled egg at his brother during an outbreak of arguing, and for tempers to combust all over again. At the sight of the eggy splatters on the window and wall, Dan's patience finally evaporated. 'Boys!' he cried in dismay, only for Ethan to take offence at being included in the scolding when he hadn't thrown *anything*. He'd gone storming off upstairs, leaving the rest of his breakfast untouched. So no, babysitting hadn't been a total success overall.

Aware that Zoe was due back at any moment, Dan frantically cleaned everything up, then tried to make amends between his nephews, wanting the house to be harmonious when their mother returned. It wasn't to be, though. Both boys were white-faced and surly, no doubt as a direct result of Dan's lax bedtime-enforcement the night before. They were still so angry too, he realized. Angry with the world and how it was possible that their dad could be snatched away from them without warning. The revelation was sobering, especially as Dan had been secretly priding himself on how much time he'd spent with them. He'd been kidding himself, though, if he thought that had changed anything. Taking his nephews and niece out a couple of times to fun activities wasn't anywhere near enough to make up for the loss of their dad. Didn't even register, in fact. For the first time since he had begun his sabbatical, Dan felt the weight of what he was trying to achieve and wondered if it was even possible.

Still, at least he had given Zoe a night away, he reminded himself, drying the egg pan and putting it back in the cupboard. Even if she did look wan and queasy as she arrived back at the house soon afterwards, her eyes narrowing at the edges, as if the weak morning light alone was triggering an automatic headache upgrade from God-awful to Life-threatening.

'Good night?' he asked, as she headed for the espresso machine.

'Mostly,' she said cryptically.

He decided not to hang around too long – sometimes a hangover was best managed in private – but then, just as he was about to leave, she surprised him with the news that she was taking the kids to her mum's place in south Wales the following week. 'Oh,' he said, deflating a little. Was that disappointment he was feeling? 'For the whole week?'

'Yeah, we're heading off on Monday. I need a break, to be honest. I need my mum. Plus my brother lives nearby too, and he and his husband have been so supportive. It'll be good to spend a bit of time with them all.'

So supportive, Dan repeated in his head, unable to prevent a sting of jealousy. More supportive than him? he wanted to ask, as if it was some kind of competition. He found himself wondering if Ethan would confide in his other uncle – his gay uncle – as he had done with Dan, and felt jealous of that too. Which was fairly pathetic of him, admittedly. 'Oh right,' he said. 'Nice,' he remembered to add. Damn it, though, this was going to bring his stats right down on the Patrick plan. 'Can I do anything for you while you're away?' he asked, hovering by the door. 'I could pop by and keep an eye on the place now and then, if you want. Do some gardening or . . . ?'

He was clutching at straws – especially as he'd offered his lawnmowing services once before and she'd given him short shrift – so he was surprised when Zoe leaned against the wall, looking thankful.

'Oh, would you? The garden, I mean. Everything's gone mad suddenly and I haven't had the energy to get it under control. Thanks, Dan. Here, let me give you the spare key.' She opened a drawer, pulling out a bunch of keys. 'These two are for the front door,' she said, dumping them in his outstretched hand. 'But don't worry if you're busy – it's only if you have time.'

He couldn't speak for a moment, because the keys now weighing down his palm were attached to a familiar battered Fulham Football Club keyring. Patrick's old house keys, which presumably had been retrieved from his jacket pocket in the mortuary. Goosebumps prickled along Dan's arms even though the house was warm. 'Thanks,' he managed to say. 'No problem. Well, have a great time and I guess I'll see you on . . . ?' He didn't know when he was going to see her again, he realized.

'Um, well, a fortnight today, I suppose. Gabe's birthday party,' she replied.

'Gabe's . . . ?' Shit. Why did he not know his own niece's and nephews' birthdays?

'Didn't he give you the invitation? Sorry, I should have said earlier. He really wants you to be there,' Zoe said, at which point the sun seemed to come out around Dan's head and a jubilant fanfare sounded. 'And so do I – I could use an extra pair of hands, if you don't mind. Let me get you the details.'

Dan stuffed the keys in his pocket, his spirits lifting once more as she went in search of the invitation. Gabe wanted him there at the party. Zoe wanted him there at the party. This was good: he was useful to them. Needed, even. Then she returned with a small colourful piece of paper.

'A superheroes party. Cool,' he said, still chuffed at this clear sign of acceptance.

'Yeah,' Zoe said. Maybe it was the hangover, but she had suddenly gone kind of furtive. Shifty, even. Then she blurted out, 'There is just one thing actually. Gabe's asked everyone to dress up and . . . Well, ages ago, when he first started talking about wanting a superhero party, Patrick had promised to dress up too. So we were wondering – would you?'

It took a moment for the penny to drop. 'Would I . . . dress up? As a superhero? What, in tights and stuff?'

'Well, yeah, basically. Could you bear it? And help with the games and everything?' She bit her lip. 'I know it's a lot to ask and you might have other plans, but . . .' Her eyes pleaded with him. 'Gabe would really like it.'

'Sure,' Dan found himself saying, powerless to refuse her. Stepping into not only Patrick's shoes but his fancy dress costume too – absolutely. Also, hello? Dressing up as a superhero: did it get any more symbolic than that? 'Of course I will,' he said.

Dan hadn't seen his friends since the night in the pub that had ended in his own face-down drunkenness and vomiting, but although he'd tried to keep a low profile and avoid future social gatherings, the others weren't so willing to let that happen. They'd clearly discussed the situation behind his back and decided that an intervention was necessary, because they'd all been on his case this week. Steve was going on at him about joining the rowing club – 'You'd be doing me a favour, I need someone there who's as shit as me' – while Neil kept texting him details of crappy-sounding punk bands that were playing in the area, and Mark had been steadily badgering him about going running together. So far Dan had managed to ignore all of their requests, until on Saturday morning he arrived home from Zoe's to find Mark jogging up the road with a look on his face that said he was not about to take no for an answer.

'Come on, lightweight, get your trainers on – let's do this,' he said, clapping his hands like a PE teacher.

Dan must still have been feeling a glow from his new superhero mission, because to both his own and Mark's surprise, he acquiesced. Having dug out some knackered old shorts and a new, previously unworn T-shirt bought for his

South American travels, it wasn't long before the two of them were jogging over Hammersmith Bridge together. Once Dan's initial breathlessness had eased, they chatted away about nothing and everything: football, politics, the new car Mark had been eyeing up. Dan's lungs ached with this unusual burst of exercise, but the blood was singing through his veins as their feet pounded along in unison. Below them on the river was a bunch of kids in kayaks, their shrill, excited voices drifting up on the breeze, as well as one of the old steamboats full of tourists. Dan couldn't remember the last time he'd crossed the bridge on foot, with the luxury of being able to look down and around.

'All right?' Mark asked as they reached the other side and swerved onto the river path skirting the wetland centre. It was drizzling, but Dan appreciated the cool mist of water on his face and hair.

'Yeah,' he said. 'Yeah, this is good. Thanks.' Being out here had released the spectre of Rebecca from his head, too. He'd spent most of the night swinging between agony at having sent her his combative message, and defiance, telling himself it was no more than she deserved. Had she read it yet? How would she reply, now that she knew he knew? Dan exhaled slowly, trying to breathe her right out. *Go away, Rebecca. You've done enough damage.*

As if sensing that he needed distracting, Mark asked about Zoe and the kids, and Dan found that he had plenty to say. Spending more time with them recently meant they had become much more vividly coloured in for him; they had become Ethan, Gabe and Bea, real people, rather than three children who briefly intersected his life now and then. 'And guess what, I've got to dress up as a superhero for Gabe's party in a fortnight,' he said at the end.

Mark hooted with laughter. 'Christ, my eyes are burning at the thought,' he replied. 'Are we talking Lycra tights and all or . . . ?'

'Yep,' said Dan. 'I just hope I don't make any of the kids cry at the sight.'

'Or the mums swoon,' Mark smirked.

Dan snorted. 'I'm pretty sure that won't be happening. Unless it's through horror alone.'

'Dan? Dan Sheppard!' came a voice just then, and Dan looked round to see that a man with a chocolate-brown Labrador was waving at him nearby.

'Gareth!' Dan said in surprise, thudding to a halt. Gareth Chappell was a colleague of his, but their paths usually crossed amidst the sterility of the air-conditioned office floor, clad in suits and ties, rather than outside on the riverbank, with Dan wearing sweaty running gear. 'How are you? Oh – this is Mark, by the way. Mark – Gareth, from work.'

'All right,' said Mark, consulting a fitness tracker on his watch, then continuing to jog on the spot.

'Hi there,' said Gareth, before turning back to Dan. 'All

good. Work's crazy as ever, you know how it is.' There was a short pause and then he asked, 'So how was Thailand? *Was* it Thailand? Are you back in the office again soon?'

'Beginning of June,' Dan replied, reaching down to pet the dog, which was nudging at his leg. Its ears were like damp suede beneath his fingers. He straightened, aware that Gareth was waiting for elaboration. 'I'm working on . . . some other stuff for the time being.'

Gareth raised an eyebrow. 'Moonlighting, eh? Just kidding. Well, you're not missing much. Duncan Smith got fired for fraud, so an audit team has swooped in and are poking into everything. It's like living under the Stasi – all the rumours and secrecy. Anyway! Yes, all right, Mungo,' he said as the dog began pulling at the lead. 'Better go. Good to see you.'

'Likewise,' said Dan, setting off once more.

'I'd forgotten you weren't working,' Mark said, as they jogged along again. 'How are you feeling about going back?'

Dan lengthened his stride a little. 'I hadn't really been thinking about it,' he confessed. In the last few weeks he had barely thought about work at all, he realized, least of all wonder what was happening there without him. His desk appeared in his head like a vision; his desk and filing cabinet, the computer screen and phone, silently awaiting his return. The three suits hanging in his dark wardrobe, ties like snakes dangling from a hanger. That life all felt so far away, as if it belonged to someone else entirely. Those early-morning starts, squeezing into the Circle Line train compartments; sardine cans of commuters that whizzed the bleary-eyed nine-to-five army to identikit air-conditioned office blocks, so that they could sit at identikit desks and type into identikit keyboards. Drink coffee. Bitch about their colleagues (fraudulent or not). Fill in forms, attend meetings, take phone calls, go home, then do it all over again, for forty-seven weeks of the year.

That had been his world, more or less. He had worked so hard that work had absorbed 90 per cent of his energy, leaving little space for anything else of significance or value. All the money he'd earned was piled up in his account because he had no time to spend it – or anybody to spend it with. It was only now, having detached himself from the treadmill, that he realized how infrequently he had seen his parents and the rest of the family in the last few years. How rarely he interacted with anyone out of the office environment, for that matter.

On the last day of work before his sabbatical was due to begin, he had packed up his belongings, trepidatious about not being there for three whole months. It had been so strange, walking out of the building, aware that he wouldn't be in touch with his clients or colleagues for such a long period of time. Deep down, he couldn't shake off a lurking anxiety that, without the central pole of the office holding up his life as usual, the rest of it might collapse like a broken tent, however far he travelled. Yet stepping into Patrick's shoes recently had made office life seem unimportant. Trivial, even. The past few weeks had been chaotic, sure – babysitting last night being a prime example – but he felt as if he was experiencing new riches, inhabiting a fuller, more textured existence.

Not that this could continue, obviously. Once back at work, normality would swing in and he'd have to peel himself away from Zoe's and the kids' lives again. Just when the children could really do with some consistency, as well, not to mention extra love.

'I don't think I want to work any more, come to think of it,' he said to Mark as they swerved to avoid a large puddle.

'Yeah, you, me and every middle-aged bloke I know,' said Mark, rather pessimistically. 'Roll on retirement, right?'

Dan's phone started ringing and he managed to wrestle it from his back pocket while maintaining pace. *Pain In Arse,* he read on the screen and groaned before deflecting it to voicemail. Being at the beck and call of Patrick's tenants – however sweet they might be – was definitely something he wouldn't be missing when he returned to his office job. Rosemary could wait. Right now, he just needed to run.

Chapter Twenty-Two

By the time it was seven o'clock on Saturday night, Dan was starving. He'd put off Rosemary for as long as possible – was he not allowed a day to himself? – but cracked late afternoon, when he finally listened to her message and heard how her voice was wavering as if she were on the verge of tears. Call him an idiot, but off he went with tool-box and gritted teeth, to sort out whatever it was this time. A leaking radiator and a new damp patch on the bedroom ceiling, as it turned out, which she was convinced must be due to a slate having come loose on the roof.

Having dealt with her concerns and then grudgingly accepted a coffee and a jam tart, he was on his way home now, tired after the sleepless night he'd had at Zoe's and looking forward to being back on his own sofa, where he could enjoy doing absolutely nothing. It was dark and driz-zling, the windscreen wipers of his car making scraping sounds where the rubber trim was starting to perish, and he cursed the traffic that seemed to have swallowed up the streets. Then, braking to stop in a long queue at the traffic lights, he noticed the hot pink dress on the woman standing at the bus stop (yes, okay, and the woman's legs) and in the next moment realized that the person he was staring at was Lydia. Coming to a halt, he looked again, wondering if his imagination was playing tricks on him, but no, it was definitely her, looking cold and a bit fed-up as she stood there shivering in a navy denim jacket, clutching a small silver gift bag, but no umbrella.

Thank you, Fate, Dan thought, rolling down his window. He couldn't believe how cheerful he felt to see her, a splash of colour against the dismal evening. 'Can I give you a lift?' he called.

Her face crumpled with relief as she saw him. 'Oh God, yes please, that would be amazing,' she said, hurrying over. 'I've been waiting here for twenty minutes, I don't know what's going on with the buses tonight.' As she let herself into the passenger seat, Dan smelled her perfume: spicy and reminiscent of winter evenings and wood-smoke. Her long brown hair was loose around her shoulders, speckled with raindrops, and she clipped in her seatbelt, then kicked off her high heels in the footwell. 'Thank you,' she added, setting the gift bag down by her feet. 'What a horrible night!'

'I know,' Dan said, conscious of how close they were sitting to one another in the small, confined space. His mind went unhelpfully blank, conversational skills deserting him.

Lydia was first to break the silence. 'Wow, it's so tidy in here!' she said, gazing around. 'Is it a new car?'

'No, I'm just—' He felt embarrassed, seeing it through her eyes. Was she taking the piss? Yes, he had a mini car-vacuum and he wasn't ashamed to admit it. A tiny bit self-conscious, perhaps, because Rebecca had always teased him about his neatness, to the point where she had rolled her eyes up to heaven and muttered things under her breath towards the end of their marriage. But what was wrong with looking after your possessions properly? 'It's quite old, actually,' he mumbled, adding, 'Where are you off to?' as the traffic light turned green and the cars in front began to move.

'Lucinda's,' she replied. 'Do you know it? The cocktail bar off Chiswick High Road. Is that okay? Were you going in that direction anyway?'

'Yeah, sort of,' he said, even though that wasn't strictly true. 'No problem.' He glanced across at her, taking in her pink lipstick and mascara. She had done something to her eyes, which made them look bigger and browner, and he felt kind of pedestrian in comparison, sitting there in a plain checked shirt and jeans. *Say something*, he ordered himself, dreading another awkward silence taking hold. 'You look nice,' he managed. 'Off on a date or something?'

'Not exactly,' she replied. 'It's a friend's sixtieth-birthday party. Jonathan, my boss – the guy you met in the shop the other day?'

'Right,' Dan said, thinking of office parties he'd been to in the past. Stilted affairs for the most part, with everyone wondering what they had in common, other than their clients and bitching about the receptionist. Rubbish at small talk, Dan had never managed to endure the faked jollity for long. 'So you've got to be on your best behaviour, have you?' he added.

Lydia laughed. 'No way! Jonathan won't be. He's my godfather as well as my boss, and his parties are legendary for all the debauchery. Give it five minutes and someone will be dancing on the bar, that kind of thing.' She pulled down the passenger mirror and examined her lipstick. 'In fact it took him a while to find a venue because his two favourite bars refused the booking, after the outrageous parties he's held there before.'

'Okaaaay,' said Dan. '*That* kind of party.' His own Saturday-night plans seemed disappointingly vanilla all of a sudden.

'How about you – off anywhere exciting?' Lydia asked, as if reading his mind. She snapped the mirror shut and looked over at him.

'No,' he said, wishing he had a different, more impressive answer. 'I've just finished work,' he added, feeling the need to justify himself. 'My evening is going to feature a takeaway pizza, several beers and the telly, I should think.'

'You wild thing, you,' she teased. 'Had a busy day then? Got rid of that tree yet?'

'That . . . ? Oh, the tree. I forgot I'd told you about that. No. Not yet. It's on my list, but . . .' He pulled a face. 'You know how it is: some jobs you just keep putting off, hoping they'll go away.'

'Yep. Replacing light bulbs. Taking broken stuff to the dump . . . Don't get me started. Or rather – somebody, please, for the love of God, get me started.'

He laughed. 'Sounds familiar.'

'Maybe you need to make an event of it,' she suggested. 'The tree, I mean. Turn the whole thing into a ceremony: use the wood for a bonfire, toast marshmallows, that sort of jazz. I'll help, if you want,' she added, warming to her own idea. 'I love a bit of fire-starting. Not to mention chainsaws.'

'Thanks,' he said. 'I'll bear that in mind.'

He didn't feel he could tell her about the babysitting saga, much as he wanted to offload on someone – it felt wrong to talk about Patrick's other children with Lydia – but their conversation flowed easily otherwise. He talked about going running with Mark and the visit to Rosemary, while she regaled him with torrid tales of her dad getting back on the dating scene, including the panicked phone call she'd received from him halfway through one such evening when the date in question went into labour.

'Went into *labour*?' Dan repeated, mind boggling at the

unexpected twist in the tale. 'Blimey, there's so much to unpack in that story, I don't even know what to ask you first.'

'I know! Thank goodness he's only got my daughter to entertain tonight,' Lydia giggled. 'Oh, left here, by the way,' she said, peering forward through the gloom. 'Then it's the next road on the right, I think. Wait – slow down. This one? No, sorry. Must be the next one. Yes, there it is.'

And there it was: Lucinda's, a brightly lit bar with the name in neon-pink loopy handwriting above. Dan found a spot to park and pulled over, wishing the journey could have been longer. 'Well, have a good evening,' he said, feeling formal all of a sudden.

'Thanks for the lift,' she said, unclipping her seatbelt. Then she hesitated, as if weighing something up. 'Come in for a drink, if you want,' she offered after a moment.

'Oh.' A list of reasons why not flashed instantly through his head – he was knackered and hungry, he wasn't dressed for a party, he wouldn't know anyone there – but then he looked at Lydia again, so pretty and smiling, eyes bright, and suddenly felt sick of being the cautious type of person whose default answer was always no. He thought of Tiggy's last Facebook posting describing how she'd completed the exhilarating-sounding Death Road mountain-bike trip – *New motto: say yes to EVERYTHING!*, she'd written. Why not? 'Okay, yeah,' he said tentatively. 'If you don't think Jonathan would mind?'

She blew out her lips in a small laugh. 'As if. His motto is almost certainly "The more, the merrier". He won't mind at all. Is that a yes, then?'

'Yes,' Dan said and then, because his voice still sounded doubtful, repeated himself with more conviction. 'Yes. Great!'

Lucinda's was heaving when they went in. Black-and-gold feathery bunting hung in bold zigzags across the main room, and massive gold number-60 helium balloons bobbed on strings where they'd been tied to the bar. Eighties pop boomed from speakers and there was a crush of guests, some glamorous and bohemian, but others thankfully in jeans and shirts, like Dan. He felt slightly overwhelmed as he followed Lydia inside. Dazzled, even. There was such an exuberant buzz in the air that he half-expected to become intoxicated simply by breathing in.

'What can I get you?' asked Lydia as they made their way through to the bar. 'Oh, there's Jonathan, look. Hey, Jon! Happy birthday!'

Dan followed her as she went over to hug him, and saw Jonathan's eyes narrow a fraction as he noticed Dan in her wake. 'Dan gave me a lift,' Lydia explained. 'Remember, he came in the shop the other day? I invited him in for a drink – hope that's all right.'

'Of course,' said Jonathan. His voice was smooth and charming, but his gaze lingered on Dan just a fraction longer than was comfortable. 'Yes, you took Lydia out to the pub, didn't you?' he said. 'I never quite got to the bottom of what that was all about.'

'There's nothing to get to the bottom of,' Lydia said quickly, shooting a look at Dan. 'Can I get you a drink, Jon? Oh – and here's your present. Hope you like it.'

He softened. 'Thanks, darling,' he said. 'Don't tell everyone, but it's a free bar for a while, so get in there quick. Have something lovely and expensive on me.' He held up an empty glass. 'Mine's a Caipirinha, if you're insisting.'

'Oh, we are,' said Lydia. 'Come on, Dan.'

If he had been intimidated about joining a stranger's party at first, the feeling didn't last long. Having studied the cocktail list, Lydia opted for a Manhattan while Dan picked something called a Lion of Soho, and these slipped down so easily that it wasn't long before they were choosing more drinks, and Dan had decided to leave his car there for the night and get a cab home. They got chatting to a drag-queen friend of Jonathan called Bella Doner – 'Like the kebab, darling' – whose filthy stories soon had them cackling helplessly. More cocktails were ordered and then a song that Lydia liked started up. 'Come on!' she whooped and, before Dan could argue, she'd pulled him onto the dance floor and forced him to dance with her. When had he last danced? He couldn't even remember, and yet, despite not being a natural mover and starting off feeling wooden and somewhat self-conscious, it rapidly began to feel like the most excellent thing to do suddenly: to throw himself around with this beautiful laughing woman, her pink dress flying out as she twirled and spun.

A few cocktails later, someone produced a microphone and started up a karaoke session, something Dan would normally have cringed at and hidden away from – and yet, to his astonishment, when Lydia said, 'I've put our names down for a duet, by the way – "Islands in the Stream" or "Don't Go Breaking My Heart", which do you prefer?', he didn't even make a run for it, throwing excuses over his shoulder. He must have been already half-drunk – or at least giddy on the atmosphere – because instead he found himself answering, 'Kenny and Dolly, OF COURSE'; and then, when it was their turn, he bellowed the song out in a terrible harmony with her, which earned them a round of applause as well as more than a few winces from those in the room who actually liked music.

Afterwards there were more drinks – random jabbing at the cocktail menu by now, rather than careful consideration – followed by more dancing, and it occurred to Dan all of a sudden that he was happy. That he felt light and free, for the first time in months, as if he had left all his worries and problems at the door of Lucinda's when walking in. 'I'm having the best time,' he bawled into Lydia's ear, as some disco track or other came to an end and they paused for breath on the dance floor.

'Me too!' she yelled back, cheeks flushed, mascara smudging around her eyes. 'Shall we have another drink?'

'Hell, yeah!'

He could live like this too, he thought dazedly, queuing for drinks. He could have colour and music and dancing in his life all the time, if he chose. If he allowed such things in again. The idea was liberating. Exciting. Tempting. 'I'm going to change my life, you know,' he confessed drunkenly to Lydia as they waited in the crush. 'I'm actually going to do that.'

'Your wife? I didn't know you were married,' she shouted back.

'My *life*!' he yelled, just as the two women onstage bawling out a karaoke version of 'Bohemian Rhapsody' reached the end of the song. 'I'm going to change my *life*!'

He'd shouted louder than he meant to and heads turned, then a man with cropped peroxide hair along the bar punched the air and whooped, 'Yeah, baby!' at him, while a woman in a jewelled cape to his right cheered, 'Do it!' and everyone laughed.

Dan's exuberance continued to glow around him – he felt invincible, unable to stop smiling – right until the moment when, returning from the Gents a short while later, his way was blocked by Jonathan. 'Don't you muck about with her, all right?' he said, a pleasant expression on his face, but his voice and eyes bearing an unmistakable warning.

Dan was jolted out of his happy mood as if he'd been tripped up. 'What? It's not like that,' he said, taken aback.

Jonathan took a step closer, looming over Dan; he was a good two inches taller and as wide as a shed door. 'That girl is precious to me, understand? And I don't want to come over like a heavy, but she's had a rough time. Thanks to your brother, I believe.'

All the wind was taken from Dan's sails. 'Right. Although—'

'I promised her mum. Break her heart, you'll be dealing with me. Yes?'

'Yes! But—'

'Good.' He moved past Dan towards a couple of blokes in rugby tops, switching seamlessly back into the genial host once more. 'Bob! Alex! What took you so long, you fat fuckers?' he yelled.

Dan meanwhile slipped away, feeling chastened, as if the bubble around him had been well and truly popped. Maybe it was time to go. Jonathan was no doubt only being protective of his god-daughter, but Dan felt as if he might have outstayed his welcome anyway. He found Lydia on the dance floor with a couple of older women and went over to her. 'I'm going to head off,' he said. 'But thanks for—'

'You're going?' she interrupted him. 'Already? Stay and dance, Dan!'

'Yeah, Dan,' echoed one of the other women. She was

wearing a Cleopatra-style wig that had slipped slightly on her head. 'Stay and dance!'

'I'd better—' He glanced over to see that Jonathan was looking at him and felt a prickle of irritation. *Yeah, all right, I'm going*, he thought. 'Nah, I should shoot off,' he told Lydia. 'Thanks for asking me in, though, I've had such a good night.'

'Yeah, me too,' she said, then towed him off the dance floor to a quieter corner. 'I'm glad we did this.'

'Same,' he replied, then hesitated, no longer in such a hurry to leave. She was standing right there in front of him, her hair all mussed up from dancing, her make-up sliding off her face, but radiant and dimpled and smiling. He felt like taking her in his arms and kissing her, he realized, but that was almost certainly a terrible idea. Not least because Jonathan was likely to appear behind him at any moment and haul him off by the scruff of the neck. 'Lydia, I . . .' he began, unsure what he wanted to say. He felt enchanted by her. Dizzied. Was this how Patrick had felt? he wondered, only to instantly regret his own question in the next moment. *Don't think about him.*

She put her arms around his middle, so close he could smell the coconutty scent of her hair. 'I really like you, Dan,' she said. 'I'm glad we met.'

'Yes,' he said hoarsely. He mustn't kiss her. He must not. She was drunk, and kissing would only muddy the waters, complicate things even further. *Do not kiss her*, he told himself desperately, even though he could feel himself leaning towards her, gazing at her mouth.

'TEN!' A shout went up just then and they jolted apart again. 'NINE! EIGHT!'

'What's going on?' Dan asked, blinking as the spell broke. The music had been switched off and a crowd had gathered around Jonathan.

'SEVEN!'

'Birthday countdown,' Lydia said, slipping her arms free. 'SIX!' she yelled. 'It's Jon's actual – FIVE! – birthday tomorrow. FOUR!'

'THREE! TWO! ONE!' yelled the crowd. 'Happy birthday!'

Someone brought through a cake alight with candles, while a man with a silver cowboy hat sat down at the piano and played a thunderous version of 'Happy Birthday', to which everyone sang along. Dan recognized an exit cue when he saw one and squeezed Lydia's hand. 'Bye,' he said, leaning to kiss her on the cheek. 'See you soon.'

The sky was starlit as he stepped outside and he gulped in the cold night air. He had done the right thing, leaving now before anything happened, he told himself. He had done absolutely the right thing, and the only thing possible under the circumstances.

So why then, he thought, ordering a cab and wrapping his arms around himself for warmth as he waited, did going home alone feel so wrong?

Chapter Twenty-Three

From the sublime to the ridiculous, or rather from the sublime to the fire hazard: Dan woke up the next morning with a pounding hangover to an urgent phone call on Patrick's work mobile. The Hossains, tenants in Shepherd's Bush, had just had a scare because their washing machine had burst into flames forty minutes earlier. The fire was out, but the kitchen was a mess. Could he help?

This, needless to say, was not the relaxing start to a Sunday that Dan had hoped for, especially as he'd slept so badly. Thoughts of Lydia had tumbled through his mind all night, questions unanswered, emotions churning. That moment when they'd stood so close together, her arms slotted around him, when every part of him wanted nothing more than to kiss her . . . If the countdown hadn't interrupted them then, he was sure they would have kissed. And what then?

Oh God. It was the 'what then?' that kept him awake, the

memory of her body warm against his, the smell of her hair, her smile . . .

Stop, he thought, hitting his forehead with the flat of his hand. Having thrown some clothes on, he knocked back two paracetamol with orange juice glugged straight from the carton. He absolutely could not start thinking of Lydia in any romantic terms, given who she was. His first loyalty had to be to Zoe, 100 per cent. But he wasn't mistaken, was he, that there had been something between himself and Lydia last night? Surely she wouldn't have put her arms around him like that if she felt complete indifference towards him? Or was he simply a Patrick substitute? *You look like him,* she had said the first time they met. Had the two brothers become muddled for her, in that drunken moment?

Perhaps it was just as well he had the Hossains' exploding washing machine to deal with, he thought, cycling off along the quiet streets a few minutes later, his car still stranded in Chiswick. A wrecked kitchen would distract him from his confused feelings, at least.

He hadn't had any dealings with this particular family yet, but as he reached the terraced street, his heart sank into his trainers when he counted along the house numbers and realized that theirs was the property with the cracked front window, the badly painted front door and the wet streaks beneath the guttering. Inside, the place wasn't a whole lot more appealing, he discovered, as Mr Hossain – Tamal – let him in and led him through to the blackened, smoke-stinking kitchen.

'It burst into *flames*,' Tamal said, gesturing at the scorched machine. He was tall and bearded, bristling with shock and bad temper, as well you might be, had something blown up unexpectedly in your house early on a Sunday morning. 'I've got *kids*, man. The whole place could have gone up. Smoke everywhere. Jana's taken them round to her mum's, because our youngest has got asthma. It's not good enough. Do you hear what I'm saying?'

Dan did absolutely hear what he was saying and apologized profusely, promising he'd get rid of the ruined machine and have a new one plumbed in as soon as possible. The picture grew worse every time he looked at another part of the small, squalid kitchen: with damp casting a shadow across one wall, the cupboard that was missing a door, and the ripped, tatty lino that now had a huge burn mark from the fire, although someone had done their best to clean it. Bloody hell, Patrick. It was a shithole, whichever way you looked at it – and what was more, he'd been charging the Hossains a lot of money to live here.

'This is my brother's business – I've only recently taken it on,' Dan explained, 'but it looks like there's a lot of other work that needs doing here too.'

Tamal snorted. 'You don't say. My little girl's got bites all

the way up her arms from something or other. The bedroom at the top has mould growing behind the wardrobe
where the roof leaks. Your brother doesn't want to know,
though. Too busy, he always says. Last time I spoke to him
was – what? Six or seven weeks ago. I laid it on the line, but
even then he didn't bother responding. I've given up asking,
to be honest, but today . . .' He spread his hands with a
fierce, impotent sort of despair. 'Kind of the last straw.'

Dan felt mortified. Horrified, actually, that Patrick could
have let things slide so badly for this family; and ashamed
that he hadn't been in touch with them himself before now.
'I'm sorry,' he said. 'You're right – it's not good enough. The
thing is, he died; coming up for seven weeks ago actually.
That's why he's not been in touch.'

'Sorry,' Tamal mumbled and Dan shrugged it off, trying
to prioritize what needed doing. Have the roof fixed, get a
dehumidifier to help with the damp in the meantime,
arrange for pest control to come in and kill off whatever
was biting the little girl . . . He found himself imagining
Bea's arms covered in scarlet flea bites or a bedbug rash, and
felt worse than ever. It would cost a fortune, but everything
needed to be done and he was pretty sure Zoe would be
okay about sanctioning the payments. No one should have
to live like this.

'First things first, let's get the washing machine into the

front yard, then maybe you could walk me round the rest of the house, so that I can start making a list.'

Perhaps he should have taken his brother's side, Dan thought as the two of them shuffled the stinking, burned washing machine out from under the sink and heaved it towards the front door. Perhaps he should have defended Patrick more staunchly, come up with some excuse for why he had allowed this house to fall into such disrepair – but the words stuck in Dan's throat. What was wrong with you? he thought angrily of his brother, as Tamal gave him a tour of the miserable place and Dan added *Broken bannister, loose stair carpet, leaking toilet, draughty windows, ancient plumbing* to the list of things that needed attention. Oh, and was that some bare wiring in the little girl's bedroom? Yes, it was. For crying out loud, this place was a deathtrap. Accidents waiting to happen around every corner.

'I'm going to sort this out,' he said to Tamal, feeling sickened with each new revelation. 'I promise.'

But Tamal had heard it all before, judging by his quiet coldness. *Prove it then*, his eyes said as Dan left.

Once they'd said goodbye, Dan cycled around the corner, then stopped to lean over the handlebars and breathe deeply. 'What the hell, Patrick?' he muttered into the quiet street. 'What the fuck?' He had felt embarrassed by his brother's shortcomings in there – a horrible thing to say, but true. 'You cheap shitbag,' he said. 'Again and again you let people down. And what for?'

He thought of everything Patrick had had going for him – Zoe and the children, a beautiful house, a thriving business – and what a wonderful life this had added up to. Why, then, had he felt the need to piss all over other people's lives: Lydia and Jemima, Tamal and his family . . . No doubt there were others Dan wasn't even aware of. Why hadn't Patrick cared more? Why hadn't it been enough for him?

Something Tamal had said was niggling away at him, a light flashing in a dim corner of Dan's brain. Then he remembered how, when he'd gone to meet Patrick that very last night, his brother had been on the phone when Dan arrived. He'd looked stressed as he noticed Dan approach, then curled around his phone defensively. What had he said? *Yes, all right, all right, give me a break,* or something. He'd seemed rattled, anyway. Agitated. He'd smoothed over his feelings as soon as Dan asked if he was okay, of course – but *had* Patrick been okay? Had it been a fed-up tenant – perhaps Tamal himself – getting heavy with him? Had Patrick felt cornered, defeated by his workload, driven to the edge?

Dan put a hand to his head, not liking to think about his brother in that state. Why hadn't he tried harder to get to the bottom of whatever had been going on? Why hadn't Patrick been able to confide in him, if he felt under pressure? Instead they'd had that stupid, pointless argument where Dan had pushed him away. What if it had all been too much and Patrick had snapped? People did, didn't they? Middle-aged men especially, if they'd reached the end of their rope.

He sighed, wishing there was some way he could know what had been going through his brother's head at the end, wishing he could understand. 'What happened?' he muttered under his breath as he went to pick up his car. 'What happened that night?'

Dwelling on it was no use, so he threw himself into practical work instead, driving to the nearest Currys, where he ordered a new washing machine to be delivered and plumbed in for the Hossains, next-day service, with the old machine taken away. He added a fridge-freezer to the order for good measure, remembering how their existing one had looked positively medieval in age. It was a start, he told himself, texting Tamal to give him the news, adding that, if need be, he could wait in for the delivery tomorrow himself.

Afterwards he felt slightly at a loss for what to do. He drove back towards his flat until an impulse sent him off the motorway at Chiswick roundabout in the direction of Kew Bridge, then heading towards the cemetery, in the hope that it would bring him the comfort he needed.

The cemetery was hushed and still. It had been raining earlier that morning and the trees were sodden, their new leaves dripping each time a breeze shook the branches, but the sun seemed set to break through the clouds any moment, creating a pearlescent, marbled effect in the sky. Dandelions and bluebells sprouted between the aged headstones with some cheering yellow tulips growing out of one grassed-over grave. Ahead of him, a squirrel ran nimbly along the branch of a cherry tree that frothed with candyfloss-pink blossom.

Dan's breath deepened amidst the calm and his inner turmoil began to recede, his fists unclenching as he walked along. It was okay, he told himself. It was all going to be okay. However conflicted his feelings about his brother on a personal level, he could still continue with his good-deeds schedule for Zoe's sake, for the children, he decided. For Lydia and Jemima too, and for the tenants. He would do Patrick's jobs for him, only better. Anything to get through the days.

Then his thoughts spooled back to the night before and he found himself wondering what Lydia was doing today. Already it seemed like a dream: the two of them dancing and singing karaoke duets amidst the black-and-gold party decorations. He'd felt so free and untethered, as if nothing else mattered. He thought of the smell of her hair, how she'd smiled at him and said, 'I'm glad we did this.' Maybe he should take her up on her offer to help with the tree in his garden, he thought, until he remembered that he was supposed to be backing off. That the whole thing was impossible.

That if anything happened between them, it would only make the situation a hundred times more complicated. Lydia had already been dumped on by Patrick. Whatever else he did, Dan was not going to mess her around, end of story.

He quickened his pace, heading for the Garden of Remembrance where Zoe had had a plaque installed. His parents visited the cemetery every week without fail, and he knew that Zoe had brought the kids too a number of times to pay their respects and talk to Patrick, but Dan hadn't made the journey here before. He wasn't sure why. Partly because it seemed a very public way to demonstrate your grief – announcing in effect to the rest of the world: Here I am, being sad about my loved one who died, witness my sorrow – when, given the choice, he would always rather deal with stuff in a private space. Apart from today, apparently.

The Garden of Remembrance seemed empty when he arrived, but then he noticed a woman in a pale-blue coat sitting on a bench, hands in her lap. He didn't recognize her and assumed she was the relative of someone else altogether, so he was taken aback when she peered at him, then stood up and asked, 'Are you Patrick Sheppard's brother?'

'Yes,' he said, trying to place her in his mind. Gingery hair, late thirties, slender, anxious-looking . . . Nope. Not ringing any bells. 'I'm sorry,' he said, 'my memory's terrible. Have we met?'

She pulled a tissue from her coat pocket and dabbed her

eyes. 'I was at the funeral,' she said. 'My husband and I, we were friends of him and Zoe. He was such a great guy.'

Oh, here we go. Just what he didn't need. 'Yes,' he said, feeling tired. So much for the quiet reflection he'd hoped to have with his brother here.

'But how *are* you? The grieving process is so slow, isn't it? You must still be in bits,' said the woman, gazing at him with keen sympathy. There was something distastefully eager about her manner, he thought, stepping back and trying not to shudder. Parasitic, even. One of those people who wanted to feast on the sufferings of others, who loved hearing all the tragic details. It was surprising how many of them he'd come across in the last couple of months.

He was unwilling to throw her any titbits. 'I'm keeping busy,' he replied shortly. Keeping busy, trying to deal with the fallout from Patrick's life, secrets and all. Tormenting himself with thoughts of Patrick's last moments. 'Anyway.' He wasn't going to hang around discussing his brother with this woman he didn't even know. 'Should I mention to Zoe that I bumped into you or—'

It was strange, but her face stiffened at Zoe's name. Her nostrils actually flared like a spooked horse. *Interesting.* 'Er . . .' She faltered for a second, but then her composure returned. 'No, there's no need, I'll probably see her next week at school. Thanks, though.' She pantomimed looking at her watch. 'Oh, gosh! I lost track of the time,' she said.

'Better go.' She stood up and brushed herself down, returning to the role of grief-stricken friend. 'So sorry for your loss,' she said, putting a hand lightly on Dan's arm for a moment, before walking away.

Dan watched her go, her perfume drifting through the air behind her, pungent and kind of sickly. Then he sank into the nearest bench with a frown. That had been odd, he thought to himself. Something about it didn't quite ring true. It was almost as if she'd been acting a part.

Tilting his head back, he stared up at the sky, still chewing over the exchange. Then he sighed as the obvious struck him. 'You didn't, did you, Patrick?' he asked under his breath. 'Come on, man. Seriously? Again?' He groaned, hoping he was jumping to conclusions. But as he looked over again at the redheaded woman, now just about vanishing from sight, he had a horrible sensation of déjà vu. 'I don't want to know,' he said aloud. 'This time I'm not getting involved. Understand?'

Chapter Twenty-Four

As the next week began, Dan made it his business to show Tamal and Jana Hossain that he could keep his word. He was there at the house on Monday when their new white goods were delivered, and hung around while the washing machine was plumbed in, until he was satisfied it worked properly. A couple of roofers and a handyman arrived on Tuesday in order to provide quotes for the various repairs, with Dan intending to book in one of the roofers to start as soon as possible. Also due that week was a visit from a pest-control service, in the hope of finding out what was biting the Hossains' daughter. In the meantime, Dan had shelled out for a new vacuum cleaner that was advertised as being the best for children with allergies, and ordered a replacement lino for the kitchen to be fitted the following week. He'd told Tamal and Jana that he would paint the place from top to bottom as well, once all the work had been completed.

It was satisfying to see progress being made, not to

mention a real difference to the family's lives; it felt like paying off a debt, righting a wrong. Plus it kept him busy – too busy to think about Lydia very much (probably a good thing) and too busy to dwell on Rebecca, and what she had made of his message. There was so much to do, in fact, that it wasn't until Wednesday that he was free to drop round to Zoe's, as promised. Talk about stepping into Patrick's shoes, he almost felt as if he *was* Patrick as he let himself into the house with his brother's own set of keys. 'Hello?' he called, even though he was pretty sure that Zoe had said she wouldn't be back until Easter Monday.

The rooms felt oddly quiet without their usual noisy residents present. The night before, Dan had looked at his social media to see that Zoe had uploaded various photos and video clips of her and the kids with her parents and brother in Penarth, and he'd pored over them all. There were the two boys on the beach, running over shingle with their coats flapping out behind them in the wind, like superhero capes. (Which reminded him: he must sort out his own fancy-dress costume for Gabe's party.) There was Bea in yellow wellies at the edge of the surf, turning round to wave at the camera, a new gap visible in her front teeth. There was a lovely shot of Zoe with her arms around two men – one who had the exact same nose as her, presumably her brother Niall, and the other with a pop-star dark quiff and a stubbled jaw, whom she'd tagged as 'Marc': Niall's husband,

Dan guessed. He'd zoomed in on a group shot of the family, checking each of their faces for tension, but they had all been smiling and laughing, relaxed and happy. *Good*. Dan was so relieved he didn't even feel a pinprick of jealousy this time.

Gathering up the post and leaving it in a pile on the side-table, he walked through the house, his fingertips trailing along the wall. If Patrick's spirit was anywhere, it would be here, rather than in the breezy memorial garden, he thought. His brother's coat still hung on the peg, and he smiled handsomely down from the wedding and family photos on display. Even his trainers were visible in the shoe basket, Dan noticed. On a whim, he slid off his own jacket and put on Patrick's coat, just to see what it was like. The insides of the sleeves were cold against his arms, but he fancied he could detect a whiff of aftershave still clinging to the fabric. It was a size too big for him, of course: too broad on the shoulders, too long around his body. As a boy, Dan had always looked forward to becoming as big and strong as his brother but he'd never quite caught up. Outliving him didn't really count as a consolation prize, he supposed.

Catching his reflection in the hall mirror, he felt shifty about wearing Patrick's coat, as if he might be caught and reprimanded for it. He took it off again and carefully hung it back up with the others, wondering how long Zoe would keep it there. Presumably Patrick's side of the wardrobe was still stuffed with his shirts and suit jackets as well, the drawers in their chest filled with his T-shirts, jeans, socks and pants. When did you make the decision to start removing the physical stuff from your home? he wondered. It must surely help to bring about some closure and acceptance, but at the same time the clearing of possessions was so final; a huge letting go. Perhaps the scale of the operation was what was putting Zoe off, he thought, making his way through the kitchen and out to the shed. Could he help her in this? He would test the waters with a tentative suggestion, he decided, imagining that it might be the sort of chore it was very hard to begin alone.

Unlocking the garden shed, he heaved out the lawnmower, which was dusty and festooned with lacy cobwebs, then tracked down an extension lead and plugged it in. Spring had arrived in the back garden since he'd last been here: there were white tulips in the borders and the magnolia tree was dripping with crumpled star-shaped flowers. The blue sky was torn up with vapour trails from aeroplanes above and the air was warm and sweet-scented, like a blessing. Wednesday morning and here he was, outside mowing a lawn with the sun on his face and the smell of grass clippings rising up around him. In just over a month he'd be installed in his office again and probably wouldn't even notice the weather any more, apart from when he walked to the Tube station and back each day.

The garden wasn't large enough for the task to take long, but Dan made a thorough job of it, cleaning and sharpening the blades afterwards, before returning the mower to the shed. Now what? he wondered, winding the extension cable around the reel. He went back inside, still half-expecting to hear shouts from the children or to see Zoe drifting around like an anxious wraith. He couldn't help noticing once more how scruffy the kitchen was these days, how neglected and sad it still felt in here. The whole room could really do with a lick of paint and spring-clean, just to lift everyone's spirits. Then he thought of how he had transformed the White-cliffe Road property with a few cans of emulsion and gloss and wondered . . . Well, he could do the same for Zoe, couldn't he? He could easily spruce the place up as a nice surprise for when she came back.

The idea gained momentum like a car moving up through the gears. Let's face it, she hadn't even taken Patrick's coat down in the hall yet, he told himself, so painting and decorating were hardly priorities for her right now. Whereas he had a few days at his disposal and so . . . He paced around, feeling feverish with all his good intentions. Should he?

His eye fell on the grubby skirting boards, the scrapes and scuffs on the walls, the greasy marks that were still there from when Gabe had thrown scrambled egg at his brother back at the weekend. He imagined Zoe coming home from her trip away and gasping as she walked into a clean, bright kitchen. How happy she would be, how grateful! Another thing that she no longer had to think about, because he'd got there first and done it for her.

It was a no-brainer. Of course he was going to do this. Whistling to himself, Dan grabbed his car keys, planning to head straight out for the nearest DIY store, but then his phone rang. *Rebecca*, it said on the screen and he felt a lurch inside. Ah. This was almost certainly going to be an unpleasant conversation. Or not? Maybe she was ringing to grovel, full of shame. *Please don't tell Rory, I beg you,* he imagined her snivelling. It could happen, right?

He leaned against the hall wall, took a deep breath and answered the call. 'Hello?'

'Danny, what the *fuck*?' was her opening gambit. She sounded furious rather than grovelling. 'I've been trying to work out how to reply to your obnoxious message on Facebook, but today I just thought: do you know what, I need to speak to him and find out what the hell he is on about. Were you pissed? Having a nervous breakdown? I mean, what is your problem?'

Her voice was very loud in his ear, with a shrill quality that he recognized from the dying days of their marriage, and he had a flashback to the argument they'd had in a Notting Hill tapas restaurant, the one that had ended with her flinging down her napkin and yelling, 'I can't do this any more!'

'What's my problem?' he repeated, trying to pump himself up. Not a combative person by nature, he was nonetheless secure in his place on the moral high ground this time. *She's the one in the wrong here*, said a voice in his head. *She brought this on herself.* 'My problem is that you went behind my back with my *brother*, Bex.' *You and all the other women, by the sound of things.* 'He told me. So if anyone's got a problem—'

She made a scornful sort of noise, before wading right in over the top of him. 'You sanctimonious prick. How dare you speak to me like that? I've never done anything with your brother. I didn't even *like* your brother. There – I said it. I slagged off a dead person. Sorry, but it's true. And NOTH-ING HAPPENED, okay, because I was married to *you*. Call me what you like, but I was never unfaithful to you. *Never.*'

She was practically shouting by the end of this little speech, but Dan suppressed a faint twinge of doubt and stiffened his resolve. Yeah, well, she would say that, wouldn't she? 'That's not what Patrick told me,' he said coldly.

'Let's hear it then,' she said. 'What did he tell you? I do love a good story. Some classic fiction. Bit of fantasy. Wait – no spoilers, let me guess. So . . . I made a pass at him or something. I fancied him and tried it on. Am I right? Is that what he told you?' She laughed, but it was harsh and unkind, not a pleasant sound. 'And you believed him. Well, that's lovely. Very decent of you.'

'He said . . .' Rebecca's fierce self-righteousness was

disarming; it had taken the wind right out of his sails. 'Yeah, it was something like that,' he mumbled. He glanced over at the nearest photo on the hall wall: of Patrick and Zoe's wedding day, their faces so tender, so loving. Then he was back to that last evening in the pub with Patrick, the rain lashing against the black window, the two of them onto their fourth or fifth pints. *She wasn't exactly loyal when you two were married, was she?* Patrick had said. *If you know what I mean.*

Dan could still picture him saying the words, a smirk playing on his lips. He'd assumed that Patrick was telling the truth when he said this – because why would anyone lie about *that*, for one thing? – but now the ground beneath him seemed to be unstable, the world dropping away. *Had* Patrick lied? Rebecca seemed pretty adamant that these claims were unfounded. But if none of that was true, then it meant . . .

'And you *believed* him,' she was saying again, voice dripping with scorn. 'Thanks a bunch. Jesus, Dan, I—' Then the sound became muffled as if she had moved the phone away from her mouth. 'It's okay, I'm fine,' he heard her say to someone else. 'Yes, all right, I suppose so.' Then she was back on the line, clipped and frosty. 'My husband wants me to stop talking to you. This imbecilic argument is probably doing terrible things to my blood pressure. So—'

The argument was slipping away from him, turning into something else completely: a bad joke, with Dan the punchline. He felt a twist of guilt that he might just have been deeply offensive to the woman he'd once loved most. Had he really got this wrong? Why would Patrick have lied? Embattled, he felt compelled to land one last blow instead. 'Ah, yes, I saw you were pregnant,' he sneered. 'An accident, was it? I'm guessing so, seeing as you'd always said that you never wanted—'

But she'd gone, the call disconnected, and he couldn't really blame her. The adrenalin drained out of him, and shame slid through his veins in its place; he wished he hadn't sunk to such a scummy parting shot. Jeering at her happiness was cheap – it was mean of him.

He let out a long shaky breath. Standing there alone, his head was a tumult of terrible thoughts. Pieces of a puzzle coming together to form a dreadful new picture. And now he had compounded everything by insulting his ex-wife and making that nasty remark about her pregnancy, like an absolute wanker.

He *was* an absolute wanker. He had got everything wrong. He rubbed his face with his hand, wishing he could rewind all those weeks, to have a second try at the night when everything unravelled.

It had started back in February with the dead tree in Dan's back garden. The neighbours had complained about it after a branch fell off into their garden and broke their solar-powered fountain, and he'd promised to cut it down before his flight to Santiago in a few days' time.

'Yeah, no problem,' Patrick said when Dan asked him for the favour. Getting the big old sycamore out of the ground was definitely going to be a two-man job. 'Are we still on for a beer Thursday night, by the way? I could stop over after-wards, if so, and we can get the tree done first thing Friday.'

They were all set. Dan had hired a ladder and chainsaw ready for the next day, and they met up in The Rutland Arms, a pub down by the river. And at first everything was good that evening. Normal. The pub seemed particularly cosy, with the cold wintry rain pelting against the windows outside, and the two of them chatted about Zoe and the kids, their dad's news about his knee-replacement op, Dan's travel plans, the half-marathon Patrick was training for and all the rest of it, while they sank pint after pint. Dan had been jubilant and excited, having just finished work for the sabbatical, and felt as if he already had one foot on the plane. Another drink? Yeah, why not. The rain was falling harder and neither of them felt inclined to move yet.

Conversation turned to Dan's forthcoming adventure. 'Think of all those women you're going to pull,' Patrick had teased. 'You'll be making up for lost time, I bet. After all these years of living like a monk!'

'I'm not – it's not that kind of a trip,' Dan protested.

'Yeah, but . . . Come on. It's been years now since you and Bex split. You must be gagging for it by now.'

'*Three* years. It's hardly—'

'Exactly, and how many women have you seen since then?'

They'd had this conversation before and it was always galling, always pushed Dan onto the defensive. What was it about smug, happily married people that made them feel they had the right to interfere and criticize? Splitting up from Rebecca had been the worst thing ever to hit Dan; he'd felt as if his life had fallen apart, segmenting like a peeled orange. What was he supposed to do: march straight out after signing the divorce papers and start chatting up other women, like their marriage had never happened, didn't matter to him? 'Look,' he said, 'it's not about—'

'Because she didn't waste time moping around. Eh? I mean, she wasn't exactly loyal when you two were married, was she? If you know what I mean.'

Dan had drunk enough by then for the pub to be blurring softly at the corners, his head pleasantly fuzzy, but his brother's words cut clean through the alcohol like an ice-pick. *No*, he thought. *I don't know what you mean. What the hell do you mean?* He stared at Patrick. 'What are you saying?' he asked.

It was the smirk on Patrick's face that rankled most. The cocky look he was wearing, like this was all one big laugh. 'Well – you know. That time she tried it on with me,' he said.

The time she – *what?* Dan thought for a moment he must have misheard. Please God let him have misheard. He felt stunningly sober now, every particle of his body standing to attention. '*What* did you just say?'

'Shit. Didn't she tell you? I thought—' Patrick's brain had obviously caught up with his mouth because his bravado now gave way to bluster, his smirk buckling into awkwardness. 'I mean – it wasn't anything, really. Not like an affair. But yeah, she made a move. There was this . . . you know. Thing.'

'This *thing*,' Dan repeated, feeling sick as he imagined Rebecca making eyes at his brother. Turning that creamy freckled face of hers towards him, quirking an eyebrow with a suggestion in her gaze. She often wore her long auburn hair in a thick side-plait, and Dan could picture her twirling the end of it idly round her fingers. He'd always loved Rebecca's hair. He'd loved every bit of her.

'I guess I'm hard to resist. Right?' Give him the benefit of the doubt – perhaps he was trying to make a joke of it, lighten the mood – but, for whatever reason, Patrick was now puffing his chest out like some kind of randy ape. Like the stupid, dick-driven alpha male he was.

Dan laughed, but there was zero mirth in the sound. 'You're unreal.'

'What?'

'You heard me.' And then it was all bursting out of him, the shock and hurt and rage. 'You're actually bragging about having my ex-wife – the woman I loved – making a move on you. Like you think that's funny! Tell me, why did you even go there with this story tonight – to put me down? To make me feel like shit? It's always been like that with you, hasn't it? You can't help yourself. I bet it was the other way round, anyway. I bet it was *you* flirting with *her*, I bet it was—'

'Hey! Whoa!' Patrick had his hands in the air. 'Calm down, Dan, don't get your knickers in a twist.'

Yeah, and there it was, right on cue: the old *Calm down. Don't be so sensitive.* Any minute now, Patrick would say that it was only a bit of banter, or something equally moronic, and then Dan would probably have to punch him. 'Oh, fuck off. I'm going home,' he said, rising unsteadily to his feet. Without looking back, he went striding towards the door, shoving his arms into his jacket.

Patrick had caught up with him by the time he'd stepped outside, mouth wet where he must have drained his last half-pint in a fast gulp. He'd never been one to waste good beer. 'Wait! What's got into you? Jesus! It was only one night. I mean—'

'I don't want to know,' Dan yelled, pushing him away. Patrick staggered – it had been a hard push – but Dan was too angry to care. One night? Which night? And what exactly had they done all night? Every time Patrick made another glib comment, the situation became worse. Nausea surged up Dan's throat as he pictured the two of them in a clinch, Rebecca's soft, wide mouth against Patrick's, their arms twining around each other's backs. He couldn't bear it. 'For God's sake, I don't want to hear any more. Just shut up.'

He was fuming, practically trembling with rage by now. Patrick had often taken Dan's toys through childhood: broken them, lost them, been careless with them. A nice shirt Dan had saved up for as a teenager – Patrick had borrowed it without asking, and left it stained and crumpled on his bedroom floor afterwards. The motorbike Dan bought, aged twenty, his pride and joy – Patrick had taken it 'out for a spin' and returned it with a dent in the exhaust and silvery scrapes along the frame. He'd always had to show who was boss, who was the older brother. But Dan had never dreamed Patrick would stoop so low as to go there with Rebecca, his *wife*. To be so unbothered about how Dan might feel that he could recount it as a funny story. Did he have *any* feelings in there, or was he all just one enormous pulsing ego?

Patrick followed him as Dan stalked off along the path. The dark sky was punctuated with yellow street lights, the river wide and black on their left, and a chilly breeze sent an empty beer bottle clinking along the concrete. The rain blew into their faces, but Dan turned up his jacket collar and walked faster.

'Come on,' Patrick wheedled from behind. 'Look, I'm sorry, okay? I'm sorry.'

Finally he had thought to say sorry. Well, it was too late now. Everyone knew that an apology counted for nothing if you only made it out of obligation. 'Sorry for what? Sleeping with my wife or being stupid enough to tell me?' Dan's fists were clenched by his sides; he was imagining breaking his brother's handsome nose, wrecking his face, pummelling the shit out of him. 'Don't answer that. In fact don't say anything else. Go home. I don't want to see you.'

'What do you mean, you don't want to—I'm your *brother*. I'm meant to be cutting down your dead tree tomorrow morning, remember, so—'

Dan whirled round, glaring at him. 'Forget the tree. Just go. You're not welcome at my place any more.'

He knew he was being melodramatic, sounding like a five-year-old, but he couldn't stop himself. He wanted to punish Patrick, for once in his life. To snatch some power back again by refusing him, rejecting him. He was due to fly to Chile in a matter of days and, right now, it didn't seem far enough.

Patrick's face was yellowy beneath the street light, so it was hard to read his expression. He shrugged. 'Suit yourself,' he said, then walked past Dan and further along the path.

Dan watched him go for a moment, then turned off to the right, winding through the estate that led back to the main Hammersmith drag and towards his flat. Rage beat impotently through him at the fact that his brother hadn't even bothered to put up a fight. Smarting that Patrick hadn't tried harder to seek forgiveness. *Suit yourself*, indeed. What would suit Dan would be for the betrayal never to have happened in the first place, or at least for the whole tawdry saga to have remained silent and secret within Patrick's guilty conscience, jabbing at him now and then as a reminder of what a shit he was. A furious growl escaped his throat as he kicked out at a nearby bin, instantly regretting it for the corresponding pain that shot up his leg. That was Patrick's fault too. It was all Patrick's fault!

'I can't believe you let him walk home on his own,' Zoe raged the day before the funeral, when emotions were running high. 'What kind of brother are you? Why couldn't you let him stay – be the bigger man?'

It was a good question. One that had haunted Dan ever since. And one to which he had absolutely no answer. *It's your fault*, she was effectively saying. *This is your fault. I blame you!*

Yet now, in a devastating new twist, it turned out that the entire fight with Patrick had been built on a lie after all. A pointless, mean lie that Patrick had told him, in order to – well, what? Make Dan feel crap, no doubt. Cut off his balls just before he left on his travels. Burst his bubble good and proper.

'You fucking idiot,' he muttered under his breath, still standing there in the cool hall of his brother's house, with the family photos gazing silently down at him. He punched the wall, utterly distraught. What a waste, he thought, as tears pooled in his eyes and began spilling down his face. Tears of frustration and disbelief and wretchedness. Had Patrick really died for nothing, for a stupid *lie*? He gulped for air, crying properly now. His first tears since Patrick's death and they weren't even fully for his brother, but for himself too, for the horrific irony of the situation. 'Well, that backfired, didn't it?' he shouted miserably into the emptiness. 'The joke's on you this time, Patrick.'

But it wasn't funny. And he wasn't laughing. Not even slightly.

Chapter Twenty-Five

The reverberations of the phone call with Rebecca continued to slam through Dan over the next few days. He felt
numb with shock, as if nothing touched him. He didn't see
or speak to anyone, just dazedly went and bought tins of
cream emulsion and white gloss and set about repainting
Zoe's kitchen like a robot, every brushstroke a silent *But
why?* in his head. Had it all been a massive wind-up? If so,
why had Patrick let it get so out of hand? Why, when Dan
lost his cool and pushed him away, didn't Patrick own up,
say that it was a stupid joke? Granted, it wouldn't have been
amusing, but at least they could have put the matter to bed,
so to speak, rather than leave things festering. Rather than
have Patrick stalking off alone into the night – towards his
death, as it turned out.

He'd been in a weird mood all evening, though, come to
think of it. Preoccupied and kind of brittle. He'd teased Dan
about Tiggy, insisting that she must fancy him and vice
versa, despite Dan demurring that Tiggy really wasn't his

type. 'Ah, you won't be saying that after *dos cervezas*, though, will you?' he said, elbowing Dan. 'Eh?' Then Patrick's phone had beeped with some message or other, after which his tone had changed abruptly. 'Don't listen to me, though, Dan. I'm a fuck-up, really. You go off and shag your way round the Andes while I just fuck it all up here.'

Patrick did get like this sometimes when he was drunk – Eeyorishly glum and prone to negative introspection – but Dan had just assumed he was wasted and hadn't paid too much attention. Patrick's life was the ideal after all: what did he have to complain about, really? Clearly something must have been going on in his head, though, for him to have come up with that whole story about Rebecca.

His thoughts returned to the phone call Patrick had been in the middle of when Dan arrived at the pub that night, how agitated his brother had seemed. Had Patrick been under some enormous strain that he wanted to talk about, but didn't know how? Had his brash claims later on been a misguided cry for help?

Dan hated that there were still so many loose ends around his brother's death, so many uncertainties. He hated not knowing what had happened to him that night, how Patrick had ended up in the river at all, and why. They'd all assumed it must have been a tragic accident – that or a violent mugging – but now Dan found himself wondering anew. What torments had Patrick been suffering that he hadn't been able to speak about? Why had he acted so badly, so out of character?

I'm sorry, he texted Rebecca on Saturday morning, feeling a pang of remorse for his tirade. Sorry too that he had shown his true colours at the end of the phone call, with the nasty pay-off about her pregnancy. He had never thought of himself as a cruel person until now. *Really sorry, Bex. I should have had more faith in you. Patrick must have made it up to hurt me – I don't know why. That was my last conversation with him, so it's been on my mind. Sorry I said those things to you. I'm a bit of a mess. Hope you are well and happy.*

There. Humble and fulsome. She probably wouldn't reply – maybe she'd even blocked him – but at least he had apologized. And painting the kitchen was proving to be soothing: a straightforward, fairly mindless task and another act of atonement for the tangle of events that had been Patrick's end. Afterwards, yes, he was glad he'd bothered to put in the effort. He'd given the entire kitchen two coats of cream paint with white gloss for the woodwork, and it was, although he said so himself, one hell of an improvement. The walls gleamed in the April sunshine and the room felt lighter, brighter and a more hopeful place to be. Call it a new beginning, he thought, with a ripple of pride in his own work. A clean slate. Zoe would be delighted when she returned on Monday.

For the finishing touch, he went out to the supermarket and picked up bread and milk for them – *thoughtful*, he praised himself – as well as an Easter egg for each of the children, as a nice surprise. Then, because it only seemed fair, he chose an egg for Jemima too, feeling a strange tightening in his chest as he added it to the trio. Well, why not? She was family after all, this mystery little niece of his. And yes, okay, because he had been looking for a reason to get in touch with Lydia again since the night of Jonathan's party. He had been unable to stop thinking about her; his memories vivid of the two of them dancing so wildly, the lurid cocktails they'd dared each other to try, and her body so close to his, the smell of her coconut shampoo. *I have a horrible feeling I might have embarrassed myself last night – I blame those cocktails!* Lydia had texted the morning after and he'd agonized over his response, wanting to be witty and charming in reply, yet ultimately feeling that he had to keep his distance. *Great night!* was all he wrote in the end, bland and nothingy. She hadn't messaged again.

Still, at least he had an excuse to get in touch with her now, and it came wrapped in shiny foil. *I have something for Jemima,* he'd texted. *If you're working, I could drop it off at the shop?*

Lydia had replied shortly afterwards: *Week off! You could drop it round at the flat instead?* – and then added her address.

So here he was now, parking outside her apartment

block and walking up to the main door, his heart actually thumping, he realized, putting a hand to it as he pressed the bell. Was this really the good idea it had seemed, back when he'd stood there in front of the shelves of confectionery? Would Lydia answer the door, glance down at the Easter egg in his hands and give him a look that said, *I see straight through you, mate*? He'd never had a good poker face, frankly.

'It's Dan,' he said, when he heard her voice over the intercom, then the door mechanism buzzed and he was able to push it open and walk in. Her flat was on the first floor, she'd said, so he went up the stairs, chocolate offering in hand. When he reached the landing she was standing in her open doorway, wearing a red dress patterned with blue birds of paradise, with her hair coiled up in two twists on either side of her head. The style made him think of Princess Leia, which was faintly erotic in itself.

'Hi there,' she said. Her feet were bare, the toenails painted pastel blue, he noticed. 'Do you want to come in?'

'Er . . .' He hesitated, holding up the Easter egg. 'I just wanted to drop this round, but—' Why was he talking himself out of the invitation? 'Yes please,' he said, as a small pirate came barrelling up to him, complete with eye-patch and felt-tipped stubble. Jemima, presumably. Her upturned nose was the spit of Bea's, he noticed. 'Hello there,' he said. 'I mean – shiver me timbers, who in the name of Davy Jones is this terrifying pirate?'

She held up a bendy foam cutlass with impressive menace; unmistakably Patrick's daughter, with her hard stare and sweeping dark eyelashes. The thought made him feel strange. 'Arrrr!' she growled.

'Jemima's going to a party later this afternoon,' Lydia explained. 'Get out of the way, love, let Dan come through the door. And watch that cutlass, will you – I don't want you to stab anyone, let alone someone who's turned up with a present.'

Jemima's one visible eye lit up immediately. 'Question: did somebody say . . . *present?*' she asked.

'Do you know, I think they did,' Dan replied, finding it almost impossible to keep a straight face. On first impressions, this new niece of his was pretty adorable. He held up the Easter egg on his palm, as if tempting a pony with a sugar lump.

Jemima's gaze swung from the Easter egg to her mother, then back to Dan. 'For *me?*' she asked, hopping from foot to foot.

'For tomorrow,' Lydia said. 'From . . .' She hesitated, caught Dan's eye and then said, 'From Uncle Dan.'

'Thank you! Thank you! Thank you!' Jemima cried, bouncing up and down. Then she stopped and glanced suspiciously from Dan to her mum again. 'Wait. Question: is he your new boyfriend or something?'

Dan almost choked at such an ambush of a question. 'No!' said Lydia, turning pink.

'No,' Dan agreed gruffly, hoping his face wasn't betraying his feelings.

'Hmm,' said Jemima, apparently unconvinced. 'Only Dylan at school said *his* mum is always bringing round these *uncles* and then they turn out to be her *boyfriends*.' She swung her cutlass through the air, then whirled away down the hall. 'Anyway, bye,' she yelled over her shoulder. 'Thank you!'

Lydia cleared her throat, rolling her eyes. 'Sorry about that. She's over-excited about the party and showing off. Um, did I offer you a coffee?' She put a hand to her face. 'I'm all flustered now. Why are kids so embarrassing?'

Dan laughed. 'I think it's in the job description. Coffee would be great, please.'

He followed her along a narrow hallway, painted bright pink and hung with photographs of Lydia and Jemima, as well as a Lego Batman poster and some splodgy finger-paintings. Through an open door on the left Dan caught sight of a cosy living room, with jade-green wallpaper patterned with palm leaves, a bookcase stuffed with paperbacks and a dark-purple sofa, heaped with cushions. A sewing machine and piles of fabric took up one table, along with an old-fashioned sewing box, a bit like his mum's. Further on was a small modern kitchen with prints and postcards all over the walls, plants ranged along the windowsill and the sweet, heavy smell of syrup in the air. 'We've been making flapjacks, sorry about the mess,' Lydia said, flapping a hand at a pile of washing up by the sink. A tray of caramel-coloured oaty flapjacks sat cooling in a tin nearby. 'Do you want one? They're a bit gooey. Between you and me, I think my assistant was somewhat heavy-handed with the golden syrup.'

'Yes please,' he said, his gaze darting around the walls. Some of the things up there struck him as odd – why would anyone stick old dressmaking patterns on the wall? he wondered – but others told stories: a Good Spelling certificate on the fridge; aged black-and-white wedding photos, presumably of Lydia's parents; and a large map of Sydney, with a small framed handwritten list beside it. *Favourite places to take Lyddie,* he read, feeling curious. *Bronte Beach. Murphy's Café. Rosie's Threads . . .*

'So you've recovered from last Saturday then,' Lydia said, cutting the flapjacks into rectangles.

Dan turned back from the list, feeling as if he'd been prying. 'Yes, just about,' he said. 'The six o'clock emergency call from one of Patrick's tenants the next morning was pretty sobering.'

'Oh no, nightmare,' she said, laughing in sympathy. She slid four flapjacks onto a plate. 'Here – tuck in. I'll make some coffee. Does that happen a lot, then? Emergency calls around the clock from irate residents?'

'More often than you'd think,' he replied, biting into the flapjack. 'Oh, wow,' he said, as its sweetness hit him. 'These are *good*.' His phone started ringing just then and he pulled it out of his pocket, only to see the words *Pain In Arse* on the screen. *You are kidding me,* he thought, trying not to grind his teeth in frustration. 'Talking of which,' he said, feeling certain that Rosemary would be phoning about some non-existent problem again, like the squeaking floorboards incident, and that it wouldn't be unreasonable of him to ignore the call. But then he remembered how lonely she had seemed last time and sighed, knowing that he was a push-over. 'Here's one right now. Excuse me a minute.' He swiped to answer it. 'Hello?'

'Daniel? It's Rosemary Verlaine here. I'm ever so sorry to bother you at the weekend like this, but . . .' Her voice quavered. 'I've gone and fallen over and I'm finding it quite hard to get up again.'

His cynicism vanished at once. 'Rosemary! Are you hurt? Should I call an ambulance?'

'Heavens, no, I don't want to make a fuss, only I tried ringing Alan – you know, my nephew – but he's not picking up the phone. I think he said they were going to Marbella for the Easter weekend, you see, so he probably doesn't want to hear from a silly old woman on his holidays, but . . .'

She sounded upset, tearful even; a different person from the charming, chatty Rosemary he knew from past visits. 'I'll come over,' he said, before she had to ask. He'd have to go back to his flat and grab her keys from the box of Patrick-related stuff so that he could let himself in, he thought quickly. 'I'll be about forty minutes; can you hang on that long? Are you sure you wouldn't rather I called an ambulance – got someone to you sooner?'

He was dimly aware of Lydia looking anxiously at him, while Rosemary replied. 'Thank you, Daniel, you're very kind. No need for any bother with ambulances or anything. I've just slipped and bumped my head, but I'm not dying on the floor, I promise. Sorry to be so tiresome, dear, only I didn't know who else to call.'

Dan sighed. His parents were like this too. Even when his mum had been seriously ill with pneumonia a few years ago, she'd fretted endlessly about 'being a bother' and 'making a fuss', and now Rosemary was doing the same. But if he rang an ambulance and they arrived before him, she wouldn't be able to let them in, by the sound of it, and they'd have to break the door down. 'I'll be there as soon as I can,' he promised.

Chapter Twenty-Six

Damn it, Dan thought, driving away a few minutes later. Of course he didn't begrudge Rosemary for calling him, but the timing could have been better. Just as he'd successfully engineered a visit to Lydia's place, he'd been wrenched straight out of there again. Then he felt bad for his own churlishness. It wasn't as if Rosemary had chosen to fall over and hurt herself.

Having arrived at her flat and let himself in, it quickly became apparent that her 'not wanting a fuss' was wishful thinking. Dan wasn't any kind of nurse or doctor, but it was obvious even to him that she had broken her wrist and was in a lot of pain from her hip too. He knew that a broken hip was pretty catastrophic for an elderly person; his grandmother had fallen and fractured hers when she was eighty, and he could still remember overhearing the doctor gravely telling his dad, 'A broken hip is basically a death sentence for a woman her age, I'm afraid.'

'I need to get you to the hospital,' he said, kneeling down

beside Rosemary. She was lying in an awkward twist on the carpet, dust motes twirling in a nearby shaft of sunshine. 'And I'd take you in my car, but I don't want to risk making things worse by moving you, so I'm going to call for help.'

Rosemary must have been feeling really bad because she didn't even argue, merely nodded then shut her eyes. There were mascara marks beneath her lashes, Dan noticed, as he called 999. Had she been crying as she lay here alone? He couldn't bear the thought.

'What a fool,' she sighed, once he'd assured her the paramedics were on their way. 'And now I've ruined your weekend as well. But please – there's no need for you to wait around here any longer; just leave the door on the latch so that the ambulance people can get in, and I'll be fine.'

'As if,' he scoffed. 'I'm not leaving you like this.' Oh God, was that urine he could smell? How long had she been lying here anyway? He felt doubly wretched for his bad-tempered reaction earlier, when she must be suffering such embarrassment as well as pain right now. Should he mention it or would that only make her feel worse? The latter, he decided. 'Can I do anything while we wait?' he asked humbly. 'Do you want me to get you something to eat or drink?' Then a thought occurred to him. If she needed surgery – if her hip *was* fractured, for instance – then she probably shouldn't be having either. Weren't you supposed to be nil by mouth before an operation?

'I'm okay,' she said, which saved that dilemma anyway. She closed her eyes again, as if she'd used up all her energy with his arrival. The skin of her eyelids was translucent, her face very pale and her hair fell in loose hanks around her shoulders. It was the first time he'd seen her without her chignon, Dan realized; she must have made an effort for him when he'd been here previously. There was something about this that he found particularly heartbreaking.

The paramedics arrived within ten minutes, confirming that Rosemary's wrist was broken. Dan could tell they were concerned about possible concussion, and her hip pain as well. They gave her some painkillers before manoeuvring her skilfully onto a stretcher and out to the waiting ambulance, then they set off to A&E, with Dan promising to lock up and follow on behind. 'Daniel, there's no need, I'll be quite all right,' Rosemary quavered in protest, but Dan merely raised an eyebrow and told her he'd see her at the hospital, and that was that.

A short while later, having eventually found somewhere to park, he tracked her down in the X-ray waiting area, still looking ashen-faced as she lay on a trolley, but insisting that she would be absolutely fine on her own, and that he really didn't need to be there. 'I know I don't need to be here,' he replied, 'but if this had happened to my mum and I couldn't get to the hospital, I would want somebody to sit with her, okay? So no more quibbling. I'm staying.'

'Goodness,' said Rosemary and he was relieved to see a faint twinkle return to her eyes. 'It's rather thrilling when you get all stern, Daniel. I quite like it, you know.'

He laughed and was about to reply when his phone bleeped with a text from Lydia. 'Excuse me a minute,' he said, unable to resist opening it at once.

How is she? Hope you are both okay x, he read.

'Sorry, I just need to . . .' he said, firing off a quick reply with the details. Nice of her to bother asking, he thought, feeling warm inside.

He looked up to see that Rosemary was peering at him in an interested sort of way. 'Is that your lady friend?' she asked.

'What? Why do you ask that?' he blustered in response.

'I can tell from your face.' She had definitely perked up now, Dan thought, trying not to roll his eyes. 'Is this the one you were not quite talking about the other week then? What's her name? Or his name for that matter, obviously. I'm quite modern about these things, you know.'

Dan felt himself turn red. What was this: Jump to Conclusions Day? First Jemima lobbing in difficult questions about him and Lydia, now Rosemary . . . The barrage of nosiness was almost enough to make a man panic and run away.

'You might as well tell me,' she said. 'We could be stuck here for hours, judging by that queue. Why not take pity on a poor old woman and talk me through your love-life to while away the time? Take my mind off things.'

On a good day there was nothing 'poor old woman'-ish about Rosemary and they both knew it, but Dan could tell it would be impossible to try and wriggle out of this conversation, now that she had the bit between her teeth.

'Well . . .' he began. 'It's quite a long story, actually.'

'My favourite kind,' she said, looking delighted. 'Tell me *everything.*'

It took a while for the whole tale to emerge, interrupted as it was by a series of X-rays, first of Rosemary's wrist and then of her hip. 'So that's about the size of it,' Dan finished, once they had been moved to a curtained-off cubicle to wait for a doctor.

'But you like her,' Rosemary pressed, eyes beadily on him.

'Well, yes,' he said. 'But . . .'

'So what's the problem? She sounds a very nice girl. And your sister-in-law will understand, given time.'

'I'm not so sure,' Dan said glumly. 'I mean, this is the woman that Patrick cheated on Zoe with. Who had his child. Trust me, Zoe's better off not knowing about any of that. It would destroy her. Which means nothing can ever happen with Lydia.' He spread his hands. 'Zoe already blames me for Patrick's death. I can't risk blowing things up completely over this.'

Rosemary blinked. 'She blames you for his *death*? But why?'

He'd walked right into that one. 'It's another long story,' he muttered.

'Gracious, Daniel, you're like a living soap opera,' she told him. But then, seeing his downcast expression, she reached out to pat his arm cautiously with her good hand. 'I'm sorry. This must all have been very turbulent for you. But why on earth would Zoe blame you for whatever happened to Patrick?'

Dan didn't have to tell her the whole thing, he knew that. And yet there was something about Rosemary's concerned, listening face that made him feel powerless to change the subject. Plus he was still trying to make sense of everything after the phone call with Rebecca. Out it spilled: the argument over Rebecca; Dan digging his heels in for once and turning his brother away.

'Good gracious,' said Rosemary. 'You have been through the wringer, haven't you? I *am* sorry.'

Dan wasn't sure he could bear her sympathy, with everything so fresh in his mind. 'I'm trying to put things right,' he told her, followed by a brief explanation of his spreadsheet.

'So it's a bit like picking up Brownie points for good deeds?' she asked.

'Yes, I suppose so,' he replied, although he would have preferred a slightly more manly analogy. 'I'm trying to help in lots of different ways, each one a secret apology. Like looking after her kids and taking on Patrick's workload – things he would normally have done himself. Some extras too: for instance, painting the kitchen as a surprise while Zoe's away and—'

Her eyes narrowed. 'You painted the kitchen as a *surprise*?' she said. 'Without asking her first?'

'Er . . . yeah?' Dan replied, wondering why she was looking so dubious. 'I thought she'd be—'

Before he could say 'pleased', the curtain was pulled aside at that moment and a doctor walked in, carrying a file of notes. 'Mrs Verlaine?' she said. 'I'm Dr McCarthy. I've just been looking at your X-rays, and have some good news, but also some bad news.'

Rosemary gave Dan a meaningful look. 'To be continued,' she said, then turned her attention back to the doctor. 'Hello, dear, thank you so much. I'm very sorry to be a bother. What beautiful nail varnish that is, if you don't mind me saying. It's *Ms* Verlaine, by the way. Never married. Unfortunately for all those men!'

The doctor smiled briefly. 'Let's start with the good news, Ms Verlaine: your hip isn't broken, although I gather you're experiencing some pain there. I imagine it's badly bruised, but may I take a look?'

Dan stood up, taking this as his cue to leave. 'I'll wait outside.'

'He's embarrassed because I've been on his case about his love-life,' he heard Rosemary saying to the doctor as he made his way back through the curtain. '*And* because he won't want to see my old legs, either. Or anything else, for that matter!'

Safely on the other side of the curtain, Dan rolled his eyes again, even though it was hard to argue with either of Rosemary's statements. He heard the rustle of clothing and then the doctor speaking in a low voice, and what sounded like Rosemary whimpering in pain a couple of times, which was horrible to hear.

He pulled his phone out from his jeans pocket, needing something to do with his hands, and clicked on a sports app to see what was happening in the football that afternoon. He had started keeping an eye on how Fulham were doing, so that he had another thing to talk to Gabe about. But before the page had even loaded, he heard a voice saying, 'Dan?' and looked up, only to see, astonished, that Lydia was there in the hospital corridor, walking towards him.

'Hi,' he said, taken aback. He almost wanted to rub his fists into his eyes and check again, like a cartoon character, because he couldn't quite believe what he was seeing. 'What are you doing here?'

She was carrying a cloth bag, which she handed over to him. 'It sounded as if you might be here a while, so I brought you some provisions. How is she? And are you okay?'

He was so touched that he couldn't actually speak for a moment. 'That's so kind of you. Thank you.' He could see clingfilmed sandwiches inside the bag as well as a couple of apples, plus a tinfoil-wrapped package. 'She's in there,' he added, indicating the curtain with his head. 'Her hip's not broken at least, but—'

'Daniel?' he heard Rosemary call at that moment. 'Who are you talking to?'

'Er . . .' His mouth went dry. Oh no. He did *not* want the two of them to meet, not after he'd just poured his feelings out to Rosemary. Knowing her, she wouldn't be able to resist stirring things up with great glee. 'A friend,' he called back, pulling a face at Lydia.

'Um . . . hello,' Lydia said.

Goodness knows what the doctor made of her patient's through-the-curtain nosiness, but then it got worse because they heard Rosemary saying to her in thrilled tones, 'Well, I never, I think that might be the beautiful lady-friend that Daniel's been telling me all about. This *is* exciting!'

Dan cringed. Talk about wishing the ground could swallow you up. 'We can hear you, you know,' he said, unable to look at Lydia any more. 'Sorry,' he mumbled in her vague direction.

'If you could keep still a moment please,' the doctor said to Rosemary, who clearly wasn't paying any attention, because she was too busy issuing instructions of her own.

'Well, open the curtain then, Daniel. Come in! I'd like to say hello properly, seeing as she's made such an effort.'

Dan shot Lydia an agonized look, although she seemed more on the verge of laughter than being embarrassed or offended. 'It's fine,' she hissed.

'Are you sure you're decent in there?' Dan checked, only to have a very impatient *'Yes!'* in response. 'Okay then,' he sighed, mouthing, 'Really sorry about this' to Lydia. Then he pulled back the curtain. 'Lydia, Rosemary. Rosemary, Lydia,' he said. 'Lydia has kindly brought us some food.'

'What a darling,' Rosemary sighed, looking Lydia up and down and nodding with approval, before making a very unsubtle thumbs-up sign to Dan. Give me strength, he thought, trying not to groan aloud. 'So you're Lydia,' Rosemary said. 'And you've come all this way to see Daniel. Well, I never. You must like him a great deal.'

'Rosemary, that's enough – behave yourself,' Dan said. There was only so much blatant mischief-making he could take.

'As I was just telling Ms Verlaine,' Dr McCarthy said, 'her wrist is broken in two places and she'll need to stay in for surgery. Are you the next of kin?' she asked Dan.

'No,' he said. 'I'm her . . .' He glanced over at Rosemary, who was propped up on the bed with a blanket covering her legs. 'Landlord, I suppose. And friend.'

'Okay, so we're going to admit Ms Verlaine for the night, treat that wrist as soon as possible and keep an eye on her,' the doctor said. 'There are no visible signs of a head injury, but we will continue to monitor her for the time being. Ms Verlaine, is there anyone we could contact for you? Perhaps somebody who could bring you a couple of items from home – toiletries and a nightdress, that sort of thing?'

'Er . . .' said Rosemary, and Dan could tell she was about to launch into her 'not wanting to be a bother' spiel again.

'I can go back and get a few things for you,' he said. 'If you'd like me to, I mean.'

Rosemary's mouth wobbled a little. 'Thank you, darling, that would be so kind, if you don't mind.' Of course in the next minute she was looking over at Lydia with an eyebrow raised. 'He's a proper gentleman, isn't he? Heavens, if I wasn't so ancient, I'd be after him myself.'

The doctor said she would add Rosemary to the list for surgery and that yes, it was fine to eat and drink before the operation, as she'd only be having a local anaesthetic. She would see if there was space on a ward for her, but in the meantime they could stay put. Then she went off to her next patient, looking rather glad to escape, Dan thought.

Rosemary turned her full attention on Lydia. 'That's a beautiful dress you're wearing, dear,' she said.

Lydia's hand flew up to her chest. 'Oh, thank you,' she said, looking pleased. 'I made it myself.'

'Did you? Very good! I love the mandarin collar,' Rosemary said, peering beadily. 'And the frogging across the throat is divine. Goodness, you are clever.' She turned to

Dan, who had only managed to follow half of the conversation. 'I used to teach at the London College of Fashion, I'll have you know. I haven't always been a mouldy oldie.'

'Rosemary!' scolded Dan. 'Nobody thinks that.'

'Oh my God,' said Lydia. 'Seriously? I applied to study there.'

'What, and they turned you down? What idiots,' Rosemary clucked. 'That dress really is very good, you know. And I'm a curmudgeon – I wouldn't say it if I didn't mean it.'

'Thank you. They did offer me a place, but . . . well, life got in the way,' said Lydia. She looked sad for a moment, then rearranged her face. 'Anyway, I'd better go. I need to pick up Jemima from her party in twenty minutes. Can't keep a pirate waiting.'

'Good to see you,' Dan said. Should he lean in and give her a hug? No, she was already moving towards the curtain and out of there. 'Um, shall I walk you to your car?' he asked.

'I got the bus,' she said. 'It's fine. Bye. Hope you feel better soon, Rosemary.'

'Thank you,' Rosemary said. Barely had Lydia closed the curtain and left than she was leaning forward, eyes bright, and saying to Dan, 'Well, fancy that. How lovely of her. And by the way, she definitely likes you back, Daniel. Definitely!'

'Rosemary!' Dan hissed, glancing at the curtain, which wasn't exactly soundproof. Truly, had there ever been a less discreet person in the history of the world? 'Let's see what's in here then,' he said to distract her, and unpacked the picnic that Lydia had brought. The tinfoil package contained four flapjacks, he discovered, and the smell took him back to the warmth of her kitchen earlier on. It seemed a long time ago already. 'Cheese or ham?' he asked Rosemary, proffering the sandwiches.

'Thank you,' she said, plucking one from the clingfilm.

'And now you'd better tell me about this fabulous career of yours,' he said to her, sitting down on the plastic chair beside the bed. 'You dark horse, you. London College of Fashion, eh? You kept that quiet.'

There was a far-away gleam in her eye, perhaps as she reflected on past glories. 'Well,' she said, smiling. 'Seeing as you asked . . .'

'Wait,' he said, shuffling about in the chair to get comfortable. 'Okay. I'm ready. Tell me everything.'

Rosemary spluttered on her sandwich. 'Oh, Daniel,' she said fondly. 'I *am* glad you're here.'

He smiled back at her. 'Me too,' he replied.

Chapter Twenty-Seven

It was Easter Sunday, and Rebecca had left a voicemail on Dan's phone: *I'm sorry too,* she said. *Sorry for what you're going through, and for what I said about Patrick. He gave me a ton of shit in the street once after we split up, did you know that? I'm not telling you this to have a pop, more to remind you that he did love you. Remember that speech he made at our wedding? I still get goosebumps thinking about it. Anyway, I hope you're okay and that Zoe's bearing up. Take care.*

Her words were so unexpectedly nice that they brought tears to Dan's eyes and he ended up listening to the message three times over as he drove to the hospital. Patrick had never mentioned the incident in the street – Dan felt quite saucer-eyed just imagining the scene (what had been *said?*) – but hearing about it now made him feel good too. Comforted. And for Rebecca to bother leaving him the message at all meant a lot to him. She had seen past his ugly words and had been kind. He felt . . . not mended exactly, but as if something broken was finally healing.

Having delivered home a patched-up Rosemary, he found himself looking around her flat with renewed interest, now that he knew more about her life story: the rags-to-riches tale of her having been an impoverished dressmaker who began designing her own fashions in the Sixties, selling them first in Portobello Market before being taken under the wing of an influential woman who was already working in the fashion industry. She went on to launch a range of clothes in a Carnaby Street boutique, branched out into costume design for the theatre and then the movie industry, as well as being invited to lecture on prestigious design courses in London and New York.

She always dressed immaculately – he'd noticed that much – but now Dan registered the sewing machine on a corner table in the living room, the design books on the shelves, the stylish decor of the place, and it fitted with the story she had told him. Sad, though, that the tale did not have a happier ending. 'So how come you ended up renting a flat from my brother?' he'd asked the day before, curiosity getting the better of his tact. 'I mean – sorry, that came out wrong—'

She waved aside his blustering. 'It's called a fall from grace,' she replied with a sigh, before going on to detail how she'd clashed with a couple of big industry names – 'once you're out, you're out, darling, that's the problem' – then made some bad investment decisions and, basically, spent all the money without having much of a savings safety net. 'Born with nothing, die with nothing, that'll be me,' she said with a laugh. 'I never bought a house or started a pension, I just enjoyed myself and had a marvellous time. And do you know what else? I don't regret a minute of it.'

It had been sobering for Dan, having to completely rethink his perception of Rosemary to include this whole colourful back-story, to realize that her life had once been vibrant and exciting. In her prime she'd been a powerhouse, a dazzling young woman bursting with creativity – only to be reduced, years later, to the label of 'Pain In Arse' on her landlord's phone. Dan had patronized her, been irritated by her, but in fact she had achieved way more with her life than he – or Patrick – had managed.

Having promised to drop in and see her again soon, he headed on to his parents' house, where his mum was hosting Easter lunch. 'It'll be about twenty minutes,' Liz said, apron-clad and pink in the cheeks as she kissed him on arrival. A comforting smell of roast lamb and mint sauce wafted out from the kitchen, and as she led him through to get him a drink, Dan could see that the special red table-cloth had made its biannual appearance (Christmas and Easter only) on the dining-room table, along with a jug of yellow tulips.

'You look nice,' Dan said, taking in his mum's floral dress and coiffed hair.

'Yes, well,' she said, with a self-conscious shrug, 'I felt like making an effort today. For church. And – well, for me too, I suppose.'

'Good,' said Dan, sliding a bottle of wine into the fridge. Seeing her looking more like her old self again was so comforting that he actually had a lump in his throat. It was only a dress and some blow-drying, at the end of the day, but it also signalled her strength, her courage. The world seemed a tiny bit more normal, now that Liz Sheppard had her lipstick on again.

'Your aunt and uncle are in the living room, if you want to say hello,' she went on, as if that was quite enough talk about herself. 'Although' – she wagged a finger at him – 'don't you go moving that bloody photograph again, son. I'm on to you. Every time!'

'The—Oh,' he said. *Rumbled.* 'I hate that photo,' he muttered as the image swam up in his mind: Patrick grabbing him in a headlock on the beach, victorious and jeering. The look of frightened servitude in his own eyes. He could practically hear the mocking cries of the seagulls in the sky above, even now.

'Why do you hate it?' she asked in surprise. 'It's one of my favourites.'

Dan couldn't believe that she had to ask. 'Because he's picking on me. He's practically strangling me, by the look of things, and grinning about it, like it's all a big game. It makes me feel humiliated, that's all.' His face felt hot. More emotional honesty. It was actually quite liberating, though, being able to express yourself with such frankness. To *say* stuff out loud. Who knew?

'What? No,' she said, shaking her head. 'That wasn't what happened at all. He'd just rescued you from another boy, who was – I don't know, throwing stones at you, roughing you up a bit. Don't you remember?'

Dan stared at her blankly, having no idea, no memory, of what she was talking about. 'That's not how I remember it,' he said.

'Yes! Definitely. Ask your dad, if you don't believe me. We had gone to Brighton for the day and were down on the beach – you boys rushed off with a load of other kids to play while your dad and I were setting out the picnic. This boy made you cry about something anyway, and Patrick saw that you were upset, went over there and sorted everything out. He was protecting you, Daniel! Then he brought you back over to where we were sitting, all triumphant and pleased with himself. That was why Dad took the picture, because he wanted to capture the moment.'

Dan couldn't speak for a few seconds. He couldn't take it in, couldn't square this story with his own version of events. Previously the photograph had always represented Patrick's superiority over him, Dan the loser. It was unsettling to hear his mum recounting a wholly different story. 'Are you sure?' he asked eventually.

'One hundred per cent! Your dad will say the same if you ask him. Patrick was a good brother to you, Daniel! We were proud of the way he used to look after you like that.' She pulled open the oven door, which released a great plume of steam, then leaned forward to check the roast potatoes. 'So leave that picture where it is now, and be grateful for him, okay?' she added in a muffled voice.

Dan was still in a daze. 'Okay,' he said.

The following day, Easter Monday, Dan decided to give himself a break. He had worked tirelessly over the last few weeks, pouring all his energy into picking up the slack in his brother's absence, doing his best to make up for Patrick not being there. Today, though, he would please himself for a change. Look after number one. The plan could have a day off.

First things first: inspired by Mark, he went for a long invigorating run along the river and back again, followed by a hot shower and a massive fry-up. Then he spent some time out in his garden, cutting the grass and tidying up the straggling honeysuckle. The tree was still there, as dead as ever, but he kept his back to it most of the time, and that was all right. Besides, he was going to get round to sorting it out any day now.

Ever since he'd been looking after Patrick's properties,

Dan had picked up the habit of glancing over a place with a critical eye, seeking potential problems that needed attention. Today he found himself doing exactly this with his own flat, seeing it anew. The kitchen window frames, for instance, were starting to rot where the paint had flaked away, and the rear guttering was looking kind of rickety, so he spent a pleasant hour or so making a list of what needed to be done. The handyman he'd taken on to deal with the Hossains' house was doing a good job so far, he'd noticed; he would ask him to provide a quote for the work that needed tackling here as well.

By the time he broke for lunch he was feeling pleased about how productive he was being, how satisfying it felt to get on top of the life admin like this. The secrets he had carried around with him since Patrick's death had been weighty and cumbersome, but today he felt less burdened, as if he had temporarily put them to one side. It felt good to focus on his own matters for a change; he hadn't realized how caught up he had been in other people's lives until now.

Then the doorbell rang.

Easter Monday was an odd time to have an unexpected caller, he thought, as he went to answer it. Unless it was some religious nut trying to give him a pamphlet about Jesus, he supposed. Back when he and Rebecca had been together, friends of hers would occasionally drop round with a bottle of wine or a bag of pastries from the bakery – *Just passing!* – but that had all stopped when they split up, of course. Hardly anyone ever came round to see him, he realized with a jolt as he reached the door. In fact when was the last time anyone else had even been in this flat, other than himself?

'Zoe!' he said in surprise, opening the door and seeing her there.

She was red in the face as she walked in and shut the door behind her. 'The children are in the car and I don't want them to see me shouting at you,' she said. Her hands were curled into fists, he noticed in alarm, and her expression was extremely fierce. 'But what the hell, Dan? What the hell were you playing at?'

He swallowed. Oh my God. Had she found out about Lydia? he thought with a flash of panic. But then he remembered Rosemary's reaction when he'd told her what he'd done. *Without asking her first?* 'Is this about . . . the kitchen?' he guessed.

'Too bloody right it's about the kitchen,' she said. 'What were you thinking? It's not your house! Why on earth did you think it was your place to do that?'

'Because . . .' His nerve faltered. Oh, shit. Had he made a terrible mistake? 'I thought it would be a nice . . . surprise?'

'It was a surprise, all right. Not exactly the surprise I wanted, either, having just driven all the way back from south Wales.' She glared at him and folded her arms across her chest, perhaps to stop herself from punching him. 'Patrick was the last person to paint that kitchen,' she went on. 'And that was fine because, you know, he lived there too. But—'

'I'm sorry,' he mumbled. 'I thought it would—'

'You painted over our height chart, did you realize that?' she yelled. 'We've been marking the kids' heights for years and years.' Tears appeared in her eyes. 'And you painted over that. It was precious to me. It was so, so precious!'

With a horrible jolt Dan remembered the strange series of lines pencilled against the door jamb that he had blithely gloss-painted over. His mind had been on the fallout from Rebecca's call; he hadn't thought to question what they might be. No wonder Zoe was upset. 'I'm sorry,' he said again, feeling wretched. 'I didn't realize. But I honestly thought you would be pleased.'

There was a short silence, which told Dan – as if he didn't already know – that no, Zoe was not pleased. She was very, very far from being pleased in fact. 'I know you want to help. And you've been very helpful,' she said, although the words were snarled rather than said with any fondness, 'but you totally overstepped the mark there. How would you feel' – and now she was striding down the hall and into the kitchen – 'if I did the same to you?' He followed her, his stomach turning over as he remembered that the good-deeds spreadsheet was right there on the fridge, each column care-fully filled with achievements, but she was like an unstoppable force. 'If I just changed these crappy blinds of yours without asking?' She flicked at them with contempt. 'If I ripped up your shitty lino and put a different one down, without even checking you liked it?' She kicked at it. 'If I took out your cupboards. Replaced your fridge—' And then – oh God, she was standing right in front of it before he could stop her. An image came to mind of him rugby-tackling her away, but then it was too late. 'Hey,' she said, peering closer. Her voice changed to something sharp and cold. 'What the hell *is* this? The *Patrick plan*?'

Dan's knees felt as if they could no longer support him all of a sudden. His head swam with attempts to excuse himself, but nothing seemed valid. 'I . . .'

'Mending Mrs Henderson's boiler. Taking Ethan to sculpture club,' she read aloud. 'Fixing Zoe's car. What *is* this? Meeting Lydia – who the fuck is Lydia?'

Dan shut his eyes, wishing this was not happening. It was like a bad dream, except it was playing out in real life, right now.

'Skateboarding with Gabe. Easter egg for kids,' Zoe went on reading. 'Oh – here we are. Painting Zoe's kitchen.' She snatched the chart off the fridge and swung round with it, eyes like lasers searing into him. 'Dan. Help me out here. I really need to know what the *hell* this is all about.'

Oh Christ. When the day had been going so well too. 'I . . . I was just trying to help,' he said weakly.

'Awarding yourself points for each thing you did? How big of you.' Zoe didn't seem able to take her eyes off the paper she was holding. 'Buying the kids fish and chips for tea – when even *was* this?'

'Er . . . It was when you stormed out that first night,' he confessed.

Her eyes blazed. 'What? I left a perfectly good dinner cooking,' she reminded him angrily. 'And you felt you had to ditch it and buy them all junk food instead?'

'It wasn't like that,' he said. 'The sausages burned . . . I ruined it. Not on purpose! And I wanted to treat them, so—'

'Wanted to win them over, more like,' she sneered, turning back to the list. 'Tenant visit; VAT return completed; visit to Mum and Dad . . . Jesus, Dan, can't you even go and see your own *parents* without patting yourself on the back? I mean, I thought you were doing these things out of kindness. Because you liked spending time with us. What an idiot I must be. Ha!'

'I do like spending time with—'

'Because it was only ever about you, right? You've made this whole thing about you. Dan to the rescue!' she sneered.

'I just wanted to step in for Patrick,' he said. 'To try and make life easier for you and the kids.'

'To ease your conscience, you mean,' she said. 'And who

is Lydia anyway? Is she one of the tenants? Only I don't remember hearing her name before.'

There was a terrible pause. The easy option dangled in front of Dan like a lifebelt offered to a drowning man. He could simply say yes, couldn't he? Yes, she's a tenant; tell a white lie, so as not to make this any worse?

'Dan?' she prompted. 'Who is she?'

He leaned against the worktop and stared down at the floor, the words sticking in his throat. He couldn't do it to her.

'Dan!' she yelled. 'For fuck's sake, what is it? You're freaking me out now. Tell me!'

Dan's stomach shrivelled. Should he go there? 'She . . .' He couldn't. But Zoe was glaring so fiercely at him that the words fell out anyway. 'She told me that she and Patrick had a fling,' he said miserably and the air around them seemed to seize, as if the room was holding its breath. No turning back now. 'And she has a daughter. Patrick's daughter.'

'*What?*' Zoe flinched as if she'd been slapped and took a step back. She was blinking fast, a hand flying up to her throat. 'I don't believe you.'

'Zoe—'

'Why would you say such a vile thing to me? Why would you do that, Dan?' She screwed up the paper and hurled it to the floor. 'God, you have got some nerve. You've always been jealous of him, haven't you? So pathetically jealous!

Even when he's dead, you're trying to get one over on him by saying these disgusting things!'

He ventured another glance at her, only to see Zoe's features contorted by a mix of rage and hatred. 'Look, I was as shocked as you are,' he said feebly, but she was still going.

'Well, guess what? You're not Patrick. You've never been as good as Patrick! And do you know what? You should live your own life for a change, rather than trying to hang on the coat-tails of your dead brother. My dead husband! Appropriating his life, his work, his *family*, like you have any right to do that. Even worse, bad-mouthing him like that to me. How dare you say those things about him? He was worth ten of you. A thousand of you!'

'Zoe, I—'

'If you have ever cared about me or the kids, you will never say another word about this woman in my presence or to anyone else, do you hear me?' With that, she stormed from the room, marching back towards the front door. 'Just leave us alone!' was her parting shot as she slammed out of the house.

Chapter Twenty-Eight

The walls seemed to echo with Zoe's departure. Dan didn't move for a few moments, trying to absorb the shock. His eye fell on the crumpled piece of paper on the floor that had been his main purpose in recent weeks, and he let out a low groan of despair that he could have got everything so very wrong. *You should live your own life for a change*, Zoe had yelled, and the words kept stinging because they were true. He had stepped into Patrick's shoes and he had enjoyed it, taking on the mantle of the busy property developer, the caring dad. Look at me, how well I'm doing this, he had crowed to himself as he sorted out everyone's problems and gave them his attention. He had even, on occasion, relished a stab of pride at how much better he was at dealing with situations than Patrick had been. The Hossains, yes, but also the moment when Ethan had come out to him. The big hero! Wasn't it telling that he'd felt a spurt of competitive one-upmanship even then?

Now Zoe was calling Dan out on it, and she was right.

He had gone too far, overstepped a boundary. It wasn't much of a competition, after all, when your competitor was dead. And then he had made everything a hundred times worse by telling her about Lydia. He grimaced, remembering how she had flinched, the shock and hurt on her face. The secret was well and truly out now, but he didn't feel any lighter for it. In fact he only felt sickened by himself for blurting out the truth so clumsily – and for what? For Zoe to turn on him, tear him down. He kept thinking about the contempt in her eyes and could hardly bear it.

He reached over, picked up the printed spreadsheet and began ripping it into pieces. Like a stupid chart could ever make up for the loss of a loved one: a father, husband, son. All those jobs and favours Dan had been so eager to complete – they felt meaningless in the face of his sheer ineptitude. How would he be able to put things right now? He couldn't imagine Zoe ever forgiving him for this.

The flat seemed to be closing in around him, so he grabbed his keys and jacket, then went out, suddenly needing to gulp in lungfuls of fresh air. He stuffed his hands in his pockets and headed in the direction of the river, under the flyover that thundered with end-of-bank-holiday traffic and down towards Lower Mall. A plane hung in the sky on its way to Heathrow, and Dan found himself wishing he had left the country and gone to South America after all, and not got involved with any of this. Imagine! He'd never have become entangled with Patrick's business, or the tenants, or the paperwork, or the seven hours spent in hospital waiting rooms on Saturday. He'd be tanned and lean after days spent hiking the Inca Trail, his Spanish would have improved tenfold, he'd have explored jungles and mountains and great beaches and met people from around the world. Maybe fallen in love beneath the vast star-spangled skies of the pampas. He'd be carefree. A different man.

Then again, if he had gone to South America, he wouldn't have met Lydia, a voice in his head pointed out. He wouldn't have got to know his nephews and nieces any better, he wouldn't have spent all this extra time with his own parents, he wouldn't have gone skateboarding or learned about sculptures or unicorns. Was it too corny of him to say that he wouldn't have learned about all the different ways you could love people? Probably, but it was true.

He leaned against the wall, gazing wretchedly down at the river below, watching a clutch of gulls peck at the mud and shingle of its banks. A couple of men in hi-vis tops were out in kayaks, paddling steadily through the water alongside one another. Brothers? he wondered. Or just friends? Was it ever possible to be both?

His dad had taken him and Patrick mudlarking a couple of times when they were boys and they'd found a clay pipe once. He couldn't remember which of them had discovered it now, only that they both wanted it and had such a terrible fight about who was going to keep it that the pipe had got broken, and their exasperated father had said he wouldn't take them out again if they were going to be such brats. So they'd both ended up losing out, twice over.

He was worth ten of you. A thousand of you! Zoe shouted in his head, and Dan cringed afresh. Oh God. What had he done?

He walked past the rowing club, the pubs, a house that was rather optimistically called 'Beach House' and on towards the Dove Pier. He paused to gaze out at all the houseboats moored there, some with amazing gardens growing on their decks, others with buckets and ropes and pulleys piled up. He thought about his own, far less romantic home; somewhere to sleep and eat breakfast, a holding place in between stints at the office. But he didn't want to live like that any more.

Leave us alone, Zoe had yelled and he wondered uneasily about the extent to which she meant this. Did she want him to stop working on Patrick's houses? Drop contact with the tenants and leave all of that to her? Worse – did she mean for him to no longer see the children? She had seemed so hurt and angry that he could imagine her driving them home, saying, 'You're not going to see Uncle Dan again, do you understand? We're better off without him.' The thought was unbearable.

'Sorry,' he groaned under his breath: to Patrick, to Zoe, to the kids. He wished she had let him explain: that, okay, maybe filling the columns of the chart with practical favours and assistance had started out as an obligation, a framework that he felt safe within, but the project had quickly grown into one of love. That he had cherished being part of their family, felt himself become a better person for it. That, yes, he might have helped them out here and there, but they had given him so much in return.

He slumped onto a bench in Furnivall Gardens, feeling numb as the world carried on around him. Cyclists skimmed by. An elderly couple walked a rheumy-eyed poodle. A Lycra-clad woman with pink headphones jogged past, checking something on a fitness tracker.

He didn't know what to do with himself. It was a bank holiday and the rest of the country seemed to be entertaining themselves just fine, but he felt frozen to the spot, unable to make any decisions. Without his good-deeds spreadsheet shoring up the week, he had lost all sense of purpose. He felt as if the mask he'd been wearing over the last month had been ripped away, revealing a small, shabby person beneath. If he wasn't careful he might end up like this for the rest of his life: alone and bitter. His thoughts turned to Rosemary, lying on the floor after her fall, embarrassed and smelling of piss, with only her landlord to help her. It was like a warning premonition, a glimpse into a possible future that awaited him. So what should he do?

★

'Mummy,' said Bea, clambering up onto the bed next to Zoe and lying beside her. 'Why are you crying? Are you sad about Daddy?'

Zoe had managed to wrestle down her distress all the way back from Dan's house, but now that she was home and lying on her own bed, it was no longer possible to maintain the floodgates. Every time she shut her eyes she kept seeing Dan's stupid stricken face and, worse, his printed spreadsheet keeping score of all the things he'd done for her in the last month, like she was some kind of charity case. To think that she'd begun to warm to him again lately, rely on him. Confide in him, even – and yet it was all for a printed list stuck up there on his fridge, his warped means of making himself feel better about the part he'd played in Patrick's death. It was just so cold, so calculating. What had happened to doing things for other people out of the goodness of your heart? As for the rubbish Dan had said about Patrick, it didn't even make sense. Dan had always been gullible when it came to women – look how Rebecca had treated him – but even so, he had got this spectacularly wrong. Zoe felt insulted that he could even have believed such nonsense.

'Yes, darling,' she managed to croak, pulling Bea in close to her. 'I'm sad about Daddy today.'

'I'm sad too, because it's school tomorrow. And I miss my Nain and Taid. And the beach, and Uncle Niall and

Fozzie.' Bea wriggled up a little so that their faces were very close and stroked Zoe's cheek. 'We're both sad together, aren't we, Mummy?'

'We are, my love,' Zoe said, her eyes brimming with tears again. 'We're sad together. Let's hold each other tight for a moment.'

They lay there, arms across one another, Bea nestling her head under Zoe's chin. Forget Dan, she told herself, feeling comfort from her daughter's empathy, as well as the warm softness of her body. Forget his naff plan and his terrible accusations. She didn't need him or his so-called help. She had family and friends standing loyally by her; she had her children and her memories of Patrick to keep herself strong. They'd had such a lovely time in Penarth, with the children laughing and more relaxed than she'd seen them in ages. All three of them had seemed different people, haring around on the beach together with the dog, whooping and screeching. Ethan had lost the bags under his eyes for once. Gabe hadn't started a single fight. Bea had slept soundly in her own bed every night. So had Zoe. The warm welcome they'd received had cast a calming enchantment on them all – only for Zoe to completely lose her shit on returning home to see what Dan had done to the kitchen. But she could return to that calm place, she reminded herself. In her head, if not in person. She could breathe deeply and imagine the sea and remember the lightness she had felt, crunching across the beach in pursuit of her racing children.

'You're doing great,' her mum told her as they hugged goodbye that morning. 'And we're always here, whenever you need us.'

She sighed, wondering if her mum would still think she was doing so great if she'd seen her just now, over at Dan's. Had she overreacted to the paint job? It had been such a shock to walk in there and find the place transformed like that; it hadn't felt like her home any more. Rationally, she knew Dan was only trying to be kind, but it felt like an intrusion, as if he was judging her and her messy house – and being too quick off the mark to smarten them up. Maybe it was petty, but she'd wanted to hang on to every-thing Patrick had ever done for her, preserve it for as long as possible, rather than paint it out of sight. She knew that the height chart they'd created over the years was not the most important thing in the world – it was just lines on a wall – but it had meant something to her, representing the years and years of family life, her children growing up, and the five of them sharing that time together.

She had flipped, anyway. Lost that famous temper of hers. Bundled everyone back in the car and driven over to Dan's house like a maniac. And then, when she saw that moronic list of his, it had been like an arrow to the heart. *What – you thought I was doing this because I liked you all? Not really!*

Her memory kept replaying the scene in her head and she tightened her arms around Bea as she reached the most dreadful moment of all, when he started making accusations about Patrick and some woman or other. Was he deliberately trying to hurt her? He must have got the wrong end of the stick, fallen for a con artist. He must have!

Wait. Something occurred to her. *Lydia*, he had said. Where had she heard that name before?

Bea wriggled free just then. 'Too hot, Mummy.'

'Sorry.' She hadn't realized quite how tightly she had been squeezing the poor thing.

Bea studied her intently, her breathing loud and warm against Zoe's face. 'If Daddy was here, I know what he would say: Come on, you two, enough moping around now.'

Zoe gulped because her daughter's intonation was so like Patrick's, it was as if he were in the room with them, conjured up by the little girl's impression.

'You are absolutely right,' she said, trying to get a grip on her feelings. *Enough moping around now.* Yes, that was exactly what Patrick would have said – and he'd have been right. This was the last day of the school holidays. She would block out the horrible conversation with Dan as best she could and slap on a brave face. She could do that. Hell, she was an expert by now.

Sitting up, Zoe hugged her daughter, trying to squash her sadness back down. 'Thank you, Bea,' she said. 'That was just what I needed to hear. No more moping.' She swallowed hard, pushed her damp hair out of her eyes and squared her shoulders. But as she and Bea went downstairs together in search of something fun to do, Dan's words kept sliding insidiously into her head. *She told me that she and Patrick had a fling. She has a daughter.* It couldn't be true, could it? It just couldn't!

All the same, Zoe couldn't help but rack her brains to remember where she'd met someone called Lydia recently. Because as soon as she remembered, this woman – this liar! – would be sorry.

Chapter Twenty-Nine

Hi, massive apologies again. It honestly came from wanting to be a good brother-in-law and uncle, that's all. I'm sorry. I am happy to continue looking after the business until I'm back at work, but will drop off all the paperwork etc. if you'd rather I didn't do it any more. Dan

Another day, another apologetic text. Overcome by the guilty feeling he had bungled everything, Dan had contacted Zoe on Monday evening, but no reply had come and he didn't dare push the matter. Did she hate him? It had certainly looked that way when she stormed out of his house. The last thing he wanted was to hurt her, but he was pretty sure he had. Very badly. Again.

It was sod's law that a delivery arrived for him that morning, which turned out to be the superhero costume he'd ordered for Gabe's party the following weekend: Thor, Gabe's favourite. The costume came with a red flowing cape, padded six-pack moulded armour, a blonde wig and a plastic hammer. How ironic. He stuffed it all back in the packaging, unable to look at it. Was he still even welcome at the party?

Over in the shop, Lydia's eye was caught by a woman walking past the window with long brown hair, like her mum's, and she was catapulted straight back into one of her favourite memories. She must have been about twelve when she first got to grips with her mum's sewing machine and discovered the joys of making cushion covers and a simple tote bag, and then one day Eleanor had taken her to Goldhawk Road, just the two of them, to browse around the many fabric shops there.

Eleanor Fox had been a fantastic needlewoman, making clothes for the whole family, her own wedding dress even. The low hum of the sewing machine had been the sound that Lydia fell asleep to all through her childhood. 'I think you're ready to start using proper dressmaking patterns,' Eleanor had said thrillingly, as they entered the first shop, and Lydia's heart had leapt to see all the rolls and rolls of different fabrics lined up, so many shades and patterns. Her mum had squeezed Lydia's hand as if she shared her daughter's excitement. 'Let's treat ourselves.'

She could still remember the sewing pattern she'd chosen that day – she probably still had it somewhere in a box of craft stuff. A simple round-necked dress with a high–low hemline. 'Ooh, nice,' her mum said approvingly. 'Now, what fabric would you like?'

The finished dress would not have won any prizes, admittedly – it suffered from some wayward, clumsy seams and the zip at the back never quite sat flat – but it marked the start of a love-affair in earnest between Lydia and the needle. Over the years it became a ritual: she and Eleanor taking the bus to Goldhawk Road together to choose a new pattern each, fabric and buttons and thread. 'When you're older – maybe eighteen – I'll take you to my favourite sewing shop in Sydney,' her mum had once said, over a post-shopping hot chocolate in a café near the bus stop. 'Would you like that?'

Forever after, Lydia had associated the taste of hot chocolate with sheer happiness. 'Really? I would *love* that,' she had replied.

Sewing remained a communication channel between mother and daughter for the rest of the time they had together. When Lydia was fifteen, Eleanor bought her her own sewing machine, and the two of them often commandeered the kitchen table in the evenings so that they could sew away companionably together. They made each other birthday and Christmas gifts – a skirt, a bag, embroidered cushion covers. 'I'm so jealous,' her mum sighed when Lydia showed her the prospectus for the London College of Fashion. 'Hey, do you think they'd let an oldie like me enrol too? Wouldn't that be something?' Even when her mum became ill and lost her hair, Lydia made her light chiffon scarves to wrap around her head, every stitch an *I love you*, every seam a *Please get better.*

The shop door jangled just then and Lydia blinked out of her reverie. She'd been miles away, she realized, turning to greet the customer. But said customer was already speaking, loud and angry.

'What the hell,' she asked, marching up to the counter, 'is your fucking game?'

Lydia stared in shock. First, because nobody ever raised their voice in this shop; and second, because the customer in front of her was Zoe, Patrick's wife, looking puce in the face, fists clenched as if she was about to hit her. 'W-what?' she stuttered.

'It *is* you, isn't it? On Dan's chart. Lydia. You must think I'm some kind of idiot.'

'I . . . No,' said Lydia, trying to get her head around this. *Dan's chart?* 'I don't—'

'You planned this from the start, I'm guessing. You took advantage of me. Found out who I was and then went planting lies left, right and centre.'

'What? No!' Was the woman crazy? This furious outburst was the exact inverse of Zoe's first appearance in the shop when she'd been limp with grief, practically unable to support her own weight, her face puffy with tears. Now she was rigid with anger, eyes blazing, one finger stabbing the air with each accusation. 'I've no idea what this is all about,' Lydia stammered.

'Yeah, *right.*' The words dripped with sarcasm. 'Lying that you had a child with my husband? You're like some kind of parasite. You disgust me!'

'Everything all right?' said Jonathan coming in from the back room. He was carrying a coffee each for Lydia and himself, and his startled gaze swung from one woman to the next. Then his eyes narrowed. 'Can I help you?' he asked, a hint of steel entering his voice.

'Ask your psychopath colleague,' Zoe said, trembling. 'I should sue you for slander,' she added, turning back to Lydia. 'How could you? Preying on a vulnerable woman, trying to get your hands on my money, I'm guessing – well, forget it!' Then without warning she grabbed the nearest object off the shelf beside her – a tall dip-dyed vase – and hurled it at Lydia. Lydia ducked, but the vase hit the wall behind her and shattered into pieces.

'For fuck's sake!' Jonathan shouted, putting down the mugs and striding over towards Zoe. 'Get out of my shop right now or I'm calling the police. Lydia, are you all right? Are you hurt?'

Gulping and tearful, Zoe wheeled around towards the exit. Just as she was pushing the door open, Lydia recovered herself enough to shout, 'I'm not lying. It's all true. *It's all TRUE!'*

The door slammed behind Zoe, and Lydia's knees began to shake. Jonathan came over and put an arm round her. 'Who was that lunatic? Are you okay?' he asked. Lydia was trembling all over, her heart pounding. 'What on earth was all *that* about?'

Dan was out running again, this time along the riverside in Barnes, when his phone rang. He slowed to a walk, fumbling to retrieve it from his pocket. 'Hello,' he said, breath puffing out of him.

'I've just had your sister-in-law in the shop,' Lydia said without preamble. 'Red in the face and screaming at me. Threw a hundred-pound vase at my head too, which smashed everywhere. Why didn't you think to warn me she knew? Not that she was *admitting* to knowing anything, she seemed to be completely in denial. Accused me of making the whole thing up.'

'Oh God,' said Dan, stopping completely. All the blood rushed to his head. 'How did she . . . ? Shit.' Then he remembered the crumpled spreadsheet. *Who the fuck is Lydia?* He groaned. Zoe must have gone flicking through her mental folder of Lydias, recalled his reaction when he first saw that business card on her fridge and put two and two together, he guessed. 'Wait, did you say she'd thrown a *vase* at your *head*?'

he asked, catching up with Lydia's words. Had Zoe become completely deranged? 'Are you all right?'

'Yeah. No harm done. Well, apart from the vase. And me feeling really embarrassed in front of Jonathan.'

Dan exhaled, a long rush of dismay. 'I'm so sorry,' he said. 'Zoe and I had a bit of a bust-up yesterday – she came over and . . . Well, everything's gone wrong, basically. She's really angry with me. And yes, when she saw your name, I briefly told her about you – that Jemima was Patrick's daughter, but she wouldn't believe me and—'

'Hold on. Where did she see my name?' Lydia asked. 'I don't understand. She said something about a . . . a chart?'

Dan shut his eyes. 'She . . . ah. Yes. Well. I sort of drew one up: for myself, listing the things I was doing as part of my plan.'

There was a pause where he imagined Lydia screwing up her face in a frown. 'What – and I was on the chart?' She sounded suspicious now.

'Yes, but—' He struggled to find the right words. 'You know I talked to you about my sabbatical? How I was sort of picking up the slack, with Patrick not being around for the last two months I was off work, and—'

'So I was part of that?' Suspicion had given way to indignation, he detected. Injury, even. 'Jemima and I, we were just "slack"?'

'No!' God, he wished he wasn't having this conversation

out on Putney Embankment, with people shooting him curious looks as they went by. He began walking again, speaking in a lower voice, his head turned away from passers-by. 'No, of course not. It was more that I was trying to fill in for my brother. Doing things he would have done – and beyond. And—'

'Let me get this straight, because I'm really confused,' Lydia said, cutting in. 'At the end of next month, or whenever you go back to work, you were going to wash your hands of me and Jemima, and this chart? Time's up, job done?'

'No. Absolutely not!' His heart was pounding. 'I don't want that. Do you?'

There was a terrifying pause when she didn't reply immediately.

Unable to bear the silence, Dan ploughed straight on, desperate to explain himself. 'I'm sorry,' he said again. 'About all of this. I'm really, really sorry. Honestly. I put you on the spreadsheet initially because you were sort of a job to deal with at first – a mystery on the bank statement to clear up. But then I met you and got to know you, and . . . things changed. I promise. I want to keep seeing you, whatever happens. I want to be a part of your life. Jemima's, too.'

She sighed down the phone and his heart clenched at the sound. Was that good or bad? Contemptuous or weary? 'Right,' Lydia said eventually. 'Look, I'd better get back to work. Just thought you should know what had happened.

I mean, she was seriously out of control. That was a big, hefty vase as well. If it had hit me . . .'

'I'm sorry,' he said yet again, because it seemed like the only thing he had left to offer. 'I'll talk to her,' he added, even though he was fairly sure Zoe wouldn't want to listen.

Then they said goodbye and he put his phone away, setting off once more, in the hope of finding the former rhythm of his run. It was no use, though. His legs felt heavy and his mind was whirling in all directions, trying to imagine the scene in Lydia's shop: Zoe bursting in, shouting at Lydia and throwing a vase at her . . . It seemed grotesque, impossible. He had never known Zoe act in such a violent or wild manner before.

He had done this to her, he thought unhappily, jogging through a puddle and barely noticing as the muddy water splattered up his shins. He was responsible. What was worse was the fact that he had no clue how to put any of this right again.

Chapter Thirty

Sometime later when Dan arrived home, panting and still not having found any solutions to his problems, he was surprised to see a familiar figure standing at his front door, pressing the buzzer. 'Mum?' he said as he approached.

She turned round, looking relieved. 'There you are! I was starting to think I had the wrong number. Hello there. I won't hug you, you look a bit sweaty for that right now. Everything okay?'

He was so taken aback to see her that it took him a moment to fumble his key into the lock. She never usually came to visit. Don't say Zoe had gone steaming and ranting over to his parents' place as well? he thought in dismay. 'Yeah, sure,' he said. 'How are you? Dad's all right, is he?'

'He's fine,' she replied. 'I just thought – well, there I was, a few weeks ago, commenting on how rare it was having you come and visit us, and I realized I never come to see you, either. So here I am. Mending my ways. I've brought some rhubarb from the garden, by the way.' She brandished a carrier bag, which had pink rhubarb sticks poking out the top. 'Thought you could make yourself a crumble, I remembered how much you loved it as a boy. Really tasty with a bit of stem ginger added – that's my tip.'

'Thanks, Mum.' He'd finally got the door open and ushered her inside. 'Go on through. I'll have a quick shower, if you don't mind – I'll be five minutes.'

'Good idea,' she said. 'I'll put this in the fridge for you.'

A few minutes later, hair still damp and skin pink from the hot water, he emerged to find her out in the garden, examining the dead sycamore. 'Oh,' he said, stepping outside to join her. 'Yeah. I've been meaning to do something about that.'

'It must have been damaged by the wind originally,' she said, running a finger along the rough wood where a branch had broken off. 'Fungus would have come in through this wound, look, and killed it. You should get rid of it, Daniel, it's not going to come back to life any time soon.'

'Yeah, I know,' he said, looking down at his feet. 'I'll sort it out, Mum.'

She gazed around the rest of the garden with a practised eye, bending to pluck some chickweed from the nearest border. 'South-facing, isn't it?' she went on, nodding to herself. 'You could make this a lovely spot, you know, if you pull your finger out. These flowerbeds could be full of colour and wildlife by midsummer. That honeysuckle's healthy enough, and you could plant a couple of roses too, maybe a nice peony – fill up the gaps with some annuals. I've got loads of seeds I can give you.'

Her face was animated; she had always loved planting and growing. Even in their old family home with its tiny back yard, he could remember her watering her pots and window boxes, making use of every inch of space. Indoors, too, she had got him and Patrick growing cress and broad beans in pots on the windowsill with varying degrees of success. She was never happier, she'd once told him, than when her hands were deep in compost.

'Come on, we could make a start now,' she went on. 'Weed these beds ready for planting. Have you got a couple of trowels?'

Under his mum's instruction, Dan soon found himself kneeling at the edge of a flowerbed, pulling up valerian shoots, red robin and a plant that was apparently called enchanter's nightshade. Arriving home, his head had been jangling with Lydia's phone call and alarm over Zoe, but there was something soothing about being outside, having the sun on his shoulders, that took the edge off his stress. A fat pink earthworm squiggled beneath his fingers, a bird trilled from a tree nearby. He hoped Zoe was able to feel similar calm soon, wherever she was now. He hoped she wasn't about to come bursting over the fence in order to throw stuff at him too.

'I was thinking about that photograph by the way,' his mum said, from the nearby flowerbed. 'Why you didn't like it. And I found myself remembering that . . . Well, he did go through a bit of an aggressive stage around then, your brother. Got into trouble at primary school a few times for fighting.'

Dan swivelled his eyes over to her. 'Did he?' He remembered Patrick being something of a golden boy at primary school. Everyone loved him.

'Yes. Pushing boundaries, probably. Getting a bit too big for his boots. So I could understand why you might have always thought he was picking on you. In that photograph, I mean.' She tossed some large leafy intruder behind her, head still bent over the flowerbed.

'Right. Yes.' Blimey. This was a bit of a key change from the whole-hearted Patrick adoration that he was used to.

'Your dad and I were discussing it last night: how, when someone dies, you only ever talk about the good stuff. What a great person they were, so loving and kind and hard-working. That's the temptation, isn't it, to glorify them, make them into saints?' She turned then, a rueful smile on her face. 'But we all know that's rubbish, don't we? Because nobody's that perfect. Least of all your brother.'

This was so unexpected Dan wasn't quite sure what to say. 'No,' he agreed after a moment.

'I mean, we all loved him, of course, that's not in any doubt, but Patrick definitely wasn't a saint. All the lip he gave me as a lad. So unreliable too – do you remember what a flake he was before he settled down with Zoe? Sometimes whole months would go by and I wouldn't hear from him.' She rolled her eyes. 'But nobody's perfect, like I said. We're all just muddling along, trying to do our best. Getting it wrong sometimes – but that's life.'

'Yeah,' he said. And then, feeling the need to confess, he added, 'I've got a few things wrong recently.'

She put her trowel down. 'Have you? Like what?'

He stared down at the grass. 'I was trying to help Zoe out and so I drew up this sort of plan, to organize everything.' It sounded so lame now, when he said it aloud. 'I wanted to be more like Patrick,' he blurted out. 'I was trying to do the things he would have been around to do, but then Zoe saw the plan and got really angry.'

'She got angry? When you were trying to help?'

This was not the moment to get into the whole Lydia angle. 'I went about it a bit clumsily, I guess,' he mumbled. *The Patrick plan?* Zoe cried scornfully in his head, eyes glittering. 'I think I've really upset her.'

His mum reached out and put a hand on his arm. 'Do you know, Daniel, when you came over to see me and your dad the other week and you said that you were standing in for Patrick . . . well, you don't need to do that, okay? Not for me, not for Zoe. Stick to being your own self, because that's good enough, do you hear me? You don't have to come round and try to be anyone else, or look for jobs you can do, or anything like that. Just be you. That's all I want. As for Zoe – well, it's not my place to say what she wants, but I'm sure that would be enough for her too.'

Her face had become quite stern with this little speech, her chin pointy and determined as if she was not about to put up with any argument. Dan had a lump in his throat by the end of it. 'Thanks, Mum,' he said.

'Now, are you going to make your old mother a bit of lunch after all this work, or do I have to do everything myself around here?' she demanded.

And they were back to normal. 'Good idea,' he said, getting to his feet. Her words of love were exactly what he needed, he realized, walking towards the kitchen, wondering if he had enough eggs for an omelette. You could waste a lot of time thinking you were second best, the least favourite child, as he had always done – and for what? It had been a pointless exercise in self-pity. *Just be you*, his mum had told him, and it felt like the warmest of hugs, a proper stamp of approval. He'd reciprocate by making her the best omelette of her life, he vowed, then maybe think about how to put everything else right.

Meanwhile, Zoe was having what felt like a breakdown. It had been brewing inside her ever since Dan had dared to say those terrible things in her presence – things she could not, would not, believe – and then today, when she finally made the connection between the Lydia of his accusations and the woman she had met in the shop, the anger had burst up out of her like a boiling fountain of rage. You heard about these people and their long cons, leeching on troubled souls and getting fat from their misery and savings – oh, she'd read the stories in newspapers and online. That was clearly what had happened here. Obviously. The conniving bitch in question must have taken one look at the weeping Zoe and rubbed her hands with glee. Some Internet digging later, Lydia had latched on to idiot, gullible Dan, who had been only too keen to believe the worst of his brother.

Having worked all this out, Zoe had been like a woman possessed. She had driven to Chiswick, parked illegally on double yellow lines (so sue me, she thought, unable to care as she locked the car) and then the sheer power of her fury had sent her shouting, fists clenched, into the shop where she'd first come across that woman. That liar.

Zoe wasn't proud of the scene that unfolded, mind. She'd intended to go in, coldly powerful, to look this woman in the eye and make herself clear: *I know what you're doing and you don't fool me. It stops right here.* But something had gone wrong, a circuit in her brain fusing with the white heat of her anger perhaps, because she'd ended up screeching like a banshee and throwing – actually *throwing* – a chunky vase at the bitch's head. She was shaken afterwards. Could hardly walk back to the car because her whole body was trembling with the shock of what she'd done.

Zoe has a bit of a temper, her secondary-school teacher had written in one of her reports. *Zoe is too hot-headed and needs to think before she speaks!* another had observed. Her mum was fond of recounting stories about Zoe's fiery nature as a little girl – 'You were just like the girl in the nursery rhyme,' she had often said. 'When she was good, she was very, very good. But when she was bad, she was HORRID!'

Well, she'd been horrid today, all right. She had gone full batshit-crazy at another woman, in public. Ever since Patrick had died, in fact, her anger had been like a wild horse, unstoppable in its galloping. Driving home from Lydia's shop, heart thumping, adrenalin still pumping on overload, she felt dazed by what she had done, as if it had been an out-of-body experience. The smash of the vase hitting the wall kept ringing in her ears like a warning bell. She could have really hurt the woman, if her aim had been any better.

Good! said the anger that still simmered inside her. *And it would serve her right.*

Yeah, but Ethan, Gabe and Bea were relying on her, Zoe reminded herself. Imagine if the woman had been badly hurt and the police had come knocking as a result, charging Zoe with assault – or, worse, murder. She might still be reported for damages or affray; a criminal record could ruin her career, her reputation, her whole life. What had she been *thinking*? Maybe her boys weren't the only ones who needed some anger-management counselling. If she carried on like this, she would self-destruct.

Once home, she went inside, feeling sombre and ashamed, hoping she could draw a line under the scene, write it off as a bad day. Wishing she could stop dwelling on how the woman – Lydia – had called after her, her voice clear as a bell: *I'm not lying. It's all true. It's all TRUE!*

It couldn't be true, though, Zoe tried to tell herself, but her hands were shaking as she began gathering together the creased piles of laundry that needed seeing to, focusing hard on the discarded school shirts and pyjamas as if she needed to study them for a very important test. A sob escaped her throat. *Please. Don't let this be true.* She found herself thinking about the day she'd come back from school, only a bit older than Bea, to find that her dad had left them, gone off with Annabel Clarke from the newsagent's. How her mum had cried at night for three whole weeks, and how they'd all never stopped waiting for him to come home again. In hindsight, that might have been when the anger began, she realized now, stuffing Ethan's dressing gown into the laundry basket with another muffled sob.

Then the doorbell rang and her heart started pounding. It was the police, come to arrest her, she guessed. Or maybe it was Lydia, having tracked her down – an even bigger vase in hand – ready to duke this one out in a proper brawl.

Wrenching the door open, ready to defend herself, she saw someone else altogether: Mari, from school. 'Oh,' she said, the adrenalin draining away. She wearily remembered how Mari had asked her for coffee a few weeks ago, and how she had politely refused. Perhaps she hadn't been clear enough at the time. 'Hi,' she added without any enthusiasm.

Mari's nose was pink, as if she had a cold, and there was something nervy about the way she kept flicking glances at Zoe, then away again. 'Um . . . is it all right if I come in?' she asked. 'Sorry to bother you. There's just something on my mind. I need to talk to you.'

'Sure,' said Zoe, wishing she hadn't opened the door. She wasn't in the mood for any sympathetic *How ARE you?*s right now. 'Come in,' she added, already feeling defeated.

They sat in the living room, Mari having refused offers of a drink. She definitely seemed twitchy, perching on the edge of her chair, shoulders a little hunched, eyes flitting around at everything.

'So how are things?' Zoe asked, hoping this wouldn't take long.

Mari crossed then uncrossed her legs. Her hands were in her lap, her head angled down in what looked like . . . well, it actually looked a lot like penitence, Zoe thought, frowning. Which was odd.

'I don't know how to say this,' Mari began, raising her gaze. Her face was bone-white, bloodless. 'But I can't keep it to myself any longer. I . . .' She ground her hands together in her lap as if she was strangling someone. Wringing a bird's neck. 'Remember the other week when I saw you and asked if we could have a chat? It was because . . .' She actually looked as if she was going to throw up. 'You see, the thing is, Zoe, I had an affair. With Patrick.'

Zoe blinked hard, unable to process what she'd just heard. Wait a minute. *What?* This was not what she'd been expecting. 'I don't think so,' she said faintly. This couldn't be happening, she told herself. She refused to believe it. 'No, you didn't.'

'And on the day he died . . .' Mari shut her eyes briefly, her mascaraed lashes spidery against her pale cheeks, 'I found out that I was pregnant. With his baby.'

'*No*,' said Zoe wildly. Unable to keep still, she rose to her feet, full of agitated energy, and paced across the room. 'Stop it. Did Dan put you up to this? Did *Lydia*?'

'When you saw me in the doctor's waiting room a few weeks ago, I was there because . . .' Again with the strangling hands. Zoe felt like slapping at them. 'Because I was booking an appointment for an abortion.' Tears filmed her eyes and then went trickling down her face. 'I'm sorry, Zoe. I know you don't want to hear this—'

'Too right I don't.' Zoe gulped for breath. There didn't

seem to be enough air left in the room. 'How dare you come to my house and make these despicable allegations?'

'Because it *happened*, all right? And I loved him too.' Her face was wretched and tear-stained, and Zoe had a sudden memory flash of Mari weeping at Patrick's funeral, how over-the-top it had seemed at the time.

'I don't believe you,' Zoe said, trying to shore up her defences. Her heart was pounding. 'And if you don't leave my house right now, then I might do something I regret. Go on, get out!'

'I had an abortion. I wish I hadn't, but I did.' She gave a sob. 'I upset Patrick the night he went missing – we had a massive row on the phone and I've been blaming myself ever since. I'm so sorry. I'm really, really s—'

'No, you're not. You're not sorry at all.' Zoe's temper was rising again; she seemed to have no control over herself any more. 'Patrick loved me. He wouldn't have – you're talking shit.'

'I'm not! I can prove it. He . . . he had a scar on his elbow from where he fell off some rocks as a teenager.' Tears streamed down her face. 'There's a birthmark on his hip, shaped like a heart. Um, his dog, growing up, was called . . .' She floundered. 'Argh, it's on the tip of my tongue. His parents are Derek and Liz, his dog was called—'

'Okay, time's up, you need to go now,' Zoe said. The room seemed to be tilting beneath her as if she'd just stepped off a roller coaster. 'This proves nothing other than that you are completely psycho. Get out of my house.'

'Brandy! That was it – Brandy! And—'

'Get out,' Zoe said, and then she was screaming. 'Get out! Get OUT!'

Mari scuttled from the room and Zoe flung herself onto the sofa as the front door banged shut, feeling as if she wanted to keep on screaming until she went limp. She clutched at her own head. Why was this happening to her? Zoe had married Patrick because he was loyal, because he was a good person. She could not – would not – accept that she had married a man like her own philandering dad. Patrick was a flirt, sure. He was friendly to men *and* women, everyone had loved him, but that didn't mean . . . She swallowed hard, blood pounding in her ears. Surely that didn't mean . . . ?

She pulled a cushion over her head, her thoughts whirling. It was true about the scar on his elbow, mind you. And Patrick did have a birthmark on his hip, shaped like a heart. How would Mari have known *that*?

Nausea turned her stomach because now she was imagining the other woman in bed with him, draped across Patrick's naked body, tracing a finger across his skin, outlining that birthmark and commenting on it, just as Zoe had done years earlier when they first started dating. No. *No.* It couldn't be true, though. She refused point-blank to believe it could be true. 'I refuse!' she said aloud to the cushions. 'No!'

She *had* to refuse. She could not for a second let herself believe that there might be so much as a scrap of truth in this. Because if she began to doubt her own marriage, her own husband, if she allowed such ideas to worm their way into all she had held precious, then . . . She gasped, dizzied by the awful possibilities currently rippling out around her. Everything she had ever relied upon and trusted felt perilously shaky right now, as if the walls were a mirage, her life flimsy and unreal. Images flashed through her head of Patrick laughing with her female friends; how the school mums used to giggle and bat their eyelashes at him at class assemblies and Christmas concerts; how sometimes he'd disappear for hours on end and she wouldn't be able to get hold of him. He'd always come up with a plausible excuse, though, that was the thing. She'd believed him every time. But was that because the alternative – a life of doubt and suspicion – had been too awful to contemplate? Had trusting him been an act of weakness and denial all along?

Groaning, she wrapped her arms around herself, remembering how she'd bumped into Mari in the cemetery a few weeks ago, how it hadn't occurred to her to wonder why the other woman was there at all. She must have gone to pay her respects, just like Zoe. The thought made her feel like puking.

She shut her eyes, but Mari's face floated up into her mind. *Brandy! That was it – Brandy!* the woman cried, shrill with triumph.

Zoe didn't half feel like a brandy herself right now. If it wasn't for the fact that she had to pick up the children from school later and face all the other parents, she would totally be face-down in a bottle of brandy, drinking to blot out the horror of today. Instead she went to her phone.

'Clare,' she said, when she got through to her best friend. Reassurance, that's what she needed. Reassurance from someone who knew. 'I need to ask you something and I want you to tell me the truth.'

'You sound very serious! Of course,' said Clare. 'What is it?'

Clare was not a liar. She was the sort of person who would tell you, honestly but kindly, if your bum looked too big in a pair of lift-'n'-shape jeans, and if your hairstyle *really* suited you or if the hairdresser had just been over-complimenting you for the extra tip. She'd even give you the full hand-on-heart lowdown on whether you'd acted out of line at the school quiz night. And so Zoe was confident Clare would be able to answer this question with her usual direct-ness, and make all the bad stuff go away.

'Have you,' she began, 'at any time ever had doubts about me and Patrick? Him being faithful, I mean. Be honest.'

But instead of the immediate 'No! Of course not. Babe, what *is* this?' she had been expecting, there followed a pause that lasted too long. A pause that made Zoe feel as if she'd walked right to the edge of a precipice, only to find it crumbling beneath her feet. Her heart seemed to be lodged in her throat, her stomach on spin-dry.

'Clare?' she whispered. 'Are you still there?'

'I'm here,' said Clare, sounding uncharacteristically awkward. 'Um, are you at home right now? I'm actually off this afternoon, so I'll come over. Sit tight, all right? I'll be five minutes.'

Zoe put the phone down, her mouth opening in wordless alarm, her spine cold, her heart as weak and fluttery as an injured bird. She had a horrible, prickling premonition that her day was about to get a whole lot worse before it got any better.

Chapter Thirty-One

Dan's apologetic text to Zoe had been met with a silence that said it all: *I don't forgive you*. And so, with a heavy heart, he boxed up the paperwork from Patrick's business, ready to return everything to Kew. He had tried but failed – the story of his life right there, he thought. *Daniel shows promise but never quite manages to apply himself,* as his teachers had said all those years ago. They'd got that right, anyway.

Putting the box in the car, he headed off, deciding to make a couple of stops en route. First, to the Hossains' house, where work was well under way. In the ten days since the washing machine had caught fire, the pest-control team had been round to exterminate all the unwanted bugs, gleaming new kitchen lino had been laid, the stair carpet had been replaced and the damp treated. Tamal was at work when Dan rang the bell, but when he introduced himself to Jana, she shook him by the hand, thanking him for everything that had been done, and took him round the house, showing him the improvements. A pistachio cake was cooling on the side in the kitchen and when Dan commented on how good it smelled, she insisted on wrapping the whole thing in grease-proof paper and packing it in a tin for him. 'Please – I want you to have it,' she said, ignoring his subsequent protests about how he couldn't possibly, and pressing it into his hands.

'Any more problems, it'll be the same phone number, but my sister-in-law Zoe will be taking care of things from now on,' he said, the cake tin warm in his arms. He rapped on the lid a little self-consciously. 'Thanks again for this. Very kind.'

'Thank *you*,' she said again, ruffling the hair of a small dark-eyed little girl who was sitting on the floor, method-ically pulling plastic pots out of a cupboard. 'It's much better here now already. Right, Lila?'

It was gratifying and humbling how pleased Dan felt, getting back into his car afterwards. If he'd done nothing else right, at least he had helped this family by making their house a nicer place to live. That must count for something, he told himself.

Next stop – Rosemary, looking more cheerful than the last time he had seen her and enjoying being indignant about the fact that her doctor had suggested she have some help while her wrist was in plaster. 'Like I'm completely useless,' she snorted disparagingly.

It was a shame, therefore, that Dan had to spoil the mood by telling her that Zoe would be taking on the property man-agement from now on. 'Oh no! But I like seeing you and having our chats,' she pouted. This was as they sat in the living room together, Desmond kneading her lap with his huge ginger paws, a look of slit-eyed bliss on his fat furry face. 'Can't you carry on looking after my flat – let her do the others?'

'Probably not,' Dan said. 'I'm due back at my office job in a month anyway, and this was only ever meant to be a temporary thing.' He felt unexpectedly forlorn at the prospect.

'Well, listen,' said Rosemary, digging into an enormous beaded purse, 'at least let me give you a little something. Here.' She pulled out three ten-pound notes and held them towards him. 'Take that lovely girl out on me. My way of saying thank you, for all you've done.'

'Rosemary, no, I couldn't,' he said. Was there something particularly hangdog about his face today that was inspiring the tenants to force gifts upon him? he wondered. 'Honestly – you keep it.'

'No, I insist. You can give her my phone number too, if you think she'd like some sewing chat. I wonder why she didn't take up the place on the course? If the London College of Fashion offered her one, she must have been very good, you know.'

'Her mum died the summer she was taking A-levels,' Dan said. 'I don't think her exams were a top priority.'

'Oh, that *is* a shame. Well! Never too late. Tell her to come round and I'll give her some tutoring. I'd like that, actually. I thought she was very nice.' She peered at Dan, gimlet-eyed, when he didn't respond immediately. 'What? Oh, Daniel. Don't tell me you've blown this little love-affair already?'

'It isn't a love-affair,' he said. 'We're just friends, but . . .' Then he sighed, because Rosemary was annoyingly good at leaving a long anticipatory pause that was almost impossible not to fill. 'I've kind of ruined everything,' he muttered. 'With Lydia, with my sister-in-law, the lot. I should have stayed in my quiet, boring office job rather than attempting anything more challenging.'

Rosemary made a scoffing noise. 'Goodness, you *are* feeling sorry for yourself,' she said. 'Come on, then. You might as well share the story while you've still got me to ask for advice. Let's hear it.'

He sank gratefully into a chair. If someone had told Dan six months ago that he would have turned to an eighty-something-year-old woman during an emotional crisis of confidence, he would have thought they were on hallucinogenics. But here he was, pouring his heart out with the latest instalment of the soap opera that had become his life, ending up with how the good-deeds plan had hit the buffers in full Technicolor terribleness and Zoe had gone berserk.

She reached over and squeezed his hand. 'You're a good lad,' she said. 'A very kind person. But mercy me, I do feel sorry for your sister-in-law. Poor woman. This is a dreadful mess, isn't it?'

'Yes,' he agreed. 'I'm on my way over there actually, to drop off the paperwork and keys to the properties. Jury's still out on whether she'll actually answer the door and speak to me, though.'

Rosemary frowned. 'She must be very hurt,' she said. 'But *he's* the one who's caused that, not you. And she'll know that, deep down. Hearing that her husband betrayed her must have been the most awful shock, but she can't even confront him with that now. It's not surprising, really, that she's taken it out on you instead.'

Dan nodded, mulling it over. 'So what do I do?'

'You treat her like a sister, and you keep on being there for her. Apologize for the – excuse me, Daniel – for the rather crass "plan" you drew up, be sincere, keep offering your help. She'll realize that you mean what you say, and she'll come round eventually.' Rosemary glanced at the clock on the mantelpiece, then pushed Desmond off her knee. 'Gosh, where did the time go? That's your fault for yapping on, Daniel. Now I'm going to be late for my art class.'

'Your . . . what?'

'Art class. Is something wrong with your ears as well?' She did her best to brush the orange cat-hair from her skirt. 'Desmond, I'm going to have to shave you one of these days if you insist on shedding your beautiful fur everywhere. Right. I'd better go.'

'I didn't realize you went to any classes,' Dan said, feeling as if he were being shooed out of the place.

'I didn't,' she replied, picking up a smart maroon handbag with a massive gold buckle. 'But falling over like that gave me rather a turn. I've become a bit lonely, I think. Cut myself off from the world. I hadn't realized quite how much, until I was lying there on the carpet, with nobody to call.'

'Ahem,' said Daniel. 'Apart from your caring landlord, that is.'

'Well, obviously!' She beamed at him, herding him towards the door. 'Apart from you. So I gave myself a bit of a pep talk and decided: Bugger it, I'm not past it yet. I need some more pals to see me through the years. Hence art class today. And a choir meeting tomorrow. I hear there's a local ladies' sewing club too, called – what is it again? "Stitch and bitch", that's it. Or is it "Bitch and stitch"? Anyway, I'm definitely going to join them for some lovely stitching and excellent bitching.' She looked delighted with this new attitude, smiling at herself in the hall mirror as she touched up her lipstick.

'Rosemary, this all sounds brilliant,' Dan said.

'Doesn't it?' she replied modestly. Then she patted her hair into shape and picked up her keys. 'Won't be long, Desmond,' she called, as she opened the front door. Then she raised a neatly plucked eyebrow at Dan. 'You should try it yourself: hobbies, I mean,' she said. 'Maybe that's what's been missing?'

Following a sleepless night, Zoe had scuttled out on the school run to drop Gabe and Bea first thing, head down and avoiding eye contact, then came straight home and got back into bed, where she lay scrolling through old video clips of Patrick on her phone until she couldn't take it any more. She was still there now, numb and shell-shocked, only having moved in order to turn the wedding-day photo she kept on the bedside table face-down. Her heart felt as if it was breaking all over again, shattering into splinters. Had Patrick ever loved her? she wondered miserably. Had he meant a single word of those vows they'd made? She never would have cheated on him: never. It hadn't even crossed her mind to look at another man once she met him. She had loved him so, so deeply. But had it all been a game to him?

Yesterday had gone from shock to horror, before totally hitting the skids. If Zoe had hoped that Clare would make everything better, she soon realized she had been deluding herself.

'Look, I would have told you at the time if I thought it would have been helpful, but . . . well. The thing with Mari? I can believe it, I'm afraid,' Clare had said, blunt but sorrowful. She'd hardly been able to look Zoe in the eye since she'd arrived. The two of them were sitting on the sofa together, and she took both of Zoe's hands in hers and held them tight. 'I'm really sorry.'

Zoe had stopped breathing, or so it seemed. *I can believe it, I'm afraid.* 'What are you saying?' she managed to croak.

Clare stared down at her star-printed leggings. She had become obsessed with yoga classes recently, but in the annoying, evangelical sort of way that made Zoe feel like tearing open another family bag of Chilli Sensations and cramming massive handfuls into her mouth. 'There was that school auction-of-promises night about a year ago, do you remember?' she said after a moment. 'You had to go home early because one of the kids was poorly or something, but Patrick stayed on. Everyone was really pissed. I went to the loo at one point, and he and Mari . . . I wouldn't say they were in a clinch as such, but they were standing talking together and they were very close. Like, she had her back to the wall and he was practically pressed against her. They sprang apart when I walked up, obviously, but I had a bad feeling about it.'

Zoe felt herself inflating a little again. 'That's it? They were just standing next to each other?' A bad feeling was *nothing*. Patrick was a flirty person – big deal.

'Um, not quite.' Clare's hands, still clasped around Zoe's, were warm and starting to feel sweaty. 'I saw them another time as well. I was over in Shepherd's Bush, on my way to my brother's house, and I saw Patrick's van parked up.'

'So? He has tenants over there. He was probably—'

'She was sitting in the front seat with him. They each had a takeaway coffee and were sort of . . . snuggled together.' Clare swallowed. 'Then she leaned forward and touched his face.'

Zoe shut her eyes. Face-touching was pretty intimate, she had to concede. In the early days of their relationship, whole evenings had passed where the two of them had lain in bed, touching each other like that. Tiny, personal strokes, delighting in the other's skin, learning the respective language of each other's faces, bodies, hair.

'I mean, I didn't say anything to you, because she might have been brushing a bit of pastry off his cheek or . . . an eyelash.' Clare was sounding defensive now, as if she half-expected Zoe to launch into a full *Why the hell didn't you tell me?* accusation. 'It wasn't as if they were kissing passionately or boffing away on the dashboard, but . . .'

No words seemed to be available to Zoe. She felt as if her whole life – her lovely, perfect life – was pixelating before her eyes. Pixelating and breaking up, disintegrating. The man she had loved was not the person she'd always thought. The man she had loved had pressed himself against Mari O'Connor, cosied up in the cab of his van with her, allowed her to trace the outline of his heart-shaped birthmark. Worse, he had got her pregnant. So did that mean that Lydia . . . ?

Oh God. Now Zoe was shaking all over. She thought

412

about the many times she'd searched for a sign from Patrick after his death, some kind of message – well, here it was: a Molotov cocktail chucked through the window, blowing up before her eyes. So if Mari had been telling the truth, then maybe Lydia had too, she thought dazedly. And if Lydia was telling the truth, then there was another child of Patrick's out there: a half-sibling to Ethan, Gabe and Bea . . .

'I'm going to—' she gulped, wrestling herself free from Clare's grasp and running out to the loo, where she threw up again and again. No, she thought desperately. No, no, please no. She didn't want this to be happening. 'I can't bear it,' she sobbed as Clare came in to find her kneeling on the bathroom floor. 'I just can't bear it if this is true.'

But Clare's kind hand on her back, and sympathetic silence, only told her that she was going to have to bear it, like it or not.

The doorbell rang downstairs now and Zoe groaned in frustration. For crying out loud! She was having a private nervous breakdown up here. Why couldn't everyone leave her alone?

She was tempted to ignore the caller, in case it was Mari again – or, worse, some other woman that Patrick had wronged her with – but forced herself out of bed and down the stairs with supreme effort. If it was a delivery person with a present for Gabe's upcoming birthday, she'd only end up having to trek out and pick it up from the sorting office, which would be extremely irritating, she figured.

Dan was on the doorstep, carrying a box of stuff. The same box of stuff connected to Patrick's business that she'd given him a month earlier, by the look of things. A great weariness enveloped Zoe. She felt very much like ramming the entire box into the dustbin.

'Hi,' said Dan. He looked nervous but determined. 'Um, right. So here it all is. Let me know if there's anything you're not clear about, or if I can do anything else. I know I messed up, Zoe. I know you're mad at me. But I hope that one day we can . . .' He paused. 'Are you all right?'

'No,' she gulped. She was so relieved to see his kind face that her anger with him dissolved; the painted kitchen and his stupid chart no longer seeming important. Her chin wobbled with the effort of trying not to burst into tears again. 'I'm sorry, Dan. About everything. I . . .' She took the box from him, because she didn't know what else to say. Her hands were shaking. A tear plopped from her eyes onto the folders and laptop inside. 'Oh God. Sorry.'

'It's okay,' he said. His hands twitched by his sides as if he was wondering whether or not he should try to give her a hug. He must have been too scared after their last encounter, though, because he just shuffled his feet around awkwardly and asked, 'Do you want to chat or . . . ?'

Did she want to chat? Not really. Zoe wanted to dig a big

hole and make all of this go away, forever. Stick her fingers in her ears so that she couldn't hear any more accusations or gossip. Maybe leave the country for good measure, start over somewhere else, where nobody knew her. 'I don't know,' she mumbled, putting the box down on the floor and scrubbing her eyes with her sleeve.

'Have you eaten anything?' he asked after a moment. 'Why don't I take you for lunch somewhere?' He was peering at her with concern. 'How about The Greyhound? I haven't been there for ages. Fancy it?'

She drew breath, realizing that she was starving. Remembering that she had once had the best chicken pie of her life at The Greyhound and that it might be exactly what she needed right now. They could always go and sit in the garden if she felt like crying again, she supposed. 'Yes please,' she said in a tiny voice.

At least something seemed to be going her way today because – hallelujah – the chicken pie was still on the menu at The Greyhound and it tasted every bit as delicious as she remembered. With each forkful of pastry and gravy and mash, Zoe felt her equilibrium gradually start to return, little by little, crumb by crumb. Dan kept the conversation going by talking through the tenants he'd been dealing with, listing various problems that had arisen and solutions he had found, but it was very much filler-chat, when they both knew there were far more serious subjects lurking unspoken.

What the hell, she thought after a while, fortified by food. It was time to address the big old elephant in the room. 'So,' she said, when he paused for breath, 'maybe we should talk about other things. Like, what you were saying the other day. About this Lydia woman.'

Dan blanched, but then a moment later he nodded and met her gaze across the table, his eyes anxious but kind. 'Okay.'

'I . . .' God, this was hard. 'I didn't want to believe you,' Zoe stammered. 'But something else has happened since then – *someone* else, I should say – and now . . .' She put her knife and fork down, pleating her fingers together in her lap. 'Now I'm not so sure.'

Halfway through a chip, he stiffened at her words, not looking at her as he chewed and swallowed. 'I know it's horrendous, but I'm pretty certain Lydia's not lying,' he said eventually. 'Her daughter is the spit of Patrick, for one thing.'

Tears brimmed in Zoe's eyes again and she dabbed at them with the napkin. 'Do you think he actually loved me, Dan?' she asked, her lip trembling. 'At all?'

His expression was gratifyingly shocked, at least. 'Of course! Oh my God, *yes*. Yes, Zoe. So much. He adored you.' He could hardly say it enough times. 'I promise you. He was mad about you. One hundred per cent.'

'Then why . . . ?' She picked up her fork again and

416

swooshed it glumly through the mashed potato. 'Why would he cheat on me? If he loved me so much?'

There was a small, miserable silence. 'I honestly don't know,' he replied. 'I've asked myself the same thing a hundred times. I swear – I was so shocked when I discovered Lydia's name in the list of business-account payees and found out who she was.'

She stared at him. 'He was *paying* her?'

Judging by his expression, he knew he'd put his foot in it. 'Oh. Yes,' he said awkwardly. 'There was a monthly maintenance payment going out to her. For J—, her daughter. That's how I found out in the first place, because I was doing the VAT return.' He stabbed another chip. 'It wasn't because Patrick was still seeing her or anything, though. Apparently, he finished whatever relationship they had as soon as she got pregnant and was paying her off, basically. Paying her to keep quiet and stay out of his life.'

Ugh. The more Zoe found out about her husband's secrets, the worse the situation became. And this must be why Dan went so weird on her the other week when she mentioned Patrick's paperwork, she realized. Christ. So many layers of deceit. 'You know,' she said dully, 'all this time I've been really regretting not saying anything about Patrick at the funeral. Not giving a proper eulogy on the day. I've been writing one in my head ever since, to say when we scatter the ashes – the most loyal, loving, wonderful husband and father . . . That sort of thing.' She gave a horrible bark of a laugh that felt more like a sob. 'But how can I say it now? How can I say those words?'

Dan put his cutlery down and took her hand over the table. 'Look, Patrick did some stupid things, all right? Really stupid things that neither of us understands. But that doesn't mean he didn't love you and the kids any less. And that you didn't love *him* any less. The way you felt about him was real – and that's still valid. What you two had was good. He *did* love you. He just had this . . . this weakness, I guess, that meant he couldn't be satisfied.' He shrugged. 'I don't get it, either. But that doesn't mean all the good stuff between you didn't happen.'

She knew he was doing his best to comfort her, but she was too numb for his words to change anything right now. Perhaps it was time to talk about something different, find a lighter, easier conversation to have instead. But then again, she figured, maybe this was the perfect moment to get it all out there on the table. To hear every detail, however grim that might be. No more secrets. The worst had already happened, right?

'The night Patrick died,' she began slowly, 'we had an argument. Just a silly one about whether or not the kids should go to university. If he'd come back the next day we'd have made up, it would have been forgotten, but it's been killing me ever since, thinking that he might have died angry with me. Was he—' She broke off, shooting an agonized look at Dan. 'Was he slagging me off to you in the pub that night? I've always wondered if that's why you wouldn't tell me what happened.'

Dan shook his head. 'No. He didn't slag you off.' He wrinkled his forehead, thinking hard. 'He . . . What did he say about you? He mentioned something about you doing well at work, I think. That you'd found a school you really liked?'

She nodded, remembering how the row had started.

'He definitely didn't slag you off, though. He seemed proud of you, if anything. Hey!' He looked alarmed by the way her face had fallen. 'That's a good thing, isn't it?'

She hadn't realized until now quite how much tension she'd been holding about their argument. 'Yes,' she agreed shakily. 'That's a good thing. I was so worried that . . .' Emotion overwhelmed her. 'You know when you have a row and it blows up, and you say stuff you don't really mean? I never got the chance to tell him I was sorry. Neither did he. And . . .'

'Oh, Zo! You should have said something sooner.' Dan looked mortified. 'If he died angry with anyone, it was with me, not you. I promise.'

'He argued with Mari too – this other woman he was seeing,' she replied miserably, her stomach twisting as she imagined Patrick pinballing from one person to the next, row after row. Had it all been too much for him, in the end?

Despite everything, she hated the thought of him feeling cornered and desperate on that last night. If only he'd made it home, they could have sorted everything out between them, couldn't they? She blew her nose, trying to gather herself. 'Do you want to tell me about it?' she asked Dan in a low voice. 'Seeing as this has turned into a warts-and-all confession?'

It was his turn to look anguished then, gazing down at what was left of his fish and chips, poking a fork at the last few peas. 'I swore I was never going to get into this with you,' he mumbled, 'but . . . okay. He told me that he and Rebecca . . . Well, that they went behind my back. And yours, too. That's why I lost it.'

Zoe gaped. Yet another can of worms she wished she hadn't opened. Patrick and *Dan's wife*? 'He told you . . .' she repeated, unable to say the words aloud because they were so awful. Had Patrick possessed *any* kind of conscience or shame? Every time she thought she had hit rock-bottom, it turned out there was another level to fall. How many other women *were* there in the shadows?

'It wasn't true, though,' Dan added hurriedly. 'Okay? I have since found out – via Rebecca, who tore a strip off me for asking – that they didn't sleep together or anything else. Patrick made up the entire thing.' He raised his palms in a weary gesture. 'I have no idea why. Your guess is as good as mine. Maybe it was because I was about to go off travelling and have some fun for once, and he . . .' He shrugged. 'I dunno. Felt the need to try and piss on my fireworks. Like brothers do, now and then.'

Zoe was reeling. 'Oh, Dan. And that's why you didn't let him stay at your place.'

'That's why I didn't let him stay at my place.'

Her head swam as she felt a flash of the tumult that he too must have undergone. And Dan had kept the whole thing to himself in order to protect her, when he must have been through hell, she realized. 'What a nightmare,' she said, remembering how haunted he'd looked at the funeral, how the colour had all but leached out of him. How furious she had been, blaming him for what had happened. When all along . . .

'Yep,' he said. 'So now you know.'

They looked at each other, wordless. 'Fuck it,' she said. 'I need a drink. I'm going to ask Clare to pick up the kids from school. Ethan can get the bus to his club for once. Shall we get shit-faced, just the two of us?'

'That's the best idea I've heard all day,' he replied.

Chapter Thirty-Two

Dan had warned Lydia that she could expect a second, very different visit from Zoe at some point following their so-called Lunch Date of Truth – 'I think she feels pretty bad about the way she behaved,' he'd said. All the same, when the shop bell jangled and Lydia saw the other woman coming in, she felt completely sick with nerves at whatever was about to happen. Not to mention bracing herself for the possibility of having to duck reflexively once again.

Jonathan too recognized Zoe and immediately moved to stand beside Lydia, arms folded. For someone whose natural instinct was for jollity, he could do stern pretty well, it transpired. 'I sincerely hope this is not going to be a repeat of your last appearance,' he said, in an impressively head-teacherish voice. 'Because I'm not about to stand here and let you attack my staff, do you understand?'

Zoe hung her head, clutching her own hands as if needing to cling to something. She was wearing a white linen shirt and jeans with the exact same Zara leopard-print pumps that

Bridget always wore. In a different life they might have been friends, Lydia thought.

'I've come to apologize,' Zoe said, looking directly at Lydia. 'I'm really sorry.' She bit her lip. 'I'm not trying to make excuses, but I've been under a lot of stress recently. Clearly I shouldn't have acted the way I did, though. So I'm sorry.'

She seemed genuine at least. She also seemed a lot smaller and more tired than the last time she'd turned up here. Quietly spoken. Lydia didn't want to stare, but it looked as if she'd only put mascara on her left eyelashes and had forgotten about the right ones. Was it possible to bear a grudge against someone who couldn't even get it together to do their make-up properly? 'Okay,' she said eventually.

'I'll pay for the vase, obviously.' Zoe rummaged in her bag for her purse. 'How much do I owe you?'

Lydia and Jonathan exchanged a glance. 'Jon – could we have a minute, do you think?' Lydia asked.

He eyeballed Zoe with a hard stare, clearly not fully trusting her. She put her hands up, still holding her purse. 'I'm not here to cause trouble,' she said. 'I promise.'

'You'd better not,' Jonathan said severely, before turning back to Lydia. 'Have a break, if you want. Go and get a coffee or something.'

'Thanks, Jon,' Lydia replied. 'If you're up for that?' she asked Zoe. Her heart was thumping, wondering how this was going to go. Her instinct was that all the fight had gone from Zoe, but you never could tell.

'Okay,' said Zoe. She glanced back at Jonathan, looking uncertain. 'Should I pay for the vase first or—'

'You can buy Lydia a bloody good coffee instead,' he replied. 'And be nice to her, for heaven's sake. She's done nothing wrong.' He jerked his head towards the door. 'Call me if you need anything,' he said to Lydia as she grabbed her jacket and they left.

There was a café next door to the shop, but the staff in there all knew Lydia and she couldn't bear the thought of any of them eavesdropping on what was potentially a dynamite-packed conversation, so she suggested the Italian place at the bottom of the road that did the best latte in the postcode. She was going to need rocket fuel to get through this little chat, she guessed.

They ordered drinks and sat down, neither of them quite able to meet the other's eye. 'So how shall we do this?' Zoe asked. She looked incredibly nervous, Lydia thought, drained of colour apart from some very red lipstick that she had presumably put on for courage. For her part, Lydia was only glad she had bothered to do her make-up properly herself that morning – both lashes coated in mascara, for starters – and that she was wearing her favourite olive-green jumpsuit, which had been an absolute bugger to make, but was the most flattering item in her wardrobe.

'Um . . .' Lydia said, thinking fast. The stakes felt dizzyingly high right now; she had to find the words to navigate her way through. 'I guess I want you to know that I had no idea Patrick was married when he and I . . . you know. On my life, I had no clue.'

Zoe nodded. 'Dan said as much. But thank you.' There were such bags under her eyes, Lydia noticed. Bags that even a ton of foundation and concealer couldn't disguise. This woman must be completely shattered, she thought, feeling a stab of sympathy for her, despite the circumstances. *Because of* the circumstances as well, if she was honest. She found herself wanting to be generous in defeat, to give this broken woman some kind of comfort, if possible.

'Getting pregnant was an accident,' she went on, 'but Patrick was quick to choose you over me. That was made very clear to me: his loyalties definitely lay with you.'

Zoe fiddled with the salt cellar, a scornful breath puffing from her lips. 'I'm not sure "loyalty" is really a word I could use about my husband now,' she replied. A moment passed. 'I'm sorry he was a shit to you,' she added in a low voice.

There was a lump in Lydia's throat. 'I'm sorry he was a shit to you, too,' she said. They looked at each other and, for the first time, the barriers of mistrust seemed to lower a fraction, replaced by what felt like a slender thread of mutual understanding. They had both been wronged by the same man, after all. They had both adored him too. Despite everything, there was some common ground to be had.

A moment passed and then Zoe cleared her throat. 'Tell me about your daughter,' she said.

Lydia hesitated. 'Are you sure? It won't be too weird for you?'

Zoe's body language was taut, as if she were steeling herself to receive a blow, but she nodded all the same. She had guts, it was undeniable. 'We're going to have to do this, aren't we?' she said. 'We can't pretend that this isn't how things are.' Her mouth buckled a little. 'I mean, part of me would love to pretend, obviously. I was desperate for none of this to be real, but . . .' She broke off, pressing her lips together.

'We're grown-ups,' Lydia finished for her, and her own words took her by surprise. Hadn't she been fretting the other week that she wasn't a proper grown-up? Maybe she was making a better fist of it than she'd thought – *thinking things through*, as her mum had always advised. 'All the same,' she added, seeing tears glimmering in Zoe's eyes, 'we don't have to do this here and now if you'd rather take some time.'

Zoe shook her head. 'Let's rip the plaster right off,' she said. 'I can handle it.'

'Well, in that case . . .' Lydia opened her phone and showed Zoe the photo on the home screen of Jemima upside-down mid-cartwheel, hair flying everywhere, face screwed up in concentration. 'This is Jemima. She's seven years old, loves sport and dogs, is friendly and brave, constantly trying to find me someone to marry, even if that's my best female friend . . .'

And so it begins, she thought, feeling nervous and a little trepidatious as she flicked through her gallery to find more photographs, and the two of them began to exchange fragments about each other's lives. Zoe produced pictures of her children and Lydia found herself poring over them. *Jemima's brothers and sister*, she marvelled, gazing at every detail of their faces. This would not be an easy road for her and Zoe to walk down, that was for sure, but at least they were both trying to make it work. Could she ask for any more at this point?

It was only as Lydia finished her coffee that she realized they'd been sitting there for forty minutes and she should probably get back to work. There was a limit to Jonathan's generosity, particularly so close to lunchtime. 'I should head off,' she said, 'but thank you for this chat. I really mean it. I know the situation isn't great, but thanks for – well, for not hating me, I guess.' She grimaced at her own naive positivity. For all she knew, Zoe *did* hate her, but had a better poker face than Lydia gave her credit for.

Zoe's expression was certainly hard to read now. 'You've got Dan to thank for that,' she said. There was a pause. 'Um, I'm not sure where we go from here,' she went on. 'What do you want out of this? Ideally?'

Lydia gulped. She had been so busy feeling sorry for Zoe that she hadn't actually considered her own self in the matter. 'Um . . .'

'I don't mean financially,' Zoe said quickly and then it was her turn to pull a face. 'Although I suppose we'll have to talk about that at some point too.' She bit her lip. 'God, this is so strange, isn't it? I don't know the right thing to do. How to feel.'

'No,' Lydia agreed. 'Me neither.' She thought for a moment. 'I can see that your children might be upset to hear about Jemima and me, whereas for Jemima, the stakes aren't so high. She would be over the moon to have a half-sister and half-brothers, in fact. So let's take any next steps at your pace. Whenever you're ready.'

'Thanks.' Zoe's eyes looked wet again. 'I don't know how I'm going to tell them,' she confessed. 'Mind you, saying that, Bea would love a sister too. She's always going on about how annoying brothers are.'

They exchanged small, anxious smiles. It was a mess, but neither of them was afraid. Perhaps that was all that could be hoped for right now. 'By the way, could you give me Dan's address?' Lydia asked, changing the subject. 'I've got something for him. A surprise.'

Zoe hesitated a fraction – maybe she didn't completely trust her after all – but then reeled off a street name and number. She gave Lydia an appraising look. 'What's the deal with you and him, anyway?' she asked. 'He was very nice about you over lunch yesterday, but then again we were completely pissed by that point.'

Lydia tried to keep her face neutral. *He's got the brains, I've got the looks,* Patrick had said about Dan all those years ago, and she'd laughed coquettishly at the time. *I know which I prefer,* she'd replied, pressing herself against him. Funny how a bit of time and distance could change your mind about things.

'We're just friends,' she said, getting to her feet. Her complicated feelings for Dan meant it was impossible to answer honestly in one single snappy sentence. She really liked him – and for a few heady moments at Jonathan's party she had wanted very much to kiss him – but she recognized that they were both holding the other at bay, because the repercussions were potentially so difficult, so messy. Not that Zoe needed to know any of this right now, obviously. Lydia didn't want the other woman getting the wrong idea about her either. *First you have a fling with my husband, now you're going after my brother-in-law . . .* It really wasn't like that. It wasn't like that at all.

Walking back to the shop a few minutes later, Lydia felt light with possibilities, though. As if good things might be on the horizon. Okay, so she had told a tiny white lie to Zoe about having 'got something' for Dan, but she knew exactly what that thing *was,* it was simply a matter of organization.

She pulled out her phone again, feeling fizzy with the prospect of a plan. 'Dad? Can you do me a favour?' she asked. 'No, everything's fine. I just need to borrow something and I'm hoping one of your mates can help me out . . .'

Chapter Thirty-Three

It was only when Dan was parking the car, back home on Saturday afternoon following Gabe's birthday party, that he realized he was still wearing his Thor wig. He pulled it from his head, snorting a laugh. Perhaps that was why he'd been getting funny looks all the way back from the leisure centre. Still, it had been worth the embarrassment of the costume and all the comments from the mums dropping their kids off, to see what a great time Gabe had. 'A skateboard, whoa! That's so cool!' he'd cried, opening the present from Dan. Zoe appeared to be putting her face in her hands, but perhaps that was due to sheer joy at her brother-in-law's generosity. He hoped so anyway.

The party had gone really well, despite being two of the most exhausting and deafening hours of Dan's life. After the terrible Zoe showdown, he had assumed his name had been scrubbed off the guest list, *persona non grata*, but he had been reinstated after their Greyhound bonding session. 'Too right you're coming,' Zoe had said when he asked. 'You're not getting out of it that easily.' Then her voice softened. 'Besides,' she said, 'the kids all love their Uncle Dan. They talk about you all the time, you know – about the fun things you've been doing with them, but the big stuff too. Like Ethan telling me the other night that he'd come out to you and that you'd been brilliant. So thank you.'

Dan's heart had cracked a little with pride. *The kids all love their Uncle Dan.* It was truly one of the best sentences he'd ever heard in his life. 'You're welcome,' he'd said. 'It's my pleasure.'

A taxi pulled up alongside him now as he was locking the car. 'Fancy seeing you here,' called Lydia out of the window.

He stared at her in surprise. 'Hi!' he said. 'What are you doing here?'

She was paying the driver and didn't reply immediately, but then opened the back door of the cab and got out, turning and reaching back inside to remove . . . What the hell?

'Just thought I'd pop round with my chainsaw,' she said, then laughed. 'You should see the look on your face. What? Does this not happen very often then?'

'Women with chainsaws arriving at my house? Funnily enough, no – you're the first,' he said. Then the penny dropped. 'Oh, right. This is about the tree, is it?'

'This is about the tree,' she confirmed. There wasn't only a chainsaw, it turned out. She'd arrived with a full kit, including hard hats, safety goggles and protective headphones for them to wear. She dumped a box of stuff on the pavement, shut the cab door and called thanks to the driver. 'Shall we?' she asked, looking down at the chainsaw, then back to Dan. 'I've always fancied having a go with one of these.'

He was still trying to get his head round the fact that she'd rocked up here with so much gear. Where had she even got it from? 'Is this what you do in your spare time or something?' he asked. 'Moonlighting as a tree surgeon?' A laugh bubbled up from his throat at her delighted expression. She was even wearing what was presumably her tree-removing outfit: burgundy dungarees over a Breton top with monkey boots, her hair swung up in a ponytail. God, he fancied her, he thought. 'You seem *very* pleased with yourself, you know. Some people might even say "smug".'

'Hell, yeah, too right I'm smug!' she replied. '*And* pleased with myself. And pretty glad that you weren't out when I arrived, either. That would have spoiled the whole thing.' She grinned at him, dimples flashing in her cheeks. 'So are we going in then or what?'

He pulled his door keys from his pocket, then picked up the box of equipment she'd brought. It weighed a ton. 'Do I have a choice? Come on, then. We're going in.'

He was conscious of his home's plain decor as they went inside, especially compared to Lydia's own flat, with all its colours and textures, the memories and stories that were on display in each room. Here there were no memories and stories to see, no insight into his personality revealed at all, he realized. Even his mum had commented on how soulless it was, when she'd come round the other day.

'I've been meaning to decorate,' he mumbled, as they went through to the kitchen.

'Wow, it's so tidy, Dan, it's like walking into a serial killer's house,' she said. 'Joking,' she added quickly. 'But whoa, your recycling is so *organized*! Amazing.'

He eyed her – was she teasing him? he wondered – but she seemed to be sincere, marvelling over his sorting system. 'Um . . . thanks?' he ventured.

'Nice garden,' she went on, walking over to the window. She was so animated, he thought; he really liked that about her. The way she brought life and energy to a conversation, to a place. Even his miserable kitchen felt more interesting with her there. 'Lucky you,' she was saying. 'Ah, and there's the tree, I see. Not for much longer, though. Right? Shall we set this bad boy on it?' She brandished the chainsaw as if she was about to start carving up the back door with it, and Dan's laugh became slightly more nervous. 'Kidding again. Don't worry,' she said, seeing his expression. 'How are you, anyway? And' – her eyes widened suddenly – 'Christ, what are you *wearing* by the way?'

In the shock of seeing her, he had completely forgotten about his Thor costume, visible in all its fake-armour, padded-chest glory, now that he'd unzipped his jacket. 'Didn't I mention I'm into cosplay?' he said, pulling the wig out of his pocket and plonking it back on his head. 'Yeah, I always dress like this on a Saturday afternoon.'

She burst out laughing. 'Looks good on you,' she said. 'And the blonde hair . . . yes. I'm digging it. Er, should I be scared right now? I'm actually feeling a tiny bit scared. And wishing I'd said a proper goodbye to my daughter when I dropped her at her grandad's. Was I right about the serial-killer thing after all?'

'Gabe's birthday party,' he said, taking the wig off once more. 'The only scary thing about it was how many of his mates challenged me to fights and tried to punch my inflated pecs. Oh, and how weird and giggly some of the mums got too. Have these people never seen a man in a red cape and skin-tight nylon chainmail leggings before, for heaven's sake?'

Lydia's mouth twitched as he struck a pose, one foot on a kitchen chair, flexing his muscles. 'Those poor women, they didn't stand a chance,' she teased. Then her expression became serious. 'Talking of your in-laws, I saw Zoe the other day,' she went on. 'It was . . . surprisingly okay. Thanks for whatever you said to her.'

'Good. She said that the two of you had spoken.'

'And . . . ? What did she think?'

'Well, we didn't chat long, because we were trying to

corral twenty ten-year-old boys around a soft-play obstacle course, but she seemed to think it went okay too. Who would have thought?' They smiled at each other. 'Right. I'm feeling a bit self-conscious in this get-up now, so I'm going to go and put some normal clothes on, then shall we tool up and get started?'

Lydia plucked a pair of safety goggles from the box and put them on, with a thumbs-up. 'Let's do this thing.'

A short while later, as they began working through a list of helpful instructions that Lydia had printed out from a tree-surgery website, Dan couldn't help thinking how much more easy-going and amicable it was doing this sort of task with her, rather than with Patrick, as originally planned. If he and his brother had ever managed to remove the dead sycamore, you could bet there would have been arguing over who got to use the chainsaw, jostling over who got to take the lead, an ongoing contest about who was the best at cutting the dead wood, who could lift the heaviest pieces, who got lumbered with all the clearing up. Of course neither of them would have done anything as effeminate as consulting actual instructions, either. That said, Dan found himself missing his brother very much again. Wishing that Patrick was still around to be annoying in that brotherly way. But here they were anyway. Life went on.

Once they'd made a plan and got started, the actual

taking down of the tree was unexpectedly straightforward. They removed the branches first, then sawed the trunk down chunk by chunk, until all that remained was the stump. 'The website I looked at suggested drilling holes into that and using some Epsom-salt mix to get rid of it,' Lydia said, as they made a pile of dead wood alongside the shed, for Dan to take to the dump at some point. Then she blushed. 'Sorry. I got quite into the whole research thing. Even watched a couple of YouTube videos on the subject. Usually the only online tutorials I look at are for making stuff – turns out that destroying stuff is really good fun too.'

'I know what you mean,' Dan said, heaving a last log onto the heap. 'Quite satisfying, isn't it?' He straightened up and brushed the sawdust off his jeans. 'Thank you, by the way. For all of this.' He turned to look at the garden, taking in how much emptier it seemed now. Bigger. Sometimes it wasn't until you removed a problem that you could see how much it had dominated everything else. 'It was so thoughtful of you. God knows when I would have got round to doing it, otherwise.'

'No worries,' she said.

He hesitated, not wanting their time together to be over just yet. He liked having her here. 'So . . . do you have to rush off? Only I've got some beers in the fridge, if you fancy one. Or coffee? Actually, maybe we should have a coffee, then I'll be able to drive you back with all this stuff later on.'

'I'd love a beer,' she said, apparently ignoring his last suggestion. 'And there's no rush with the gear. I borrowed it
from a couple of my dad's mates; it's not like I've paid a hire
charge or anything.' She pulled a funny face. 'And Dad's just
been dumped by a text, so he's happy to have Jem for the
rest of the day, he said. Take his mind off the heartbreak.'

'Wait,' said Dan, unable to keep track of the man's con-
voluted love-life, 'is this the same date who went into labour
a few weeks ago?'

'No, this was the new one. Only lasted until the starters,
before she vanished.' Lydia snorted. 'That's what you get
when you go on Tinder and lie about your age, apparently.'

'I'll bear that in mind,' said Dan. 'In the meantime – two
beers coming up.'

Lydia must have been rummaging around in the shed
while he was in the kitchen, because when he returned
bearing a bottle for them each, she had unearthed a couple
of ancient patio chairs, left behind by the previous owners
of the flat. Having unfolded them, she was now brushing
muck and cobwebs off their seats. 'Is this okay?' she asked.
'It feels so long since we've had proper sunshine, we should
make the most of it.'

'Good idea,' said Dan, handing her a beer. They clinked
the bottles together and gulped down a mouthful each.

'So how's Rosemary?' Lydia asked. 'Is she out of hospital

yet? I was so chuffed she liked my dress, you know.' She had dimples when she smiled, a flush of pride on her face.

Was he staring at her too much? He couldn't take his eyes off her.

'Yeah, she's fine and back home again,' Dan said. 'In fact she asked me to say that she'd be very happy to give you sewing tuition any time. She said you must have been good, if the college offered you a place.'

Lydia had the beer bottle to her lips, but lowered it immediately. 'What did you just say?'

'I mean, don't feel obliged to, obviously, it was only an idea,' Dan went on hurriedly. 'And Rosemary *is* a bit of a handful – she might not let you leave her flat once you cross her threshold, but—'

'Are you kidding? I would love to have sewing tuition from her. Oh my God!' Lydia's eyes shone. 'Did she really say that? You're not forcing me on her, are you?'

'No, definitely not, it was all her idea. She liked you. And your dress.'

'Wow.' She beamed. 'Really – wow. This is proper dream-come-true stuff. Thank you.' She gazed up at the sky. 'Fifteen years late, but it's happening, Mum. *Yes!*'

'Tell me about your mum,' he said, seeing her wistfulness. 'That must have been hard, losing her when you were so young.'

'Oh, she was lovely,' Lydia said at once. 'Beautiful, Australian, bohemian, kind. One of those people who make you feel special – who get you. She always really got me. You know? I still miss her.'

As she moved her hand, the sun flashed on her silver ring, the one that looked like a tiny Viking helmet – only Dan realized at that moment that it wasn't meant to be any kind of tiny Viking helmet, it was a miniature of Sydney Opera House. 'Do you still have family in Australia?' he asked, remembering the list that had been framed on her kitchen wall. *Favourite places to take Lyddie.* It must have been written by her mum, he guessed, feeling a pang for her loss.

Lydia shook her head. 'Not any more. Mum was an only child and her parents never really got over losing her, by the sound of things. Came over for the funeral and had a massive row with my dad – blamed him, basically, for stealing her away from them. Dad was upset and broke off contact. I'm pretty sure they're dead now, unfortunately.' She swigged from her beer and tucked her hair behind her ear. 'Anyway, that's enough doom and gloom for one day. How are things with you? What's happening with the rest of your sabbatical? You've got – what, a month left now?'

He ignored the question because a brilliant idea had just occurred to him. 'Listen, I've got some money,' he said recklessly, before he could even think about what he was saying. 'I'll pay for you to go to Sydney.'

Lydia stared at him, completely taken aback. 'What? No, don't be daft.'

'Yeah. I mean it. There was a bit left to me in Patrick's will. It would be enough for you and Jem to get plane tickets over there. You should go! Retrace your mum's footsteps, explore her home city.'

'I . . .' She seemed genuinely stunned. 'Dan, that's ridiculously kind, but—'

'I don't need the money,' he said. 'It's Patrick's money anyway. Think of it as him doing one nice thing for you. Belatedly.'

She drank from the beer bottle, looking agonized, then shook her head. 'I can't,' she said. 'Thank you, but . . . It's too much. I'll probably kick myself for this later, because I do really want to go, but if I take your money—'

'Patrick's money.'

'Whatever, I would still feel in debt to you. I—' She broke off, an internal argument playing out on her face, but then shook her head once more. 'Thank you. It's so, so kind of you. Insanely kind. And I really appreciate the offer, but I think it's something I need to do for myself. I need to find a way to make it my trip, if that makes sense.'

He was feeling a bit of an idiot now. As if he'd overplayed his hand. And he could totally see what she meant. Of course she wanted the trip to be on her own terms.

'Okay,' he said. 'Was that weird of me? Sorry. It seemed a good idea as I was saying the words, but . . .'

'It *was* a good idea. It was a lovely idea.' She put her beer down and took one of his hands between hers. 'You're a lovely man.'

All the breath seemed to leave him at that moment. 'Thank you,' he said, his heart quickening. 'You're lovely too. Really incredibly lovely.' A shaft of sunlight was angling onto her face, lighting her cheekbones, and she was smiling at him. All he wanted to do was kiss her, hold her. Should he? Would it be crossing a forbidden boundary? He hadn't felt this way about a woman for so long. So, so long. 'Lydia . . .' he said, almost in a groan, and then his body apparently decided for him, because he was leaning towards her, their lips meeting. He could smell her coconut shampoo as they kissed, her mouth soft against his. Blood drummed urgently through him and he slid his hands around her back. Oh my God. They were the only two people in the world suddenly. His heart seemed to be overflowing; fireworks bursting and soaring in his head. How had he forgotten how good a first kiss could be?

They broke apart after a moment and looked at each other breathlessly. Her pupils were huge. 'Is this okay?' she asked, their heads still close together.

'What do you mean, because of—' The passion died away in him a little, a flame turned down. Because of Patrick, he thought but didn't say. And Zoe. And how difficult this might make everything; how weird it might become. Pessimism began to seep in. 'Oh. Should we be doing this?'

Her reply was to lean forward and kiss him again, deeper and with more intensity. 'Yes,' she managed to say as the kiss showed no signs of ending. 'Yes, we bloody well should.'

Lydia and Patrick hadn't lasted long, he reminded himself. It had been years ago. And he would do everything differently. His way. 'I completely agree,' he said.

Chapter Thirty-Four

Catching a glimpse of her red sweaty face in the mirrored wall opposite as she took up the Warrior pose, Zoe realized that, for the first time since the night Patrick vanished, she was actually feeling okay. Tentatively okay. Admittedly her thighs were killing her, her bum ached from the long series of Bridges and Planks that she and her classmates had been forced through and she was totally regretting not having put on extra deodorant that morning. Despite all of that, when exhorted by the yoga teacher just now to listen to her body, Zoe felt as if hers was giving her a valiant thumbs-up. So was her head. She had been so engrossed in the challenges of the hot-yoga class that Clare had dragged her along to, in fact, that she hadn't thought about Patrick or the children, or Lydia, once so far. She hadn't had a chance to, what with the extreme concentration and sweating that was happening right now. This was progress, she decided.

It was the middle of May, her favourite month of the year, and she'd got out of bed that morning feeling what she dimly recognized as optimism once more. Okay, so it wasn't exactly a pompom-shaking, wholehearted WOO-YEAH about the world, more a determined gritting of the teeth, a squaring of the shoulders that made her feel as if she could cope. That she *would* cope. This too was progress.

The last few weeks felt like a giant leap forward in terms of progress, come to that, an upward curve once more. By chance, after the raucous but successful party for Gabe's birthday, she'd bumped into Felicia Perez in the leisure-centre car park. Felicia was a head teacher she'd worked for previously, who mentioned that her school had an upcoming maternity-cover vacancy and would Zoe be interested? Zoe was. She had been meaning to start putting out feelers for work, so to be presented with an opportunity like this was particularly fortuitous. Plus it was an ideal way back into teaching: three days a week in a spirited year-two class, beginning after the May half-term. Perfect. Whether her application was successful or not, Zoe had now decided to set this as the deadline to get everything else sorted out. It felt possible. Life in general was starting to feel possible after the long, dark months she had survived.

Taking on Patrick's business was going to be too much for her, she had realized, so she had arranged for the lettings agent to manage the properties as well as organizing the rentals. The tenants could stay put, giving her useful extra income, with the properties representing good investments for the children's futures. With one exception. There was currently one unoccupied flat on Whitecliffe Road that she had decided to sell and give the proceeds straight to Lydia and Jemima, in lieu of any further maintenance money from Patrick. She had talked the idea through with her brother, the most practical, level-headed person she knew, and it seemed like a fair solution. 'Are you sure? It's very generous, Zo, but you don't have to,' he had advised her. 'The will has already been granted probate, right? So Lydia would be on shaky ground if she tried to contest it.'

Zoe didn't want to wrangle with Lydia about money. She didn't want the other woman to feel hard done by and for the two of them to end up arguing in court, or for the little girl to be cheated out of her father's pretty sizeable earnings. When she and Lydia had sat down in that Italian café and talked, honestly and openly, it had felt a completely different experience from the excruciating exchange she'd had with Mari. Lydia had been kind to her. Lydia had always been kind, come to think of it. 'I'm sure,' Zoe told her brother.

She blinked, realizing that everyone else in the class had moved into Triangle pose, arms stretched wide, bending over to reach their ankle with the lower hand, and Zoe hastily copied Clare's positioning. From her new angle, she could see a blackbird alighting on the branch of a tree outside, head cocked slightly as if it was trying to peer in. 'Eyes to the ceiling,' the teacher called. 'Keep your jaw soft, don't forget to breathe.'

Zoe gazed up at the ceiling and breathed. A month ago she would have looked at that blackbird and wondered if it might be a sign from Patrick, she thought to herself. She had been so desperate previously – obsessed even – about receiving any kind of sign from him, a message from beyond the grave that said he loved her and was sorry. But now here she was, dripping with sweat in a hot-yoga studio, her body working hard for her, breathing, strong, and maybe she didn't need any sign after all. Maybe this *was* the sign. She and the children were gradually coming through the long tunnel of bereavement together, united and bearing up. After singing in the car at the top of her voice had proved so cathartic, she'd joined a choir that one of the mums from school had started – with some initial trepidation, admittedly, but she was already finding singing to be uplifting, especially as part of a group. The other members were friendly and fun, and Zoe was pretty sure some of them didn't even know about Patrick, which made things easier. Most importantly, following the interminable weeks of inertia, she had finally bitten the bullet and contacted a therapist. With her help, Zoe was beginning to make peace with what had happened, with the man her husband had really been, and to let go of all the bad stuff, session by session.

'Some men are not cut out for marriage,' her mum had

said sadly when Zoe poured her heart out over the phone. 'Your dad was the same. He was a great bloke, really fun to be around, but he couldn't handle the commitment of marriage and family life. He just wasn't good at that side of things. Some people aren't. But Patrick did love you, darling. It was there for everyone to see. He loved you and the children so much. Unfortunately, he seemed to have his demons as well though.'

Zoe didn't want to feel angry with Patrick for the rest of her life. Forgiveness still seemed a way off, but she had made a pact with herself to hang on to her loving memories and try to let go of the betrayals, to ignore those demons of his for now. He *had* loved her. The rest she would come to terms with in her own time.

Everything would work out, she kept telling herself. One day at a time.

It was all she could do, but it was enough.

'Last day of freedom,' said Lydia, licking her ice-cream. 'How does it feel?'

Dan gazed out at the horizon and put his arm round her. The weeks had passed and tomorrow morning he was due back at his desk. Suit on. Travelcard renewed. Office politics resumed. 'I don't want this to end,' he confessed. 'Can we just stay here instead?'

He, Lydia and Jemima had driven down to Hayling Island

for a day at the seaside, at Lydia's suggestion. 'So you can tell your colleagues you've at least been *somewhere*,' she had said. 'South America, south Hampshire . . . they're practically interchangeable really.'

Dan might not have travelled very far distance-wise, but all the same the last three months had definitely been a journey – through the hell of grief and guilt initially, with unexpected stops along the way. If his planned trip to the southern hemisphere had been about expanding his horizons, stepping out of his comfort zone and trying new things, then you could say that he'd achieved all of those and more, without leaving the country. He had gone skateboarding and dancing, he'd been a landlord and a superhero, a chauffeur, a unicorn, a confidant and confessor. Stepping into Patrick's shoes had been life-changing but, above all, it had shown him how to be himself. For once he didn't need a spreadsheet to chart this progress.

'I can't stay here,' Lydia reminded him now, leaning against his shoulder. 'I've got my hot date with Rosemary and her sewing machine in the morning. I'm not missing that for anything – even a night camping out on this beach with you, I'm afraid. Priorities.'

He kissed the top of her head. 'Fair enough,' he said. Lydia and Rosemary had become fast friends, by the sound of things, working together over the whirr of the sewing machine, experimenting with different fabrics and styles and studying the work of famous designers. Rosemary was delighted to have the company and was apparently a patient, enthusiastic teacher, encouraging and supportive, yet honest in her critique. She was already talking about contacts of hers who might be able to offer Lydia paid internships once her skills were at a certain level.

'I feel as if all my synapses are lighting up whenever I'm with her,' Lydia had said when she and Dan went out for dinner a few evenings ago. 'That I'm learning so much, just from a couple of hours each time. My brain hasn't had this much excitement for years.'

'Oh, really?' he'd said, pretending to take this personally, and she'd laughed and poked him with a breadstick.

'You know what I mean,' she said. 'Being with you is a different kind of excitement. There are more ways than one to get your kicks.'

There was truth in this: truth it had taken him a while to appreciate. *Get some hobbies, Daniel*, Rosemary had told him when she embarked on her own spree of social bravery, and he had realized the wisdom in her advice. His previously stagnant life had become immeasurably richer through filling it with new people and activities over the last few months, and he wanted to keep it that way once he returned to the office. You could hold down any kind of job if the rest of your life was full and interesting, he hoped.

To that end, Dan had taken up Steve's offer to join the

rowing club with him, and was regularly running alongside Mark, who was competing in a half-marathon in September. With Lydia's input, he had also begun to transform his flat from a boring box into somewhere that actually resembled a home. So far he had painted the living room the pale blue of a dawn sky and had hung up a series of framed prints and photos, including some that Ethan had taken during their sculpture walk. (His nephew had been delighted, especially when Dan chucked him twenty quid to get them blown up and printed in the school darkroom.) Meanwhile, Lydia had run up some curtains for him on her sewing machine, and his mum had arrived with a box of house plants that she promised it was almost impossible to kill. 'Plants always lift the spirits,' she said, arranging them along the windowsill. She'd also bought him a rowan sapling for the back garden, which they planted together. Every time he looked at its young, frond-like leaves, he felt a quickening of hope. Life went on.

That wasn't all. Having forged new bonds with Ethan, Gabe and Bea, Dan was not about to vanish from their lives in a hurry. Zoe was due to return to teaching after half-term, and Dan planned to use his company's flexible-working scheme to finish early on Tuesdays, so that he could pick up the younger children from school then. He'd suggested taking Bea to the City Farm for pony-riding classes (the nearest he could get to finding *real* unicorns) as well as being responsible for Gabe's Saturday-morning skateboarding sessions. On Wednesdays he'd be working from home so that he could continue driving Ethan to the sculpture club, thus keeping up to date with his nephew's life as well as his own musical education. There was a Sunday workshop coming up soon at the club, parents and carers welcome, and Dan had been temporarily lost for words when Ethan mumbled an offhand invitation for him to come along. 'Mum doesn't have a clue about art, but I thought you might fancy it? You're always badgering me about what we do in there,' he'd said, with that funny mixture of teenage bravado and vulnerability. Dan had agreed like a shot. Being invited was like receiving some kind of medal, one that he would wear with pride.

'He sounds great,' Lydia had said, on hearing about Ethan. 'My kind of kid. Oh, I hope I can meet him soon. And Jemima will love Gabe – she's just started playing football at school and talks about nothing else. Plus she's desperate for a sister to play with.'

Zoe was still building up to telling the children about their new half-sister – Bea had recently entered a particularly clingy phase, she said, and it wasn't the right time – but Dan had broken the news about Lydia and Jemima to his parents who, once over the shock, were keen to get to know their new granddaughter and her mum. 'I'm so sad for Zoe that Patrick could have done such a thing – but goodness,

I'm so happy for *me* that there's another grandchild to love,' Liz confessed to Dan. 'Is that selfish?'

'I think it's called being human,' Dan had reassured her. 'And Jemima's never had a grandma. It'll be lovely for her too, remember.'

The biggest difference to Dan's new post-sabbatical life was that he intended to spend lots of time with Lydia. As much time as possible. She, out of everyone, had painted his world with vivid new colours; she made his life brighter and more fun. Until now he hadn't thought much about the future, plodding through each day as it came, but now he wanted to look ahead, make plans, start dreaming again. The two of them were still taking it slowly, feeling their way gradually into a relationship, but only because it felt too important to rush. The Patrick thing would always be there between them, but Dan was trying not to dwell on it. At least it would provide an interesting answer to the old 'How did you two meet?' question, he supposed. 'It's not important,' Lydia had assured him. 'And don't worry, if anyone asks, I'm totally going to say that you're better than him. In every way. Okay?'

He opened his mouth to protest that it hadn't even crossed his mind, but Lydia already knew how competitive the two of them had been. Of course it had crossed his mind. 'Good to hear,' he replied instead, feeling only a tiny bit sheepish.

He really liked her, that was the main thing. Lydia was funny and surprising, loyal and kind. He thought about her all the time. He wanted to make her happy. He had met her dad and Bridget, both of whom seemed delighted for them. Even Zoe had given the relationship her blessing, however bittersweet Dan knew it must be for her. She had also been incredibly generous to Lydia. The sale of the Whitecliffe Road flat would not only mean financial stability for Lydia and Jemima, but also gave Lydia the chance to book the trip to Sydney that she'd always dreamed of – that coming winter, hopefully. 'Play your cards right,' she'd said to Dan with a raised eyebrow, 'and there might even be space for you on the plane as well.' He could think of nothing he'd like more.

Out of the blue he'd had a Facebook message from Rebecca recently: *Saw you holding hands with a woman across Ravenscourt Park the other day*, she had written. *You look happy, Dan. I'm glad for you. No hard feelings.*

No hard feelings, he had replied, and to his astonishment, he realized that at last he could think about her without bitterness, without rancour. For the first time since their divorce, he felt as if an aching wound had healed. As if he had finally moved on from the pain.

He was coming to terms with the loss of his brother, too. He would probably never know why Patrick had said those things to him on their last evening together, but he wouldn't let that define their relationship, or how he would go on thinking about Patrick. *Nobody's perfect*, his mum had said. *We're all muddling along, trying to do our best. Getting it wrong sometimes – but that's life.* Patrick had got it wrong at times, Dan had got it wrong too, but it didn't make them bad people. Just people.

A week ago, his parents, Zoe and the kids had come round for dinner and while Ethan showed his grandad an animation he'd made on his phone, and Liz supervised Gabe juggling and Bea attempting handstands in the garden, Zoe surprised Dan by giving him a large brown envelope. She'd finally got round to clearing out some of Patrick's old clothes and things that she didn't want to keep or pass on to the children. 'And I found this,' she said. 'In a box with all sorts of precious things – first Valentine cards we'd sent each other and your great-grandad's war medals, and some Father's Day pictures the children had drawn, that sort of thing. I thought you might want it.'

Dan had opened the envelope to find a photo from his graduation day up in York, outside Central Hall. Patrick had protested the whole time about being there, teasing Dan about his gown and mortar board, scoffing at the university traditions, constantly overplaying his own lack of further education – 'What do I know? I'm just a builder, common as muck, me' – until Dan had been completely sick of him and wished Patrick hadn't bothered coming. He felt unexpectedly touched now to discover that his brother had not only taken photos, but had kept one. In a box of 'precious things', no less.

This must have shown on his face because Zoe had put a hand on his shoulder. 'He was dead proud of you, you know, Dan. I bet Patrick never told you that, did he, but he was always praising you in front of the kids, saying how clever he thought you were.'

No, he hadn't said that to Dan's face, not once. He hadn't been that kind of brother. But all the same it gave Dan the warmest of feelings to hear Zoe's words. He hadn't realized how much he had needed that warmth until then – and it was good. Really good.

He gave Lydia another squeeze now and they both laughed as Jemima, racing back up the beach towards them, trod in a huge mound of stinking, slippery seaweed and shrieked in dismay. 'YUUUUUUUCCCCCK!' she wailed, peeling slimy strands off her bare arms with a look of revulsion. 'Gross!'

'God, I feel happy,' Dan said suddenly, as they sat there, the sun bright and warm on their skin, the sea pounding cheerfully into shore. Whatever had happened in the past seemed irrelevant here in this moment, a cloud that had burned away in the heat of the day. The future stretched ahead of them as far out as the horizon, twinkling like sunlight on the water.

'Me too,' Lydia said, and squeezed him right back.

Epilogue

It was almost midnight and the Thames was rolling along, black as tar, wrinkling and smoothing itself beneath the starlit sky. The houseboats were shadowy shapes at their moorings as frost scattered icy glitter across rooftops and railings, silvering each trembling blade of grass. High above, a crescent moon gleamed, as lustrous as wedding satin.

Patrick walked unsteadily down the river path, hands shoved in his pockets, head bowed. His world seemed to have tilted on its axis and he wasn't sure how to right himself again. First there had been the breathless phone call from Mari that afternoon – *I've got something to tell you* – leaving him with the prickling sense that luck was slipping between his fingers, that maybe the charm he'd always relied upon might not be enough to rescue him this time. Then, feeling cornered, he had lashed out needlessly, hurting people he loved with his words: Zoe initially, as they had that stupid row about university, which, even as he was arguing, he knew was bollocks. Of *course* he wanted his kids to do well – he'd

457

be the proudest man alive if they achieved so much! – but he had argued for argument's sake, from some desire to punish her because he knew he should be punishing himself. He was a bad person. The worst. And then Dan had wound him up, being so enthusiastic about going travelling, leaving Patrick feeling jealous. Yeah, jealous of his brother's adventures. Because he was stuck here with Zoe and the kids, and another one on the way, and this time he couldn't just cut her loose, as he had done in a panic with Lydia. This time it was Mari, who lived three streets away, with children at the same school as his kids, which made everything more complicated.

What was he going to do? Had he blown everything? *It's definitely yours,* Mari had sobbed. *John had a vasectomy last year. He'll kill me if he finds out what we've done!* Patrick felt terrible about it. She'd been so miserable in that marriage, he had felt like some kind of hero, swooping in and rescuing her, making her smile again. He didn't feel much of a hero now, though. They'd ended up having an argument the second time she phoned, when he was in the pub waiting for Dan. Christ, what a mess.

A scouring wind skimmed off the river against his face and somewhere in the distance a fox shrieked, as high-pitched and unnerving as a child's scream. Patrick hunched deeper into the collar of his coat, wishing he was already at home, the front door bolted, the heating pipes cooling with their soft clicks and creaks, lying warm and safe in bed with the woman he loved. But did he even deserve to be there any more, after what he had done? He had fallen for Mari too, that was the thing. There was something so fragile and pretty about her that made him want to look after her. But how could he? How had he let things go so far again? What was wrong with him that he kept doing this to himself?

Suddenly there were footsteps scuffling behind him. A shout. 'Oi! Mate.'

He turned to see a homeless guy with no front teeth, probably about the same age as him. 'Don't suppose you could spare a few quid, could you?' the man asked. He was wearing jogging bottoms and a filthy T-shirt, his trainers split on the toes. He smelled terrible, of sweat and booze and hard times.

Patrick swallowed, aware that this man could easily have been him, if things had been different. If he hadn't met the right woman, lucked in on a couple of cheap properties and made some easy money. And who knew – if Zoe found out about Mari and kicked him out, this could be a vision of his future self: alone, unmoored and desperate. Patrick dug out his wallet and pulled all the notes from it, fifty quid or so. 'Have the lot,' he said, putting it into the other man's grimy palm and walking on.

The act of generosity made him feel momentarily better, as if perhaps he wasn't all bad. He started to walk quicker, thinking about how he was going to turn everything round.

He'd have to apologize to Dan in the morning, tell him he'd made up those comments about Rebecca out of spite. *Sorry,* he'd say. *I was being a prick – I was jealous, that's all.* Imagine being so honest and generous! He would do it, though. More importantly, he would make it up to Zoe too, say sorry for their pointless argument, treat her better from now on. After that, he would let Mari down as gently as possible, take her to a clinic far out of town, if that was what she wanted, and hold her hand, then tell her they had to stop seeing each other. He couldn't risk losing Zoe, he'd say, regretful but determined. And then he would redouble his efforts at home. He had been weak before, but would keep to the straight and narrow from this day onwards. No more playing away, he promised himself. Because he loved Zoe so much. He never wanted to hurt her, never!

Just as he was thinking this, he saw some wild daffodils in the moonlight, growing in a clump at the bottom of the riverbank. Zoe's favourite flower! He would pick them for her because he loved her. Because, from now on, he was going to be the best and most appreciative husband. From now on, it was only her for him. He meant it this time.

He slithered unsteadily down the steep bank towards the daffodils. The ground was very wet after all the rain they'd had recently, the mud dangerously soft, but he really wanted to do this, to pick the flowers for his wife. But then with a sudden loss of balance, his feet skidded straight out from under him and he lurched, arms windmilling, powerless to stop himself falling. He toppled over and the momentum carried him into the water, his head bashing hard against a rock in the shallows as he fell.

His mind went out like a light, his body motionless in the swollen black river, face-down. The breeze shook the bowed heads of the daffodils, and a few bubbles rose to the surface of the water, glistening silver under the light of the moon. *Pop. Pop. Pop.*

The current dragged Patrick's body further into the river, water soaking through his clothes and into his shoes, his pockets, his lungs. Then the river swallowed him right up and he was gone.

NOW:

Seven months to the day since Patrick took his last stunned breaths, a woman was walking along a leafy West London street, trailing perfume, late to meet her husband for their anniversary dinner. Her heels clicked as she hurried along, replaying in her head the chatty phone call from their eldest daughter that had delayed her, smiling as she imagined relaying all the news to her husband across the restaurant table once she arrived. So deep in thought was she that she didn't realize the fastening of the silver brooch pinned to her coat lapel was gradually working itself looser with each step, the pin eventually easing from the velvety fabric and falling to the pavement with a tiny clink. The woman didn't notice, continuing her journey, and the brooch remained there in the autumnal dusk, stepped over unseen by passers-by, sniffed at by a spaniel on its evening walk as the indigo shadows gathered and thickened into night-time.

The next morning, a different woman walked down her front path. She was dressed smartly in a teal shift dress that had been made especially for her by her brother-in-law's girlfriend, with her favourite indigo scarf knotted around her neck. Her head was full of lesson plans for that day's teaching until she spotted the brooch glinting there in the mild September sunshine. She crouched down and picked it up, exclaiming as she saw that it was a small silver brooch in the shape of a daffodil. Her favourite flower.

'What's that, Mummy?' asked a little girl with pink butterfly slides in her hair. (Butterflies were her new thing. Unicorns were so last week.)

'Someone must have dropped it,' the woman said, glancing up and down the street. Her heart was racing. Could it be? she thought, goosebumps prickling her skin. At last?

'What is it?' asked her younger son, who was fiddling with his bike helmet. He had recently been allowed to skateboard to school, under strict instructions not to show off or attempt any tricks until he was well inside the school gates.

Nobody had any huge confidence that these instructions would be closely followed for very long, but so far at least, so good.

'Why is everyone standing around?' her eldest son asked grumpily, wheeling his bike up behind them. 'I'm going to be late. Remember I'm going round to Jay's after school,' he called over one shoulder as he hooked a leg over his bike and pedalled away. Jay was a new friend – possibly a boy-friend, the woman had been thinking to herself, but whether he was or not, he seemed to make her son happy. That was all that mattered.

'Bye, love, have a good day,' the woman shouted after him. Her eyes shone as she gazed down at the brooch in her hand again. 'It's a sign,' she said happily. 'I know it is.' Then for some reason unknown to her children, she smiled up at the sky and blew a kiss into the air. 'Thank you,' she called, still gazing upwards. 'Thank you!' A moment later, seeing their confused expressions, she ruffled her daughter's hair and knocked gently on her son's protective helmet. 'Come on, then. Off to school we go.'

The boy wrinkled his nose at her as they set off. 'You're being weird, Mum,' he informed her, gliding away on his skateboard.

The girl slid a hand into hers. 'Are you actually okay, Mummy?' she asked, gazing up wonderingly.

Zoe smiled again and squeezed Bea's hand.

Remembering the perfect blue-sky Pembrokeshire day last month when they'd scattered Patrick's ashes and she'd found the right words for her eulogy. Thinking back to the Sunday a few weeks earlier when Dan, Lydia and Jemima had come to lunch for the first time and, after the initial few minutes of awkwardness, everyone had got along pretty well. Looking forward to whatever the future held next. 'Yes,' she said, as they started walking. 'I actually am.'

Acknowledgements

Massive thanks as ever to my superstar agent, Lizzy Kremer, for brilliant editorial notes and support throughout. Thanks too to the rest of the David Higham team, especially Maddalena Cavaciuti (for similarly great notes!) and Emma Jamison, Alice Howe and Margaux Vialleron . . . I appreciate everything you all do.

Thanks to everyone at Pan Macmillan – Caroline Hogg, Charlotte Williams, Stuart Dwyer, Rosie Wilson, Kate Bullows, Mel Four, Kate Tolley, Sara Lloyd, Elle Gibbons, Claire Evans and Mandy Greenfield to name but a few. It's a pleasure to work with you all.

Extra thanks to Karen Ball (Speckled Pen) for editorial expertise and so many excellent suggestions and prompts. You helped make this a better book – I'm so grateful.

Love and thanks to all my author friends, not only for the lunches and wine but also for the laughs, solidarity and gossip. Ronnie, Milly, Mimi, Rosie, Cally, Jill, Emma,

Kate, Victoria, Kirsty, Harriet, Jo, Anna, Cathy, Linda, Lynne . . . what a fantastic bunch of women you are.

Thanks to Vicki for all the pep talks (and my balloons!).

Special thanks to my lovely readers whose kind words of encouragement keep me going through the tricky writing days. Every friendly email and message of support is so appreciated – thank you if any have come from you!

Last but definitely not least, huge thanks to my family – to Martin, Hannah, Tom and Holly, who have been there throughout all the highs and lows of author life. I couldn't do it without you!